JUST A KISS AWAY

Felicity couldn't stop laughing at the preposterous story. It seemed he was embellishing his story just to make her keep on laughing.

She touched his shoulder as if to admonish him for his teasing. "Shame on you."

"I love to hear you laugh," Jared said. "Any man would love to hear that laugh. And you how what else they'd love?"

Felicity didn't like the sudden huskiness of his voice, "Um, it's getting late," she said. "I should go . . ."

Jared smiled wickedly. "Did you think I was going to say they'd love a kiss?"

She cleared her throat and paused before she dared speak. "No. I knew you wouldn't say anything so bold."

"So of course I wouldn't tell you I wanted to kiss you. . . ."

"Of course not. You're a gentleman."

"And gentlemen don't kiss?"

"Surely not ladies they hardly know."

"I didn't think so," he said, almost bringing another laugh from Felicity with his forlorn look. "That's why I, for one, would never say such a thing."

"Good night, Captain," Felicity said.

Jared grinned as he watched her move toward the house. It was going to take some time, he thought, but he was confident of the end results. All she needed was a bit of convincing, and this cool little miss would soon grow hot and hungry in his arms.

BOOK YOUR PLACE ON OUR WEBSITE AND MAKE THE READING CONNECTION!

We've created a customized website just for our very special readers, where you can get the inside scoop on everything that's going on with Zebra, Pinnacle and Kensington books.

When you come online, you'll have the exciting opportunity to:

- View covers of upcoming books
- Read sample chapters
- Learn about our future publishing schedule (listed by publication month *and author*)
- Find out when your favorite authors will be visiting a city near you
- Search for and order backlist books from our online catalog
- Check out author bios and background information
- Send e-mail to your favorite authors
- Meet the Kensington staff online
- Join us in weekly chats with authors, readers and other guests
- Get writing guidelines
- AND MUCH MORE!

**Visit our website at
http://www.zebrabooks.com**

Only For
Love

Patricia Pellicane

Zebra Books
Kensington Publishing Corp.
http://www.zebrabooks.com

ZEBRA BOOKS are published by

Kensington Publishing Corp.
850 Third Avenue
New York, NY 10022

First Printing: June, 1998
10 9 8 7 6 5 4 3 2 1

Printed in the United States of America

To Kathleen Drymon—The best friend ever.
And to Mary, my mother, for her patience and love.

One

Someone was at the door. Felicity Dryson frowned as the knock sounded again.

If only she could reach . . . "Fluffy, come here sweetheart," she said, trying to disguise her annoyance lest the puppy hear and never come from his hiding place. If she didn't get him outside soon, there was sure to be another accident.

Her hand closed over a small mound of fur, touching his collar and the leather leash twisted twice around the desk leg. Felicity tugged the puppy from his hiding place, cuddled him in her arm, and hurried toward her front door.

She opened it just as the man raised his hand to knock again. "Yes?" Felicity asked automatically, even knowing as she did that there was no need to inquire as to the man's wants. English officers had come to her door with disgusting regularity for close to three years now, more frequently of late, since Major Wood had taken up residence some six months ago. This one was no doubt bent on joining the man who had sat alone in her formal sitting room.

Felicity put the puppy down as the man asked, "Major Wood?"

"Inside," she said as she nodded behind her and a bit toward her right. "He's in the . . ." Felicity gasped as the man, moving as if to pass her, stumbled and appeared to lose his balance as he came crashing against her, shoving her slight frame between him and the outside wall.

"Don't move," the man said as he leaned against her. To Felicity's way of thinking the remark was unnecessary at best, for there was no way she could move an inch with this lout crushing the breath from her.

Captain Jared Walker, a doctor attached to the King's Dragoons now stationed in New York, smiled as he looked into honey brown eyes that had first widened with surprise, then grew narrow with obvious annoyance. Her face had been flushed with exertion when she'd answered his knock, her mobcap slightly askew, while red hair, curling wildly from beneath the bit of lace, fell over a creamy cheek. Dressed in a modest pink gown, she looked like a strawberry confection. For just a second Captain Walker wondered if this woman would taste as good as she looked. And then the clean scent of lavender soap and her own sweet breath rose to invade his senses, and he knew she'd taste even better. Feeling no need to hurry to extricate himself, Jared teased, "Do all colonists have so intriguing a way of making a man feel welcome?"

Felicity knew had he been another, the predicament she now found herself in might have been mildly amusing. But Felicity couldn't find anything the least bit humorous about being crushed by an Englisher. It wasn't that she hated the British: she was intelligent enough to know they were not all the disreputable beasts some thought. What she hated was their cause and the fact that they had occupied her city since the Battle of Long Island some three years back and her home as well. She hated their unbearable haughty attitude that all could only hope to be British, that they and their kind could do no wrong, and their overbearing, insufferable pride. Felicity reconsidered. All right, maybe she did hate them a little.

"We're apt to accomplish little by standing here, sir."

"You think so?" Captain Walker asked, a definite twinkle in his dark eyes. A twinkle Felicity had no wish to investigate further, for the captain obviously imagined his present position agreeable in the extreme.

Jared straightened but didn't move away from her. The puppy

ran out from between them, and back into the house, no doubt beneath her desk.

"Thank you," she said primly. Well, as primly as a lady could while realizing that this fool had yet to take a second step back.

Jared allowed some space between them at last as he looked with some surprise at the unwelcome, distinctly aromatic deposit the dog had left behind, smeared over the toe of one boot. He muttered a sound of disgust.

"Billy is in the kitchen. He'll clean you up," she said as she moved into the house again, heading for the stairs, her room, and the privacy to change.

Jared was about to ask where the kitchen was, when she nodded toward the hallway, then seemed to reconsider. Felicity knew Billy well enough to realize the boy wouldn't hesitate to use whatever was close at hand to clean the officer's boot, and she didn't want to sacrifice a perfectly good apron. Enough had been sacrificed to these cursed English. "Wait a minute, I'll get you a rag."

With Jared at her heels, Felicity opened the door to her linen closet. She gave a silent gasp at the scene unfolding before her eyes and, stunned into immobility, stood there for a long moment taking in the fact that a man and woman stood inside the closet locked in a heated embrace. Having never found herself in quite so mortifying a position before, Felicity could only manage to blink her surprise. It wasn't until seconds ticked by that she began to wonder what to do. Should she close the door with neither knowing of her interruption, or ignore the scene unfolding and reach inside for a rag? As it turned out she took just a little too long to make up her mind, and Jared made it up for her.

"Oh, excuse us," Jared said behind her as he watched a fellow officer and the pretty serving maid clutched together in passion. The girl spun from the man's arms in shock at being discovered.

Felicity might have been looking for a rag, but Jared was looking at a pair of small neat breasts, fully exposed to his view until the girl made a startled sound, apparently realizing seconds too late her state of undress, and turned again into her lover's arms. She buried her face into his open shirt, just as Felicity snatched a rag from a shelf and slammed the door shut.

"I thought you locked it?" came a muffled deep voice from behind the door.

"I thought *you* locked it," the girl returned.

Felicity thought her cheeks might be stained pink forever, for she knew she'd never get over the scene just witnessed. She took a deep breath and swore she'd have a word with Becky tomorrow. If the man wouldn't make an honest woman of the girl, then perhaps Major Wood would have a word with him.

Jared strangled on his amusement. It was only at his choking sounds that Felicity remembered the man's presence. She turned to glare into smiling dark brown eyes.

Until this moment Felicity had seen only a uniform. The man in it had gone quite unnoticed, blending in with the hundred others who occupied her city. He was tall. Felicity shrugged aside the thought, knowing anyone could be considered tall when compared to her diminutive form. His hair was dark, his skin almost bronzed, his nose narrow, his mouth wide, and his dark eyes fringed in ridiculously long lashes. Beautiful was not a word one directed toward a man, yet she couldn't find another quite so appropriate.

While Felicity's good sense lapsed for just a moment, Jared allowed himself the pleasure of returning the favor. He had from the first realized that this woman was a pretty little thing, and knew firsthand that her body was soft and neatly packaged beneath that modest gown. But it wasn't until now that he understood just how lovely she truly was. She had red hair, but her lashes, thick and brown, almost exactly matched her eyes in rich color of honey. Her mouth was wide, and as she bit a pink lip, he noticed small white teeth. Jared frowned at the sight of those lips, and then as his gaze rose to meet hers again he realized she was glaring at him.

That the woman did not find the scene just encountered quite as hilarious as he, was obvious. Jared fought to stall off his laughter at her prim, "Have you found something amusing, sir?"

"No, mistress. Nothing at all."

Felicity silently cursed her red hair and fair complexion as she felt the heat in her cheeks grow to fiery proportions, no doubt setting them, as well as her entire face, ablaze. She was mortified. Lord, what must this man think of her and her household? Not only had he been witness to a half-naked woman carrying on in a most disgraceful fashion in her linen closet, but Felicity had compounded her embarrassment by boldly staring at the man and had allowed him to catch her at it.

A moment later Felicity reconsidered her silent question. This was her house, and what she or her servants did was hardly any of his affair. He was an English officer, and she didn't care what the man thought.

Her tone was dismissive as she nodded just over his right shoulder. "The kitchen is through there." She shoved the rag into his stomach. "Tell Billy to get you some soap and water."

Jared held back his laughter until she turned the corner and moved up the stairs to her room.

Fifteen minutes later Jared stepped into the formal sitting room to greet his old school chum. "When did you get in?" Sam Wood asked.

"This afternoon."

"You settled yet?"

Jared nodded. "Marcy found us rooms over on Amsterdam."

"You brought Marcy with you?" Sam laughed at the thought of the old man braving an ocean voyage. "What is he, eighty by now?"

"He'd whip your ass if he heard you say that."

Sam laughed again as he pushed a glass of brandy into his friend's hand, while remembering the times when as a boy Marcy had threatened to do just that. Sam couldn't remember ever seeing a manservant half so muscular and uncivilized in appearance, yet able to match any gentleman in speech and manners. "I'd wager he could still do it, too."

Jared looked at the glass of amber liquid with some appreciation. "By the looks of him, he could." He glanced at his friend, then at the glass. "How are you getting this stuff?" The taxes levied against French imports made luxuries like this almost nonexistent. Jared knew a major's salary did not permit such extravagance. There was no way that Sam could have come across Napoleon brandy legally.

Sam laughed. "I have friends in high places."

Jared narrowed his gaze. "You mean swinging in high places?"

"My wife bought me a case for my birthday."

Jared smiled, remembering the lovely Mary. "How is she?"

"About to have our third any day."

"Good God, man, can't you keep your hands to yourself for a bit? You've only been married four years."

"It's not my hands doing the deed, I'm afraid." Sam grinned. "You being a doctor should know that."

The two men laughed, and across the hall, in a smaller, less formal sitting room, Felicity smiled as she worked over her needlepoint.

"We should close the doors, I think," said her cousin Alvina Davies. Her father Thomas had asked Alvina to come and share his home some two years back, a week before he had finally signed allegiance to the King. Sign it or lose everything, he was told. That very afternoon, Thomas had left to join Washington's forces.

"No, dear. It grows close in here with the doors shut." Felicity knew her cousin worried over a young lady's sensibilities. She should not be privy to such talk, she knew, and under normal conditions she wouldn't have hesitated to close the doors. But not when the English were about. Not when she might hear a scrap of information shared between those ridiculously wigged and powdered fools.

Felicity frowned as she remembered the encounter earlier that evening. All right, so he hadn't worn a wig, but had brought his long dark hair to the nape of his neck and tied it with something. Felicity scowled at the thought that he was any less feminine in manner than his fellow lace-handkerchiefed officers. She scoffed. He hadn't turned from her, not so she could remember in any case, so she hadn't gotten a good look, but she could well imagine a velvet ribbon holding his hair in place. He probably wore lace and satin while alone in his rooms. Felicity laughed aloud at the picture brought to mind.

A moment later she realized she and her cousin were no longer alone; Major Wood stood in the doorway. "Would you ladies care to join us?" he asked. "One of my officers found a bottle of sherry today, which should be to your liking, Mrs. Davies."

Felicity thought she might have liked this man had it not been for his politics. He was a congenial sort and not nearly as presumptuous as the last Englishman to quarter himself in her home. The major had not taken over the running of her house and except for insisting on her company during the evening meal, Major Wood had pretty much allowed her to come and go as she pleased. Felicity soon came to know that he missed his wife sorely, and she could not find it in her to refuse him this one directive.

In the evening he often invited her and her cousin to join him and his officers for a drink before bed. On occasion, Felicity obliged, but not tonight. She did not want to see the young officer, nor linger in his presence. She couldn't have said why. She simply thought it wise to keep her distance, even if it meant her cousin should forgo a coveted glass of sherry.

Since Alvina was particularly partial to sherry, and Felicity could see from the corner of her eye that her cousin was coming to her feet, she felt a twinge of regret as she said, "Thank you, Major, but I think not tonight. My eyes feel the strain of my work. I think I'd best find my bed before a headache takes hold."

"Another time then," Major Wood said as he gave a brief bow and left the ladies to their own company.

"Where are your spectacles? You always get a headache without them."

"I'm sorry. I forgot." Felicity wondered how that could be. She could hardly see without them and yet she had managed to work for almost an hour without remembering to put them on.

Alvina sighed and came from her seat. She had her own sherry awaiting her in her room and thought perhaps it shouldn't await her attention too much longer. After all, there was little an old woman could look forward to. Little enough to bring cheer into a lonely life.

Jared grinned as his friend returned alone. "I told you she wouldn't come."

Felicity and Alvina were just leaving the sitting room when she overheard what she took for an absurdly cocky comment. She took the older woman's hand and, despite Alvina's look of surprise, said nothing as she directed her toward the formal sitting room.

Sam frowned. "What did you do to her?" Sam was in love with his wife and yet he found he had grown oddly charmed by the tiny woman who lived in this house, no doubt because she reminded him so much of Mary. As he felt more like a brother than a lover toward her, he wouldn't take kindly to any man abusing her, not even his old friend.

"Me? I didn't do a thing. It was her dog."

Sam sat opposite his friend and grinned. "Go ahead. Tell me Fluffy attacked you. This has got to be good."

"Well not exactly."

"What then, exactly."

"Why would you think I wouldn't come?"

Jared and Major Wood came instantly to their feet at the sudden appearance of the two women. "I thought you might be upset with me."

"Surely not. Have you done anything to upset me, Captain?" she asked with a bit more feeling than Sam deemed necessary.

"Not on purpose."

"What happened?" Major Wood asked, a deep frown creasing his tanned forehead.

"Fluffy was a bit more . . . frisky than usual tonight."

Jared figured she was close enough to the truth to satisfy and did not elaborate.

Sam sipped at his cognac as he watched Felicity ignore his friend. That she ignored him with purposeful inattention was obvious. Sam could only wonder what had truly happened?

There was fire here, just bubbling beneath the surface of cordial, if sometimes stilted conversation. Jared had a lazy look of innocence about him, a look far too innocent to be believable, while Felicity strove to ignore the man at every turn. These two might be unaware of the fact, but Sam knew passions were about to erupt. It was then that he made his decision: Tonight he'd send off a letter telling Mary to come.

Felicity stepped through the hidden doorway to the lush gardens beyond the mansion. She seldom took this route, knowing to do so chanced discovery. But tonight she cast her usual precautions aside. Tonight she couldn't face the four officers quartered in her home. She couldn't smile demurely and keep up the pretense. Tonight, after spending almost a full twenty-four hours with a dying man, seeing to his needs, administering him in his pain, urging him to hold on, only to watch in helpless frustration as he gave up his struggles at last, she needed a few moments to collect herself, lest the preening redcoats gathered inside know the full force of her fury.

If only there had been a surgeon, perhaps he could have done something. But there were none. All able-bodied men, including physicians, surgeons, and druggists had left the city three years ago, when the Battle of Long Island had secured New York as a British stronghold. Yes, there were physicians still practicing here, but none who weren't Tories and sure to turn both her and the dying man in. Felicity couldn't grant him much, but she could, at least, allow the man to die free.

It was late and yet lights still blazed from most every room of her home. All of her guests were still up and about. It had been a thoughtless act to use the hidden doorway. What if one of the men had stepped outside? What if she'd been seen?

Felicity sighed and moved from the cover of shrubs into the warm moonlit night, heading for the garden at the back of her home and the privacy of a secluded bench. She never noticed the uniformed soldier standing partially obscured beneath a thickly branched oak, as she hurried to the far corner of her garden.

Felicity sighed again as her thoughts returned to the man inside, hidden in the chimney room. Who was he? What was his name? Had he a family somewhere? Would a wife wail her heartache upon realizing her loss?

Joshua and Brian, her two contacts, had brought the man in about one o'clock this morning. And Felicity hadn't left his side, but for the time it took to find bandages for his wounds and water for his thirst. Now, as she found a moment to rest, she trembled with exhaustion. She probably should have gone directly to bed, and she'd do just that as soon as Joshua or Brian came back. She expected one of them momentarily, for they always came near eleven. Tonight they'd be anxious to see how the injured man fared.

Jared had, only moments before, stepped outside for a smoke. As he lit his pipe his thoughts turned yet again to the lady in residence, wondering if he'd get a chance to see her tonight. Wondering what she did with her time, who she spent it with. Damn, it had been almost a month since their first meeting and things had not gotten any better between them. No matter how amicable he made himself, the lady spurned his company.

He'd never had a problem attracting women before, so what was her problem? Why wouldn't she give herself the chance to know him?

Jared's mouth tightened at the thought. He'd never had to beg for a woman's attention before, and he'd had just about enough of waiting.

As he puffed on his pipe, he blinked at the vision through a cloud of smoke. Was he seeing things? Could it be the woman in question had just moved through a solid wall of brick?

Jared found himself following the gentle swish of her skirt as she moved off into the darkness. A moment later he saw her sitting on a bench, eyes closed, her head tipped back as if asleep. Dark smudges of exhaustion under her eyes marred a perfect creamy complexion, while the delicate bones of her face appeared more prominent in the silvery moonlight. She looked ill, and Jared felt instantly alarmed.

"What have you been doing? Are you all right?"

Felicity, believing herself alone, knew a moment of shock upon hearing a man's voice coming out of the dark. She gave a soft sound of alarm and came instantly to her feet, only to find her legs unable to hold her slight weight. Just as she was about to crumple to the ground, Jared dropped his pipe and reached for her.

Felicity was far from a weak woman. In truth she was stronger than most and could equal any fellow colonist in her zeal of patriotism. Still there were moments when a woman found herself in desperate need of comfort, and this appeared to be one of them.

It didn't matter, for the moment, that she was standing in the arms of a British officer, a man who, because of his loyalty to a hated King, was an enemy to her cause. Felicity had just watched a man die, and she needed human contact more than she needed her next breath. She needed to touch someone who was alive, and in so doing she couldn't hold back her tears.

Jared felt her body soften against his. He'd been dreaming of this moment for weeks, yet he knew the reason behind her sudden acquiescence was not the answer to his prayers. Indeed, she appeared quite unable to stand on her own.

"Mistress," he whispered above a lacy mobcap and sweetly scented red curls. "Tell me what ails."

It was only at his words that Felicity realized her scandalous position. She'd never before stood so close to a man as to press her body to his. She sighed, knowing exhaustion influenced her actions in the extreme. She knew as well had he not spoken she could have, for a few brief moments at least, indulged in this forbidden luxury. "Forgive me. I didn't mean . . ." She murmured the half sentence as she tried to disengage herself from his hold. "It's just that you startled me." From her pocket she took a lacy handkerchief and dabbed at a tear.

Jared, with his hands on her shoulders, held her at arm's length and searched her face. Had he frightened her to the point of tears? "Are you sure? You appeared so weak."

Felicity smiled and tried her best to make light of an awkward moment. "Indeed?" she lied. "I turned my ankle when I stood up. Perhaps you mistook that for weakness."

"Did you? Let me see," Jared said as he guided her to sit again.

"Surely not," Felicity said obviously aghast at the mere thought of a man seeing, never mind touching her ankle.

Jared smiled at her modesty and waved aside her dismay. "Do not fear, mistress," he said as he knelt before her. "Have you forgotten, I am a doctor?"

It would take but a touch for him to realize the lie. "It was only a slight turn," she said, her voice oddly strained, almost pleading for him to desist. "It's all right now."

"Good," Jared returned. Kneeling before her, he lifted her foot to rest against a thick thigh. "Then this won't take but a minute."

Jared examined a trim ankle with well-trained fingers. He did not need full light to know nothing was amiss here, that her ankle was fine. She was lying, and for a moment he couldn't understand why. And then he smiled, realizing the ploy: She was a lady, and a lady could not chance her reputation by honestly admitting to her wants. Like hundreds of others, she played the game.

So, he hadn't misread the signs. Perhaps the smiles she directed toward him held no more dazzling light than those bestowed upon others, but he knew the lady was interested. "I can find nothing wrong."

"It was a very small turn," she said in a very small voice.

Felicity fought back her moan of shame, even as she thanked the Lord for the darkness. There was no telling what this man must think. He had to know she was lying. How in the world was she ever going to face him again?

"Is it sore?" Jared asked as he twisted her foot gently to the right and left.

"It's fine now."

"Would you like me to help you inside? I could carry you."

"I can manage, I'm sure."

"It wouldn't take but a minute, and a little thing like you would be no . . ."

Felicity interrupted his comment with, "The truth is, Captain Walker, I came out here for a few moments of solitude."

Jared frowned. The woman was confusing in the extreme. He had no doubt what she had been about, but apparently she had for some reason changed her mind. That she wanted him to leave was obvious. Only he wasn't about to accede to that particular and not so subtle request. There was no telling when he'd get another chance to be alone with her.

He fished around in the dark looking for the pipe he'd dropped. "What are you doing?"

"Looking for my pipe."

"Here? Now?"

"I dropped it here. Where would you have me look for it?"

Felicity almost said, "In China," but instantly thought better of the sarcastic remark. It wouldn't do for the captain to become suspicious. She couldn't make it known just how much she longed to be without his company, lest she chance some questions. Questions that would indeed be hard to answer.

She breathed a sigh as she realized she worried for naught. If Brian or Joshua came by a bit early, they would hear their conversation and leave. Tomorrow night would be soon enough to move the body, she supposed.

Felicity never noticed her sigh, but Jared did and without asking permission sat at her side. "Something is the matter. Why are you so tired?"

"It's late."

Jared nodded at her response, knowing some women were a bit more delicate than others. Judging by this one's slender form, she just might need more rest and care than most. "You should go to bed."

"I will. Did you find your pipe?"

Jared smiled and patted his pocket.

"I wouldn't mind if you smoked," she said. "The smell reminds me of my father."

Jared reached for his pipe and tobacco pouch. "Do you expect him home soon?"

As far as the English knew, Thomas Dryson had gone to one of the islands on business. While there, he had succumbed to some mysterious illness. To tell the truth of the matter—and that her father was fighting alongside Washington and was possibly even at this moment peering down the scope of his rifle in an effort to rid this land of its unwanted guests—would be to forfeit all his assets, leaving his daughter destitute. "The doctors say he's not well enough to travel yet."

"He's been ill for a long time."

Felicity only nodded, for her father had been gone for two years. She knew her story was growing thin, but she had no choice but to continue the charade. "He hasn't been ill all this time. He was trading at first."

"Did they mention the disease exactly?"

"No. I don't think they knew what it was."

Jared nodded, wondering what kind of doctors the man had in attendance, even as his gaze narrowed with what Felicity took for suspicion. "Well, perhaps they did know," she quickly added, "but didn't want to frighten me."

He nodded again, and Felicity almost smiled as the faintly puzzled look left his eyes.

"Where is he?"

"Martinique."

"Why haven't you gone to him?"

"I wanted to, of course, but Father insisted that I stay at home. With the conflict and all, he thought it might be too dangerous. Besides, he said there was a chance that I could come down with the fever."

They sat in silence as Jared puffed on his pipe. He was racking his brain trying to think of something, some subject they could converse upon. She was stiff and obviously uncomfortable. Jared wanted her to relax, but couldn't for the life of him think what might do the trick.

"It's beautiful out here, isn't it."

Felicity nodded.

"Warm night."

She only nodded again.

Suddenly he laughed as he peered through the smoke. "I saw you before at the back of the house. It looked like you stepped through the wall."

"What?" Felicity croaked out the word, feeling her heart begin to race with fear. Is that why he was here? Had he insisted on staying at her side in order to taunt her with subtle and veiled comments? Would he now tell her he knew what she was about? Was he even now quietly awaiting Brian's arrival and eventual capture?

"I said it looked like you stepped through the wall. It must have been the smoke." Jared laughed at the nonsensical thought. "Imagine being able to walk through walls?"

"I don't think I've ever thought about it."

"Oh you must have. Weren't you ever confined to your room as a child?"

"I suppose." Felicity was afraid to say anything. She couldn't imagine what this man was up to, unless it was no good.

"Well? Don't all children fantasize about being able to leave their rooms without their parents ever knowing? How else would they do it, but by gaining the power to walk through walls?"

Felicity smiled. A moment later she realized it was only her own guilty thoughts that had brought about her suspicions. She laughed with relief, knowing the man hadn't a clue as to the truth of things. "It's been a long time since I was a child."

Jared looked at her for a long moment before saying, "It hasn't been that long. Do it again."

"What? Become a child?"

He smiled and moved almost imperceptibly closer. "Laugh."

Felicity did not trust the look in his eyes. They were entirely too dark, too appealing. She shook her head. No, not appealing. The man might be good to look at, but he was English. And that lone fact settled any thoughts of attraction she might have entertained.

"No? Why not?"

Felicity didn't know what he was talking about until she realized he had mistaken her movement for an answer to his question, rather than a response to her own thoughts. "You haven't said anything amusing. What would I laugh at?"

"You could laugh because you are a beautiful woman, and beautiful women should always laugh."

Felicity shot him a warning glance and almost sighed with relief to see him retreat. Her relief didn't last long however. The man had only backed off so he could turn in his seat and lean closer than ever. Felicity inched toward the edge of the bench.

"All right. How about laughing for the sheer joy of living?"

"That wouldn't be appropriate, I think."

"Why not?"

"Because too many are at this moment suffering."

Jared nodded. "You're right." He seemed to think a moment before saying, "Suppose I told you an amusing story. Would you laugh?"

Felicity chuckled at the eagerness displayed. Somehow the man had grown boyish before her eyes. She'd been forced to live under the same roof with British soldiers for close to three years and had not until this moment imagined an Englisher to possess such charm. "I might."

Jared grinned and leaned a bit closer, as if to tell her the story in confidence. Felicity didn't trust him. She backed away again. "Do you know Sergeant Major Simpson?"

The sergeant was often in her home. "Is he . . . ?"

"The fat one."

Felicity nodded.

"Well, it seems our esteemed sergeant is not particularly liked. At least not among his men."

Felicity smiled, waiting for him to go on. When he appeared to lose his train of thought, as his gaze lingered for some moments on her mouth, she prompted with a gently spoken, "And?"

It was almost Jared's undoing, for her breath brushed gently against his lips and all he could think was to feel it again, to breathe it while touching her mouth with his. It took a bit of effort, but he finally got his thoughts in order. "And? Ah, yes, and one or two of the most unhappy to be under his command, decided that the sergeant could use a bit of color."

Felicity's eyes widened with surprise. "Really? He looks very colorful to me. His nose is always red as are his cheeks."

"Wrong color. They were thinking a bit darker, something closer to black."

Felicity bit her lip, unable to keep her smile at bay while watching his barely restrained laughter. "What did they do?"

"They waited until he was asleep, a sleep they helped to induce with something added to his drink, I've no doubt. And then they smeared shoe polish over his face, spelling out a rude word. By morning it had pretty well set."

Felicity laughed. "That was terribly mean, don't you think?"

Jared grinned, for the story had brought about exactly what he wanted. "It would have been if it were true."

She laughed again, her eyes widening a bit in surprise. "You made it up?"

Jared nodded proudly. "Every word."

Another laugh. "Why?"

"Because I couldn't think of anything amusing, and I needed to hear you laugh."

Felicity touched his shoulder as if to admonish him for his teasing. "Shame on you. I won't be able to look at the man again without laughing."

"He won't mind. Any man would love to hear that laugh. And you know what else they'd love?"

Felicity didn't like the sudden huskiness that had entered his voice and came instantly to her feet. She ran her fingers over her hair and cap, neatening the curls that refused to stay in place. She adjusted her neckcloth and then smoothed the wrinkles from her skirt. "Um, it's getting late," she said, "I should go in."

"They'd love a tall glass of ale and a good smoke."

Her gaze moved to his, and she couldn't hold back her grin at his playful words. Words that appeared to be quite innocent on the whole and yet somehow held a thread of wickedness. Felicity felt as if she were overmatched, drawn into a game where she knew not the rules, a game she could only lose. The best thing, the only thing she could do was to beat a hasty retreat. "Well, good night, Captain."

Jared was standing before her when he said, "Did you think I was going to say they'd love a kiss?"

She swallowed and cleared her throat, before she said, "No. I knew you wouldn't say anything so bold."

"I wouldn't tell you I wanted to kiss you then?"

Felicity took a half step back, forcing aside her smile at his woeful expression. "I doubt it. You're a gentleman."

"And gentlemen don't kiss?"

"Surely not ladies they hardly know."

"I didn't think so," he said, almost bringing another laugh from the lady with his forlorn look. "That's why I, for one, would never say such a thing."

"Good night, Captain."

Jared grinned as he watched the lady move toward the house. It was going to take some time, he thought, but he was confident of the end results. All she needed was a bit of convincing, and this cool little miss would soon grow hot and hungry in his arms.

Two

Felicity couldn't quite rid herself of the smile. It stayed with her as she told her servants good night, reminding them as always to lock up. It stayed as she wished as much to the small group of soldiers gathered in the sitting room, as she mounted the stairs and finally found herself alone. Captain Walker had looked so hopeful and then so dejected upon realizing he wouldn't be kissing her after all, that she had barely controlled the need to laugh aloud.

Felicity had known him for almost a month. Apparently he and Major Wood were close friends, having been school chums in their youth. For weeks now he had come almost nightly to her home, to play cards, to talk, and to share a drink with his friends. Granted he often looked her way, but she hadn't imagined his interest. Until tonight she'd taken as only simple cordiality his nods and smiles as he wished her a good night.

The two sitting rooms were separated by a wide hallway that ran the length of the house. Most often Felicity could hear the officers' conversations as the doors to neither room were ever closed. It caused her nothing short of amazement that the officers never thought to close those doors. Not even while discussing matters pertinent to the war effort. Apparently they thought the ladies across the hall hard of hearing, or perhaps so meager in intelligence as not to understand words spoken in clear English.

* * *

Felicity had been asleep for less than an hour when a hand shoved gently at her shoulder. She came instantly awake to find a shadowy form looming over her bed. She felt no fear, for she knew the man standing there.

Brian Adams was more like an uncle than a friend of her father's. He was older than her father by perhaps ten years, and yet the man possessed all the vigor and vitality of a man in his prime. He was dark, short, hardly more than three inches taller than Felicity, and thickly set, with muscular arms so strong as to break a man in half or soothe a little girl who had taken her first fall from her horse. Brian had lived in the colonies for close to twenty years but had never lost his accent, and here in the dark quiet of night, it appeared more pronounced than ever. "He died, did he, lassie?"

Felicity only nodded as she came to her feet and reached for her robe. She tied it at her waist before following the man to her closet. A moment later a wall was silently pushed aside, and the two moved down a flight of stairs that led to the basement and a room hidden behind a wall of brick.

Felicity had no idea why the man who had built this house had thought to add a hidden room, stairways that led from the attic to the basement and outside, plus walls that moved at a twist of certain bricks. Perhaps he had been a smuggler. Perhaps he had cause to hide his treasures from the watchful eye of customs inspectors. All she knew for a fact was she'd discovered the room as a child, played in it on rainy days, and felt no fear as she descended the stairs to the dark damp cellar and warm chimney room.

Even in the winter the room was warm. Now, because of the summer months, it was hot, for the fire in the kitchen was never allowed to go out and had been stoked for the night.

Joshua was waiting for them, standing beside the table. Along one wall stood a cot; upon it a dead man lay covered with a sheet. Joshua nodded in greeting. He was tall, blond, with sparkling blue eyes that might have smiled had the circumstances been better. He spoke in a cultured fashion. Felicity thought him to be well educated, but did not inquire. The less she knew about the man the better. His gaze moved to Felicity at her entrance. "I didn't have much hope."

Felicity nodded, knowing a wound taken to the middle of a man's chest rarely allowed a man an alternate course. It was almost a given, no matter the effort taken, that he would die. "What was his name?"

"Said it was John. That's all I know."

Felicity shook her head at the terrible waste. It was obvious to any who looked at the man that he had somehow escaped from one of the dreaded English prisons. His near-skeletal remains told that much. But starvation hadn't killed him. A steel ball had done the job. Entering his back, it had probably hit a lung, for the man had slid in and out of consciousness all day, even as he gasped to the end for every breath taken. Felicity had administered to many men who, after escaping prison, had been brought to her home while means were made to find them safe passage. A few had been badly injured, and some had died, but she thought this death the hardest she'd ever witnessed. "His wife will never know."

"She will when he don't come back," Joshua said as he hauled the corpse to his shoulder. "I got two coming this week. You got enough?"

Felicity knew he meant food and blankets, perhaps even a little whiskey or port. She nodded as she smiled into serious blue eyes. "The redcoats don't miss the food. There's more than enough, but Major Wood did give me a strange look when the last of the port showed up missing."

Joshua laughed. "They be thinking the little lady can hold a pint or two, I take it."

Felicity wrinkled her nose at the thought of drinking that awful brew. She had a small glass of sherry on occasion, but because sherry was in short supply since the beginning of this conflict, Felicity rarely indulged. She shrugged as both men smiled. "I care little what they think. If he blames the servants, I'll admit to it."

* * *

Felicity entered the teahouse, and smiled as Jimmy Remmington came toward her. It had, for the last three years, gone undetected that Jimmy Remmington was an important part of Washington's Culper spy ring, that his teahouse was often used as a drop or pickup while passing on information. Felicity had no message today. She was merely meeting a friend.

"Good afternoon, Miss Dryson. Your friend is waiting in the back room."

Jimmy Remmington smiled again as he escorted Felicity to her table. On the way he spoke almost conversationally. "The cakes you ordered came in today. I was going to send a boy over with them tonight."

No one, especially not the red-coated soldiers sitting to the left and right of her path, admiring the lovely red-haired lady, understood the coded words. That the delivery of cakes meant a packet. And tonight meant the packet was to be dropped near English headquarters before tomorrow morning.

Washington, a brilliant strategist, had devised a scheme to allow the enemy, which was heavily based in New York, an occasional glimpse of his intent. In doing so, he could sometimes maneuver the English at his will.

The plan was unbelievably simple, and Felicity wondered how the English had yet to catch on. A packet of official-looking papers, signed by the General himself, would be dropped *by accident* where someone of authority could find it. To Felicity's knowledge this happened on a regular basis, but the information obtained was usually a bit late in coming. Whatever had been planned had already been put into effect. But there were occasions when it appeared the papers had been found in time.

Washington has used this ploy when moving his troops past New York. A day or so before his appearance, it was *learned* that his intent was to attack the city. As garrison after garrison readied itself behind barricades for the attack, the General merely slipped by the fortifications and into New Jersey, leaving the English quite bewildered.

Felicity smiled at the man's cunning. "Thank you, Mr. Remmington. I'll take them with me, then."

Carolyn Carpenter was Felicity's closest friend. The two were the same age, and had attended the same finishing school, but that was where the similarities ended. Carolyn wasn't at all pretty. Those of a generous nature might have allowed that her features were pleasant, for she had startling blue eyes, a thin nose, and a mouth that was a bit too wide. She was tall for a woman, dark when fair was in fashion. Still none of her missing attributes appeared to matter, for her social life was active in the extreme.

Carolyn was a bit more worldly than Felicity and despite her less than perfect attributes had a new man in her life nearly every week. This particular week she had lost her heart to an English soldier attached to Clinton's staff, a lowly lieutenant, but Carolyn professed him to be the most handsome yet. A man with a great future ahead of him. "I think I'm really in love this time."

"You said that the last time," Felicity felt the need to remind. She might have added that her friend had felt the same the last half dozen times, but decided the gentle reminder was enough.

Carolyn made a face as she remembered her last. "I know. He was a beast, wasn't he? Imagine never telling me about his wife and children. It's a good thing I found out in time."

Felicity wasn't sure what her friend meant by in time and decided it was probably best not to ask. "I was under the impression that officers were supposed to be gentlemen."

"So they say, but I think you can find a scoundrel among the best."

"Especially if you look hard enough," Felicity murmured into her cup.

"Meaning I usually pick the wrong one? I know, but not this time."

"Meaning you are often taken by a man's looks and never think to consider his character."

Carolyn sighed. "I know, but that uniform sends me into a tizzy. I can't imagine anything more handsome."

The fact of the matter was, Carolyn liked men. And because she obviously did, men liked her in return. Politics never entered into her thoughts. All she could see, all she knew was the desirability of a man in tight white trousers, a red coat, and knee-high, polished black boots.

"Every man in here will look at me with envy if you invite me to join you."

Felicity looked up to find Captain Walker standing at their table. His dark gaze was warm as it settled on her face. "Are all the sick and injured well today?"

Jared grinned and sat without waiting for the asked-for invitation, knowing this woman wasn't about to issue it. "My staff is watching over them while I take a minute."

Felicity introduced the officer to her wide-eyed friend, and Captain Walker, although wishing he were alone with the lady, played the part of perfect gentleman as he divided his conversation between the two ladies.

Carolyn thought the man the best she'd seen yet and, were it not for David, might have known a tinge of envy that he seemed so taken with her friend.

A half hour later Carolyn glanced at the watch pinned to her bodice and gasped as she came suddenly to her feet. "Lord, I had no idea it was so late. David is coming for dinner, and I have to change."

She glanced at her friend. "Will you come, too? I want you to meet him."

And at Felicity's hesitation, she urged, "Please, Fel? You can tell me if I'm right this time."

Felicity gave a reluctant nod, and then, had she known the right words, would have mentally savored a curse, when Carolyn added, "And you as well, Captain. We'll have a lovely night of it. After dinner we could play cards."

Felicity almost moaned as the man answered with, "I'd be delighted, Miss Carpenter."

Carolyn was about to give him directions when she suddenly said, "If you call for Felicity, she can tell you the way." And giving her friend no opportunity to object, she said, "At eight then." A moment later she hurried from the teahouse.

"Eight o'clock and she has to start dressing now? I wonder what she will wear."

Felicity realized she had no recourse. She didn't want to dine with him. Her father was fighting for the cause, and she in her own way was doing her share. How could she justify becoming involved with the enemy? She couldn't. Therefore, she had to take steps to make sure it did not happen.

Still, it was only a dinner, and she supposed she could bear his company through one meal. Besides, Carolyn was bound to be upset if she begged off at the last minute. She'd go tonight, but in doing so she'd make it perfectly clear that she had no interest in Captain Walker. If he were the gentleman his uniform professed him to be, he'd understand her resolve and keep his distance. Felicity put aside her thoughts to concentrate on his question. "Something exquisite, I'm sure."

"Perhaps, but it won't matter."

"And I'm supposed to ask you why not, am I correct?"

Jared grinned. Did she know what it did to a man's stomach when she looked at him from beneath those thick dark lashes? This was the first time he'd ever found her so amicable, and he could only hope she'd stay that way, right up to and including the carriage ride home. "You are."

Felicity couldn't hold back her laughter. "All right. Why not?"

"Because she can't outshine you, no matter what she wears."

"Thank you, but she's not trying to outshine me. She's in love, and dressing for a man."

"Is the feeling mutual?"

"I don't know. Why?"

"Because if he sees you, he's bound to lose his heart."

Felicity shot him a look of disbelief. "You're being ridiculous."

"Am I? What would you say if I told you that every man quartered in your home is in love with you."

Felicity's cheeks stained a soft pink. "I'd say you're speaking utter nonsense."

"Even Sam feels a certain tenderness."

Felicity's eyes widened and she gave a small gasp. "Rubbish! What an awful thing to say. Sam . . . I mean, Major Wood has been a perfect gentleman. He's never once . . ." She shook her head.

"I don't mean he loves you that way. Perhaps he feels more like a friend, or a brother, but if it weren't for Mary, I'm sure . . ."

"And I'm sure this conversation has gone on long enough. Perhaps you thought to compliment me, Captain, but I can tell you all I feel is embarrassment."

"You have no reason to. You are a beautiful woman, and beautiful people often find themselves admired, don't you agree?"

Felicity blinked at his comment, then her gaze filled with laughter. "Meaning you are equally besieged?"

"Do you think it couldn't happen?"

"I've no doubt it could."

"Why?"

Felicity only shrugged; he had managed to trick her into saying far too much.

"Come now, Miss Dryson, I thought you were made of sterner stuff. Are you afraid to tell me?"

"You have only to look in a mirror, Captain. You know as well as I know that you are a handsome man."

"Was that so hard to say?"

"Harder than you could ever imagine."

Jared laughed. "I'm beginning to suspect that you are a stubborn woman. I think my only alternative is to get to know you better." He gave a slight shrug, "You know, just to be sure."

"I'm not an easy woman to know, Captain."

"I'm most diligent when the need arises."

Felicity couldn't say exactly how he did it, but she was most certain his smile, a thoroughly lazy smile at that, and the sudden low husk of his voice had just caused her stomach to lurch and a slight tingling to run down her spine, as if she were embarking upon a fearsome journey, which of course she wasn't.

He was teasing her, but for some reason she couldn't take that teasing in stride. He was not like other men. Felicity almost laughed aloud as she realized her thoughts. How could she have gotten the impression that he was different? She had no knowledge of his person and had but only once or twice found herself engaged in conversation with him.

The fact was, the man confused her, or at least her reaction to him confused her. Felicity wasn't sure which, but she was sure about one thing. She'd stayed long enough. "I'd better go. I have a few errands to run before dinner."

"I could go with you."

"You have to go back to work. And don't worry about tonight. I'll give Carolyn your apologies."

Jared's eyes widened with surprise. If he'd had any doubt that she was less than delighted at spending the evening together, she had just cleared up the matter. Only it wasn't going to be that easy. Jared knew what he wanted when he saw it. And he'd wanted this lady since the first moment he'd laid eyes on her.

Felicity almost groaned at another flash of that somehow tempting grin of his. "That's very kind of you, but there's no need, Miss Dryson. I'll call for you about half past seven."

Customs and manners are often relaxed in times of war, but Felicity felt no need to alter her usual course. It didn't matter to her that coaches came and went during all hours of the night, delivering to eating establishments unprotected young women who could easily become prey to their English admirers. Felicity knew a lady's responsibilities. There was no way she would dine alone with a man. No way she would put her honor in jeopardy by riding in a coach to a dinner alone with a man. Especially not that man.

Jared was unaware of the lady's intent and had during the long afternoon fantasized in some detail about their ride home and the possible intimacy they might share. So it came as something of a surprise when he realized that Mrs. Davies would accompany them.

His disappointment was gone in a flicker of an eye, but Felicity caught it. She smiled and asked with some feigned sensitivity. "Is everything all right, Captain?"

"Everything is perfectly fine, mistress," Jared returned even as he promised himself that the light of laughter in her eyes would shine and soon, but for an entirely different reason.

"You're not feeling indisposed are you? I could make your apologies if . . ."

"Not at all," Jared said, as a smile touched the corners of his mouth.

Felicity turned quickly away. She didn't want to watch him smile. Lately when he smiled her stomach seemed to lurch and flutter uncomfortably. Felicity knew that was impossible and yet it had happened earlier today as well. She took a deep steadying breath, daring to look his way again, and swore the tenderness, the gentle laughter in those dark eyes, affected her not in the least. She stiffened her spine and swore she didn't feel confused as the dancing laughter in those dark eyes acknowledged she had won in this case, but promised she wouldn't forever escape his intent.

"Are we ready then?" Jared asked, knowing a duel of flashing eyes was not the way to win out against this lady. She could possess all the determination and strength in the world, but his day would surely come.

There were six of them at dinner. Carolyn's grandmother, an elderly, but spry lady joined them. Felicity was surprised at finding the lady present. That Carolyn often dined alone with a man was common knowledge at least between the two friends.

That she did not tonight caused Felicity some interest. Apparently Carolyn was serious this time. Certainly she wanted the man to think the best of her.

The dinner party was most enjoyable, the conversation flowed easily, for Carolyn always had something to say, someone to mention, some amusing tale to relate. Felicity never realized her guard slipped a bit as she sampled one glass of wine too many. Even had she realized it, she wouldn't have worried over the fact, for she felt well protected and perhaps just a bit too confident in her supposition. "I don't remember ever tasting wine this good."

Lieutenant Tennison had brought the wine. It had been given to him by a lady friend some years back, but the lieutenant was a gentleman and because a gentleman was discreet, he merely said, "It's been in the family for years." Which was true enough.

"Would you mind if we had our tea outside on the terrace?" Carolyn asked her guests.

All with the exception of the Misses Davies and Carpenter agreed. Both mentioned the dampness of the night and decided that they'd have their tea later. Mrs. Carpenter invited Alvina upstairs to her private rooms. So it was that the elderly ladies remained inside and a setting for four was arranged on the terrace table.

Felicity felt not a hint of foreboding.

The four spent a very pleasant few minutes enjoying their tea and further conversation before the garden was mentioned and Lieutenant Tennison asked if Carolyn wouldn't mind showing him the pretty sight.

The wine might have cast Felicity into a charming lighthearted mood, but it did not slow her thinking. She knew well enough what a man might expect if a woman agreed to accompany him in a turn around her garden at night. Carolyn agreed, and Felicity knew what that meant. The two wanted to be alone for a bit, but that would mean she and the captain would also be alone.

Felicity decided both couples were equally needy of exercise.

"That sounds like a lovely idea. Let's all go." She glanced at Jared's knowing grin. It was obvious he knew what she was about, only Felicity didn't much care what the captain knew. "You should see the garden, Captain. Carolyn can boast of the best in New York."

Jared came to his feet and offered Felicity his arm, which she ignored. "Mrs. Carpenter works most of it herself. It's her pride and joy. If you mention the word garden, she's sure to go on about it for hours."

"I'll be careful then," Jared said while that most annoying grin curved his mouth again. Felicity knew he knew what she was about and didn't care. She was talking too much and perhaps a bit too loudly, but she didn't care about that either.

She hurried her steps as she realized the distance between the two couples was growing at an alarming rate. "Hurry up, they're getting too far ahead."

"I believe they want to be ahead. Don't you, Miss Dryson?"

Felicity only knew what *she* wanted, and that was not to be alone with this man. Then she realized she was overreacting.

Jared broke the long moment of silence with, "You're right about the garden, Miss Dryson. It is beautiful. I'd like to take a closer look in the daytime."

"I'll tell Carolyn. Perhaps you could come for tea."

"Perhaps."

"Oh David," came a muffled groan suddenly quite clear and all too close. Felicity hardly had the time to understand the meaning behind that intimate moan before Jared instantly turned them from the sound, directing them to the opposite side of the garden.

"Yes, it is beautiful here. Perhaps I will come to tea."

They came to a stop. A small bench sat in an alcove of shrubbery. Above the bench a tall tree stretched steady limbs forming a private shadowy half circle. Felicity never realized they had stopped walking. All she could think was how embarrassing to come across a couple in the midst of an intimate moment.

"You're very quiet. Is something the matter?"

"No. I was thinking, is all."

"About what?"

"About how I'm going to kill her the first chance I get."

Jared laughed, and Felicity couldn't help but smile. "You wouldn't be half so embarrassed if we were about the same thing."

"I wouldn't be embarrassed at all if I hadn't come tonight."

"Why did you invite Mrs. Davies?"

"She and Mrs. Carpenter are old friends."

"It couldn't be that you were afraid to be alone with me, could it?"

"Certainly not. I'm alone with you now, aren't I?"

"You are." Jared didn't miss the fact that Felicity bit her lip. If she wasn't afraid, she was certainly nervous. And considering what he had in mind, she had every right.

"What have I to be afraid of?"

He took a step toward her and smiled as she only blinked at his daring. "Perhaps you thought I might kiss you."

"It never entered my mind." She lied outright, uncaring of the fact that he had to know it was a lie. What was the matter with her feet? Why wouldn't they move?

"Are you sure?"

"I wouldn't have come at all if I thought that." Well, she wouldn't have left the safety of Carolyn's house at least.

"You mean you would have claimed an illness?"

He was standing too close. Mingled among the blooming roses came his scent, and Felicity, although she was loath to admit it, thought it much outdid any flower she'd ever enjoyed. "Exactly."

"But I'm a doctor. I would have known the truth of it."

"Exactly," Felicity said with no little misery.

Jared placed his hands at her waist and grinned as he closed the small distance between them. Their bodies almost touched, and Felicity knew some surprise at a sudden sense of disappointment. Had she wanted him closer? Surely not. And why hadn't she slipped from his gentle hold?

Jared grinned and Felicity almost moaned. *Lord, why does he have to smile like that?* "So you did give it some thought."

"Give what some thought?"

She was finding it harder to concentrate. Jared felt no pity for her dilemma, for he'd known the same for some time now. "Feigning illness."

"Perhaps."

"Why?"

"Because I didn't want this to happen."

"What to happen?" he asked as his head lowered and his mouth brushed gently against her forehead.

His breath smelled so clean. Did he know how hot it was against her skin? "I didn't want to find us alone."

"Why?" he asked as his mouth moved to her temple, then seemed suddenly and quite naturally at her cheek.

Felicity was having a hard time keeping her thoughts in order. She should have moved when she had the chance, only she'd never really had the chance. "Because it's not proper, of course."

"Of course," Jared might have said the words in agreement, but his actions told quite another story. "And you had no fear that I might kiss you?"

"None at all." Her voice trembled, but she seemed unaware of the fact. "You would ask for permission."

"If I did, would you give it?"

"No."

"I didn't think so."

His mouth was at her jaw now, and Felicity thought the touch of a man's lips on a lady's jaw to be a delightful experience. She swallowed as his mouth moved to her neck, never realizing how she moved to allow him easier access. "What are you doing?"

"I'm not kissing you. You'll have to tell me when you want a kiss."

Felicity laughed at that. "A lady would never want a kiss."

"Do you think ladies don't like kissing?"

"Some do, I suppose," came on a breathless sigh.

Felicity never realized how soft she'd grown in his arms. Never knew that she was leaning against him. "I feel a little weak."

"We could sit."

Felicity didn't know why exactly, but she thought that wouldn't be wise and said so.

"I could hold you tighter then, just so you don't fall."

"That might be better," she said without thinking.

Felicity wouldn't notice until later that she was at the moment doing an excellent job of not thinking.

"If you put your arms around my neck, it might . . ." Jared had no need to finish his sentence for Felicity immediately obliged. "That's better."

"Do people always talk like this? I mean, so close?"

"It's the best time to talk, don't you think?"

"I can't think at all. I must be ill."

"Why?"

"Because I drank too much wine."

Jared knew she had only had two glasses and hadn't finished the second. It wasn't alcohol that caused her this intoxication.

"Are you having a hard time breathing?"

"I think so."

"Thinking?"

"I don't know."

"I thought so. Do you know what that means?"

"No."

"It means you want me to kiss you."

Felicity smiled as his mouth left her neck and came within inches of hers. She felt suddenly terribly wicked, terribly good as she smiled into his dark eyes. "It couldn't mean that."

"Why don't we try it, and you can tell me if I'm right."

"I've never kissed a man before."

"Never?" Jared couldn't hold back the astonishment he knew. How could a woman who looked like her manage to live twenty years without once being kissed? Were all the men in these colonies blind? Surely there had to have been one time, just one kiss.

Jared had no idea that Felicity was raised with a strict code of morality. Stricter perhaps than most. "A lady doesn't kiss a man unless he's her fiancé."

Warning bells went off in Jared's brain. Was she hinting at marriage? Was she holding out for a ring before allowing even a kiss? He'd thought that old-fashioned way of thinking had gone out years ago.

He wondered if it mattered? He wondered if he wanted her enough to marry her and, before he could finish the thought, knew he did not. But he could convince her to see to his way of thinking. Of that he had no doubt.

"That's not true. Many women kiss just because kissing feels good."

The words were harsh enough to bring Felicity from her daze almost instantly. She blinked her surprise to find them face-to-face with less than two inches separating their mouths. What in the world was she doing? What was she allowing him to do? Felicity pushed against him, finding it was she who was forced to take a step back. "Then why are you sniffing at *my* heels, Captain? Go find one." With that she turned and left him in the garden to find his own way back.

Three

Felicity placed her packages on the table in the foyer and was in the midst of removing her gloves when suddenly she was swept into strong arms that swung her in a circle wide enough to allow Jared an enticing glimpse of neat trim ankles. "She's coming! God, I can hardly wait."

"Excuse me?" Felicity gasped.

"Mary's coming. She had the baby, another boy," he beamed proudly and in his absolute delight squeezed her so tightly Felicity thought her ribs might crack.

"Congratulations, Major," she grunted breathlessly, even as she tried to disengage herself from his bear hug. Her effects went unnoticed however, for Sam Wood was thinking of another lady, a lady with equally bright red hair, about to set sail and join him at his lonely post.

"God, I can't wait to see her again."

"Do you think you could put me down now?"

"Oh," the major exclaimed, apparently having only just realized he was indeed holding the woman. "Was I holding you too tight? I'm sorry."

Felicity smiled. She didn't care if this man was British or not. It was impossible not to like him. "Will she be staying here?"

Sam frowned before he realized what she meant. Ever since he'd gotten her letter, Sam had had a time of it keeping his concentration. "Mary? Perhaps at first, but we'll have to find other accommodations. She's bringing the children with her."

"Three children," Felicity said, her voice holding just a thread of envy. "How lovely for you."

Sam laughed at her remark. Obviously the girl didn't have the slightest idea what children could do to a well-run household, not counting the hours their care often took his adorable wife from his side. "And about to get lovelier, I'm sure." He laughed at his remark, then insisted, "You have to join me for a drink."

"It's time for tea."

"We'll have a drink first and then Becky can bring in the tea."

Becky had married the young officer a week after Felicity came upon them in the closet. As it turned out, the young man had a titled brother, but he himself was as poor as a church mouse and would be making the army his career. Apparently Becky didn't care a whit. All that mattered to the young girl was that they loved each other. Still, with only a lieutenant's salary to count on, Becky thought it wise to continue with her duties, at least for the time being.

Felicity was delighted with her decision and more than a little relieved, for she dreaded advertising for help again.

Major Wood, in his joy, had forgotten to ask permission and practically dragged her into the sitting room. It was only after she entered the more formal room that she realized Captain Walker was present. "Good afternoon, Captain," Felicity said a bit stiffly. They hadn't spoken for some time, not since that awful time in Carolyn's garden some two weeks back. He still came to the house almost nightly, but he hadn't again engaged her in conversation, for Felicity took pains to stay out of his way. "Have you heard the good news?"

"I haven't heard anything else for the last half hour. The man grows monotonous when someone mentions the name Mary. Be sure you don't say it."

Across the room Sam, while preparing their celebration drinks, chuckled.

Felicity's smile grew less stiff at the sound, and she found herself relaxing for the first time since noticing the captain. "He is excited, isn't he?"

"Looks like a man in love, wouldn't you say?"

"I'll thank the two of you to stop talking about me as if I'm not here," Sam said good-naturedly as he brought three snifters from the table.

They toasted his new son. They toasted the woman he loved. They toasted love in general. The snifters were empty, and before he could refill them, Felicity insisted, lest she spend the remainder of the day in bed with a headache, they do the rest of their toasting with tea.

"Have you ever been in love, Felicity?" Sam asked just after downing another small cake in one huge bite.

Felicity couldn't help but notice the major's use of her Christian name, but she couldn't find fault under these happy circumstances. "I thought I was once."

"But you weren't?" This came from the captain.

Felicity put aside a sudden disquieting feeling. Surely he hadn't meant to use that particular tone of voice. She smiled for his benefit. "No, just a young girl's temporary infatuation."

"How temporary? Were you engaged?" he asked, his tone bordering on the belligerent. And only Felicity knew the meaning behind those words. She longed to tell him yes, knowing what yes meant, but she wouldn't lie, not even to better this beast.

"What happened to him?" he asked.

"He married someone else. Why?"

"Happily married, I hope." Again that annoying, demanding tone of voice.

Felicity narrowed her gaze, and said very softly, "I'm sure. I'm also sure there is a reason behind these questions. Perhaps you are practicing the art of detecting? Are you growing bored with medicine, Captain, and looking to change your profession?"

"No, just writing a book," Jared said as he leaned back in his chair and grinned as if he'd gotten in the last word.

"Stop teasing the girl, Jared," Sam admonished. "I'm rarely allowed her company, and I'll not have you ruin this tea." The major grinned again. "Besides, I'm happy, and I want everyone to be happy along with me."

"People in love are disgustingly smug and complacent, wouldn't you agree? They think because they're happy, the world is a glorious place."

"Although some might think so," she said obviously pertaining to him, "being happy is not a fault, Captain. And I know for a fact that the world is quite glorious."

"How much of it have you seen?"

"I've been to France, England, and to visit my mother's relatives in Ireland."

Jared's gaze seemed to widen a bit at the mention of the Emerald Isle. "What did you think of Ireland?"

"I thought it was beautiful. It's greener than I would have imagined, and the people are delightful."

"You like the Irish, do you?"

"Very much. Why?"

Jared grinned. "Like you, my mother was Irish."

Felicity didn't much appreciate the comparison. She and Jared were nothing alike. Nothing at all, and if he was trying to find some compatibility, he might as well give it up right now. Felicity answered his grin with a smile that looked slightly sick.

Jared only laughed.

It was late. Brian and Joshua had said tonight at one, and it was already half past the hour. Had something gone wrong? Felicity knew the men came from the British prisons in the city, but she hadn't a notion as to how either Brian or Joshua met up with them. Perhaps they didn't just meet up. Perhaps Joshua and Brian actually broke into the prison and got the men out.

If that were the case, anything could have happened. They could be injured, or themselves imprisoned or even—she shuddered at the thought—dead.

Felicity paced the empty room and sighed her relief when after another ten minutes she finally heard the sounds of muffled grunts and footsteps. Joshua almost fell into the room. There were two men with him and Brian following close behind. The escapees were obviously shaken, afraid, terribly thin and weak, but uninjured. Joshua was bleeding. An almost-perfect circle had formed just below his shoulder. Even with dark clothes and in bad light, it was easy enough to see he'd been seriously injured. His face was ashen, and around his mouth were tight lines of pain.

The men sat on the floor as Brian helped his friend to the cot. "We've got to get the boy some help, lassie.

"Took himself a steel ball. He'll be needin' a surgeon, and I know of none who will not report us."

Felicity felt a moment's panic. He couldn't die. Hadn't enough died for this cause? "Wait a minute. Let me think," Felicity said as she began to pace again, this time stepping over the exhausted men's legs as she moved from one end of the room to the other. "I know a surgeon."

"Will he help us?"

Felicity smiled as a plan began to form. "He's English, but I think the end of a pistol would persuade him to help."

"I'll get him. Tell me where."

"I'll go with you. This won't be easy." Felicity had to get her hands on male attire. There was no way she could manage what had to be accomplished dressed as a woman. Captain Walker must never suspect. Only where could she . . . ? A light seemed to dawn, and Felicity realized how simply her plan could be accomplished. Her father's clothes were in the attic. All she had to do was get past the sleeping officers and dress. It was easier than anyone might have supposed, for the secret stairway ran all the way to the top floor of the mansion.

Fifteen minutes after she left the small room, Felicity returned, dressed as a man, her hair tied back and covered with a black neckerchief. Another remained in her pocket to cover her face later, while a hat had been pulled low over her head, disguising the fact that a woman stood before them. "Do I look like a man?"

Brian grinned at her outfit. "He'll never recognize you, lassie. But don't talk unless you have to."

Felicity couldn't chance it. If Captain Walker answered the door, and recognized her, all would be lost. Brian would have to knock and ask for the captain.

Felicity stood at the corner of the building, hidden in the shadows of an alley as Brian knocked. It took a moment before a servant answered, but Brian was finally heard to say, "Tell Captain Walker, Miss Dryson has taken ill. Seriously ill."

The man nodded, and the door closed. Seconds later Brian was at her side. "I hope you know what you're doing. We never should have mentioned your name."

"It doesn't matter. Everyone knows where he spends most of his nights. I only hope your message matters enough to bring him out."

"Aye, I wouldn't want to tangle with his man. The fellow looked about seven feet tall and almost as wide."

Felicity grinned at the exaggeration, then caught her breath in a gasp as Jared ran from the building with a small bag in hand. He hadn't bothered to button either his shirt or jacket, and the material blew out behind him as he hurried down the empty street. "Let me call a cab," his servant called out from the doorway.

"I can make it there before one comes along. Go back to bed."

Jared heard the door close just as he approached the alley. A second later a gun was shoved hard against his back, and a sinister whisper, "Take it easy, man, and no harm will come to ye," came from behind.

Jared was shoved against the alley wall. The man behind him might have been short in stature, but he possessed amazing strength. Jared grunted as his head hit the wall. "Jesus, man. Not now. I'm a surgeon, and a woman is in need of my care."

"No. The woman is fine."

It took a moment for the words to penetrate Jared's panic. For his heart to regain its normal rhythm. Jared was conscious of a sense of relief, still it wasn't easy to trust, especially hard when a gun was pressed to one's back. And Jared had to be sure. "How do you know?"

"I left the message."

"What's her name?"

"Miss Dryson," came the response.

It was only then that Jared realized the ploy. The man had purposely set out to bring him from his rooms by mentioning Felicity's name. Obviously someone was in need of his assistance. Someone who wanted no questions asked. Someone who knew him and the house where he spent most evenings. "Who's hurt?"

"You don't need to know who. You just need to fix him."

"Fine. Where?"

"Put this on." A canvas bag was slapped upon his shoulder and Jared cursed, knowing he had no option but to do as he was told. Especially since he'd noticed the second figure positioned to his right and the gun in his hand. There was no telling how many there were, and he wasn't about to get his head bashed, or worse, by refusing their orders.

"I can't see a thing."

"That's the point, mate."

Jared knew they were guiding him through alleys, across streets into a labyrinth of still more alleyways. He could tell by the curbs he stumbled over and the sometimes muddy, sometimes cobblestone streets beneath the heels of his boots. Still, it wasn't long before he lost all sense of direction. Jared figured they had done that on purpose, and he didn't much care. All he knew was the longer they took to get him there, the less chance his patient would have. "Hurry the hell up, will you?"

"We're almost there."

They were walking on grass now, and Jared figured the man was telling the truth. He felt shrubbery brush against his legs and then realizing there had been no steps that normally proclaimed an entry hall, he was moved directly from the grass into a building. "Stairs," the man grunted as he was turned to his left.

They were in a basement. The damp musty smell was unmistakable. Jared's companions seemed to hesitate for a moment before he was ordered to bend and Jared walked into a room. The reason for the hesitation was so both could mask the lower portion of their faces.

A man moaned, and Jared asked, "Can I take it off now?"

"Aye," came the voice, again behind him.

Jared blinked as he pulled the canvas bag away. He was in a small room. Two men sat on the floor, both obviously in bad shape, but he couldn't see any real injury. And he couldn't tell what their problem might be without further examination. "What happened?" he asked, bending toward them.

"Not those two. Him," one of his kidnappers said as he was directed toward a young man lying upon a cot. The man had been shot. Jared couldn't see much in the dim light of one lantern, but it looked serious.

"Put him on the table," he ordered as he moved aside.

The taller of the two short men did all the work as the smaller one appeared incapable of doing more than holding the man's feet, and that he did with some difficulty. Jared assumed the smaller one was only a boy. He was puny enough and didn't have the strength of a girl. "You need some exercise, boy," Jared said as he watched the lad struggle, almost dropping the injured man's foot. Jared shoved the boy aside with a grumbled, "God, you're weaker than shit."

Felicity scowled at the man's back. It was easy enough to bark out orders, she supposed. Especially when one only had to stand in place and watch his bidding done.

Joshua was finally on the table. Jared looked around the room, only to find it empty of everything he needed. "Get water, sheets, bandages, lint, and a bowl. I'll need light and lots of it. Get me all the lamps you can find."

Felicity scowled again. What was wrong with asking, or if one were forced to order another about, couldn't he manage it with a measure of civility? She scowled again, but left the room to do his bidding.

Within seconds after removing the bag, Jared realized there were no obvious doors in this room. To be sure, there was a door, but it was hidden. He watched the boy run his hand over one wall, then turn and glance in his direction, hesitating. Jared looked away, knowing there would be time later to find his way out of here.

It took Felicity two trips to gather the needed supplies. At last all appeared ready. Joshua was on the table, his bloodied shirt and coat removed.

"I'll be needing your help. How much balls you got, boy?"

Felicity realized he was talking to her, but never having heard that expression before, she couldn't understand what he was talking about. "What?" she asked, the word was begun before she remembered to lower her voice to a husky whisper. She cleared her throat and tried again.

Jared grinned. He hadn't missed the break in the boy's voice and figured he knew the reason behind it. So the boy was exactly as he appeared—hardly out of the schoolroom, with a voice that still played him false, and yet he had taken upon his small shoulders a mighty dangerous task.

"I'm wondering if you have the stomach. I'm going to need your help."

Felicity shot the man behind her a pleading look, but Brian only shook his head. "Not me, lad. I ain't got the stomach to look into someone's innards."

Felicity could have refused, she supposed, but Joshua's life was on the line. Brian looked green at the very thought of helping. The two on the floor were completely depleted in strength, hardly able to stand should the need occur. That left only her. She moved toward the table, steeling herself against the horror she was bound to witness. "I'll do it."

"Set the lamps up on the corners," came the first order as Jared opened his bag and took out an array of medical utensils and equipment, laying each alongside the other. Scalpel, curved needle, waxed shoemaker's thread, probe, ball retractor, adhesive plasters, sulfur, ointment, and a bottle of oil were set in place. And with his supplies stood a bottle of opium, a luxury indeed, for opiates were in great shortage during this conflict, most particularly on the Patriot side. Many were the poor souls who were forced to withstand the horrors of an operation with nothing more than a bottle of rum at their disposal.

"Tear one of those sheets to pieces, wet one, and clean him up."

Felicity did as she was told, ignoring to the best of her ability Jared's abominable way of ordering her about. After she wiped away most of the blood, he took a steel stick measuring about six inches long and began to probe the wound, obviously searching for the ball hidden somewhere among the soft tissue. The thought was disgusting. The actual sight of it more so. It took just about all of her strength not to gag as the probe sank two inches or more into Joshua's chest.

She thought she couldn't stand much more of this. Felicity had no idea things were about to get even worse.

Jared gave up his probing at the sound of Joshua's moan. A moment later a spoonful of opium was administered, and Jared, while waiting for the drug to take effect, looked closely over the damage done. The bullet was still lodged inside, for no exit wound was in evidence. It had entered Joshua's chest just below the collarbone, but as far as Jared could tell the bone had been left intact. The man's steady breathing indicated that no lung had been hit. *Things might work out well tonight,* Jared thought. *If no complications arise.*

Jared glanced at the youngster's hands as he wiped at the blood still oozing from the wound. A moment later he frowned. The boy's hands were delicate, slender, almost feminine. No wonder he'd had such trouble lifting the man to the table.

And then Jared noticed the small pearl ring. He blinked in astonishment, knowing it couldn't be, and yet the evidence stared him in the face.

It was her ring. He wasn't mistaken. He knew that ring, just as he knew the woman's every movement, smile, and sparkle of her honey brown eyes. Hadn't he studied her nightly? Hadn't he listened and watched from across the hall as she worked her needlepoint, talking with her cousin, while allowing him a gentle smile each time she glanced his way?

Had the boy stolen the ring? Had he crept into her room and taken it? Was he part of her household? Is that why he was chosen tonight, because he was often in Felicity's home and it was known that he was a surgeon?

Jared raised eyes suddenly filled with fury. It took most of his control to keep his hands at his sides, for the thought of this little whelp in Felicity's room caused him an anger he hadn't before suspected himself capable of. If he hadn't needed the boy's help, he would have throttled the lad despite the grisly little man with the gun.

Jared was thinking that before the night was through he'd know exactly whose face was hidden beneath that mask. Felicity should know the truth about those in her employ, lest she somehow become inadvertently involved in their insidious ventures. He was imagining how to go about it when the boy moved into the circle of light.

Not three feet separated them. For the first time Jared could see clearly the dark honey brown of her eyes and knew without a shadow of a doubt who the *boy* was. For a long moment he knew only shock, then he felt his entire body break into a sweat. She was working for the rebel cause. How did she have the courage to put herself in danger like this? Jared reconsidered his thoughts. Courage was the wrong word. It didn't take courage. It took a sense of adventure perhaps, but it took most of all a complete lack of common sense. Damn the little fool. Did she think her sweet ways and lovely face would keep her from harm's way? Did she think she could merely blink those beautiful eyes and flash an enticing smile and all would be forgiven? His mouth tightened with anger, for he wanted nothing more than to wring her foolish neck.

It was then that he made his decision. She might not know it yet, but this woman had just given up whatever role she played in the Patriot cause. He was going to move his things into her house. One way or another he was going to keep her safe. And if it took watching her day and night, so be it.

Jared knew a sense of relief at the thought and felt his anger ease and the tension in his body relax. He studied her for a long moment before he came to yet another decision. The corners of his mouth curved at the thought. He'd been trying for weeks to convince Felicity to share his bed. He might not have been so forward as to actually say the words, but they both knew what he was about. He couldn't have been more obvious, and had she been another, he would have already known the pleasure of that soft, sweet body. Only Felicity was more stubborn than most. So far all he'd gotten for his heated looks were polite, but coolly aloof smiles. Well that was at an end. He had her now, and there was no way she could escape him.

Felicity watched his dark eyes move over her masked face. He couldn't see more than her eyes and forehead and yet, judging by the look in his eyes, it appeared he'd seen enough. She hadn't a doubt that he knew who she was. She didn't know how he had recognized her, but he had, and Felicity could only wonder at the steps he might take. How strong, she wondered, were his loyalties to his King? Could she somehow convince him to see her way of thinking and join her cause? She knew a sudden sense of panic, not because he knew, but because of the way he was looking at her, because of the unspoken question and the hint of satisfaction that curved his lips.

There was no need to speak the words. Felicity knew there was but one way to keep his silence. She had known his wants from the first. Had she the courage? Could she do it? Was she strong enough to give in to the man's wants? Did the rebel cause mean so much?

Her thoughts were interrupted by a brisk, "He's ready. Stand by with a cloth to wipe the blood."

"Oh God," she hoarsely murmured, and Jared grinned. Felicity in her distress had forgotten to lower her voice. Had he any doubts of her true identity, the sound of those words had dispelled them.

Jared made a small neat incision with a scalpel. Next he reached for his retractors. Placing the edge of the curved steel just inside the wound, he motioned for Felicity to take the end and hold it so the wound gaped open. "Don't pull it too hard."

Felicity felt the need to gag, but forced the sensation aside. She had to do this. If she was doomed to be sick, then she'd simply have to wait until later.

Again a probe was introduced into the wound, and, after a moment of exploring, Jared smiled as he felt it brush against the ball. The ball remover in his hands, Jared gently extracted the steel from Joshua's body.

No sooner was the ball out than blood began to gush in pumping waves from the hole. Jared cursed, knowing an artery had been hit and the ball had, until that moment, greatly impeded the flow of blood. A damaged artery meant certain death. Could he, by some miracle, stop the bleeding? Could he find the break in time and sew it closed? Jared knew he had little chance. It had never been done before. Still, he couldn't simply stand idle and watch the man bleed to death. He had to try.

"The ball was lodged against an artery," he said without thinking. "It's been torn, and I'll have to try and close it.

"You," he called out to Brian. "Get over here. I need your help."

"But . . ." Brian answered weakly.

"I said get over here," Jared roared so loudly that Felicity wondered if the officers in their beds upstairs might not have heard.

Brian stood obediently at Jared's side. The incision was drastically lengthened and Felicity bit her lips together at the horror of pumping blood and thick parted flesh. How was she to bear this?

Brian was given another retractor and told to pull, only this time not so gently. He and Felicity held the wound open as Jared reached inside with both hands. Felicity shuddered and tried to look away, only she couldn't, for Jared kept yelling at her to wipe the blood that was hampering his vision. She had to reach inside the cavity more than once to clear the way.

He held a needle and thread. Half the time he couldn't see what he was doing. Joshua's chest cavity was filling with blood. Felicity forgot her disgust as she silently urged him to hurry. *Oh God, hurry. Please!*

And then the pumping eased until finally it stopped altogether. Felicity gulped as she realized that Jared had just done something extraordinary. Something she hadn't known it was possible to do.

Jared was thinking much along the same lines. He'd never tried to close an artery before. He felt a measure of pride at his cool thinking, then realized his silent congratulations were a bit premature. The man's chest was filled with blood, and, despite his efforts, it would be a miracle if he survived. Jared knew the first step would be to remove the blood. He took strips of the torn sheet and absorbed what he could, praying his efforts had been enough.

Next he showed Felicity how to hold the skin together as he took the curved needle and began to sew Joshua's chest closed. After the blood was wiped away, he applied lint soaked in oil. "These bandages should be changed daily and a poultice applied to draw pus."

Felicity swallowed in disgust at the thought.

"He'll be hurting bad tomorrow. You can give him this when the pain is at its worst, but no more than a teaspoon every few hours."

Felicity nodded at his instructions and slipped the bottle of opium into her jacket pocket.

Moments later, with his medical bag packed, and the canvas once again hooding Jared's head, Brian led him out of the room.

Anyone would have thought that was the end. Only Felicity knew it was but the beginning.

Four

Felicity knew he would soon approach her. She knew as well what his proposition would be. That she was as yet still free, that no squad of soldiers had come to arrest and carry her off to prison only meant that his plans for her were more illicit in nature. What she didn't know was her answer, nor the game he now thought to play.

Where had the man taken himself off to? From the first day of his arrival in her country, he had made nightly visits, spending hours with the men who occupied her home. Now that she expected him, Captain Walker hadn't been seen for three days.

Felicity doubted he suddenly found himself weighed down in his work, without an available minute left to socialize. No, he was keeping his distance for the distinct purpose of making her suffer all the more. Each day Felicity wondered if tonight would be the night. Each morning she awakened wondering the same. Her nerves were in shambles, her usual easy humor nonexistent. She couldn't think beyond what Jared might have in mind.

Nightly she kept to her room, hoping beyond hope that he might forget the unforgettable. It was only later, well after the officers had retired for the night, that Felicity dared to leave her room. Alone in her garden she paced her anxiousness into exhaustion as she sought reprieve from the heat, from the fear, from a jittery sense of the unknown.

* * *

Jared filled his pipe as he watched from the shadows of a tree. She hadn't been in the sitting room when he'd come by tonight. No doubt she was still unaware of the fact that he and his man had moved their things into the room beside her own.

Jared had every intention of following through with his silent promise. She would not come to harm. Not if he had to keep her in bed until this conflict was at an end.

Jared smiled at the thought, knowing that to keep her in bed would be no great chore. Would she come willingly? Jared shook his head. She would fight him, in the beginning at least, but not for long, for a gentle reminder of what she'd been about would soon bring her to acquiescence.

Until meeting Miss Felicity Dryson, Jared had imagined so dishonorable an act on his part quite impossible. He was not delighted to realize that put to the test, his character appeared no more moral than that of the lowest-ranking soldier. Lower perhaps. The thought disturbed, for he'd always imagined himself a man of high moral standards. Granted, he'd had his share of women, but none had entered his chambers and shared his bed under duress.

None until this one. Jared's sigh grew into a smile, for he had no doubt her initial reluctance would be short-lived. He'd felt the fire in her. He'd tasted the heat of her skin, in her soft sweet yearning, the fascination of her yielding, and knew unbearable pleasure awaited them both.

"Good evening, mistress," Jared said, unable to ignore the fact that his sudden presence had startled her into a slight jump. He smiled as she turned and glared in his direction. "I had imagined that you would have long ago taken to your bed for the night."

He was here at last, only Felicity wasn't sure his presence made things any better. She'd never felt more nervous in her life. Now, within the next few minutes, she'd know the way of his thoughts. At least the terrible waiting was at an end. "I needed a breath of fresh air."

Jared smiled. What she meant was she was far too nervous

to sleep. Well, he knew of a potion that had yet to fail to do the trick. Under the best circumstances, with just the right hand, not counting some expertise, it could relax the most jittery soul. And this moonlit setting appeared specifically made for what he had in mind.

"It is dangerous I think to wander through these gardens alone at night."

Felicity shot him a look of ridicule. "Certainly not. These walls are meant to keep the riffraff at bay."

Jared knew the riffraff remark was directed at him. "And no one could climb them?"

"To what gain? Do you imagine some ruffian in desperate need of a flower?"

Jared grinned at her response. She was a spunky little piece. He watched her full lips twist into a sneer as she imagined she'd gotten the last word, then thought of the feel of those lips soft and pliable beneath his. The thought brought on a surge of excitement. Jared figured wanting her had somehow twisted his mind, for he'd never felt attracted to a woman with a sharp tongue before. No, until this woman, his interest had always lain in the sweet, gentle, lushly curved lady who enjoyed the sport as much as he. A woman who came willingly to share in the pleasure, only to leave with eyes sparkling and a soft radiant smile of satisfaction. This woman already had sparkling eyes and the sweetest smile he'd ever seen. Only her unwillingness tarnished the picture. But Jared knew he would soon change that. He gave her his most charming smile. "And you being the prettiest and most ripe flower of all, I expect you'll be the first picked."

Felicity turned from his smile. She wasn't interested in his compliments. She doubted they were meant in any case. "It's late. I should go in."

"Not yet," he said with some authority, then softened his command with a smile and, "A few more minutes won't matter, will it?"

Felicity could stand no more. He played a game of cat and

mouse, disappearing for three days, obviously just to heighten her anxiety. And now that he had finally shown himself, he continued to play his unscrupulous game, knowing every sly word he spoke would be examined and worried over. Nothing he could do to her was worse than this war of nerves. The man knew what she was about. What she needed to know was what he was going to do about it? "All right, let's get it out in the open, shall we, Captain? What would you have for your silence?"

She might show a brave face, but the woman was afraid. Jared forced aside a niggling sense of compassion, lest he invariably lose his chance. He wanted her and knew he might otherwise have waited forever. There was no other way. He answered in a heartbeat. "You."

Felicity had known the truth of it since that night in the hidden room. She had seen the smile, the glitter in his eyes and known. But somehow, over these last three days, she had persuaded herself that he was a gentleman and she could somehow find a way out of this predicament. She shuddered at the ease in which he discussed the taking of her body, as if she were but a commodity, like a well-cooked meal, or an aromatic smoke. Still, in some ways just talking about it was a relief. She congratulated herself on the fact that her voice hardly trembled at all when she said, "Well, you're straightforward about it in any case."

Jared smiled, for he had only matched her in her bluntness. "As are you, mistress."

Felicity frowned, wondering why, or how his words made her feel better. Now that she knew what she faced, she was considerably less jittery and anxious. Now she knew only anger. "How do I know you won't tell anyway?"

"You don't. But satisfying me is your only hope."

She shot him a look of loathing. "Perhaps I'd rather rot in one of your prisons."

"Perhaps," Jared said without a shred of emotion. "The choice is certainly yours."

"Why?" she asked, unable to believe it had come down to this.

"Because I want you."

"And you always get what you want?"

Jared only smiled in response.

"I could deny it. It would be your word against mine."

"And which of us will be believed, do you think? A loyal officer of the King, or a beautiful lady?" Jared shrugged as he imagined himself the judge. "Still, you might have a chance. Beautiful ladies often win out. Are you up to trying?"

Felicity didn't have to think long on his question. She knew the answer. Trying wasn't good enough. She couldn't chance everything on a hope that she might be believed. There was too much to lose, most importantly, her very life. She swore she wouldn't beg, although the need was almost overpowering, for there wasn't a trace of compassion, understanding, or forgiveness in this man's entire countenance. Instead she warned, "I'll hate you forever for this."

"Perhaps, but for a short time, you'll love the things I do to you."

Felicity scowled at his confident remark. "You fit well into the English mode, sir. I know not one among you to be less than a cocky, insufferable, bastard."

Jared ignored her less-than-ladylike comment. It didn't for a minute diminish the need he felt for her. If anything it only intensified it. Every damn thing the woman did and said intensified it. "You can start now."

"What do you mean?"

"I mean, come over here."

Felicity did as she was told, standing angrily before him, her hands on her hips. In her anger almost daring him to do his worse, silently swearing she could bear whatever he had in mind and more. "Now what?"

"Now you can kiss me."

Jared saw the look of hate in her eyes and realized her intent.

Quickly he took her hands in his. "Hitting me won't solve your problem, mistress."

"But killing you would," she grated between clenched teeth.

Jared grinned. "Kiss me, Felicity, and see if you can do a reasonably good job of it."

It was then that Felicity fully understood. He didn't want only the use of her body. He wanted her full cooperation in his debauchery. Well, she'd die first and be glad of it. "You might as well arrest me now, Captain. There's not a man or cause in the world that could reduce me to a whore."

"What about your father?" he asked. He'd heard the softening of her voice when she spoke about the man and knew if this lady loved anyone, it was her father. Jared felt a niggling sense of shame at what he was doing, but disregarded the emotion. Throwing everything honorable aside, he swore he'd have this woman whatever it took.

"What do you mean?"

"I mean, what do you expect will happen to his home, his worldly goods, if it should become known that his daughter is working for the rebel cause?" Jared knew he wouldn't go through with his less-than-subtle threat. He had no intention of turning her in, but she couldn't know that. She couldn't ever know that.

"My father doesn't have anything to do with this," she said, her voice rising in growing fear.

"Too bad." He shrugged indifferently. "He'll suffer for it in any case."

"Insufferable beast. Bloody English swine."

"Lower your voice."

But Felicity wouldn't listen. She couldn't live with the rage inside. She had to let it out or burst into a million angry pieces.

"I hate . . ." Felicity found her words suddenly cut off by Jared's mouth pressing hard against her own. He'd kissed her only to silence her, Felicity knew, for his touch held not a shred of gentleness. And Felicity almost reveled in that, for his lack of gentleness was the only thing that kept the moment bearable.

Pain kept the hate alive. And as long as she knew hate she could best him in the end.

But then the beast grew gentle, leaving her without even that weapon to fight him. She tried to pull away, but his arm held her tightly against him, holding her in place, holding her arms at her side.

She turned her face from his mouth, only to find his lips at her cheek, his teeth nibbling at her jaw. "Captain, please." Felicity had sworn she wouldn't beg, but the words slipped out without her notice. Her pride wished them back, for she could take this. This and more. The vile beast might take what he wanted, but he'd never, never find her a willing participant.

Jared lifted her into his arms and didn't put her down again until he sat. With his back against a tree, he settled her gently upon his legs. This assault, whether gentle or rough was getting him nowhere, and he knew it. There had to be another way.

His hand at the back of her head held her face against his chest as he tried to think, as he tried to come up with a different route. There had to be something, some way he could convince her. Threats were of no use. He couldn't bring about what he wanted from her with threats. His mouth was close to her ear and sent a shiver down her spine when he spoke. "Listen to me, Felicity."

He had never before called her by her Christian name, but Felicity thought that impropriety was at the very bottom of her list of grievances. Now she had to keep up the struggle, for to relax even for a second might prove her downfall. "Are you listening?"

"Truthfully, Captain, I doubt you could say anything worth hearing."

Felicity could hear his warm chuckle, made warmer perhaps by the fact that her face was pressed against his chest.

"What if we devise a plan, you and I?"

Felicity ignored the fact that she was sitting on the man's lap. That he was holding her in a most improper fashion, that if anyone should come upon them, her reputation would be in tatters. All she knew were his words and the thin ray of hope she found in them. "What kind of plan?"

"Well, the fact is I want you in my bed."

"In truth?" she said with a small pretended gasp. Her sarcasm was obvious as she continued with, "And here I thought all along you only wanted me to join you in a game of chess."

He smiled into her red curls. "I just want you to understand all of it."

Felicity nodded. "Go on."

"But I left out the most important word. Willing. I want you willing in my bed."

Felicity shook her head. "That won't ever happen."

"It might, if you gave us a chance."

"What do you mean, a chance?"

"Suppose I forget all I know about you. Suppose I courted you and you were glad of it." Jared felt her stiffen. His hand slid from her hair, and Felicity took the opportunity to pull away. Granted she couldn't do much about her present position, not with his arms holding her securely about her waist, but she could create some reasonable space between her face and his chest. "All right, suppose you pretended to be glad of it. Suppose you even allowed me an occasional kiss. What do you think would happen?"

"Nothing."

"Are you sure?"

"Absolutely sure."

"Why don't we try it then?"

Felicity shook her head. "Captain, I don't think that would solve . . ."

He cut her off with a taunting, "Are you afraid?"

"Of what? You?" she mocked. "Hardly."

"No, I think you're afraid of you," Jared said. "I think you don't trust yourself to kiss me, lest you find yourself wanting more."

Felicity's laughter was low, silky, more sensual than he'd ever heard it before and detrimental to not only his mind but his gut.

He couldn't control his body's reaction to it and wondered if she realized his growing problem. "Captain, I would have thought a ploy like that beneath you."

Jared realized that when it came to this woman there wasn't any depth to which he might sink. Any except turning her in or forcing her to his will. He'd imagined himself capable of the latter, but when it came right down to it, he couldn't do it. He wanted her willing. She had to be willing, or neither of them would find joy in the union.

"You have, I think, for too long absented yourself from a lady's company. Ladies do not want men. Granted, they may on occasion concede to a man's wants, but that is part of wifely duty."

"Do you think so?"

"I know so."

"Then you wouldn't be averse to my little plan, would you?"

Felicity laughed again, somehow and perhaps for the first time enjoying this private moment. "What exactly would you have me do?"

"I'd have you smile and talk sweetly, just as you would to any suitor."

"To what purpose?"

"You know my intent."

She frowned. "And you know mine."

"Right, and in three months' time, if I haven't convinced you to see to my way of thinking, I'll give over and proclaim you the winner."

"And never bring up the subject of my loyalties again?"

"Never."

Felicity laughed with some delight, knowing herself to be the winner of this small skirmish. "And all I have to do is accept you as a suitor?"

"And treat me as you would any other."

Felicity grinned, knowing that should prove to be no hardship, for Jared could on occasion be charming in the extreme. It would be no chore to abide his company.

"And kiss me occasionally," he put in as a reminder. "You mustn't forget that."

Felicity felt it necessary to once again mention the root of the problem. "And my loyalties? They will . . ."

". . . never be known by anyone other than myself." Jared neglected to add that her days working for her cause were at an end. He was going to make sure of that.

Felicity held out her hand as if to seal their bargain with a handshake. "I hope you won't be too disappointed."

Jared smiled at her cocky self-assurance. "And I *know*," he put some feeling into the word, "you won't be."

Felicity ignored his comment. All she had to do was keep her wits about her and no harm would be done. All she had to do was pretend to like him, and, after three months, he would give it all up, and she would be free to continue on with her work. Felicity couldn't believe her luck.

She'd have no problem, of course, in seeing to it that the man was doomed to disappointment. She did not want him. She could never want him. To a lady like herself, it didn't matter how charming he might prove. Ladies were simply never tempted.

Her smile was radiant. Jared caught his breath at the sight of it and knew he'd lied. Three months, three years, thirty, it didn't matter. He was going to have this woman. He glanced at her hand and shook his head. "I think a kiss would seal the bargain."

He noticed her hesitation and fought to keep his laughter at bay. "You know, to get you used to what I'll be expecting."

Her gaze filled with suspicion. "You said occasionally."

"Well, as far as I can see this is an occasion."

Felicity's relief knew no bounds. She had little to fear from this man, and all her worrying had been for naught. The thought caused her a smile, and she found it nearly impossible not to laugh aloud. Surely she could accede to his wants this one time. After all, he only asked for a kiss. "I imagine one kiss wouldn't hurt." A moment later she placed her lips on his. Barely had they touched him when she pulled back.

Jared raised a dark brow at her satisfied expression. *Is that what she calls a kiss?* Jared thought. He'd gotten better from his little niece. His eyes darkened with promise as he watched her soft smile. No, this little miss was going to do better than that. A great deal better than that. "So when do you think we should do it?"

"Do what?" she asked, as she set about trying to remove herself from his lap.

"Kiss."

Felicity shifted and was about to roll to her knees. She turned back and blinked her surprise. "I just kissed you."

"No, you didn't. I'm sure I would have noticed a kiss. I always remember when a lady kisses me."

Felicity saw the curve of his lips and knew what the man was about. Greedy beggar. Still she kept her opinion to herself, and said, "Perhaps your memory is beginning to fail. After all, I expect there have been many, so many in fact that . . ."

"There haven't been that many. And I know a kiss when I get one."

"Meaning my kisses are insignificant enough to easily forget." Felicity didn't care in the least that her kiss did not affect him. She didn't want him affected. She waved aside the matter with a gentle movement of her hand. "You'll have to remember, Captain, I've hardly your expertise."

"Yes, I seem to remember a time when you said you've never kissed a man before." There was a moment of silence before Jared breathed on a tired sigh, "Well, I could show you how, I suppose."

Felicity almost laughed at his sly manner. Had she been as simpleminded as he no doubt supposed she thought she might have been tricked by it. As it was, he'd have to do better than that. "I wouldn't want to put you to any trouble."

"It wouldn't be any trouble, Miss Dryson."

Felicity wasn't sure of her feelings. She knew he was teasing

her, of course, and yet it was her lack of accomplishment that
gave the man reason. Perhaps if she had allowed a kiss or two
over the years, she might have grown proficient in the art. She
shrugged aside her thoughts. She couldn't correct that oversight
at this late date, and it hardly mattered in any case. "Perhaps
you could show me where I lack in skill." The words were hardly
out of her mouth when Felicity wished she could have called
them back. She couldn't imagine why she might have said such
a thing.

"All right," he returned far too agreeably. "First you put your
hands on my face like this." Jared framed her face with his
hands.

Felicity felt no fear, but smiled, knowing she could bring this
moment to a close with one word. "This isn't a kiss. It's touching."

"It's part of a kiss."

Felicity imagined this little lesson would bring no harm and
thought not to argue the point. She did as she was told and
knew some surprise since she rather liked the feel of his skin
beneath her hands. That was odd, wasn't it? She'd never thought
that she might like touching a man's face. It was harder, quite
a bit less soft than her own, and he needed a shave, but the
slightly scratchy sensation under her palms felt delightful. No,
delightful wasn't the word. It felt different, it felt . . .

"What is it?" he asked, noticing the look in her eyes.

"You feel different."

Jared refused to laugh, not when he was this close to having
his desires met. He wasn't about to rile her again by a careless
act. "Yes, I imagine one could say that. Now, you bring your
mouth very close to mine."

Felicity pressed her lips against his and Jared pulled back.
"Not yet. You don't touch yet."

Felicity frowned. "Why not?"

"Because first you do this," he said as his lips brushed sen-
suously against her own. Feather-soft, almost like a whisper of
a breeze they touched her.

"That's easy enough. Do we rub noses as well?"

"It's very easy, and you could if you like."

Felicity giggled. "This is so silly. Do people really do this?"

Jared smiled. "They do."

Felicity didn't believe him for a minute. "It takes a long time to kiss then?"

"It does, if you do it right."

"Yes, well that was very nice," she said, and made as if to pull away.

Feeling the movement, he held her more firmly. "I'm not finished."

Her eyes widened with some surprise. "You're not?"

"I've hardly started."

"But . . ."

"We shouldn't talk for a few minutes now. If you talk you might not remember, and the next time I'll expect you to know what comes next."

Felicity nodded and kept her silence, unable to imagine what could possibly be so difficult or complicated about a simple kiss?

He brushed his mouth over hers again and slid his tongue between her lips. She pulled back a bit, as if surprised, but did not demur as his mouth followed the movement. And then his lips pressed harder, just a little harder against her. And Felicity thought she rather liked the feeling, especially liked it when he breathed against her, making her, and especially her stomach, grow warm, and causing tingling sensations to appear in the most peculiar places. She thought the tingling a bit odd, but didn't have long to contemplate the matter, for he took her bottom lip and sucked it into his mouth.

Felicity thought that most strange. Granted she knew next to nothing about kissing, but could this be right? She might have objected, and even went so far to pull back, but Jared's hand at the back of her head, steady, gentle, but firmly in place allowed her little room to move. And then he began to run his tongue over that lip, and Felicity, concentrating on the oddity, grew so intrigued that she quite forgot to mention her objection.

Enjoying the sweet titillation, it wasn't until long moments later that she tried to think again. And when she did her thoughts were a bit fuzzy at best. Felicity frowned, wondering why that should be? She had a feeling she should be objecting here, but she couldn't quite say what she might object to. The kiss, that's right, the kiss. She should be objecting to . . . She frowned again, wondering why in the world she would do such a thing. It felt lovely, better than lovely. Only a fool would object to this.

Felicity allowed him her full cooperation. She might not have put much into the kiss, seeing as this was her first one and she could hardly be expected to know what was required of her, but she enjoyed it immensely. She did especially enjoy it when he released her bottom lip and took the top in its place. Long moments later his tongue was inside her lips, running over the sensitive moist flesh, and then her teeth, and Felicity never realized she had somehow forgotten to think if she enjoyed it. She forgot to think at all, but allowed her own natural reaction to take hold.

With a little insistence, her teeth parted and his tongue dipped deeper inside to brush against hers. Her entire body tingled with sensation, and Felicity couldn't believe how good it felt. Did everyone kiss like this? Why had she waited so long to find out?

He tasted good, like a man, like a pipe and a trace of port. Felicity hadn't thought that a man could taste quite so good.

And then her tongue touched his and he moaned and she knew he must like it easily as much as she. So she moved it again, only to hear the sound repeat itself. Only it wasn't Jared who moaned this time, was it? Felicity couldn't be sure. She wasn't sure of anything except that she wanted more.

Their mouths were open wide now, and Jared was learning her mouth, just as if the sweet lustrous warmth were some wondrous confection, something he hadn't imagined could be so good, something he couldn't imagine getting enough of.

She was terribly dizzy. No one could have blamed her if she leaned a bit closer and wrapped her arms around his neck. She did it only to steady herself. Didn't she?

She was soft, pliable in his arms, and a pulse throbbed in his throat with the wanting he knew, but Jared wasn't about to lose all control and push her further. He knew she'd be frightened if he insisted on more. No, she had to learn that the next step and the next one after that were equally as wonderful, and she had to come to crave them as much as he.

He pulled back and again took her lip into his mouth sucking gently, ever so gently, until she squirmed, obviously needing more. Next he loved her top lip and brought the kiss to an end, just as he had begun—by rubbing his lips gently against her own.

Somewhere along the way, Felicity had forgotten to breathe. It took some real effort to ask, "Is that it?" She frowned. What was the matter with her? Why couldn't she breathe right?

Jared rubbed his face into red curls, breathing in her sweetness. It was the longest and best kiss he'd ever given a woman, and Felicity had no notion that it was any different from a thousand others. Jared smiled as he imagined teaching her all the delicious ways there were to kiss and to where that would eventually lead. His voice was gravelly and rough when he returned, "That's it."

"I'm sorry now that I waited so long before learning. It's something, isn't it?"

Jared wasn't the least bit sorry she waited, for he liked nothing better than initiating her into the art. As a matter of fact he could hardly wait for the next step in this gentle seduction.

She moved from his lap and, with some effort, finally stood. Jared was quickly at her side.

"Well then," she said for no apparent reason, except that she thought something should be said and didn't have a clue as to what one said to a man after being kissed in that fashion.

Felicity was obviously shaken. So shaken in fact that she had some trouble finding her footing. And did not object when Jared reached to steady her. "And that's what you want from a kiss?" She smoothed her skirt, never glancing in his direction.

Jared smiled. The lady was having a time of it regaining her senses. Jared could only imagine if one kiss could cause this kind of response, how hot and delicious she would be once he got her into bed. "Not every time. We couldn't kiss like that in public."

She looked at him now. Glared actually. "We wouldn't be kissing in public at all." The words were said in a no-nonsense tone.

"But you could touch me in public, couldn't you?"

Felicity didn't trust him. Not in the least. And the narrowing of her gaze said as much. "What does that mean? How do you want to be touched?"

Jared could hardly keep from laughing aloud. There was no way that he could tell her exactly what he wanted, not that is without finding his face stinging from a slap, so he said instead, "Well, you could touch my sleeve, or run a hand against my chest now and then, perhaps smoothing my lapel. Maybe brush back my hair. You know, the usual way ladies touch their men."

"Only you won't be my man," she felt the need to remind.

"You're pretending, remember."

Felicity bit her lip in consternation. She wasn't at all happy with the idea. The fact of the matter was, she didn't want to touch him. She didn't want anything to do with him at all. And the longer she thought of it, the more sure she grew. "I really don't think this will work, Captain."

"Jared," he corrected. "No? Then you're ready to join me in bed? And after only one kiss?" He whistled softly between his teeth in supposed appreciation of his skills. "I must be a sight better than I thought I was."

She frowned. "You can take that superior self-confident look out of your eyes. And wipe that smile off your face as well."

"Yes, ma'am."

"I never said I was ready, and you might as well know, I never will be ready."

"Yes, ma'am," Jared repeated with what Felicity thought to be quite a bit more amusement than the situation called for. As a matter of fact, the situation called for no amusement at all. Still, she thought it best not to ask too many questions. She wasn't sure she wanted to know why he appeared so delighted.

"But if you feel it necessary to go on with this charade, I imagine I can do my share. And stop calling me ma'am."

"Shall I call you dear?" Jared thought he might like to call her that since she felt so very dear to him at this moment.

"Endearments are out of the question, Captain."

"Jared," he gently insisted. "What will I call you then?"

"You may call me Miss Dryson."

Jared fought back a grin at her prim and proper manner, so opposite of what it had been only moments before. "Do you imagine others might take that as strange?"

"All right, call me Felicity, or better yet, Miss Felicity."

"Or darling Felicity, or sweet Felicity," he teased.

She took a step back, not trusting him for a minute. "A simple Felicity will do nicely, thank you."

Jared mused over the last of her comments as he watched her turn and walk ahead of him toward the house. If he knew one thing, Jared was sure that there was nothing simple about this woman. She was the most fascinating creature he'd ever known. Her innocence was a constant delight and the first stages of passion she'd never known to exist beneath those prim ladylike manners was something he longed to explore further. On the surface she appeared to be nothing more than a well-bred lady of some means, when in fact she led a double life, traipsing through the streets at night dressed as a man, kidnapping surgeons and God knew what else, all to the advancement of her cause. No, she was far from simple. And if he wasn't very careful, he just might find himself in love with her.

Jared frowned at the thought and shook his head in silent denial. No, he wouldn't be falling in love with her. He was finished with love. It had been years since he'd even thought of the word. After the pain, the helplessness he'd known at Annie's death, he never wanted to love again. He was old enough and experienced enough to enjoy a woman's body without allowing his mind and emotions to become involved.

Besides, he enjoyed his life just as it was. He needed no woman to complete it. He had his work. An occasional woman to warm his bed at night would be enough. More than enough.

Lust and love were not the same, and he wouldn't be confusing one with the other. It didn't matter that she was lovely. There were hundreds of others just as adorable, with at least as much spunk and loyalty. All right, so temporarily her loyalty had gotten misplaced, but he would soon see to correcting that error.

There was no room for love here and certainly no need for it.

Five

Felicity frowned as she turned to lock the door only to find he had followed her into the house. The kitchen was dark, the tables, and cabinets thrown into shadows, the only light coming from the banked fire. "What are you doing? It's late."

"I know."

"Well, shouldn't you go to your rooms?"

Jared smiled at her confusion. "I was thinking I might."

"So?" she asked, obviously waiting for him to leave.

"So, if you don't want another lesson, you should let me pass."

"What?"

"I said . . ."

"I know what you said. What did you mean?"

"I mean, it's dark down here, and we are apparently alone, so we could try one more kiss, just so I know you have it right."

She shook her head, even as she took a step back. "I mean about passing."

"What?" Jared had a time of it controlling his need to laugh. He knew of course the root of her confusion. She didn't know he was staying in her house and had no idea why he should have followed her inside. Still, he felt in no hurry to clear things up. Jared rather liked watching her as she tried to solve a problem. Her eyes would narrow, and her mouth would thin in concentration. The truth of the matter was that Jared rather liked watching her all the time.

"You said I should let you pass."

"Oh, well I can't very well get to my rooms if I don't climb the stairs, now can I?"

It took a moment before realization dawned, and Felicity moaned the word, "Noooo," as she leaned heavily against the closed door, her back to him. The sound was nothing less than a mournful cry as her gaze rose to the ceiling and perhaps the heavens beyond as if asking the Lord why. "Which one did you take?"

"The room next to yours."

"Wonderful." She breathed on a sigh of disgust, knowing because he was part of the occupying force, she had absolutely no choice in the matter and no amount of complaint on her part would make any difference. These cursed English could do just about anything they cared to do, and the colonists had no choice but to allow it. "Just wonderful. And when were you thinking of telling me?"

"I just did."

Felicity groaned at the thought of another Tory under her roof. In fact, the most annoying of the lot. This was just what she needed.

"Don't worry, sweetheart, I'm sure you won't bother me."

Felicity scowled, shoved the lock home with a bit more force than necessary, and glared into his smile. "I suppose it's too late to ask if you might change your mind."

"Far too late. Marcy has already settled me in."

"And who is Marcy?"

"My man. He helps me with . . ."

"I know what a man's man does," she said with no little disgust.

Jared followed her through the kitchen and the darker dining room to the central stairway. There were candles lit in sconces along the wall as there would be upstairs. Felicity put each one out as she walked by. They were at her door before he spoke again. "Felicity?"

"What?" she asked. Moonlight streamed into a window at

the far end of the hall. The meager light didn't go far toward allowing a person to see clearly. She turned to squint at him through the shadowy darkness.

"Good night."

"Good night," she returned without thought.

"Ah, Felicity."

"What?" She asked again, this time her voice hiding none of her annoyance.

"This could be considered another occasion, don't you think?"

It took her a few seconds to understand his meaning. The beast wanted yet another kiss. Well, that was too bad because he wasn't getting one. She needed some time to think over her reaction to the last one—and still more time to come to terms with the fact that he had moved into her home uninvited. "Surely not."

"Well people do kiss good night, especially if they're courting."

Without answering, she opened her door and backed into the room, still facing him. Jared took that for an invitation. He shouldn't have. Had he been able to see more than a dark shadow of her form, he would have realized his mistake, by the glare of anger in her eyes.

Just as he made to follow her into her room, Felicity slammed the door, hitting him in the nose. "We'll start courting tomorrow."

Despite his pain and the blood that flowed freely into his handkerchief, Jared couldn't hold back his soft laughter.

To Felicity's disgust, when he heard the bolt slide into place, he laughed all the more.

It was more than an hour before Felicity could relax enough to lie down. And almost another hour passed before she could put from her mind the feel of his mouth against hers. It was then that she found herself in that special relaxed and floating place that promised she was only seconds from sleep. Only Felicity was not destined to sleep.

She jumped in her bed, sitting straight up at the crash that sounded from below. Fluffy, nestled comfortably at her feet, let out a low growl. It took but a second to understand that someone had broken into her house. Someone who didn't have the sense to realize that of the four bedrooms upstairs, two were occupied by British soldiers, not counting the three others who slept on the third floor.

She flung back the light cover and ran to the small table centered in her room, upon which sat a candle and flint. It took a few tries, for her hands were shaking, but Felicity finally managed to light the candle.

Next she wrapped her robe around her and ran for her door, her dog at her heels. "Stay," she said, as she entered the hall, only to hear much the same command issued to her.

"Stay right there."

Felicity gasped, for on bare feet the man had made no sound and she hadn't expected to find him suddenly outside her door, on his way downstairs.

Men were coming out of their rooms. Felicity could hear them grumbling about being disturbed at this time of night. Some held candles, some not, but all were clothed in long nightshirts and robes. All but Jared. He wore his uniform trousers and little else. Felicity blinked at the sight. Nothing else in fact. Her cheeks grew warm, for she'd never before seen a man's chest.

Downstairs a man cursed. A second later there was yet another crash, and Felicity forgot all about the startling sight of one shirtless man as she ran to join the others downstairs.

In the hallway, about six feet from the first step a man lay obviously unconscious, his face turned from her. Around his head lay the shattered remains of a lamp. The front door was closed, and even from there, Felicity could see that it was still locked.

Three steps up, Felicity's gaze caught the movement of curtains on each side of a window in the smaller sitting room. They fluttered in a gentle breeze. The window had been broken, no doubt the means of this intruder's entrance. Felicity frowned, unable to understand the man's reasoning behind the break-in. Surely had it been his intent to steal something, he would have been quieter when going about it and would hardly have used a lamp to light his way. So he hadn't broken in as a thief might have. And if he had not, it stood to reason he had something else in mind. Felicity's first thought was that it was someone who worked for the cause. Someone in desperate need. She wasn't far from wrong.

Jared glanced from the unconscious man to the woman descending the steps, for he had been thinking along much the same lines. No doubt this fellow was yet another of her comrades, laid low because of some irresponsible act. What he had to do now was make sure she did not give herself away, by even a glance of recognition.

"It's all right, Felicity. We found the intruder. He appears alone. You can breathe easily."

He said the words with some insistence and Felicity glanced in his direction, wondering what the man was about. She didn't think long on Jared's odd behavior though, for one of the officers took just that moment to turn the man to his back, and Felicity gasped as she ran the last few steps to his side. "Father! What is it? What's happened?"

Thomas Dryson burned with fever.

In the master bedroom, directly across the hall from Felicity's room, Jared leaned over his newest patient, examining the festering wound in his arm. He'd been shot, of that there was no doubt, but whoever had taken the bullet out had done a messy job of seeing to this wound, for the stitches were amateurish to say the least.

No doubt something, a fragment of the ball, a splinter of

bone, had been left behind, for the skin looked ready to explode with the festering that had since taken place.

Felicity stood opposite the doctor, her anxiety obvious in her drawn, tightly pinched features. Could Jared do something? Could he bring the fever down? Would her father live through this? Please God.

Jared glanced at the lady opposite him. For some reason she did not understand, nor, if the truth be told, care, he appeared angry. A moment later he left the room only to return within seconds with his bag of instruments. Soon after, Becky brought in water and linen towels as well as fresh lint. Apparently he had sent instruction during the time it took to move her father upstairs. Felicity had never noticed.

"You'll have to help me," Jared said. "There's no one else."

"What do I have to do?"

"His wound is festering. I have to drain it lest gangrene sets in."

Felicity swallowed at the thought, but nodded, despite the distinct weakening of her knees.

It was only then that Felicity realized she was still in her robe and nightdress "I'll change."

"We haven't got the time. Clean the skin around the wound," he said as he prepared his supplies.

Felicity moved to Jared's side, so she might more easily assist.

A moment later a scalpel slid into the tight red skin, spilling out a stream of blood and pus. Felicity swallowed in disgust, but quickly wiped the horror away. "There's a chance the arm won't have to come off, if we can clean this out and keep it that way."

The stench was awful, and although it threatened to turn Felicity's stomach, Jared seemed not to notice. He probed the wound for a long time. Probed it until he found a rotted piece of what once had been Thomas's shirt. And then he forced the wound to bleed until he was sure no other pieces of foreign matter had been left behind.

Next he sprinkled sulfur directly into the wound, praying it would stall off any further inflammation. And then, with Felicity holding the parted flesh tightly together, he sewed the wound closed again, doing a much neater job of it.

Lint soaked in oil was applied to the stitches. "I'll tell Becky to prepare a bread-and-milk poultice. If there is a need to drain still more, that should do the trick."

Felicity couldn't imagine the possibility of anything more coming from so small a wound, but nodded in response. "What about his fever? Is there something he can take?"

Jared shrugged. "The fever probably came from the wound. Now that the festering's gone, it should go down on its own. If he's not better in the morning, we'll start cold compresses."

As he washed his hands and dried them, he watched her. She looked exhausted. Fear and worry combined with the late hour had caused her creamy skin to take on a gray hue. "It's late. You should get some rest."

"I don't want to leave him. I haven't seen him in . . ." Her throat closed up, and she couldn't seem to finish as tears glistened in her eyes. It had been almost two years, and he was finally home, only Felicity didn't know if he was going to live or die. She turned away and took a deep, steadying breath, wiping at her eyes with the sleeve of her robe. "He doesn't even know I'm here."

Jared's only thought was to console her. His arms moved around her waist and from behind he brought her to lean against his chest. It did not go without notice that Felicity, in her worry, never thought to object. "He'll be all right, sweetheart," he said as he brushed his mouth over the top of her head. "The worst that can happen is he'll lose that arm." Jared knew that wasn't the worst of it. The man could lose his life as well, for many did not survive a fever such as this, never mind an amputation.

"Do you think he might?"

"I don't know. We can only wait and see." His arms tightened just a bit. "Have you ever given any thought to medicine?"

"What do you mean?"

"Twice you've helped me. You have a cool head."

Felicity smiled at the compliment. "But a weak stomach. I

hate the sight of blood, and I think I can live very nicely without seeing another abscess."

"My thoughts exactly," he said while rocking her gently against him. "Still you manage to get through it without fainting dead away."

"What choice have I? You shout orders and yell at me at every opportunity."

"Do I?" Jared grinned and lowered his head to nibble at the top of her ear. "I've been known to get a bit anxious when emergencies are at hand. Was I very bad?"

"Very," Felicity said, knowing that wasn't exactly true. He was abrupt and had the tendency to bark out commands, but he hadn't been cruel.

"And yet you said nothing until now?"

"I can take the worst you have to offer, Captain."

Jared chuckled. His words came low, filled with innuendo. "What about the best? Can you take that as well?"

Felicity didn't respond, simply because she didn't know for sure what he meant and somehow knew that to ask would only further complicate an already-complicated situation.

Jared smiled at her silence, gave her a hard squeeze, and said, "I want you to rest now, before I find myself with still another patient."

Felicity sighed even as she unknowingly nuzzled herself closer to his warmth, his strength. "I'll rest. I just want to sit with him a bit."

Jared frowned as his gaze moved over the man. His skin was browned from many hours spent in the sun. His body tight and trim from exercise. This was not some pale weakened creature who had suffered through an unidentified but recent illness. "Where was he, really?"

"What?" she asked, glancing at the man who held her. Then, realizing her position, she pulled out of his arms.

"Except for the wound, your father hasn't been ill. Where was he?"

Felicity fussed nervously, adjusting the sheet that lay over her father and needlessly wiping at the man's fevered brow. "I don't know what you mean."

"I mean if the authorities find out he was fighting for the rebel cause, they just might take everything. So, you'd best come up with something."

"He was shot. No doubt attacked by someone on his way home."

"And found himself a surgeon along the way?"

"There could have been an accident aboard ship."

Jared breathed a sigh, and asked, "Won't you breathe a bit easier when you can stop these lies?"

"I won't breathe easier until I see the last of your kind on these shores. Who do you think shot him, but a bloody Englisher?"

Jared shrugged. Apparently she hadn't taken into consideration the fact that *this* bloody Englisher had probably just saved her father's life. Jared held no political views. He was a doctor. A doctor who just happened to be born under the King's rule. Thoughts of freedom did not surge to life in his breast. He found nothing wrong with being loyal to his King. Still, he couldn't help feeling somewhat disturbed in what he was doing. He had no intentions of turning either Felicity or her father in. Did that make him a traitor? Was he putting his needs for a woman above King and country, all for the sole purpose of bedding her? Jared thought there might be more to it than that, but at the moment he was too tired to think on the reasons behind his actions. "As you said, it was probably an accident. I'll look in on him in the morning."

Jared was at the door before he glanced in her direction. He frowned as he watched her limp toward a chair. He hadn't noticed the limp before. "What's the matter?"

"Nothing. My foot hurts a little is all."

"Why?"

"I don't know." She sat and then turned her foot a bit to see to the problem. "I must have . . ." Her words dropped off to silence as she realized blood was pumping at a steady rate from the bottom of her foot.

Jared was kneeling before her. "You stepped on a piece of glass. Didn't you feel it?"

Felicity could honestly say she hadn't felt a thing. No doubt she had stepped on the glass surrounding her father downstairs, but because she'd been so upset, hadn't noticed until now. "No. Is the glass still in there?"

"Let me see."

It was only then that Felicity noticed him kneeling in front of her. It was only a cut after all. No need to make a fuss. No need for him to touch her again. "I can manage."

Jared figured he'd accomplish little more than to waste his time if he bothered to argue the point, so he simply picked her up and took her across the hall to her room. "What are you doing? Put me down." Felicity didn't want to touch his bare chest, but there was no other way to escape his hold except to put her hands on his chest and push.

Fluffy growled, but apparently the sound of his mistress's voice settled any doubts the dog might have had, for he grew quiet again.

It was dark inside. "Unless you want me to dump you on the floor, tell me where your bed is."

Felicity's arms were suddenly around his neck, holding on tightly, afraid that he just might follow through on his threat. "To your right. Be careful, Fluffy is on the bed."

Jared placed her on the bed and standing over her said, "You shouldn't sleep with your dog. It's a bad habit to get into." And before Felicity could question his comment, he said, "Roll to your stomach and stay there, while I find us some light."

A minute or so later, Jared was back with a candle and his bag. He pulled the table close to the bed, placed the candle on it, and without saying anything more he proceeded to clean and bandage her wound.

And just about the whole time he worked, Felicity complained with grunts, groans, "ows," and moans, causing her dog to sympathize with moans of his own as he nuzzled and licked at her face.

The moment Jared was done, Felicity rolled to her back. Supported by her arms, she half reclined on the bed and glared at his words.

"You're acting like a baby. The cut wasn't that deep."

"Am I? Let's cut your foot and see how you act."

Jared laughed.

Felicity moved her foot to the left and right, trying to find a position where it might stop throbbing. "It didn't hurt like this before. You made it worse."

"I got the glass out." Jared smiled. "And you're very welcome."

"I could have done it," she said, unwilling to give him his due.

"And you're welcome about your father, too." Jared grinned at her silence, and dared, "Go ahead and tell me you could have done as much."

"I wouldn't give an Englisher the pleasure of telling him anything."

Jared grinned. "Has anyone ever told you that you are a brat?"

"A lady couldn't say what you are."

Jared grinned and suddenly leaned over her, his arms on each side of her hips, actually having the temerity to touch her while supporting his weight. His position brought his body, his face, within inches of her own. And her dog, sensing no danger to his mistress, thought to join in the human play. With tail wagging, he jumped and scrambled over Felicity, trying to come close enough to lick the man above her, all with playful yelps.

"Well, since I see no lady present, perhaps you could tell me."

"Get out." There was no way that Felicity was going to back down. This was her bed, and he was the one who wasn't welcome here. He was the one who was going to move. She added without much hope, "Bite him, Fluffy."

Jared looked at the little animal and laughed at the command. "The next time you might consider a dog of more stature."

Felicity had noticed, of course, the fact that he had yet to pull on a shirt, that his bare skin was very close to her, that she had only to lift her hand to touch it, touch him. She shivered at the thought yet couldn't seem to pull her gaze away. Short dark hair sprinkled evenly over his chest and grew thicker at its center before forming a narrow line over his stomach. She'd noticed all of it before, but she hadn't noticed until this very minute that Jared, in his hurry to dress, had neglected to secure three of the top buttons of his trousers and the line of hair that bisected his stomach ran lower still. Only now, that he leaned over her and she could see . . . Felicity swallowed, not at all sure of what she was seeing. She couldn't hold back her soft gasp.

Jared followed the direction of her gaze, but instead of jumping away and correcting the oversight as a gentleman might, he merely grinned and as if daring her to look her full, stayed right where he was. "There's no need for you to blush, Felicity. Soon enough you'll be seeing that and more."

Felicity couldn't imagine what more there could be and dared not ask. "I want you out of my room." The desperation in her voice was obvious.

"And I'm going, but not without a kiss," he said, and, with no further warning, proceeded to kiss her. This kiss wasn't anything like the other. It held none of his earlier gentleness, but merely took her mouth with hunger as if she were but a lusty wench and he a man ready and willing to have his wants fulfilled. Felicity thought she should be disgusted, only she couldn't seem to summon that particular emotion. The kiss was hard, hungry, and over all too soon. Thank God, for Felicity knew had she to suffer through even one more second, she would have surely disgraced herself by reaching for that naked chest.

She breathed a sigh, never realizing the message behind it, for the kiss had been just about the most lovely thing, leaving Felicity to wonder how many kinds of kisses there were?

Jared only shot her wide-eyed look a grin as he gathered his things. Having correctly read the question in those eyes, he silently promised she'd find out soon enough.

Felicity slept not at all, but spent the next few hours limping from her room to her father's. His fever had not lessened to any marked degree, but he appeared to be resting comfortably, and a glance at his wound told her the skin around the injury appeared less puffy and was fading from angry red to pink. So far it seemed to be healing. Felicity wished she knew more about the human body. Would the abscess return? How long would it take before they'd know for sure?

Unable to give up her vigil, she changed the poultice and went to the kitchen for still another. While there she dampened cloths and used them to cool her father's chest and face. Another two hours went by before she dropped into a chair for a few minutes rest.

Jared found her early the next morning asleep in a chair beside her father's bed. He checked his patient. The fever had gone down, but was still there. Jared knew he'd been right. The abscess had caused the fever. Once the arm was on its way to being healed, the fever would disappear.

The dressing needed to be changed and another poultice applied, but first Jared would see Felicity in bed.

He brought her into his arms, cuddling her to his chest as he moved across the hall. She was totally unaware of the movement, totally unaware that she turned just a bit to snuggle her face comfortably to his neck.

In her room he sat for a moment on her bed, dislodging Fluffy from his usual position. Jared had no intention of lingering. He had things to do, patients to care for that would take up his entire day, for the hospital nearly overflowed with injured men. His mind told him to hurry, to be about his business, but his body told him something else entirely.

She felt so good against him. Surely it would not hurt if he held her for just a moment.

The house was quiet. But for those in the kitchen, no one had yet left their bed. He could spare a minute. A minute to look at her, to touch her, to breathe in a scent that would have to last him for hours.

His hand moved automatically without thought, brushing aside a rich thick curl, and his mouth touched unerringly the tempting warmth of her neck. He'd known her to be sweet, that her scent could captivate, but he hadn't imagined anything would feel or taste this good, this warm, as this woman in sleep.

Felicity moaned softly and stirred, never realizing in her sleep that she so enjoyed his touch. Later she'd convince herself that this had been naught but a dream. A very lovely dream perhaps, but a dream to be sure.

His mouth moved from her neck, along her jaw, to brush against the tempting sweetness of her lips, but he didn't kiss her. He wanted her awake for that. He wanted her to kiss him back. He ached for it. For that and more.

He looked down into her sleeping face. If he opened her robe and untied those ribbons, he might have moments to feast his eyes on her loveliness. Jared shook his head. He wouldn't do it. He couldn't do it. Not without her permission. He couldn't take advantage of her while she slept.

Jared knew his control was slipping, and despite his insistence that this could go no further, he couldn't stop himself from wanting more. He never recalled his vow not to touch her, not to look as his fingers opened the ribbons and his mouth lowered to her soft sweet flesh. He moaned a low sound of bliss. He wished he'd never have to stop. She was so lusciously soft and sweet. A few inches farther and he'd stop, he swore. All he wanted was to take the tips of womanly flesh into his mouth and he vowed he'd stop, but if he didn't soon end this insanity, he'd find himself forgetting all about the men who needed him.

It took some doing, since this was probably the last thing he wanted, but Jared turned and lifted her from his lap. A moment later she was snuggled into her mattress, covered with a summer quilt.

Breathing heavily and cursing his actions, Jared closed the door behind him. It had been a damn stupid thing to do. All the stolen moment had accomplished was to put him into a state that would take hours of work to ease.

Six

"You're far too ill to bother with business matters, Father. You can see to them later," Felicity said as she spoon-fed him clear broth. Her father had slept for three days. He was terribly weak, far too weak for what he had in mind.

"I want you to send for Mr. Struthers now, Felicity. I'm well enough to see to a few matters done."

Felicity knew her father was far from well enough. His breathing was labored, his strength nonexistent. His eyes shone with fever and the simple matter of swallowing proved almost too great a chore. Meeting with his lawyer was definitely out of the question.

"I won't hear of such nonsense. You're far from well. I want you to rest."

The fact of the matter was, Thomas Dryson had no choice but to rest. And both he and his daughter knew it, for he had not the strength to lift even his hand from the bed. But how could a man rest when wrongs needed righting? He had to talk to Struthers before it was too late.

Three days later Felicity took some delight in the fact that her patient was much improved. Still terribly weak, he was at least able to stay awake for more than a few minutes at a time. Judging by his recovery so far, as each day passed he'd be able to do a little more.

That morning, just as he had upon every wakening, he again

asked Felicity to send for his lawyer. "A few minutes spent with the man won't weaken me beyond all hope, I'm sure."

Felicity nodded in agreement. "I'll send Billy with a note."

"Tell him I have to see him as soon as possible."

"Tomorrow will be soon enough."

Thomas sighed, unable for the moment to fight his strong-willed daughter's decision. "Tomorrow then."

Felicity placed the empty bowl on the table beside his bed. "Have you eaten enough?"

"More than enough, daughter," her father returned with a loving smile. "Had I known the care I could expect, I might have gotten myself shot sooner."

Felicity frowned at the thought. "Was it very bad?" She hadn't asked before and wondered why she did now? Did she truly want to know the horrors he'd suffered through? The pain, the agony of traveling while suffering from a bullet wound?

"Most every skirmish was little more than slaughter. They line up. We line up. Before you know it, the gunsmoke was so thick on both sides you couldn't see five feet in front of you. Once, in the confusion, we even fired on our own."

Felicity shuddered. "I wish it were over. I wish they were all gone."

Thomas watched his daughter for a long moment before asking, "Have any treated you poorly in my absence?"

Thomas Dryson was terribly weak, and Felicity knew that further conversation at this point was out of the question. The more he spoke the weaker he grew.

"No, Father. They treated me perfectly well," she said, silently adding, *except for one.* "Now I want you to rest."

The object of her thoughts chose just that moment to enter the room. "Ah, I see you're awake. How are you feeling?"

"Very much better, thank you."

Thomas smiled weakly at the doctor who stopped in to check his patient before leaving for the hospital each morning and then again upon returning home in the evening.

Jared returned his smile. "Between your daughter and me, I hope you know you had little choice, but to get well."

Even though Thomas had just come from two years of battling these English, in one bloody skirmish after another, Thomas thought he rather liked the young man. The doctor had gentle dark eyes and appeared truly concerned about his patient.

Most colonists did not hate the English as a whole, but rather the tyranny directed from the Crown. Over the last few years he'd found many who were likable, many he might have, had times been different, called his friend.

Jared left his patient soon after and continued to check in on him every morning and night. It was a week later that he entered the room as always to find Felicity sitting at her father's side.

"All right, let's go."

Felicity looked up from her father's gray face to the handsome man standing at the bedroom doorway. "Excuse me?"

"I said, let's go. You've been sitting here for days. You need a breath of air."

Felicity only glanced at the man and then back to her needlepoint. Her purpose for sitting here had been twofold, one to see to her father's care, the other to avoid this man. She didn't want to see him, she didn't want to think about him. Not him, nor any man.

Mr. Struthers had come some five days back and Felicity had been asked to stay, to be privy to the conversation between her father and his lawyer, since, her father explained, the subject involved her to the extent that she was family. As Thomas Dryson began his story (the explanation for Felicity's benefit since his lawyer appeared to have full knowledge of the situation), Felicity could only stare in shocked disbelief. This couldn't have happened! But it had.

Of course Felicity was a grown woman now, old enough and mature enough she hoped to understand that many men had mistresses, but not her own father. He had worshiped her mother, and when the small frail lady had finally given up the fight to live, a year almost to the day before this conflict had begun, no one could have taken it harder than her husband. For a time there Felicity thought she might lose both parents, his sorrow being so great. But Thomas had lived and so, as she'd only days before found out, had the offspring of an illicit affair.

Apparently he'd had no contact with either mother or daughter for years, but, through his lawyer, her father had been supporting both. He had learned from Mr. Struthers that the mother had died.

Mr. Struthers was asked to find the child and bring her to the Drysons' home. A goodly sum was to be settled on the girl, and she would be treated as part of the family.

Felicity didn't care about the money, nor did she worry over the fact that a young lady, her half sister, would soon share her home. She could only care about the fact that her father had not remained faithful. In that one disastrous admission Thomas had unknowingly destroyed any chance Felicity might have known for happiness. This man who had loved his wife to madness had been unable to control his primal urges. What hope had she, then, to find faithfulness in the man of her choosing? Felicity swore she'd never give her heart to a man. Never, lest she find it torn to pieces at his act of betrayal.

Felicity felt it not her place to pass judgment on her father and kept her disappointment to herself. Still, she had grown very quiet. The light seemed to have gone from her eyes. These days her smile was a bit harder to come by. Right now as she faced Captain Jared Walker, the smile was forced. "I'm fine, thank you, Captain."

Jared walked toward his patient, needlessly checking a wound he'd only checked an hour before. "Your father is not going to get better by you sitting here willing it to be so. The arm will heal nicely with or without your fussing."

"I know that."

"So you are allowed to leave his side occasionally. You wouldn't mind if I took her away for a bit, would you, sir?"

Thomas had felt the tension between himself and his daughter ever since his lawyer's visit. He'd felt it but was at a loss as to what to say. What could a man say? How could he explain to a lady, a daughter, the need that sometimes drove a man to break sacred vows? How could he tell of it? He couldn't. And because he couldn't there seemed a rift between them. A rift that might never heal. "Not at all." Thomas knew only relief at the thought of parting from her company for a spell. "Take her for a stroll. Felicity loves the garden."

At Thomas's response, Jared, after taking her hand, gave her little choice but to accompany him from the room. It was either that or be dragged from her father's side. "What do you think you're doing?"

"I'm taking you for a walk in your garden, just as your father suggested."

"With or without my permission, I take it."

Jared ignored her less than jubilant comment. "I've had Becky prepare us something. You haven't had a decent meal in days."

"I'm not hungry, Captain, and if it's all the same to you, I'll eat something later."

"It's not all the same to me, and you'll have something now," he said, as he led her from the house.

Felicity blinked her surprise as they reached the terrace. The man had gone to a bit of trouble. Unnecessary trouble as it turned out, for she wasn't the least bit impressed. The small table on the terrace was set with china, sparkling glasses, and one candle enclosed in a glass chimney. Other candles sat on small tables positioned on the terrace. The garden beyond was dark. Lightning bugs brought a slightly festive note to the night as they danced and sparkled in merry flight. Still, Felicity, who often found delight in the smallest happenings, could find no joy in the moment.

They sat opposite one another. Jared filled her glass with pale wine. Felicity glanced at the wine and then at the man who had forced her to dine with him.

Jared smiled at the unasked question, and explained, "From an appreciative patient."

Felicity took a small sip, delighting in the gentle but crisp taste. "Very nice."

"Which of the wines do you prefer?"

"I have no preference, actually. One might say my palate is quite unsophisticated, for I can't tell one wine from another, with the exception of port." She wrinkled her nose at the thought of the strong brew.

"I haven't seen you for days."

"You've seen me every morning and evening in my father's room."

"I know. Have you been hiding there?"

"Hiding? From what?"

"Me?"

"Captain, you might believe me to be a woman of less honor than most, but I assure you that when I commit myself to do something, the act is as good as done. I was not hiding from you. I will not hide from you or any man."

Jared frowned. Something had recently greatly disturbed this lady. Something that had taken the smile from her eyes. Jared had thought at first it was merely lack of sleep, but he knew now it was more than that. "Why would I think you less than honorable?"

"Because of my involvement with certain people, certain causes."

"Oh that," Jared shrugged. "As a matter of fact you couldn't be more mistaken on that count. I think you are more honorable than most simply because of your involvement. Had you not cared, were you not sworn to honor your own beliefs, you wouldn't have chanced the things you did, am I right?"

Felicity shrugged. She didn't care what he believed of her. At the moment she didn't care much about anything.

"And I think, even though I can't agree either with your beliefs or the methods you chose to see your ends accomplished, that you were very brave to have chanced it."

"You speak in the past tense, sir."

"I do. You've chanced your last, I think."

Felicity allowed him to think what he would. She said nothing.

"I can see something has distressed you. What is it?"

"Nothing."

"Has your friend died?"

Felicity frowned. "What friend?"

"The man we operated on. In the secret room. Where was that room, anyway?"

"No, he's yet to fully recover, but he hasn't died. And unless you want me to lie to you, do not ask where the room is."

Jared grinned at her straightforward way of speaking. He only wished everyone could follow her example. How much simpler this world would be if one knew exactly where the other stood. "All right, so it's not your friend. And it can't be your father. He's well on the road to recovery. So what is it?"

"What is what?"

Jared smiled as he leaned back in his chair and studied her beautiful face. "Felicity, I was just thinking to myself how straightforward you are. And how delightful it is to be able to speak to someone without playing games. Was I wrong?"

Felicity sighed, knowing the man was bound to find out the cause of her unhappiness soon enough. Once Mr. Struthers found Margaret Rhodes, everyone would know. What difference did it make if she told him now? "My father had a mistress."

Jared smiled. "Is that so unusual? Would you deny a man the company of a lady now and then. Fathers are men, too, you know."

"I would deny him, if he were married," she said hotly. "I would if he were my own father. I would if he professed to love his wife beyond his very life."

Jared breathed a sigh and waited for her to go on. "I would when a daughter comes of the union."

"Is that the problem? Is your father claiming her?"

Felicity looked at him for a long hard moment before saying, "Did I not just tell you what the problem is?"

"All right, so you're upset because your father had an affair.

But a man's personal business is hardly any of your concern. Why should it matter to you?"

"It matters because he lied. It matters because my mother trusted him. It matters because, now that my mother is dead, he doesn't have to hide the girl any longer. He wouldn't hurt his wife, you understand, by claiming her from birth some eighteen years ago." Felicity shrugged, knowing that wasn't entirely true and didn't care. The girl was alone and needed the protection of a man. Had that not been so, Felicity might never have known the way of things. "Besides, sleeping with another woman could not have hurt my mother. She was stupid you see. She never realized his unfaithfulness." Felicity blinked her shining eyes, daring a tear to fall. She swallowed and went on, her voice growing cold and harder than ever. "I hate men. I hate every last one of you."

"Why? Because you found out your father is not the saint you've somehow made him out to be. That he's only a man. A man who can and often will make mistakes?"

"No, because my father loved my mother. I never saw love like that and probably never will again. And if he could cheat, what hope is there for the rest of us?"

Jared sighed. To this lady the episode seemed clearly cut-and-dried, with no sympathy extended toward the weakness of human nature. What was right, was right, to her way of thinking. Plain and simple. Too bad life's decisions weren't always so easy to come by. "And your solution?"

"My solution is very simple, actually. Never trust. And most definitely never marry."

"Because you're afraid to take a chance?"

"That's just my point. Marriage shouldn't be a chance. Marriage should be something solid and lasting. Something built on trust. I won't give myself to a man knowing my gift might be held in so little regard that he could the next day turn to another."

"There are a lot of men who hold true to their vows."

Felicity shook her head in disagreement as she uncovered a

plate holding a small gutted loaf of bread filled with roasted beef, gravy, and vegetables. She took a bite. "Most don't."

"I don't believe that. I think most do." A moment of silence went by before he asked, "Tell me what happened?"

"You mean you want all the sordid details?" Felicity knew he didn't mean that, but she couldn't help blurting out the hateful words.

"I mean, why? If he loved your mother so much, why look for another?"

Felicity pushed her plate away. The food was delicious, but it might as well have been straw for all the enjoyment she could find in it. "Because my mother was far from strong. The doctor said she might die if there were more babies."

Jared knew there were ways to protect a woman against pregnancy, ways that could ensure both a husband and wife great measures of satisfaction. But he knew as well the mentality of most. If Thomas Dryson knew of certain techniques, he no doubt imagined his wife too good and fine to be subjected to what he thought to be sordid conduct. Most men still lived under the supposition that a good woman wouldn't be interested in anything more than doing her duty. And if he had yearnings that might take him beyond what was considered the norm, he'd have to turn to another, since their wives were too pure to enjoy what they might have in mind.

Jared almost laughed aloud at the thought, for those men were fools. If they treated their women as they should be treated, no man would look for another, no man would ever have to.

"And you judge him to have cheated, even knowing your mother chanced her life if she obliged him in his needs?"

"Is that all there is? Is the marriage bed all of marriage?"

"Men have strong urges, Felicity. It's their nature."

"Well that's a shame, isn't it?" she snapped angrily. And then her voiced dripped sarcasm as she added, "I can't tell you how my heart aches for their plight. He made a vow, what about that?"

"I'm not saying he was right. I'm only telling you men cannot always control . . ."

"Because they are animals. Every one of them."

Jared allowed a few seconds to tick by before asking, "Is that what you really believe?"

It took a long moment before Felicity calmed down enough to answer honestly, "No, truthfully, I don't know what to believe."

"For centuries men have found it impossible to talk to women about their needs, especially if the woman is his wife. A lot of pain could have been avoided if things were clearly discussed."

"What kind of things?"

Jared thought himself quite an enlightened man and yet found himself suddenly tongue-tied at the very thought of answering her question. "Well," he finally managed, "let's just say there are ways to satisfy without chancing a woman's life."

She frowned. "I don't understand."

"And you couldn't be expected to. But you will. Once you marry some decent fellow"—Jared found himself frowning at the thought and could only wonder why—"you'll learn together the different ways."

He smiled at her obvious confusion.

Felicity looked away from his smile and sighed. "Well I'm delighted you cleared that up." She took another sip of her wine and found the roast beef tempting after all.

Jared laughed. "Of course, I could show you. That way your future husband would be delighted at the things you know."

"And I'm to believe decent young fellows are delighted to find their wives experienced?"

Jared laughed. "All right, maybe he shouldn't be quite so young."

"Or decent?"

"Or decent. Maybe he should be older and . . ."

She shook her head. "It doesn't matter. I'm not marrying anyone."

"You'll change your mind. One day you'll see a man and

your heart will flutter and you'll say, 'He's the one. He's the one I must have.' "

"And then I'll hurry to my bed and stay there until the insanity passes."

Jared grinned. "You mean because you're afraid?"

"No, because I'm wise to men and their ways."

"What about children? Don't you want to hold your own baby someday?"

She hesitated a long moment before answering on a sigh, "I've come to the conclusion that I can't have everything in life." Her smile was sad as she thought of the lonely years ahead.

"Meaning you have no interest in children?"

Felicity sighed again at what she perceived to be her greatest loss. "I would have loved children. If it weren't for this conflict, I might have married already and had three or four by now." She shrugged aside a sense of sadness for what could never be and shook her head. "But that won't happen now. Not after what I've learned of men."

"Surely . . ." he began, only to find himself cut off with, "Of course, if you can tell me how I might achieve my wants without involving myself with a man, I would be most interested."

Jared's grin turned to a delighted chuckle. "I'm afraid I know of no other way."

"Exactly."

He studied her over his glass of wine for a moment before suggesting, "What about marrying a man you don't love? You wouldn't be chancing your heart then." Jared shrugged, wondering why he continued on with the subject? And why that particular subject left him less than happy? "If he played you false, what would it matter? Best of all, you'd have your babies."

Felicity knew some surprise at his words, especially when she realized they were worth thinking on. Her expression said as much.

"Before you start looking for the right fellow, remember we have unfinished business between us."

An idea dawned, and Felicity found it particularly brilliant.

It just might be that she could solve both their problems, if he were to agree. "What are you doing after this conflict? Where will you go?"

"Back to England. There's this little hamlet about thirty miles north of London. I have an office there and a small community to see to."

"And you have no intentions of staying here?" she asked almost hopefully.

"None at all."

"You have family there?"

He nodded, not having a clue as to where her questions were leading. "A mother and brother."

"Good. Why don't we marry then?"

Felicity asked the question while Jared was in the midst of swallowing a sip of wine. He choked and coughed, gasping for air, for her question shocked in the extreme. It took some time before he was able to breathe normally again. "Why me?"

"You're perfect, actually," Felicity said, studying him from across the table. The longer she thought on it the better her plan appeared. "You're very good-looking, so your offspring should be equally endowed. You're intelligent, strong, good material I think, to father a child." She nodded as if agreeing to her own thoughts. "I know doctors as a rule are less than financially secure, but my family has money, so you wouldn't need to worry over the child's care and support. Best of all, we don't love each other. There would be no pretense there." She smiled, and then as if she had mastered some grand plan, finished with, "And after this conflict is at an end, you can go home and divorce me. It couldn't be more perfect."

Jared couldn't imagine how he could feel more insulted. He thought himself a bit experienced, and yet he'd never imagined so cold-hearted a plot. "What you mean is you need me for stud services."

Felicity's eyes widened a bit, for the man seemed suddenly angry. She hadn't expected that particular reaction and couldn't imagine why he would take unkindly to her suggestion. Perhaps she'd been a bit too blunt. She was always trying to correct that glaring fault and knew she'd have to give it some further effort. "Well, I wouldn't have put it so crudely."

"Still, it's true."

Her gaze narrowed as she reminded, "And what is it you want from me, Captain? Granted you gave little thought of children, but you wanted me in your bed. You can't deny it. At least my reasoning would be productive in the end."

Jared wouldn't deny he wanted her, had wanted her for months. Still, it wasn't as if he were using her for breeding. No, his needs were . . . Jared sighed as he realized his thoughts, . . . a bit more shallow and self-gratifying. It was then that he realized that his plan was hardly less offensive than hers. He had wanted to use her, to enjoy her body with not a care as to the outcome. For the first time in his life he could understand how a woman must feel upon being propositioned. The little witch had somehow turned the tables on him, and he couldn't help but admit he didn't like it.

"A divorced woman is frowned upon in polite society," he reminded.

Felicity shrugged. "No one need ever know. I'll simply say you have business in England and prefer to live there, while I won't leave my father." She smiled a bit smugly, as if the last piece of a puzzle had just fallen into place.

"What would happen if you should find someone you love?"

She shook her head. "That won't happen."

"But suppose it did?"

"Then word might reach me that my husband is deceased."

"How convenient," he said, and Felicity didn't miss the touch of sarcasm in his tone.

She took a sip of wine and, keeping her gaze to her glass, shrugged. "It was your suggestion, Captain. If you're not interested, I'm sure I can find another."

"And what about us?"

"What about us?"

"We have business that won't see an end for nearly three months."

Felicity shrugged again. Already sure of the outcome of their little wager, she said, "I can't see how that will hamper my plans."

"Oh you don't? I think it might."

"How?"

"The plan was to convince you to join me in bed, am I right?"

"I believe the plan was to try," she gently corrected.

"All right then, to try and convince you. How am I supposed to do it, if you are with another?"

Felicity sighed. "Fine. If it will satisfy, I'll wait three months," she said, then dismissed the matter with, "I'll make up a list. Perhaps you could help."

He frowned, not at all sure what she was talking about.

"You know, prospective applicants."

Still he appeared confused. "Men?" she offered, trying for understanding. "Men I might marry?" she clarified.

"All right," he suddenly blurted out, never realizing his intent, "I'll marry you."

Felicity grinned at the look that suddenly entered his eyes. He looked absolutely trapped and couldn't have looked more so had he just found himself in a cage. "Don't worry, Captain, I won't hold you to it." Felicity chuckled a low terrible sound.

Her laughter tore at his gut. She shouldn't be allowed to laugh like that.

Jared cursed the fact that he was doing exactly what he'd sworn never to do again. His first wife had died in childbirth and he, a doctor, had stood there watching her suffer, unable to do a thing to stop it. He'd sworn then that it wouldn't happen again. That he wouldn't love another, wouldn't fill a woman again with his seed and chance her death as well.

Granted there had been women since Annie, but those women had known how to protect themselves. And he hadn't loved them.

All right, so he didn't love Felicity Dryson either, but the terrifying fact was that he could. If they married, if there was a bond between them, he almost certainly would. And if she were to die because of him, because of his lust . . . Jared shuddered at the thought.

He wouldn't allow it this time. This time he'd take care, and, because she was an innocent, she'd never know the difference. She'd never know why she wasn't able to conceive.

Jared knew he was being unfair, knew he was beginning this marriage with an out-and-out lie, but he wasn't going to chance losing another wife. There was no other way. He couldn't, wouldn't see her with another. He'd known almost from the first that this woman would be his, only now it would be forever. And if later she still craved a child, perhaps they could visit an orphanage and pick one or two of the most needy to love. "There's no need to wait, I think. Sometime next week should fit my schedule nicely."

Seven

Bess Rhodes held the letter addressed to her deceased half sister. The paper was thick, obviously of some cost. It was definitely not a bill, or correspondence, for Margaret, but for herself and their mother, had been alone in the world, having had no friends or relatives who might send her a letter.

Bess tore open the seal. Barely educated beyond learning her letters and a smattering of numbers, Bess found she had to read the letter three times before understanding its contents. When at last she understood, she laughed in bitter irony. Margaret's father, after all these years, wanted his daughter to come and live with him, now that her mother had died and she was alone. Well the bastard had waited a bit too long, hadn't he? Damn Margaret. Bess had warned both her and their mother a hundred times to keep away from the waterfront and the sailors who prowled its docks. But no, they had only laughed and gone about their business, only their business had ended in both their deaths.

Mr. Dryson didn't know that the pox that had taken their mother had helped itself to her sister's life as well. They had died within days of each other. Both mother and daughter had been dead for two months.

Bess wrinkled the letter into a ball and threw it across the room. Angry at the unfairness of life, she began to pace. She and Margaret hadn't had a chance, just because their mother was fool enough to have had her children without the benefit of marriage. God, but she hated the rules set forth by men—the self-righteous bastards who believed it their right to have a lady or two on the side and a passel of children they'd never recognize. How dare they say she was less than nothing because a piece of paper had never been signed? She hated them all. But most of all she hated Mr. Thomas Dryson and his monthly checks.

Bess was still pacing when Lilly let Frank into the tiny house. Frank had moved in after her mother died, but he'd never once remembered to take a key with him upon leaving. His hat sailed across the room, landing on a chair as he shot his lady a wicked grin. She was dressed in black lace, see-through black lace. His favorite. "What's the matter, Bessy?" he said as he reached for her and brought her hard against him.

"Stop it, Frank. I'm not in the mood."

Frank laughed as he ran his hand over her barely veiled breasts. "You're always in the mood."

"Well, I'm not now."

"Why not?" he asked, ignoring her struggles as he reached around her, cupped her bottom and pulled her closer.

"I just got a letter from Margaret's father," she said, ignoring the fact that his hand was now on her robe, easily parting the fabric. "And I'm thinking."

"About what?"

"About how much I hate men."

Frank laughed. "You?! Hate men? You do a good job of hiding it then." Bess had been one of Frank's best girls until he decided he wanted her just for himself. It was a good thing he had, too, what with the pox having a field day around the city.

"I never said I don't like what I do with them."

"I know that."

The robe opened, and Bess allowed him to play with her body a bit, her mind not really on what he was doing.

"What did the letter say?"

"It said he wants her to come and live with him. Now after all this time, he wants to see her."

Frank shrugged as he guided her to the couch. "Too bad he waited so long." He smiled, ready to tell her about the shopkeeper and the fact that he'd handed over the money without hesitation. Frank didn't know why he hadn't thought of it before. It was so damn easy. All it took was a threat, and they all paid. He figured he could do better at this scam than with the ladies. They were always trying to cheat him, and he didn't like roughing them up. It only took a slap or two and no one would look at them for a week and Frank figured that was a week's worth of money lost. "I have something in my pocket. Something you might like."

Bess thought she knew what he meant. The man wouldn't be denied. She shrugged, and Frank grinned as her breasts swayed in his hands. "Should I find it?"

Frank only grinned again as she opened his trousers. His erection was thick and needy, but Frank was always needy. Bess thought to lengthen the moment a bit, by teasing, "Is this it? It's very . . ."

"Wrong pocket, but you can find the money later," he said as he pressed her back upon the hard cushions. Bess never wore anything more than a robe when at home, so Frank had no problem finding what he was looking for. He was done with his business in seconds, but Bess didn't mind. She knew it was her turn to be pleasured next. It would be a while before he was ready again. In the meantime, Bess would probably find release two or three times.

The lovers were just coming again to a sitting position when Lilly brought in a tray of tea. Frank grinned at the plain-looking woman, uncaring of the fact that his trousers were at his knees and his softened sex was in open view for any to see. "You sure you won't join us, Lilly? I promise you won't be sorry."

Lilly said nothing but simply walked out of the room.

"You know, she is close to being the ugliest woman I've ever set eyes on, and she ain't got nothing but bones under that dress of hers. You'd think she'd be complimented. Instead . . ."

"Leave her alone, Frank. You've got your hands full with me."

Frank laughed. At the moment he did indeed have his hands full, and he turned his appreciation on those lush curves.

"What money?" she asked, remembering his last words before he had pressed her to the couch.

"Oh yeah," he said, fishing around in his pocket and finally coming up with a thick roll of bills. "This. And all it took was a threat. Easiest money I've ever made."

Bess counted the bills as Frank poured them tea and took a huge bite out of a buttered scone. "A hundred pounds!" It was more money than she'd ever seen before. "We should put some aside, I think. We can't count on Margaret's money anymore. Once Dryson finds out about her dying, the checks will stop."

"What do you mean? You ain't going to tell him, are you?"

"No, but . . ."

"So how's he going to find out? Sign her name and cash them."

"He found out about my mother. Why wouldn't he . . . ?"

Frank frowned. An idea was forming, but he couldn't seem to grasp it fully. "Wait a minute. Stop talking. I'm thinking."

And after a few minutes, he said, "Tell me exactly what the letter said."

"Wait," Bess said as she came from his side. "I'll get it."

Frank read the letter twice before he figured it out. "How long has it been since he's seen her?"

"She was two the last time. He broke it off with my mother then and forced her to go into the streets."

Frank knew that wasn't exactly true. If Cora hadn't craved the bottle as she had, the money might have been made to last to the end of each month, with maybe a little left over for a few luxuries. Nothing but her need for men and drink had forced her into the streets.

"So he ain't got no idea what Margaret looks like, is that right?"

"I can't see how he could know."

"So," he said with a grin, waiting for her to take the bait, knowing all their problems were about to be over for good.

"So, what?"

"So if Margaret hadn't died, what would have happened?"

"What do you think? She would have gone to him. She'd be crazy not to."

"And you ain't crazy, are you, Bess?"

"What do you . . . ?" Bess's words came to a sudden stop as she realized his meaning. She asked very softly, as if others might be nearby overhearing, "Do you think I could get away with it?"

"Can't see why not. He don't know what his little girl looks like." Frank laughed. "Why she could have black hair"—he reached for her body again—"and the biggest tits a man ever laid eyes on, for all he knows."

Bess laughed as she realized he was right. No one knew what Margaret Rhodes looked like, except for a few neighbors and, of course, the men she'd once serviced. Only she didn't think any of those bothered to ask her name. "This might work."

"This will work. You know how to talk all refined like. You worked for that lady once, remember?"

Bess scowled, "How could I forget? She almost killed me when she found her husband pumpin' into me."

Frank laughed at what must have been an interesting scene. "All you have to do is act like a lady. God, we'll be rolling in money."

"But I'd have to stay in his house. That would mean you and I couldn't see each other."

"Of course we could. He ain't going to keep you a prisoner. I'll stay here, and you can visit, sometimes for a whole day."

"Lilly will leave if you bother her," she warned.

"Lilly ain't never got it like I can give it."

Bess shrugged aside the man's obvious intent. Frank didn't know Lilly like she did. Lilly did not like men. Lilly much preferred the company of women, especially in bed. Bess knew that for a fact, since she and Lilly had spent more than one pleasant evening indulging.

But Frank being a man wouldn't or couldn't believe a woman

might prefer one of her own kind over him. Bess had no doubt that he'd soon be living here alone. "I'm not cleaning up, or cooking for you when I come here. So, after she leaves you'd better find someone else."

Frank knew that would be no problem. He knew he was a good-looking man, charming, if he put his mind to it. There were women everywhere. It wouldn't take but a nod on his part to have them all over him. Frank thought he rather liked that idea. With the money Bess made, he could bring in all the women he wanted.

"We're going to have to find you some fancy duds."

"No, not fancy. I'm not rich yet, remember? I'm just a little poor bastard that *Daddy* thought to look favorably upon."

Frank grinned at her speech. "You sound like one of them, except for the curse. Remember ladies don't curse." And then noticing her gown was still open, he reached for her again, "All right, some decent stuff though. We can't have you parading around in black lace."

Bess laughed at the thought. "No, I think that would be a mistake."

As it turned out a wedding within the next week proved quite impossible. Firstly and most importantly, Thomas Dryson had to be well again, well enough to perform his fatherly duty. It was unthinkable that the honor should fall to another. That meant they'd have to wait a bit since Thomas hadn't the strength to leave his bed under his own power, never mind walk his only daughter, all right, his only legitimate daughter down the isle.

And secondly, there was the matter of wedding preparations. Felicity hadn't realized how complicated planning a wedding could be. She hadn't imagined there would be such a fuss. From the first, she'd wanted something small. A wedding that included no more than her father, her best friend, and, of course, the officers who were quartered in her home would have suited her just fine. Considering the motivation behind this planned ceremony, Felicity thought it should have been very small indeed, and yet the list of guests had thrice been added to, and Felicity couldn't help but wonder how the coming nuptials had somehow slipped from her control?

There was no sense in dressing, she thought, as she sat before the small dressing table in her room and shot her reflection a hopeless look. Mrs. Harris would be here shortly for another morning of fittings. And with the lady, Carolyn would appear to ooh and ah at just about every sketch, every sample of cloth. Today Mrs. Harris was coming for the final fitting of her wedding dress. Apparently the garment was close to being finished. Felicity found no joy in the thought. Nothing she wore would change the facts. She and Jared were to marry, but not because there was love between them. Felicity wanted children, and Jared wanted her, at least for a time, in his bed. The wedding would solve both their needs. Felicity should have known some satisfaction in the thought, but oddly enough she couldn't seem to grasp it. And she could only wonder why?

If only . . . Felicity shook aside her less-than-jubilant mood, her useless wishful thinking. She was a grown woman, not some starry-eyed young girl. There were no happily ever afters. No fairy-tale endings, no true love. This was real life. And real life meant one plain and simple fact. Men were not true and could never be trusted. Luckily for her she'd learned the way of things before losing her heart.

She smiled and nodded. She was doing the right thing. The bargain she had struck would satisfy both parties. In the end Felicity would have a baby, perhaps even two, without ever having to chance her heart. She couldn't ask for more than that.

Mrs. Harris finally arrived, Carolyn as well.

After standing for hours as one gown after another was fitted to her slight frame, she was at last fitted to her wedding dress. Felicity was adamant. The dress did not suit. She'd asked for something simple, taking almost no notice of the sketches drawn. Obviously she should have paid closer attention, for the dress proved to be far more elaborate than she might have liked.

"I'm sorry, Mrs. Harris," she said when the lady sought to add yet another row of ruffles, to a gown already overly adorned. "I thought I made myself clear on the matter. I do not want excess frills. I wanted something simple and elegant."

"But all brides . . ." Mrs. Harris, obviously upset that her efforts were not to the lady's liking, was cut off as Felicity shook her head.

"The material is beautiful, but the lace ruffles and most especially the pannier must go." Felicity, being a woman of some sophisticated style, did not always accede to fashion's passing demands. In truth she was not a young girl and would not dress as one. "I like the sleeves very much," she said, admiring the fact that they tied with gold thread between elbow and wrist only to flow into a wide circle that flared almost to her hand. "And the split skirt is lovely, especially the train. All you need do is change the underskirt. I prefer it the same creamy color, but plain." Felicity knew a plain underskirt could only emphasize the beauty of the satin gown. As it was generously laced with gold thread, as well as golden bows centered down the back of the train, it needed no further adornment.

"But you'll look . . ."

"Perfect if you do not hide this lovely material with ruffles."

Carolyn laughed as the woman, with dresses packed and hidden from inquiring eyes, soon took her leave. "I hope you know you ruined her day."

Felicity smiled at the exaggeration. "Had I allowed her a free hand you might have seen one giant ruffle walking down the aisle. God, I'm exhausted," she said as she fell across her bed and moaned into the coverlet, "I feel like a pincushion. How many times did she stick me today?"

"Only three that I noticed. Why don't you rest a bit, and I'll have Becky bring us something to eat."

"Good idea. Anything rather than dress again." Felicity had removed her chemise during the fitting and now wore only her corset and drawers. She sighed tiredly, wondering if she'd ever find the strength to dress again.

Carolyn left the room, only to knock again a moment later. Felicity rolled to her side and with her hand supporting her head called out tiredly, "Come on in. Why are you knocking?"

"A gentleman usually knocks before entering a woman's bedroom, but if you'd rather I did not," Jared shrugged, grinned at her shock, and then leaned his back comfortably against the now-closed door. As if his one intent was merely to enjoy the view.

Felicity might have been tired, but no one could have guessed as much as she leaped from the bed with a short cry of alarm and ran for the robe that lay over a chair. In her hurry to put it on, she tore the sleeve, but never stopped to examine the damage done. Her back to him, she pulled the robe tightly around her and tied it at her waist. Only then did she look at the man who lounged just inside her doorway.

Her cheeks just about blazed with embarrassment. Why hadn't she dressed again? It would have taken no more than a minute to replace her chemise and another gown. Instead, because she was tired, she'd fallen across the bed half-naked. "What do you want?"

"Felicity." His voice sounded husky and his eyes darkened to black fire, a very scary black fire, Felicity thought, as they moved over her small frame. "Take my word for it and never ask a man that particular question, especially when you're thusly dressed."

She was far too upset, but mostly too afraid to ask what he was talking about, so she nodded obediently as she asked, "What are you doing here, then?"

"Better," he said, and then, "Margaret Rhodes is here. Shall I show her to your father's room?"

Felicity turned white to her lips and staggered just a bit before Jared moved toward her, his arms quickly circling her slight form. "What's the matter? You knew she'd come eventually, didn't you?"

Felicity pressed her face into his shoulder. "I don't know why

I'm so nervous. How should I act? What should I say? What should I do? Suppose she doesn't like me. She's my sister."

"First of all, you should probably give her and your father a few minutes and then simply act as you always do." He tipped her head back with a finger beneath her chin and grinned. "Every woman should have at least one nasty little sister."

"Stop teasing and go away." She tried to push out of his arms, but Jared felt no need to let her go just yet. "I have to dress."

"Actually, you don't have to, you know." His mouth nibbled at her earlobe. "You looked beautiful without this robe. For just a second you took my breath away." Jared smiled at the memory of perfectly formed creamy white breasts. It didn't go without notice that those soft mounds of flesh were even now pressed to his chest.

Felicity moaned with embarrassment, unable to look at him. "I thought you were Carolyn."

Jared had known of course at first glance that she'd expected the knock to be her friend and continued on with his teasing conversation. "A very dangerous reaction, some might say, which could prove somewhat hazardous." Felicity frowned, but apparently her cooperation was not absolutely necessary to his continuing to tease, for he went on without it. "You know, my looking at you and not being able to breathe? Still, there's a possibility one had nothing to do with the other. If you took the robe off again, we would know for sure.

"I could sit down on the bed, just in case, and you could take it off real slow, so as not to shock my system overmuch."

"The truth is, I should probably keep it on forever. I can't see how I might have babies if the man I marry dies at the first sight of me."

Jared laughed as he pulled her tighter against him. Felicity did not object, and Jared noticed she rarely objected to his touch of late.

"I don't think I'd die," he calmly reassured. "It's not that bad."

"You mean you could breathe after all?" she blinked her dark lashes as if confused.

"Well, maybe just a little."

"Good. Now go away."

"You know, I was thinking."

Felicity shook her head and made a soft tsking sound. "Bad sign. Didn't anyone ever tell you that thinking could be even more dangerous than looking at half-naked ladies?"

Jared only grinned. He loved being able to talk to her like this. Standing close, holding her in his arms. Even if they spoke utter nonsense, it was a delightfully heady experience. "Since I'm already here, we could get to really know each other."

"I already know you."

"Not in the way I want you to know me."

"Stop teasing. I have to hurry."

Jared kissed her again and, leaving her quite shaken, turned for her door. "Wait a minute."

Jared grinned and raised and lowered his eyebrows as he asked, "Changed your mind, have you? I knew my kisses could . . ."

Felicity ignored his teasing. "What does she look like?"

The word "sultry" came instantly to his mind. The same word often made itself known when he thought of Felicity, but in a manner that intrigued rather than disgusted. Jared wouldn't tell her what he thought of Margaret's looks. He wouldn't mention the hardness of the woman's mouth, nor the artificial coloring of her cheeks, or the far-too-worldly look in kohl-darkened eyes. He said simply. "She has dark hair, and she's a little taller than you."

"Who isn't?" Felicity sighed. "Dark hair? Her mother must have been dark."

"Probably," Jared nodded in agreement, for their father was a tall man of Nordic coloring. Felicity much resembled her tiny redheaded mother.

"Is she pretty?"

Jared shrugged. Margaret Rhodes was far from pretty. She

might be attractive to a man interested in her kind, but attractive in a hard way, as a lady of the night might be attractive. And a lady of the night was exactly his first thought as he opened the door to her knock. "She doesn't look anything like you, if that's what you mean."

Felicity frowned at his vague response. "That clears everything up, doesn't it?"

Jared smiled. "You'd see for yourself soon enough, if you'd stop asking questions and get dressed."

Felicity sighed, nodded, and almost smiled as Jared winked and closed the door behind him.

Dressed in her chemise again, Felicity hunted through her wardrobe looking for the perfect dress. Carolyn came back only to find her friend tearing her closet to pieces. "What are you doing?"

"Trying to find something to wear."

"Something like what?"

"I don't know."

"What about this one?"

Felicity shot her friend a look of annoyance as she pulled another robe from the closet. "If you're not going to help me, then get out of my way."

Carolyn took her friend by the shoulders and placed her on the chair before her dressing table. "All right. Sit down and tell me what's happening, while I look."

Felicity told her friend the shocking story, only Carolyn didn't take to the news in quite the same fashion as had the daughter of the man in question. As a matter of fact her eyes seemed to light up with a bit of speculating interest. "Really? A mistress? Who would have thought?"

Felicity felt the need to remind, "Carolyn, we're talking about my father."

"Your father is a man, Fel. Didn't you ever notice?"

"You didn't notice either, until just now."

Carolyn laughed, her eyes twinkling with mischief. "That's

not true. I always thought your father was an attractive man. A bit stodgy perhaps, but very attractive."

"You're disgusting," Felicity moaned, then continued dismally, "Can't I find one person who shares my opinion?"

"What opinion is that?"

"That a man is supposed to remain faithful after marriage, of course."

"I agree. And a lot of men are faithful."

Felicity shook her head. "I don't believe it. Not anymore."

"You've had a shock, is all. You'll change your mind. Besides, if you really believed that, you wouldn't be getting married, would you?"

Felicity sighed. "You're right, I suppose."

"Of course I'm right. How about this one?" she asked, pulling one gown from the rest.

Eight

Felicity, dressed at last in a soft pink gown, brushed her hair into place as Carolyn nagged. "Come on, just let me have a look. One look. I swear I won't say a word."

"Tomorrow. Come for tea." Felicity hesitated, not wanting to expose her half sister to Carolyn's strong personality immediately. She revised the invitation to, "No, not tomorrow. The next day would be better."

"Felicity, you're supposed to be my friend," Carolyn whined. "How can you do this when you know I'm dying of curiosity."

"I'm doing it because Margaret is probably terrified. I know I would be. Give her a chance to get to know us, to feel at home."

"You know, I think I should marry your father. That would make me your stepmother. And maybe then I'd get a little respect around here."

"If you want to stay my friend, you'll take that thought out of your mind forever," she said to the woman behind her own reflection. "God, that's all I need."

There was a knock at her door. A moment later and without waiting for her to answer, Jared stepped into her room and grinned. He found Felicity fussing nervously with a wayward curl. "You look gorgeous. Ready?"

Felicity hesitated a long moment before squaring her shoulders, taking a deep breath, and nodding. She walked toward him and glanced over her shoulder. "Get rid of her."

Jared grinned as Felicity walked by him, stepped across the hall, and knocked. A second later she moved into her father's room. It wasn't until the door closed behind her that Jared realized the lady at his side had scurried from across the room and had been craning her neck trying to see into the room. Carolyn frowned as the door shut and muttered a word she had no business knowing. "You can tell her I'm not going to forgive her for this."

"What did she do?"

"She knows. And tell her I'm coming for tea tomorrow, and it will take an army to stop me."

Jared might have said, "I'll tell her," but the words would have been lost since Carolyn was already halfway down the stairs. A second later the front door slammed.

Felicity entered the room expecting to find a lady of poor but respectable gentility. She smiled brilliantly as the young woman raised dark suspicious eyes to her. The smile hid well her surprise, for her half sister wore lip and cheek rouge. Granted some ladies of elegance indulged in the cosmetic, but if so, the color was always applied with a gentle hand. Not so in this case. And because it was less than lightly used, the overall effect was one of coarseness that bordered on the vulgar.

There was a moment of silence that seemed to stretch into eternity before her father said, "Oh here you are. Come and meet Margaret. Margaret, this is Felicity, your half sister."

Felicity! *Jesus, what kind of name is that?* Bess thought as she came from a chair at the old man's bedside and reached for the small woman's offered hand. Damn if she didn't look like a Felicity, all prim and proper, with a dress almost reaching her mouth. Bess wondered if she could have gotten the neckline any higher. Probably not without choking herself.

"I'm happy to meet you, Felicia."

"It's Felicity. And I'm happy to meet you as well. Sit down, please." Felicity brought another chair from across the room. "You're going to have to tell me all about yourself. I know we'll be great friends."

Bess smiled at the woman's comment. Friends? In a horse's ass. Still, she managed to reply in what she believed to be her most cultured tone, "I'm sure we will."

"Father tells me your mother just died. I'm so sorry. I know the pain of losing a parent."

"Yeah, that was rough going for a bit, deary. I didn't know what the hell to do, you know my being alone and all."

Felicity ignored the obscenity. "That must have been terrible. Had you no relatives on your mother's side? No friends that might have helped?"

"Not a one. At least none that I know. Heard they was all a bunch a' no good bas . . ." Bess caught herself, realizing a bit too late that her speech and manner had reverted back to the streets. She tried again for refinement. "Well, from what I understand my mother was alone in the world. Still, there was always Frank." And at Felicity's puzzled look, she said, "A friend of mine. He took care of the burying."

Felicity searched for a more pleasant subject and finally asked, "Have you gone to school?"

"No, but I knows my numbers and letters if that's what you mean."

Felicity shook her head, aghast at what she'd just said. She hadn't meant it at all the way it obviously sounded, nor the way it was taken. "No, I . . . I meant only to inquire where you had gone to school. I didn't mean . . ."

"No need to get all red in the face, honey. I ain't ashamed none. My mum got me a tutor." Bess figured it might be wiser not to mention exactly how that tutor got paid for each lesson.

There was a long moment of silence as Felicity racked her brain trying to think of something else to say. Finally she thought she had something. Shopping. All women loved to shop. They'd have that in common at least. "Have you ever been to Rudolph's?"

Bess shook her head. As Rudolph's was the most uppity ladies' shop in all of New York, she'd never hoped to go there. "Nope, ain't never had . . ." Again she changed her entire manner, her speech as well. "I mean, no, his clothes are quite expensive, I've heard."

"They are, but so lovely. I was thinking of shopping there tomorrow. Perhaps you might like to join me. Afterward, we could stop for tea."

Bess grinned. She'd never shopped like a lady before. Never had a chance to stand with the la-de-das of the city and wasn't about to let this opportunity pass her by. "I'd love it."

Jared took just that moment to knock and ask if he might see Felicity on an important matter. Felicity left the room, knowing only relief to be gone from the woman's company, their strained conversation, and the ever-lengthening and decidedly uncomfortable silence that dotted a meeting that had somehow turned into a question-and-answer session. She groaned as she leaned against a wall. "God, that was awful. I think she hates me. I came right out and insulted her. I can't believe I did that."

"What do you mean?"

"I asked her if she went to school. What I meant was, what school? It wasn't until after I said it that I realized . . ."

Jared reached for her and pulled her against him. "She doesn't hate you. She's just got here. It's going to take a little time to get used to each other. If you relaxed a bit things would go much smoother."

"I know, but . . . she's so different. I hadn't expected . . ."

"In what way?"

"Well, I thought she'd be . . . Well, I knew she . . . I expected . . ." Felicity sighed. "I haven't got the faintest idea."

"She took you by surprise, is that it?"

"You might say that."

"She's a bit rough, one might even say a bit coarse, and you hadn't expected that."

Felicity shrugged. "Well, I wouldn't say coarse, exactly." At least not out loud. Felicity didn't care what her first impression might have been, she'd never say her sister was coarse.

"And even though she's wearing an expensive dress, she doesn't look expensive, am I right?"

"Well, I wouldn't have put it quite so . . ."

"And her language. Occasionally a word slips in. A street word?"

Felicity shook her head. "I'm sure that . . ."

His arms tightened around her. "You are a very charitable lady."

"Jared, she can't help it. I'm sure she's a lovely person. It's where she comes from. Anyone can see that she's trying."

"Maybe she's doing more than trying," Jared offered wondering if the woman wasn't simply playing a part. It just could be that Miss Margaret Rhodes was planning to milk this opportunity for all it was worth. Jared might have thought that was a distinct possibility, but promised himself he'd say no more on the subject, knowing time would tell if his suspicions proved correct or not.

Felicity frowned. "What does that mean?"

They moved out of each other's arms at the sound of Mrs. Davies opening her door. The woman came into the hall. Obviously she had just come from her bed, for her hair had lost its pins and had fallen into a sleepy mass of long gray knots over her robed shoulders. She leaned weakly against the doorway. "I think I slept through tea. Is dinner almost ready?"

"I don't think so, but I could ask Becky to bring you something. Would you like that?"

"That would be very nice, dear."

Jared accompanied Felicity downstairs and into the kitchen. But Milly had apparently stepped out for a moment. And the same could be said for Becky. There was a roast beef in the oven. Felicity cut two thick slices and placed them on a plate with bread and gravy. Jared moved around the kitchen searching for utensils, a cup, and tea for the water simmering close to the fire. As he closed one closet and opened another, he said, "I think if she let up a bit on the sherry, she might not sleep through her meals."

"Oh, Jared, that's not nice. I know she has a sip now and

then, but the poor thing has rheumatism so bad some days she can hardly walk."

"She has more than a sip. If you want my opinion. And that's probably why she can't walk."

"You're being mean."

"Ask Becky how many bottles she's taken from her room?"

"But . . . how can she get it? She never goes out, and everything is so scarce."

"You can get anything, sweetheart, if you have enough money and know the right people."

"Is Billy getting it for her?"

Jared had no idea who allowed the lady to indulge in her habit, but thought it more than likely that it was someone other than the youngster. "One of the officers, probably."

When the tea was ready Jared carried the tray back, with Felicity following close behind. In Alvina's room she fluffed the lady's pillows before Jared placed the tray on her lap. "Are you feeling poorly today, dear?"

"I'm better now, thank you," the older woman said.

Felicity felt a twinge of guilt. She'd been far too caught up in her own problems. Between her father's injury and subsequent illness, the fittings and preparations for her wedding, and the anxiety over meeting her half sister for the first time, Felicity had given little thought to the elderly lady. She promised herself to do better in the future. "That's good, because tomorrow morning, first thing, I'm going shopping and you have to come with me."

"Me?" Alvina was clearly surprised, "Why?"

"Because you are a lady of some refinement, and I'm going to need your help. You know"—her voice lowered for the woman's ears alone—"a bride needs to choose a personal item or two, for her wedding night."

Alvina smiled and Felicity realized she'd never seen her smile so brilliantly before. It only made Felicity feel more guilty.

Felicity and Jared soon left the lady to her meal and moved once again into the hall. Jared, taking advantage of each opportunity when alone with his lady, wrapped his arm around her waist and swung her to face him. "Now where were we?" he asked silkily, even as his dark gaze sparkled with amusement.

"We were over there," Felicity said as she nodded down the hall a bit.

Jared grinned. "I meant, what were we doing?"

"We were talking about Margaret. I promised to take her shopping tomorrow. Do you think she would feel insulted if I sort of suggested she might wear a bit less rouge?"

Jared was having a time of it paying attention to her conversation, since his lady began, as she spoke, smoothing his shirt-front in a gentle if familiar manner. The touch of her hands unconsciously but willingly upon his person produced some instant, extraordinary and quite inappropriate responses. He shifted lest his body's unwanted reaction become too obvious. "You shouldn't do that, I think," he said, the words almost choked, and then silently cursed his wayward tongue, for he'd been referring to her familiar touch, and the truth of the matter was, he ached for her to grow even more familiar.

Felicity completely misunderstood. Believing they were still talking about Margaret, she nodded, then sighed as she brushed back a bit of hair that had loosened from the rawhide tie at the nape of his neck. "You're probably right about that. There's no way I could say it without making her feel uncomfortable."

Jared realized then that they were talking about two different things. "Your father should be well enough next week. Let's not wait."

"We've already planned it for the week after. We can't change it now."

Two weeks might not seem very long to some, but they were like an eternity to him, especially when he caused himself this constant miserable ecstasy by touching her every chance he got. He should refrain, he thought, even knowing he would not, could not.

"Are you busy this afternoon?"

"No. Why?"

"I thought we might find some privacy."

"There's always the garden."

"In the daytime?" He frowned at the thought. "Actually, I was thinking about your room."

Felicity blinked in shock at the idea.

"I only wanted to kiss you. Really kiss you and without chance of interruption."

"Oh well if it's just a kiss you want, there's always the linen closet," Felicity said with a sassy grin. "I've heard tales that some have used it for just that purpose."

"How shocking," Jared teased.

"Yes, if I'm not mistaken, there was one night when I knew some surprise upon opening that door."

Jared laughed. "Your cheeks looked like candy apples that night. And after you closed the door, you leaned against it as if standing guard. Did you imagine I might knock you aside to get a better look?"

"The thought did occur."

"Did it? I wonder why?"

"Perhaps because you so enjoyed the scene."

"Felicity," he said, laughing, "a man would have to be blind not to look when a woman stands facing him naked to her waist."

"And all men would have enjoyed it equally as much?"

He gathered her closer against him and tipped her chin, so their eyes might meet. "What I most enjoyed was your blush. And what I was thinking was how I might manage to persuade one particular lady to seek out yet another closet. Perhaps one a bit less occupied."

"You thought that, did you? After all of five minutes?"

"Sweetheart, I thought that after the first ten seconds."

Felicity laughed and leaned comfortably into his arms.

It was then that Marcy came barreling up the stairs. The man was huge. With gray hair and skin that was irreparably damaged from far too many hours spent in the sun, Felicity judged him to be close to sixty years. He wore elegant clothing, but despite his style of dress, the man more resembled a street tough than a manservant. Felicity had found his manner to be most fitting to a man of his station, but those same manners directed toward his employer were more familiar than most. In fact he treated Jared more like a friend than the man who paid his wages. In some ways he rather reminded her of her cook Milly, for he seemed to take control of most every situation. "The hospital sent word that you are to hurry. Something close to a hundred men just came in shot up to hell." Marcy's flushed complexion darkened to crimson as he realized he'd just used profanity in the presence of a lady. "Sorry, Miss Dryson, I didn't mean . . ." His voice dropped off and Felicity never noticed his sheepish expression for Jared caught her attention with, "I have to go," then suddenly took her mouth with a hard hungry kiss as if it were but a common and everyday occurrence and they were quite alone.

Moments later Felicity, recovered from the devastating effects of Jared's kiss, entered her father's room again. "Oh I'm happy you came back. I've been ringing for Becky with no results."

"I think she went down to the market, Father."

Thomas nodded, and said, "I thought Margaret might like to see her room and perhaps rest a bit before dinner."

"Of course. You must be exhausted. Let me show you your room," Felicity said as she smiled at the young woman.

The two left her father to rest. As they approached the stairway, Bess frowned, realizing she would be quartered on the third floor. To her way of thinking, only servants took rooms at the top of a house. "Will I be sleeping with servants?"

Felicity looked a bit taken aback at the sharpness of her tone, and for just a second imagined she saw pure unadulterated hatred in the young woman's eyes. Felicity knew, of course, that it was but a trick of the lighting. They stood some thirty feet from a window. It was possible to imagine anything in this dimness. "Surely not. You are part of this family. I would have given you the room next to mine had not an officer already quartered himself there."

"There are four bedrooms on this floor and four again on the floor above." Gaining the third floor, Felicity opened the first door to a room decorated in blue and white. It was lovely, obviously feminine, and so the reason for its unused state, for the officers had preferred more sturdy furniture when choosing.

Bess had a time of it trying to disguise her surprise. She'd never imagined a room so luxurious, so big. It was almost as large as the little house she and her mother and sister had shared. And it was all hers, for as long as she wished it. Bess couldn't believe her luck. She thought she just might be able to stand these stuffy fools after all. "Billy will bring your bags up."

"I haven't but one small one."

Felicity smiled. "No matter. Tomorrow we'll take care of filling your closet." She turned to leave and stopped at the doorway. "There's a tub in there." She nodded toward a closed door. "After your rest, you might enjoy a bath. If so, just ring for Becky." Felicity smiled at the thought of her lackadaisical servant, but said, "She's been known to dally a bit, but she'll come eventually. I hope you'll be comfortable here."

Felicity fussed over her father, her movements slightly abrupt, her touch a bit less than gentle. She was feeding him a bowl of soup. Finally after rubbing his chin for the last time, Thomas took her hand in his and said, "All right, come out with it, daughter."

"What do you mean?"

"I mean if you continue to rub my chin like this, I won't need a shave in the morning."

"Was I too rough? I'm sorry."

Felicity might have said the words, but she wasn't feeling very sorry at the moment. What she was feeling was anger.

"Why are you upset? What happened?"

"Nothing."

"Is it Margaret? Has she said something, done something?"

"No."

"Sit down," Thomas said.

It was time to clear the air.

"Father, I'd rather you didn't . . . It's really none of my business."

"Yes, we can agree on that, but there are things you should know."

Felicity sighed, staring at the bed, not the man in it, she waited for him to begin.

"I loved your mother, Felicity. I hope you know that."

"Did you?" Felicity asked with more than a touch of belligerence. A second later she bit her lip and looked away. "I'm sorry. I didn't mean that."

"Yes you did, and I quite understand your animosity. What you don't understand is how much I loved her. She was delicate, sweet, an altogether adorable lady. You are very much like her, except she did not have half your good health. She had a very hard time when you were born. The doctors warned that should she have another, she would surely die." Thomas breathed a sigh at the thought. "I couldn't take the chance. I couldn't ever lose her."

"So you turned to another," Felicity couldn't hide the disgust in her tone. She knew she didn't have the right to judge him, and yet she couldn't help but assess his actions. Obviously they did not suit.

"I did, once. It was a long time before I could forgive myself."

"But you finally did, I take it."

"Felicity," he warned for her tone was quite sarcastic.

"I'm sorry," she murmured.

"If your mother forgave me, I can't see why . . ."

Felicity came instantly to her feet. "You told her?" she asked, aghast at the very thought. "Why would you do that? Why would you bring pain to the woman you love?"

"Sit down," he said again, the second time a bit more sternly than the first. "I did not tell her. She came across a letter."

Felicity moaned, unable to imagine how her mother must have suffered at his treachery.

"Your mother understood that a man has certain needs."

Felicity wanted only to rage at men and their ridiculous needs. Were those needs more important than right, than honor, than love? Surely not, and yet they often put them ahead of everything. Felicity silently congratulated herself, glad she'd never been subjected to a man and his cursed needs. She'd feel nothing for her husband, and, if he chose to bestow a bit of those needs on another, it wouldn't affect her in the least.

Felicity believed herself to be an intelligent woman. Intelligent enough to take lessons learned from others and use them to her own advantage. A moment of silence went by before Felicity said, "It's not my place to forgive you, Father."

"Granted," he said obviously annoyed. "What I ask from you is understanding."

"Oh I understand," she said. "I believe I understand quite well."

"Still, you're angry with me."

"No doubt that will pass," she said, unable to deny the fact.

"Despite your annoyances with me, Felicity, I must ask you to accept your sister. To make her feel welcome, at home here. After all, she's hardly to blame in this affair."

"I know, and I promise I'll do my best."

Felicity wouldn't know for some time that her best was hardly good enough.

Felicity thought to make a quick trip to the chimney room hidden in the cellar. Last night Brian had awakened her again, announcing the arrival of three who had escaped the British. Thankfully none among them was injured this time, but all were no doubt starving. In a canvas bag she placed the last of the chicken, served at last night's dinner, three huge slices of ham, bread, cheese from the larder, and ripe apples that had been brought in from upstate for the English officers' enjoyment.

Felicity thought one apiece was quite enough for the officers, while the men below would need double that before regaining their usual strength.

In the cellar she tapped into a barrel of ale, filled a large pitcher with the foaming brew, and, with arms overflowing, managed to turn the correct brick that opened the chimney-room door.

Her offering was much appreciated, for the men had not eaten since the previous night, that being a light meal of bread and cheese. She lingered talking to the men as they ate, finding no real need to hurry, since dinner wouldn't be ready for some time yet. Margaret would be resting, Alvina and her father as well, and Jared wouldn't be back from the hospital until late. She felt momentarily at loose ends and thought that lingering in the company of these men could only lift her spirits some.

"Her name his Beth," one of the men said after Felicity's gentle inquisition. "We've been married now for three years, and I haven't spent a month all told in her company. Lucky am I if I see her for an hour here or there."

Felicity sat on a hard wooden stool as she conversed. "She must miss you sorely."

"I'm wishing I could get a message to her, but with these damn English at every corner, I don't dare."

Obviously the man prowled the city, coming and going cloaked in darkness, doing what he could to aid the cause. He could not often venture near his loved ones lest he be captured and his wife be accused of abetting a criminal.

The British did not consider the rebel forces a legitimate fighting foe. Rather they imagined this conflict the idiosyncracy of ignorant provincials, dominated by a few criminals, and believed that once those criminals were brought to justice, the entire matter would then be forgotten. In the meantime, should one of the King's wayward children be found to have less than loyal intentions toward the Crown, he would be properly chastised, not as a true adversary, but as a lowly outlaw.

Felicity was aware that the man was wanted, that there was

no doubt a price on his head. He'd been unconscious last night, having been on the receiving end of a blow taken from a rifle butt. He had to be carried by his friends into her house. She was to learn later that he was the leader of this small group and responsible only just last week for three Britishers finding their end years sooner than the Lord might have initially planned.

"A note?"

The man shook his head. "If it were found . . ." Again he shook his head, "No, I want her safe at all cost."

"Tell me where she is, and I'll repeat what needs saying."

The man gave Felicity the address. "Tell her Charlie is safe. Tell her the ship sails at midnight and to watch for the joker on board."

Felicity frowned.

"She'll know what it means."

"Anything else?"

"Tell her to kiss little Charlie for me, and I'll see her soon."

Felicity came to her feet and, after wishing the men well, knowing they'd be gone by morning, left them to finish their meal.

Felicity had not expected the driver to take her to the better part of the city. Still, she wouldn't have expected the worst either, and this was definitely the worst. Perhaps she should have waited. Brian would come by tonight. But tonight might be too late. Mr. Remmington. Felicity shook her head, knowing even if she passed the message to the owner of the teashop, it might not be understood and perhaps an opportunity would be lost. No, she had volunteered to take the message and now had no alternative but to do as much.

It was growing dark and streetlamps were being lit. In less than a half hour night would fall. Felicity shivered as she imagined herself alone in this rough part of the city at night. Still, dark or not, the streets were filled with a most unusual assortment of people. Hawkers pushed huge wagons calling out to those behind closed doors. Shopkeepers swept their sidewalks as they readied to close up for the day. Children gathered in groups played children's games, occasionally defying the fates, perhaps on a dare, as they ran between the dangerous hooves of one horse or another. Decent women, dragging their children behind, hurried home from market with the fixings for a meal in hand while others, perhaps not quite so decent, judging by the shockingly low cut of their gowns, sauntered up an avenue, twirling frilly parasols that did not match their gowns, smiling at men, some of whom grinned in return and tipped their hats in greeting.

One such woman had apparently caught the eye of an English soldier and just before the cab passed them, the woman reached for the already scandalously low neckline of her gown and pulled it lower still, freeing her upper body to the man's delighted inspection. Felicity gasped at the unbelievable sight, and her mouth gaped open for a good three minutes before she realized why it was that her jaw was beginning to ache.

The cab came to a stop. The house was clean, if in a state of slight disrepair. Garbage cluttered neither the walkway nor the sidewalk to the left and right of it. A woman answered Felicity's knock, a woman who was very obviously with child. It seemed Charlie had exaggerated a bit the lack of time spent with his new wife, considering a little girl of about two hung to her mother's long skirt.

"Yes?" the woman asked.

"Are you Beth?"

"I am."

"Are you alone?" she asked, her voice lowering.

"Yes. Why?" the woman asked a bit nervously as she took a step back, obviously readying herself to slam the door shut. It didn't matter that her caller was dressed as fine as any lady. What mattered was that she was alone and had no one and nothing to protect her and her small family but her own quick wits.

Felicity repeated the message word for word and knew some relief as the woman smiled, and said, "Thank you," just before she closed and locked her door.

Felicity hurried back to her waiting cab and knew only relief as night fell and the small vehicle sped toward her home on the opposite side of the city.

Nine

It had taken longer to find the house than Felicity had first supposed. She would be late for dinner. Lights blazed in most every room downstairs. Major Wood expected her to join him and his men at the evening meal. He would be waiting.

Felicity rushed inside but stopped so suddenly she might have hit against an invisible wall as she saw Margaret, dressed in one of Felicity's most provocative ball gowns, coming down the stairs on the arm of a grinning Captain Hastings. Only on Margaret, the gown looked far more than just provocative—it looked positively indecent.

The fact that Margaret had helped herself, without asking, to one of Felicity's gowns did not shock as much as the fact that the gown obviously did not fit. Felicity was much smaller than the woman as well as four inches shorter. And because of the ill fit, Margaret's ankles were completely exposed, as were her unusually large breasts.

Apparently the officer at her side was well aware of that fact as he seemed to be speaking to her half sister's chest rather than her face. And Margaret didn't seem to mind one bit as she smiled at the top of the man's head.

Jared took just that moment to step into the hallway as did Major Wood behind him. Both men smiled at Felicity, but a moment later Jared made a sort of choking sound as he followed the direction of his lady's gaze.

There was no way that Felicity was going to sit at a table in her own home with a woman dressed in a manner so offensive. She didn't hesitate to approach her and the bedazzled officer and stopped both on the steps with, "You'll excuse us, won't you, Captain? I need to speak with Miss Rhodes for a moment."

The captain had no choice but to oblige, especially when he saw the fire in the lady's usually gentle brown eyes. A fire that promised dire consequences should he dare to object. "Of course."

Felicity took the woman's hand and nearly dragged a reluctant Bess up the stairs. Bess, having no notion of propriety, thought she looked smashing and felt no need to take herself from the admiration that surely awaited her below. "Where are we going?"

Felicity did not respond to the question, but continued on until they reached her bedroom. With the door closed behind them, she turned on the young woman with, "Take that gown off."

"I didn't think you'd mind."

"I wouldn't have, if you had found one that fit. Your breasts are very nearly exposed. Do you think to sit at my table like that?"

"I think I'm old enough to wear what I please," she said sullenly.

"As long as you are wearing my clothes, and especially in this house, you'll wear what *I* please, or I can have Becky bring a tray to your room."

Bess knew when to back down. She had already invited the captain to her room later tonight and figured staying here just might not be such a bore after all. She hadn't realized until this afternoon that she shared the floor with three officers, two of whom at least looked eager enough to do her bidding. No, this scam promised to be too good to throw away simply because Felicity Dryson was a prissy, puritanical little fool. "All right. What do you suggest?"

"First, take that off, and I'll find you something else."

Felicity knew a moment's surprise as the woman did as she

was told. Her surprise wasn't at Margaret's almost-instant obe-
dience, but rather at the fact that the woman now stood completely at ease in her nakedness in the center of the room.
Felicity hadn't imagined that Margaret wore nothing at all under
that gown.

It took some doing, since Felicity had never seen a totally
naked woman before, but she did manage at last to control her
shock, tear her gaze away, and search her closet for something
modest and appropriate.

"Why aren't you wearing anything?" Felicity asked, her back
turned to the girl.

"Because you said to take it off."

"I mean, anything under the gown."

"Oh, I never wear anything underneath when I'm at home.
I find it more comfortable that way."

Felicity couldn't believe she was hearing this. Never wore
anything under her clothes? She hadn't imagined anyone so
improperly raised as to even think to do that. "A lady always,
and I do mean always, wears something under her gown. I do.
Everyone I know does. In the future you will do the same, unless
alone in your room."

"Of course," Bess returned obediently, once again silently
questioning the wisdom of ever coming here. If she had known
what a prig this woman would turn out to be and the restrictions
she'd be forced to bear . . . Still, there were those officers. Bess
figured she could stand Felicity's fuddy-duddy manner as long
as she had one or two . . . Bess grinned at the thought, for two
sounded just about right, of those officers to warm her bed at
night.

Felicity and Margaret returned to the waiting men, Margaret
this time clothed far more appropriately. Her neckline touched
the base of her throat, and Margaret couldn't wait to get the
damn thing off.

"I'm sorry to see that you've changed," Captain Hastings had
the temerity to remark. "You looked lovely in that color."

Before Margaret could say a word, Felicity snapped, "The dress was torn."

The captain glanced at his hostess, then directed his attention to the lady at his side. "Perhaps after it is repaired, you might honor us by wearing it ag . . ."

"I don't think so," Felicity said. "The tear cannot be repaired."

Felicity sat to the left of Major Wood, with Jared at her side. Across from her Margaret sat quite happily, it seemed, positioned between Captain Hastings and Lieutenant Waverly. Lieutenant Walters, newly married to Becky, rarely joined his fellow officers for dinner. Most always he preferred to eat with his wife, in the kitchen, only Becky had eaten earlier and tonight he sat at Felicity's table. Felicity could only wonder how the woman managed to divide her smiles among all the officers present? In her usual place at the far end of the table Alvina Davies sat quietly, perhaps too quietly, with a smile that proved a bit too vague.

Felicity gave a silent moan, knowing Jared had been right and the woman was once again deep in her cups. No doubt it had been drink all along rather than illness or age that had caused her slow wit and often awkward and decidedly off-balance movement.

Would this conflict never come to an end? Forced to consort with her enemies, forced to grow to like them, despite the fact that she would rather not have. Forced to take in illegitimate offspring and drunken old ladies, Felicity felt her life had slipped totally from her control.

The table was covered in a white-linen cloth, Irish linen if he wasn't mistaken. Crystal and china as well as silver flatware told of the elegance of this meal. Still, it did not go without Jared's notice that the conduct that should have accompanied such elegant surroundings was somewhat lacking in excellence. At the opposite side of the table, Margaret seemed to make it a point to include Lieutenant Walters in her conversation. In so doing she leaned more than once toward the man and because he sat to the right of Hastings, had thrice, to Jared's knowledge, leaned her hand upon the captain's thigh. Thankfully Felicity was blissfully unaware of the happening, for Jared knew she would be aghast at the unseemly display of such familiar behavior.

Immediately after the meal, Jared asked Captain Hastings to step outside for a moment. Hastings, reluctant to leave the lady who had allowed him an inkling of the pleasure this night surely held in store, nevertheless did as Jared asked. "What is it?"

"Miss Felicity is a lady of some strict moral code."

The captain nodded, not at all sure what his fellow officer was leading up to.

"She would not take kindly, I think, to what went on tonight beneath the table. And would no doubt report such action to the major."

"What?" Captain Hastings felt his face grow warm at the thought of the others being aware of the happenings during dinner. How intimately he'd been touched. How the lady's fingers had lingered close, almost unbearably close, to what he wanted touched most. He had eaten without thought, for all he could think was how she'd touch him later.

"I don't know, nor do I care to know exactly what that was, but I think it should never happen again, lest you find yourself quartered elsewhere."

The captain was silent.

"Of course, should the lady be so inclined, and my lady should never have knowledge of that fact, you'll find I have no objections if you find a more private situation for pleasurable encounters."

Captain Hastings nodded and instantly left to join the lively company inside. A moment later Felicity stepped outside. She stood for a long moment in the moonlight, watching the man she was to marry. He stood looking to the heavens with his hands behind his back, his dark hair glistening in the moonlight, a smoking pipe between his teeth. A most handsome man, Felicity thought, as she studied his profile. She imagined it a good thing that he would leave this land after the conflict, for she often felt a thrill of danger in his company. Yes, this man was a most dangerous sort. He had the power to steal a woman's heart. And Felicity wanted most of all to keep her heart for herself.

She must have made a sound, for Jared suddenly looked in her direction, his gaze warm, his smile warmer still brought her to his side. "Did you speak with him?"

"Yes," Jared said very slowly, wondering why she should have asked that question, and judging by the distress in her eyes, could only dread the next.

"Did you ask him to never . . ." Felicity swallowed and wondered how she was going to speak of the unspeakable. "Did you mention that I would be most pleased never to witness that kind of conduct again."

"You knew?"

"I was so embarrassed. I cannot tell my father, and yet he has every right to know what is happening in his home. What should I do?"

Jared closed the small distance between them and took her in his arms. The motion had grown commonplace over these last few days, so common in fact that Felicity never thought to deny either of them the contentment and comfort found when in this man's arms. She pressed her face to his chest. "Do nothing, sweetheart. At least for the moment."

"What is she?" she moaned into his shirt. "How can this be happening?"

"Perhaps she is a little confused and has taken the captain's obvious interest for more than what he meant it to be." Jared knew that wasn't exactly true. He knew for a fact that the woman was one of some experience. All a man had to do was look at her to know that. She knew well enough what she was about.

"But to be so bold."

"I know," he soothed. "Obviously she was raised improperly, but I'm sure once she is here a while, under your gentle influence, she'll understand what is expected of her."

Felicity moaned. "She's only eighteen. My father's too ill to see to her protection. And I don't know if I'm up to the chore."

Jared frowned. If that woman was eighteen, then he was eighty. She was closer to five-and-twenty and needed as much protection as any bitch in heat.

"She was born after you?"

"Yes, isn't that the cause of my . . ."

"Disillusionment?"

"Disgust," Felicity corrected with some strength and then, "That dress!" She shuddered at the thought of how the girl had exposed herself to every male eye in her home. "Lord, I almost fainted on the spot. I couldn't believe . . ." Felicity became aware of an odd, almost-choking sound coming from deep in his chest and pulled out of his arms. "Are you laughing?"

"Me? Certainly not. I was merely clearing my throat."

"Then why are you smiling?"

"Because you look angry enough to hit me."

"I think I shall hit you."

"Why?"

"Because you looked at her."

Jared felt his heart swell with pleasure. She was jealous. She might not know it, but she was. And a woman wouldn't be jealous unless she cared. "Felicity, I'd have to be dead not to look."

"Deny you enjoyed it."

Jared shrugged. "Another time, another place, I might have done just that."

She elbowed him in the stomach, and Jared grunted at the unexpected attack. Felicity swung on her heels and started for the house. A second later an arm came around her waist, lifted her from the ground as if she were a sack of potatoes, and, despite her kicks, brought her around the house to the privacy of her garden. "Put me down this instant!"

Jared did as asked and turned her toward him. "What are you angry about now?"

"If you want her so bad, why dally with me? She's inside,

isn't she? Shouldn't you be there as well, fawning over her like the rest?"

"I never said I wanted her. I never said anything of the kind."

"You said another time, another place."

"Right. If I had seen her before you, I might have taken from her an hour or so of enjoyment." Jared thought that probably wasn't true. His tastes ran toward the worldly, yes, but not toward the cheap, and he thought Margaret Rhodes the cheapest-looking woman he'd seen in a long time.

"You're disgusting, and I've quite changed my mind about marrying you."

Jared thought the best course of action would be an explanation, rather than to insist on the fact that they would indeed marry. "Walk with me."

"No."

Jared placed his arm around her waist and began to walk, taking her, with or without her permission, along with him. As he moved he began to speak. "Men are far less complicated than women. On the whole, especially when very young, they want but one thing. It can sometimes rule their very lives."

"And it rules yours?"

"If it did, mistress, you'd be naked right now."

"What?"

Jared ignored her shock as he continued his explanation. "But men soon come to understand they cannot continue on in their rutting ways. That there has to be more to life than taking a woman to bed. That there is more to a woman than just a body. That without that special something, the act of coupling is hardly what it could be."

"Is there a particular time when they come to understand this?"

"Usually they understand it when they meet a woman like you."

"What does that mean? What's wrong with me?"

"Nothing. The fact is, everything is right about you. If the circumstances were right, I have no doubt you could be just as

provocative as Margaret and in a far less lewd way." He smiled
into her wide eyes. "In the meantime, while in mixed company
you are every inch a lady. Bright, intelligent, ready to dazzle a
man and bring him under your spell with a gentle smile."

Jared's voice lowered as he stopped walking and turned her
into his arms. "Any man, controlled by basic urges, would lust
for someone like Margaret, but any man who knows quality
would choose you."

Felicity's short laugh was devoid of humor. "Meaning, I'm
perfect material for a wife, but for a lover you'd choose Margaret. Which is exactly why . . ."

"Apparently you haven't heard a word I've just said."

Felicity hung back, causing Jared to nearly drag her beneath
a tree, where the darker shadows would afford them considerably more privacy. He sat, his back against the tree, placing her
as he had once before upon his lap. "What are you doing?"

"You, my dear, are about to discover lust. And I'm about to
show you exactly who it is I lust for."

"Jared, don't," she said, her voice breaking as dread filled
her entire being.

"Don't be afraid. I swear I won't do anything to hurt you."

His mouth was on her throat, nibbling at her clean skin, delighting in its taste and texture, unable to bear the thought that
he'd have to wait another week before he could taste all of her.
He had every intention of being gluttonous while about that
chore.

"But suppose you lose control."

"I won't. I'm going to talk and love you through each step
until you know lust, until you crave my touch."

Felicity laughed at that, knowing his intent was indeed impossible. She was a lady, and ladies did not lust for their men.
Ladies permitted the men they married a certain degree of pleasure. Felicity hadn't learned what that pleasure involved. She
knew only that a man was supposed to explain the mystery to
his wife on their wedding night. But she'd heard women talking
about it. She'd heard matrons whisper and then giggle almost

slyly, while saying it to be only one more chore to be gotten through before the day would finally end. That was all there was to it. Felicity was sure of it.

"You don't believe me?"

"I don't believe it's possible for a woman to feel lust."

"All right, suppose we try something."

"What?" she asked, her voice filled with distrust.

"I'm going to touch you. If you don't like it, tell me to stop. But you have to promise honesty. If you do like it, you must say so."

Jared ran one finger from her throat to the modest neckline of her dress. One finger that moved unbelievably slowly and barely touched against her skin. He glanced at her face, wishing they had more light, wishing he could see the look in her eyes. "What do you think?"

"I think that was all right."

"Good. How about this?" he asked as his finger moved to her lips and lingered there for some moments before trailing again to the neckline of her dress.

"Nice."

Jared nodded. "Now this?" From under her ear his finger slid down her throat to her shoulder.

"It tickles."

"Good."

Jared created some room between them and with his hands at her waist, fingers spread wide, began to raise them slowly. "What about this?"

"I don't know."

He nodded as if she'd just confirmed his thoughts. Felicity didn't really know what to make of his reaction, but breathed a sigh of relief as his hands returned to her waist. And then without warning, his mouth took hers in a gentle kiss, a kiss that left her sweetly pliant as she allowed the pleasure. Jared waited until he felt her soften against him before he continued on in his purposeful seduction.

Felicity never noticed the movement of his fingers as his

mouth made love to hers. He licked her lips. Soon enough she found the movement oddly not enough and opened her mouth to his hungry tongue. She moaned with pleasure as he discovered again the sweetness of her. And then he released her again. She was clearly out of breath and perhaps just a bit weak.

"All right, now watch this carefully," he said as his fingertip grazed over her moistened lips and then again down to her throat going lower this time, lower than her dress should have allowed. Felicity glanced down and with some confusion took in the fact that her bodice was open and her thin, lacy chemise would have allowed him, in good light, to view her body quite easily.

"How did you?" she managed as she watched his dark finger touch her white skin. And then she forgot her question as she watched that finger, so dark, so masculine against her. "That looks nice, doesn't it?" she said without thought.

"It looks very nice," Jared agreed, just before he weakened her further with another of his devastating kisses. "You probably shouldn't kiss me like that," Felicity gasped as she was finally allowed air into her starving lungs.

"Why?"

"Because, it's making me weak and a little dizzy."

"It's supposed to. Now watch," he said as he repeated the movement of his finger from her lips down her throat, only this time he didn't allow the delicate fabric of her chemise to forestall his intent. His finger grazed her skin all the way to the tip of one breast. Jared smiled as he felt her back arch a bit. "Does that feel good?"

"I don't know."

"You promised to be honest, sweetheart."

"Yes, I think it does," she amended softly.

Jared tugged her chemise a bit lower, freeing her breast to his view. "Now watch me. Don't look away," he said as he replaced his finger with the startling heat of his mouth.

Felicity jumped and might have pulled away, had not his arms been tightly around her.

Felicity felt just an instant of panic but soon reminded herself that this was but a small experiment. That they were to be married next week. That he would never hurt her. That she could trust him, that . . . that . . . Felicity tried to remember what she'd been thinking, but couldn't quite manage the chore. The truth was this did feel lovely. Very lovely indeed.

She closed her eyes and murmured a small sound of pleasure, then followed that sound with one that might have been taken for disappointment as Jared's mouth came from her body to breathe heavily against her own. "Did that feel good?"

"Lovely," she returned as she kissed his cheek, his nose, and his brow. "Does it always feel so good?"

"Lean back a bit and I'll show you."

Felicity did as he asked, eager now to experience again the pleasure of his touch. And this time, the touch of his mouth was even better, hotter than before. Her breasts were fully exposed now, the straps of both dress and chemise down her arms, and Jared took turns with both perfect globes of flesh, nibbling here and there, kissing, sucking, loving her slowly, deliciously, with all his expertise.

She arched her back even as she wondered if he could kiss her enough, touch her enough. She'd never known anything like this, never known anything could be like this. She moaned, again and again, urging him to take her deeper, to suck harder, to bite, to lick, her hands in his hair pulling his face tighter to her flesh, silently telling of her growing desperation. And every time he did as she silently pleaded, something happened to her stomach. It was as if an invisible thread connected one part of her body to the other. Felicity thought that a strange phenomenon but did not dally overlong at the thought.

And then that wasn't enough. She wanted more, only she couldn't imagine what more meant. "Jared," she whispered weakly, pressing herself to his mouth, tearing at his hair, squirming slightly on his lap. "Jared, please."

And Jared knew what it was she longed for. He knew she wanted to further this moment. To discover all there was to the pleasure that could exist between man and woman.

He took her hands in his, leaned back, and brought her against him. Felicity tried to calm her breathing some even though her gasping closely matched his. Apparently he was equally as shaken as she.

Jared allowed only a moment to pass before he placed his hand between them on her stomach, laying it flat over the gentle swell of smooth flesh. "Here. Do you feel it here?"

Felicity nodded as her mouth moved over his throat. She'd only intended a short kiss, but it seemed the scent and feel of him, the warmth of his skin, became suddenly irresistible, and Felicity found herself really kissing him and then dared to follow his many examples, touched his skin with her tongue.

Jared groaned, "Oh, sweetheart." Loath to break this delicious moment, he nevertheless knew he had to show her the passion lying dormant deep inside. "That's desire, Felicity."

He took her hand and brought it to the hardness of his body. "Do you feel this?"

She nodded again.

He touched her stomach again. "Desire, lust, it's the same thing. It's like you need something more, am I right?"

Felicity tried to pull away, her eyes wide with surprise that he should understand so well. "This is what I felt for you since the first time I saw you."

"This strong?"

"It's grown stronger every day."

"Lord," she breathed sweetly. "How have you stood it?"

"I've stood it because I knew you would be mine eventually, and I could wait for someone like you."

Felicity was only just coming to know how hard the waiting must have been. "Next week . . ." she began

His mouth was against her throat. "You'll be in my bed. I can hardly wait."

Felicity was silent for a long moment. Long enough for Jared to ask, "What are you thinking?"

"I don't know what to think. I always thought that a lady couldn't, wouldn't feel these things."

"And now that you know she can?"

Felicity's smile was wicked, pure and simple, and Jared had a thought about what he'd just had a hand in creating. "I was thinking perhaps we could get married tomorrow."

Ten

Tomorrow would come and go, but the wedding date would remain as originally planned. Felicity knew her father would be aghast at the very thought of moving it up, for all weddings were planned months into the future. As it was, some would probably whisper that the reasons behind this hurried affair might be more than met the eye. Some, having nothing better to do with their lives, might watch for any developing signs for months, before giving up their unseemly thoughts.

Felicity changed into her nightdress and robe and brushed her hair down around her shoulders before looking in on her father for the night. He was asleep. She kissed his forehead and pulled the sheet over his chest before leaving the room and heading across the hall toward her own door. She never realized her smile, nor the warmth in her eyes, for a man seemed to be blocking that door. A man who appeared to have no intentions of moving aside. "What are you doing?"

"I'm looking for a lady. You might have seen her. She's about this big," Jared said as he placed one hand flat upon Felicity's head.

"There are a lot of women about that size," Felicity returned, her eyes glowing at the prospect of yet another delicious encounter with this man.

"The one I'm looking for has red hair."

"Oh, well that narrows it down a bit, doesn't it? No more

than a hundred thousand women have red hair, I would imagine."

"And honey brown eyes."

"Perhaps you could tell me her name. I might remember her if I heard the name."

"Her name is Felicity."

Felicity managed, to Jared's delight, to look amazed. Her eyes were wide when she said, "What a coincidence. My name is Felicity."

"Is it? How odd. Do you know my Felicity?"

Felicity did not miss the possessive pronoun and found herself growing more sure of herself, more bold, more delighted at his encounter. "I'm sorry, but I don't think I do."

"That's too bad."

"Why?"

"Well, I wanted to kiss my Felicity good night."

"You already did that."

"How do you know? You don't even know the woman."

"Oh." Felicity thought about that for a second before adding, "I supposed that you had."

Jared grinned. He touched her hair, hanging in loose waves down her back and brushed his fingertips over a throat, hardly visible above her modest gown. "You look adorable."

"Thank you. So do you."

Jared had removed his uniform coat and wore only a white shirt, trousers, and black boots. His cravat was gone, and a few buttons of his shirt were open. Felicity thought she rather liked that. Rather liked seeing his chest. Wished she could see more of it, in fact.

"If you invited me inside, I could take it off for you."

"What?" she asked, her gaze moving from his chest to his dark smiling eyes.

"My shirt. I was thinking you might like to see what's under it."

"I might," Felicity teased in return. "But if looks mean anything, you'd rather see what's under . . ." Felicity suddenly realized what she was saying and turned a brilliant shade of crimson.

Jared laughed aloud as he crushed her against him. "God, I can't believe you." What he really meant was he couldn't believe his luck in finding a woman like her.

"Oh Lord, I don't know what's gotten into me."

Jared was tempted to tell her it would be him and very soon, but decided she was red enough.

"I love it. Don't stop the next time, all right?"

"What do you mean?"

"I mean when you want to say something naughty, say it. As long as we're alone, I won't mind at all."

"Why did you have to say that?" she groaned against his throat. "Now of course I'll think of terribly naughty things to say when others are around and turn red every time."

Jared chuckled.

"And you're sure you won't mind?"

"I swear I won't. Go ahead. Say something, and I'll prove it."

Felicity laughed. "I'm not in the habit of saying naughty things to men, you know."

"I know, but for me you could, couldn't you?"

One might have thought they were talking about something quite sensible, what with the way the man was going on. Still, it seemed important to him. She only wished she knew what to say. "I wouldn't know how to begin."

"All right, you can kiss me instead."

"Can I? That sounds like a lovely thought."

"It's even lovelier when you actually do it."

"One of the soldiers might . . ."

"Everyone is asleep." Jared knew that wasn't exactly true, but everyone was in their rooms or whatever room it was they had chosen for the night.

Moments later Jared stepped away from her. He found he had to tear his arms from her or find himself inside her room. "Good night."

Felicity smiled as she stepped into her room and closed her door.

The walls and floors of the mansion being very thick, Felicity never heard the soft knock directly over her room.

To Captain Hastings's delight, Bess answered the door wearing only her black-lace robe. The moment he was inside she asked, "You wouldn't have a smoke on you, would you?"

"No, I'm sorry. I don't have anything."

Bess sighed unhappily. "Maybe the lieutenant has something."

"He doesn't smoke."

"What about a drink then? Do you have something in your room?"

"I have a bottle. I'll get it."

Hastings was back within seconds. This time he didn't knock, but walked directly into the room to find Bess lying naked on the bed. Hastings poured a bit into two glasses and sat at her side. Bess downed the whiskey in one gulp and sighed. "That's better," she said, then placing the glass on the table by her bed and without any further ado, she reached for the buttons of his trousers. "Now let's see what we have here."

Lieutenant Waverly frowned when his knocking went unanswered. The lady had specifically invited him to her room. Why then hadn't she responded to his knock? Perhaps she was dressing, or undressing, he grinned. Perhaps she was readying herself for his arrival. Waverly thought the best course of action was to let himself in, lest another pass by and realize what he was about.

He opened the door.

Waverly might have known a flashing moment of disappointment as he spied the lady and his friend rollicking upon the bed, but his disappointment only lasted until Bess noticed him standing in her doorway.

She laughed at his shock, and called from the bed, "Come in, Lieutenant."

Captain Hastings rolled from the lady. It took but an instant to realize that Margaret suffered under no shock, or embarrassment, at being so discovered—rather that she seemed to enjoy the fact of another's arrival. Hastings grinned. "Come on, Waverly, join the party."

And party they did until the sun peeked over the horizon.

Jared was almost asleep when he realized the sound above had stopped. It had begun slowly and gone on so long that he hardly noticed it. Only when it had finally stopped did he recognize it, only then that he realized someone had been rocking on a bed for close to twenty minutes straight. Jared rolled to his stomach and groaned as some minutes later the rocking began once again. It was worse than he thought. Worse than Felicity could ever imagine, for Jared knew what the sound meant. He knew no man could be ready for yet another bout of lovemaking, no, not lovemaking, sex. No man could be ready that soon for another go at the woman. That meant they were not alone. That three or perhaps more were in that bed. Something had to be done and done soon, before a line began to form outside of Margaret's room and Felicity was somehow harmed by the scandal. But what? What the hell could he do?

Jared found himself dozing again to the monotonous rocking sounds. Just before he fell asleep he thought he might speak with Sam. Perhaps he could think of what might be done.

At nine the next morning Felicity mounted the stairs to the room above her own. She knocked and then smiled, for it appeared her half sister was a heavy sleeper. This morning she'd promised to take her shopping. Should she delay their outing much longer, they'd be late getting back for tea, and Carolyn just might kill if she missed seeing her again.

Felicity opened the door to find Margaret stretched out upon the bed naked. Quickly she stepped inside and closed the door lest one of the officers walk by.

"Margaret."

No response. Bess opened her eyes, trying to remember where she was, even as she wondered who was calling her sister's name like that? She scurried to a sitting position looking wildly about the room, and then sighed with relief as she saw Felicity standing against the door. "What?"

"We're going shopping, remember?"

Bess groaned and fell forward, her words muffled against the rumpled sheets. "I can't this morning. I'll go later."

"You have to get up now. This is going to take a good part of the day."

Of course Felicity could have no idea that the woman had not gotten to sleep until just a few hours ago. Still, she couldn't help but notice her less-than-enthusiastic response. "Are you ill?"

Well, she did have a bit of a headache. It was the whiskey she had drunk last night. Perhaps she could pretend illness. Bess groaned as she came again to a sitting position, knowing she couldn't profess illness again tomorrow and she had every intention of feeling much the same then. She might as well get this day started. Perhaps she could rest later.

"No, I didn't sleep well, is all."

"You can rest this afternoon. I want to get to the shops before they become too crowded."

Felicity thought she would eventually grow used to her sister's nakedness, but such was not the case as yet. She turned away, embarrassed at the sight of the woman walking toward the commode behind the screen. "You will wear underthings, Margaret." Felicity thought she might not live through the embarrassment if she did not, for the dressing area was open to the shopkeeper, her helper, and seamstresses. A woman never stood within the curtained-off area unclothed.

"Of course," the woman said. "I'm going out, aren't I?"

"I'll see you downstairs then."

* * *

"What's your hurry?" Bess said as she was almost dragged from the table, biscuit still in hand.

Felicity did not respond, and despite her diminutive size, managed to usher the woman outside and into a waiting cab. Alvina had already been deposited inside.

Those few short words and the uncooperative way they were spoken seemed to set the tone for the rest of the morning. The two women argued over the material, the cut of cloth, ruffles, lace, the depth of necklines, the length of a skirt, the style of a dress. It went on and on. Felicity had never known such exhaustion. Alvina, unable to take in the confusion, the bickering, almost instantly found herself a chair to doze in, and there she remained for most of the morning.

Their tastes couldn't be more different and in most cases Margaret's choices were completely unsuitable. Felicity thought she dressed as an actress might and said so, so frustrated by now that she didn't care that her words were close to insulting.

Apparently it would take more than that to insult Bess, for she only nodded in agreement, believing actresses to have the most beautiful clothing imaginable. She could only hope to look as good.

Felicity placed the orders, including everything from hats and parasols to underthings, as well as nightdresses and robes while Bess sulked, knowing she would not wear half the ugly things Felicity had insisted upon. All that money going to waste. Bess thought it a shame.

"How much money did you get?"

Bess frowned at Frank lounging upon the settee, enjoying an afternoon drink. "Nothing yet," she said as she stripped down to her skin and then searched a small side table, littered with unanswered bills. "Where's my pipe? God, I'm dying for a smoke."

"Lilly probably put it away. What do you mean, nothing yet?"

"I mean *Daddy* said he'd see to an allowance, but he hasn't given over a shilling yet." She shrugged. "It's only been one day after all."

"Tell the old bastard you have debts to pay." Frank glanced at the table and nodded. "You wouldn't be lying on that score."

"Suppose he asks for the bills?"

"Say it's a private debt."

Bess nodded as she puffed away. She thought she might stop at Thomas's room the minute she got back to the mansion.

"In the meantime, there must be silver or jewelry around the house. Get a few pieces, and I'll find a buyer."

"And what can you get, a tenth of their worth? We're never going to get much that way."

"You been thinking on something in particular?"

"Maybe." Bess shrugged. The movement swayed her naked breasts and caused Frank to reach for them. She took a sip of his whiskey careful not to overindulge. She'd have some explaining to do if she returned to Felicity and her sharp eyes after visiting a sick friend, half-drunk. "The old man is sick. Something might be done to make him sicker, don't you think?"

Frank grinned. "Something might," he said in agreement. "And then you'd be a grieving daughter, ready to share in his estate."

Bess smiled at the thought. "That sounds nice, don't you think? I mean the word 'estate.' "

Hastings and Waverly stood before their obviously angry superior officer, each of them stuttering, trying to come up with some excuse. "We didn't . . ."

"I've heard that you did, sir, do not add lies to your crime."

" 'Twas no crime, Major. The girl is willing. More than willing. I swear it! We harmed no one."

"No one but a lady's reputation perhaps."

Waverly laughed. "She's no lady, sir. If you had seen . . ." His words fell to silence at Sam's furious glare.

"I was thinking of the lady who lives in this house. The

daughter of the man who owns it?" he explained. "Do you honestly believe if word got out that, innocent though she might be, her reputation would remain untarnished?"

Neither man responded, knowing of course the lady might be greatly damaged by the gossip.

"I take it you have not yet spread the news of your good fortune?"

Both men thought they might have eventually, but had not done so as yet. They hadn't even told Walters. Not that Walters would have joined them, for he had Becky with him every night.

"My wife and children are due to arrive anytime. Do you think I would allow such goings-on while they are in residence?"

Both swallowed in fear. They knew it before they heard the words, and both felt their stomachs sink in despair, knowing they had committed the unforgivable transgression and nothing was going to hold off their retribution. "I think it is time for you to join Major Andrews in the Carolinas."

"But . . ."

Sam waved a hand and shook his head, stalling off some obvious pleading. "No need to thank me, gentlemen. I know you are ready for action. You've proved that much last night, I suspect."

Sam might have laughed aloud at their expressions, for he'd rarely seen a more dejected twosome. After all, they were leaving soft jobs working in New York. It didn't take much to see that they weren't happy to be heading for the battlefield. Sam figured any man would know some real disappointment at the thought. "Don't worry, men, I'm sure there are ladies to suit all over these colonies."

"I can tell you, sir, without a doubt, that it would not happen again."

"Had you thought with your head rather than what is in your trousers, it would not have happened in the first place." Sam breathed a deep sigh. "But you're right about that, Waverly. Indeed it will not happen again. You are dismissed."

* * *

Carolyn shifted again, obviously anxious. "Where could she be?"

"I'm sure I don't know," Felicity returned, as she watched Alvina sip at a very small glass of sherry. It was her second glass. At least the second that Felicity was aware of. "Wouldn't you rather have some tea, dear?"

"I'm fine, thank you, Felicity."

Felicity thought by the looks of her she was more than fine, she was drunk. She sighed, and directed her comment toward her friend. "All she said was her neighbor was ill and she had to stop by and see her. I don't even know where that is."

"And you don't look very worried about it either."

"Why would I worry?"

"Felicity, she's a young girl. She shouldn't be allowed to roam these streets unescorted. Anything might happen to her."

"Why not? You do. At times we both do."

"I know, but she's only eighteen and her innocence must be guarded at all costs."

Felicity sighed. "The truth is, Carolyn, one cannot steal what is freely given."

Carolyn shot her friend a puzzled look. "What does that mean?"

Felicity bit her lip, knowing it was terribly unchristian of her to voice such a suspicion. The girl had no notion of proper attire, to be sure. Still she had done nothing more than flirt. "Nothing. I shouldn't have said that. I think I hear her now."

To say Carolyn was shocked at the sight of Felicity's half sister, was to put it mildly. Felicity introduced the two and sat back, ready to enjoy the show. There wasn't a doubt in her mind that Carolyn would get some answers from the girl. Whether they would be true or not was, of course, open to speculation.

Carolyn knew, of course, at first glance that this was no girl of eighteen. This was no girl at all. If she knew anything, she knew the look of a woman who had just been well loved. Not that she had ever done such a thing, of course, she silently remarked, well, except for that one time with Henry, but . . . Carolyn shook aside her thoughts. That had been a long time ago. She'd been far too young at the time and had hardly realized what was happening before it was all suddenly over. She refused to take that one indiscretion into consideration.

"You look older than eighteen."

"Do I? I take after my mother, I think."

Carolyn nodded at that. "What did you say she died of?"

"I didn't say, but it was her heart."

"Poor thing," Carolyn said without a shred of sympathy.

Bess glared at the lady. "Yes, it was awful losing the two of them like that."

Bess only realized her slip when Carolyn asked, "Two of them? Had you two mothers then?"

Felicity thought Carolyn's grilling was a bit much. Her voice dripped sarcasm and most would have found this question-and-answer session insulting to say the least. Still she had a feeling that Margaret could hold her own against most anyone and did nothing to stop the inquiry.

"My sister died as well, within a week of my mother."

Felicity gasped. "Lord, how awful. Did she have a heart condition as well?"

"Yes. It was terrible."

"How old was she?"

"Eightee . . . Twenty-eight." Bess congratulated herself on the instant correction a bit prematurely. She couldn't miss Carolyn's knowing grin, realizing the slip had not gone undetected. Forcing what she hoped was an innocent smile, she sipped from her cup. She'd have to watch herself with this one.

"Where did you go to school?"

"I was tutored at home."

"Were you? In what?"

"Oh, the usual, I suppose."

Carolyn said something in French.

Bess looked blank and said, "Excuse me?"

"Well not all of the usual, dear," she said in the haughtiest tone imaginable. "Every educated young lady is taught enough French to get by, you understand?"

Felicity thought Carolyn had crossed the line. She was being downright insulting and tried to find a way to soothe things over. "Perhaps her tutor didn't know French."

Carolyn studied the dark woman across from her for a long moment, before muttering softly, "And as far as I can tell he didn't know English either."

Felicity knew some real discomfort, but apparently she was the only one suffering the emotion. Carolyn looked as if she'd just won some particular point, while Margaret only glared.

What Bess would have liked most would have been to slap Miss Carpenter's snooty face. Her fingers fairly itched to attack and it took some thinking before the impulse was put to rest. She had to act the lady. She needed to be believed here. And ladies did not resort to violence, no matter how much they might dislike someone. No, there had to be a better way.

She had to think. She had to find a way, something that would quiet the bitch, something that would . . . Bess smiled again, only this time her smile was definitely relaxed, almost happy, and so evil, it sent shivers up Carolyn's spine.

She'd have to get word to Frank. An accident would be arranged. Nothing extreme, of course. After all, they had some specific plans for the old man, and they couldn't have people dropping like flies without raising some suspicions. Just something that would keep the bitch out of her way for a while. Bess almost chuckled at the thought. Something painful would be very nice.

"If you'll excuse me," she said coming to her feet, once again her voice perfectly cultured. "I have a slight headache and should rest."

Before Margaret reached the top of the stairs, Carolyn said, "I wonder which gutter coughed that one up."

"Carolyn!"

Alvina stirred. It was only then that Felicity realized the older woman had been asleep for some time.

"You don't really believe that woman is your half sister, do you?"

"What is that supposed to mean? Of course she is."

"Of course she is not," Carolyn said emphatically.

"What do you mean?"

Jared, approaching the sitting room, heard the last few questions. He stepped into the room and repeated, softly, "Yes, Carolyn, tell us what you mean."

"I mean she is *not* who she says she is. I'd swear it under oath."

"How could you know that?" Felicity said dismissing her friend's dramatics as exactly that.

"How old is she supposed to be? She doesn't look eighteen to me and her language, that accent. No decent woman, talks like that. Her words slip in and out of refinement like . . . like . . . I don't know what."

"She was impoverished."

"But not destitute. You said yourself that your father has been sending money for years. Still, she hasn't had any schooling. She doesn't know how to dress, fashion her hair, anything. She definitely does not come from gentility, no matter how impoverished. And lastly, her hair is black, almost raven black. What color is your father's hair?"

"She looks like her mother."

"Or her real father," Carolyn added, with a knowing twinkle in her eyes.

Felicity bit her bottom lip, and said softly, "How can we find out for sure?"

"How did your father find out about the mother?" Jared asked.

"The bank said the signatures weren't the same. They suspected forgery and were about to look into the matter when Mr. Struthers, that's father's lawyer," Felicity said for Jared's benefit, "did some checking on his own. He found out the woman had died."

"How?"

"Records at City Hall, I think."

Carolyn laughed softly. "Of course. Why didn't I think of that?" A grin split her wide mouth. "So why don't we take a look for ourselves? It might prove most interesting."

No one in the sitting room realized that their plan had been easily overheard. No one knew that a well-dressed, but obviously unrefined, young woman lingered just outside the doorway.

Eleven

Carolyn left her house early the next morning. She took no notice of the cab down the street. It appeared to most a cab like any other, with the exception that two horses rather than one had been hitched to it. Still, even with an added horse, it brought no real notice. Certainly no cause for alarm.

She waited at the curb for her driver to bring the carriage around. She was meeting with Felicity, and the two of them, perhaps accompanied by Jared if he could get away from the hospital for a bit, planned to search through the records at City Hall.

Both women realized the mission might take some time, for the record keepers were not well-known for their dedication to perfection, which meant that names were sometimes posted with the wrong date, or the right date on the wrong page, but they'd find it.

Jacob always was a bit slow, but today it seemed he was slower than usual. Carolyn tapped her foot impatiently. Slower because she was in a hurry, no doubt. Carolyn sighed as she checked the watch pinned to her tightly fitted bodice. She was already late. Had she not told the man to ready her carriage, she might have waved down the approaching cab. Only even from this distance, she could see the cabby was going too fast to stop in time. Carolyn frowned. Far too fast. What in the world did he think he was doing? This was a quiet residential street.

A street where children often played. Most drivers knew better than to fly by at this speed.

Carolyn backed up a bit, finding she was standing a bit too close for comfort to the street and the oncoming cab.

She glanced to her right. What in the world was keeping Jacob? She smiled as she saw the horse's head peek around the corner, coming up the drive of her home. At last, she thought with some relief. At last they were going to get to the bottom of . . .

Carolyn never saw what hit her. She felt a blow unlike any she'd ever imagined and thought it shook her to the very core of her being, and then knew an instant of confusion as she felt herself propelled forward into the air. Amazingly enough she felt no pain when she landed some ten feet farther along the sidewalk. On impact she heard the terrible sound of a bone snapping, but felt the sound had little to do with her.

She didn't know why, but for some reason she was lying on the ground watching the speeding cab drive off. And then from the back window she saw the face of a smiling woman. A face she thought she should have recognized. Only at the moment she couldn't seem to remember . . .

Jacob watched with horrified shock as his mistress was run down. The cab had left the street, and as if on purpose, had traveled the sidewalk and run her down.

Felicity paced her hallway, waiting for Carolyn's arrival.

"Nothing yet?" Jared asked as he came from Sam's office/sitting room.

"No. I can't understand what could have happened. She wouldn't have forgotten. I'm sure of that."

Jared reached for his pocket watch and shook his head. "I can't wait any longer."

"Good morning," Bess said as she descended the stairs. Her cheeks held a healthy glow as if she'd taken in a bit of air and perhaps some exercise as well, her eyes shining with delight. She looked positively radiant. "Are you going out already?"

"Yes," Felicity knew her cheeks were growing red. She felt so guilty, so terribly dishonest. Subterfuge, at least in this personal matter, was nothing less than appalling, and Felicity didn't much like herself at this moment. "I have an appointment."

"Perhaps you might join me then, Captain, for breakfast."

"I'm afraid not. I'm already late getting to the hospital."

Jared swooped Felicity into his arms and gave her a quick hard kiss, before whispering, "Be careful." A moment later he was gone.

"What would you have to be careful about?" Bess pried, not at all concerned that she'd just overheard something that was none of her business.

"What?" Felicity glanced at the woman who had boldly intruded upon a private moment and frowned. "Oh, Jared worries when I'm going out, is all."

"And he has every right to worry, I've been told. The city is filled with all sorts of riffraff."

Felicity frowned. Of course she'd only known the woman two days, but her half sister certainly seemed in a good mood today. After the confrontation with Carolyn yesterday afternoon and then her more than obvious disappointment upon learning that her two favorite officers would no longer be in residence, one might have thought to find her less than bubbling with delight. "You seem happy today."

"I am."

"Is there a particular reason?"

Bess smiled mysteriously. At the moment she felt good, very good indeed, for the woman that promised at almost first sight to be her archenemy was at least temporarily out of the picture. "Well for one, I received word that my neighbor is much improved this morning. I'll visit with her later, of course, but I don't think I'll have to worry any longer."

"She must be a very close friend."

"Oh, she is. I don't know what I would have done without her after my mother died.

"You said for one thing. Does that imply there is another?"

"Oh, well the second reason is, I'm happy to be here. That's a very good reason, don't you think?"

Felicity smiled and watched the woman move toward the breakfast room. She frowned, wondering if they weren't being a little hasty here. Perhaps she wasn't at all what Carolyn suspected. Maybe the girl was just confused, overwhelmed perhaps by the sudden change in her lifestyle. Certainly she could not be held to account if her mother had not chosen for her the very best of tutors. Surely her lack of knowledge concerning dress and maybe even manners could be easily overcome, with some gentle advice. Maybe they were about to embark upon a fool's errand, and Margaret was exactly who she professed to be.

It was growing late. Carolyn should have arrived some time ago. Felicity thought, like herself, her friend must have had second thoughts on the matter. No doubt a note would arrive later telling her as much. Felicity nodded in agreement with her thoughts. She put aside her morning's intent. There was no need for inquiry. Margaret just needed time. Time to acclimate herself to her new surroundings and things would work out very nicely she was sure.

Felicity entered the breakfast room. Having eaten earlier, she poured herself a cup of tea. She sat at the table across from Bess and smiled at the girl's healthy appetite.

"I take it your friend is not coming?"

Felicity frowned at the question. "How did you know I was waiting for my friend?"

With her mouth full Bess said, "You said you were going out, and I saw you pacing. I just assumed." Margaret shrugged, and, without swallowing the last, took another huge bite of jam-covered bread. A moment later she sipped a bit noisily at her tea. Bess laughed at Felicity's look of surprise. "Sorry. Sometimes I forget my manners."

Felicity said nothing as another loud slurp was heard, followed by Bess's low chuckle. "It doesn't matter, does it? I mean we are alone after all."

"I think it's best to practice when we're alone. You won't ever forget your manners if they become a habit."

"You're probably right about that," Bess said, again with her mouth full.

Felicity looked away, and Bess laughed. "I take it a lady never speaks with food in her mouth."

"It has less to do with being a lady than simple common courtesy, I think. The true mark of a lady, or gentleman for that matter, is less manners than caring about others and their feelings. Speaking with one's mouth full is unattractive."

"And a lady should always be attractive."

"Don't you think attractiveness makes for a more interesting companion during a meal?"

Bess shrugged. "Perhaps, but don't you sometimes grow tired of it all? I mean, a lady may not do this, a lady may not do that? Wouldn't you just once like to chuck it all and do what Felicity likes?"

"But I do what I like."

"And you like being a lady." Bess said the words with some disappointment, as if she might have thought better of her half sister.

"Don't you?"

"Oh, of course. I was just thinking, is all."

"What I'm doing is trying to understand you. The fact is that you are my sister and for both our father's sake and our own, I think we should make every effort to grow to like one another."

"Oh, I like you just fine," Bess lied. The fact was her feelings for her fellow man never ran deep enough to either like or dislike anyone. She merely used people to gain her own ends. As she ate she studied the lady across from her, knowing she'd be wise to make a friend of this one. Her heart was soft, and that could be used to some advantage. Bess, like many a villain, thought those soft of heart could be easily tricked, mistakenly believing kindness to be a weakness. She nodded at her thoughts. Yes, considering Thomas Dryson was soon to be but a memory, it might be to her benefit if they were friends.

"I was thinking."

Felicity raised her gaze from her cup, waiting for her to go on.

"Do you think you could teach me? You know"—Bess shrugged—"how to be a lady? I make a lot of mistakes, but I only realize them as mistakes afterward." Bess tried for insecurity and apparently managed to produce something close to it, if Felicity's look of compassion meant anything. "If you could show me a few things, maybe I could find myself a lovely gentleman like yours someday."

Felicity smiled. "Of course. It wouldn't take much effort, you know. You're already on track in some instances. Mostly all you need, I think, is practice."

She glanced at the small watch pinned to her bodice. "It looks like I have the morning free. Why don't we . . ." Felicity was interrupted by the delivery of a note. Billy stood at her side as she read it, obviously awaiting a response.

Only he never got the one he expected. Felicity, believing the note had come from Carolyn and was an excuse as to why she would not be coming, had to read it twice before the full impact of the situation made itself clear. Once it did she came instantly to her feet, knocking her chair over in the process, bringing Billy to instant attention as nearly all her color drained from her face. She stood with her hand flat against her chest as if to still a thundering heart and seemed for a moment unable to speak as her wide eyes grew glazed with apparent shock. "Is her driver still here?" she finally managed.

"Yes, miss."

"Run for Captain Walker. Tell him he's needed immediately. Tell him to meet me at Carolyn's." And when the boy simply stood there with mouth agape, Felicity roared, in a most unladylike fashion, "Hurry!"

Billy had disappeared around the corner by the time Felicity reached the front door, descended the steps, and entered Carolyn's carriage. She slammed the door and fell into the seat as the carriage lunged forward.

Carolyn lived only three blocks from Felicity's home. Still it felt like forever before the large brick house came into view. Felicity did not wait for the driver to open the door and help her out. She jumped to the sidewalk and ran up the three steps to Carolyn's home, pounding upon the door until seconds later a servant let her in. "Where is she?"

"Upstairs. The doctor . . ."

"I have one coming," Felicity said, already halfway up the long flight.

She didn't bother to knock but let herself into the darkened room. Mrs. Carpenter stood over her granddaughter's still form, weeping loudly. Felicity refused to believe it. She wasn't too late. Carolyn was not dead and no one could make her believe that she was.

"How is she?" Felicity forced herself to ask.

"I don't know. I can't make her wake up."

"But she's breathing?" Felicity asked, while wondering how her knees had not given out in relief at the old woman's nod? She walked toward the bed, hardly able to manage the chore. "Carolyn. Carolyn, can you hear me?"

No response. Felicity made the mistake of looking at the older woman, for her worried glance only seemed to add to the lady's despair and brought about a wailing sound that sent chills down Felicity's spine.

Mrs. Carpenter was obviously close to collapsing. There was no help for it. She had to be taken from the room. With her arm around the lady, Felicity guided her toward the door. Servants stood nearby, ready to run for whatever might be needed to help their mistress. Felicity asked one of them to see to the lady's care until the doctor arrived. Considering her emotions, Felicity thought nothing less than a sedative would calm the old lady. She could hear the wailing all the way down the hall.

She returned to Carolyn's bedside just as the door flew open. Jared, gasping for breath, ran into the room. He moaned a low sound of relief upon seeing her standing there apparently perfectly well. "What happened?" he asked, reaching for her, crushing her hard against him. "Billy said to get over here. I couldn't get him to talk straight, to answer my questions. I thought . . . I thought you were hurt."

"I'm fine. It's Carolyn."

It took some effort, for Jared was loath to leave the warmth of her arms. Still, he managed to step away and then glanced at the bed. "What happened?"

"She was hit by a cab. Do you think she'll . . . ?" Felicity couldn't finish as tears came to her eyes. "I don't know what I'll do if . . ."

"Calm down." Jared, at once a doctor again, showed not a speck of sympathy, knowing to do so would only fuel his lady's need to cry. "I'm going to need some help here."

Felicity swallowed back the fear, the horror of this moment, and asked, "What do you want me to do?"

"First, I have to find out the extent of the damage," Jared said as he reached for his bag and took out scissors. Without another word, he began cutting away her clothes.

"Carolyn is going to kill you for this," she warned forcing her mind from the stain that ran over the bottom part of the gown. Mud mixed with blood was obviously in evidence, but what was most terrifying was the mark of a carriage wheel that ran over both legs. The carriage hadn't just knocked her down. It had run over her. "This is one of her best gowns."

Jared grinned, never looking up from his chore as Carolyn's chemise and drawers went the same way of her gown. "Let's hope she'll soon be well enough to try." And then, glancing at his patient's legs he said, "Get me soap, water, rags, and a clean sheet," as he began to pull her cut clothing away.

Felicity ran for the servants and called out the order. Moments later the needed supplies were brought into the room.

One leg was obviously broken, perhaps the other as well, but a broken leg could be seen to later. First he had to find out why the woman wasn't awake and screaming in agony.

It took but a moment to find the cause. She'd taken a blow to her head. The area was swollen and had bled badly, her pillow absorbing most of the blood.

Felicity covered Carolyn with the sheet, only to see Jared move the sheet to her waist as he ran his hands over her, his gaze almost blank as he mentally addressed what his fingers found. Beginning at her neck he gently examined her body, feeling for broken bones, praying those bones if found had not already punctured a lung. A large bruise was forming on her midriff. Jared hadn't a doubt the horse had stepped on her there. All he could do was hope she wasn't bleeding internally. There was no way to tell for sure, at least not at the moment.

He rolled her to her side and ran his fingers down the length of her spine. Placing her again on her back, he replaced the sheet to her neck and pushed it up from the bottom as he examined the lower part of her body, again checking for broken bones. A moment later he covered her again and faced Felicity's worried expression. He knew she wanted to hear something. Jared only wished he had something to say that would erase the worry from those eyes. "She took a blow to her head."

Felicity swallowed and nodded, steeling herself for the worst. "Tell me all of it."

Jared sighed. "The injury could mean damage was done to the brain itself. If that's the case, she could need part of the bone removed so fluid can be released." Jared could see Felicity sway and cursed. "I need you with me here. Don't faint!"

Felicity reached for the bedpost and forced aside her weakness. She nodded again. "What do you want me to do?"

"Help me dress the wound. For the time being, we'll wait."

"What are you waiting for?"

"To see if she comes around. If she does, she'll probably be all right."

"Meaning if she doesn't, she won't be?"

Jared didn't answer her. Instead he said, "Some believe a patient, even though unconscious, can hear much of what is said around her. She'll be all right, won't you, Carolyn?

"Bring me more light. I can't see a damn thing."

Jared thought he might as well keep to himself the fact that Carolyn had been stepped on by the horse. And that injury alone, although no bones had been broken, might have caused irreparable damage. There was always a chance one might live through such injuries, but Jared thought they needed a miracle in this instance. Still, if she managed the task, she'd be able to walk. Once he cleaned up the head wound, he turned to her leg.

"She has a compound fracture. I haven't any splints with me, but she won't need them right away."

Jared cleaned the torn skin as well as he could, washing it with soap and water. Dry that off for me," he said as he walked to the bottom of the bed, then suddenly yanked on Carolyn's leg with all his strength. Felicity moaned as she heard the sound of bone rubbing one ragged edge against the other.

"Get behind her and hold her under her arms." Jared positioned Felicity where he wanted her. "Hold her tight. I've got to pull again."

She did as she was told, while Jared did as promised. Finally, apparently satisfied with his efforts, Jared returned to the side of the bed. Felicity's face was ashen as she made yet another moaning sound. "What's the matter?"

"That was disgusting." Felicity shuddered wondering if she'd ever forget the sound of that moving bone.

"What was disgusting?" he asked. Concentrating on what he was doing, Jared never realized the question, nor her lack of response, as he placed an eighteen-tail bandage under the leg. Seeing first to the wound, he quickly stitched the skin closed and covered the cut with oil-soaked lint. Next he began to wrap the bandage into place. "This will hold the bone. Once she is awake again, we'll use splints."

Felicity knew Jared was unaware of his abruptness. She didn't care. All she wanted was for her dearest friend to get better. "She'll be all right, won't she?"

"She will if you have anything to say about it," Jared said as he examined the other leg. Finding no damage done, he washed his hands and dried them. "Have you given any thought to my suggestion?"

"What suggestion?"

"Medicine. You're so cool-headed. You really should think about it."

"I'm only cool-headed because you won't allow me to faint."

Jared laughed. "Too bad I can't convince you to obey me in every instance."

Felicity smiled, knowing full well to what he alluded by the teasing twinkle in his eyes. "Mrs. Carpenter was very upset. Quite hysterical actually. I had to ask one of the servants to look after her. Do you think you could give her something?"

Jared nodded and left the room. He'd only just returned when David ran, wild-eyed, into the room. "Where is . . . Oh my God!" he said taking in the sight of his love with her head bandaged, her leg as well, clothed only in a thin sheet.

Jared instantly took the man into the hall. Felicity could hear them whisper, but could understand almost nothing of what was said. It wasn't until David returned, in apparent control, that Felicity understood. Just in case she could hear, Jared didn't want David upsetting his patient.

"Sit by her and talk for a while. The sound of your voice could bring her around.

"Felicity, would you like some tea?"

"Actually, I'd like some whiskey, and maybe a lot of it, if you don't mind."

Jared grinned. "One should do the trick, I think."

They were in the library before Jared asked, "Do you know what happened?"

Felicity shook her head. "Only that she was hit by a cab." The thought of her friend so seriously injured brought tears to mist her eyes. She glanced at Jared. "I thought she had changed her mind. It never occurred to me that I should worry."

"Maybe you should sit down," Jared suggested as he guided her to a large leather chair, one of two that faced a fireplace. He placed a small snifter of brandy into her shaking hand. "You'll be all right, if I leave you for a minute, won't you?"

"I'll be fine. Where are you going?"

"Someone has to know something. I'm going to ask a few questions."

While he was gone a servant brought in a tray of tea and small sandwiches. Felicity smiled fondly, knowing Jared had ordered the light snack. Felicity couldn't eat, but the tea did make her feel better.

Twenty minutes went by before Jared returned to the library with a thoughtful expression.

"What is it?" Felicity came to her feet. "Is she . . . ?"

Jared shook his head. "No, I just looked in on her and she's the same. I spoke to Jacob, her driver. He said the cab looked as if it deliberately ran her down."

Felicity frowned. "Oh, Jared, that's impossible. Perhaps it looked like that but it had to have been an accident." She shook her head. "Jacob must be mistaken."

"She has no enemies that you know of?"

"None."

"What about Margaret?"

Felicity smiled. "That's a bit far-fetched, don't you think? Granted they obviously don't like each other, well Carolyn doesn't like her, in any case, but to put this on Margaret is a bit much." Felicity poured Jared a cup of tea and offered it to him. "It was an accident, I'm sure."

Jared wasn't nearly as positive as was she. Still, he couldn't imagine any but one's most hated enemy to resort to this extreme. Perhaps Felicity was right. Having no knowledge that their conversation had been overheard, Jared assumed Margaret had nothing to gain by doing away with Carolyn, and he correctly imagined Margaret the type never to make a move unless there was some gain involved.

After finishing his tea, Jared returned to the hospital. Felicity and David spent the rest of the day alternating their time with Carolyn. It was past the dinner hour when Jared returned to check on his patient. Nothing had changed.

Jared thought another opinion might be needed. If nothing had changed by morning, he'd send for a colleague. A trepanning procedure might be necessary after all. Jared hated to do it, for he often wondered if the removal of a bit of bone from the head didn't cause more harm than good. Still, if the brain swelled, or if fluid accumulated, he knew he'd have little choice in the matter.

In the meantime, Felicity needed some rest. He said as much, looking forward to the short carriage ride home where he could comfort her, alone and in the manner of his choosing.

"I'm not leaving. One of the servants can prepare a room for me. I'll see you in the morning."

To Felicity's surprise, Jared only nodded and left. Since agreeing to marry him, he hadn't once left her company without a kiss. As a matter of fact, he hadn't touched her or kissed her since this morning, Felicity thought with a touch of disappointment. Of course Felicity hadn't expected any tenderness on his part while Carolyn lay so critically injured, but a good-night kiss might not have put the man out overmuch.

Jared let himself into the house, only to find Sam coming from the sitting room. The man was as always, even when off duty, perfectly attired.

"Where the hell is everybody?" Walters proved less than useless as a companion, since he was but a newlywed and spent damn near every minute with his young wife, once her work was done for the day. He'd yet to replace his two transferred officers. Even the lady of the house was nowhere to be found. And perhaps because she was not present, Mrs. Davies had overindulged before dinner and left him and Margaret to themselves.

Sam did prefer the company of a woman at dinner. He very much enjoyed their delicate manners and witty charm and might have greatly appreciated the evening meal had it not been for Margaret's boldness. The fact was, he had no liking for her kind of woman. Twice he'd been forced to remove her hand from his thigh. One might have thought she would understand his intent after the first time. Apparently she had not.

And now he faced the balance of the evening with the very real threat that Margaret would join him. The fact was she was not nearly the temptation she supposed herself to be, for Sam was well aware of her lack of morals. He very simply did not wish a further confrontation and was pleased at Jared's arrival.

"Carolyn had an accident. Felicity is there. I'm going back once I get her a few things."

Sam nodded, having earlier heard about the accident and then sighed his disappointment as he realized he was destined to be alone tonight, despite his wants. "Is she all right?"

"No. She's very bad, in fact." Jared shrugged. "We can only wait and see."

"Can't you stay a bit? Maybe have a drink with me?"

Jared nodded as he started up the stairs toward his and Felicity's rooms. "As soon as I pack her a few things."

His hand was on the doorknob to his room when from the corner of his eye he noticed movement. He turned to see her walking from the shadows at the end of the long hallway, having obviously just come from the floor above and her room. Jared gasped at the sight of her for she wore again the gown Felicity had professed to be torn. Her breasts were indeed huge, made to look even more so by the cut and ill fit of the gown. That she was very nearly exposed to his view seemed not to matter in the least as she smiled in her usual seductive manner.

Only her provocative posing was wasted on him, for Jared felt none of the lust he might have once known. Instead, the sight of her half-naked state only caused him to feel slightly embarrassed and somehow intensified a need for Felicity, her modesty, her clean light scent, her soft laughter, and always perfect manners. A need that he'd rarely been without since first meeting her.

Surprise at this woman's lack of modesty held Jared frozen in place as he watched her approach. She smiled as she watched his gaze move over her, believing he liked what he saw.

"Good evening, Captain," she said. "I didn't expect you back. Felicity sent word that she was staying at Carolyn's tonight. I thought you might be staying there as well."

Jared gave a mental groan. No wonder Sam had been so relieved to see him. This woman, apparently believing them alone, was on her way to the man, and Jared wondered if Sam realized the temptation this night held in store. No doubt he did. No doubt that was exactly the cause behind the man's obvious annoyance.

Her dress began to slip forward. Jared only realized then that it was open down the back. She felt the movement and held the fabric to her in a way that showed more than it covered. "Please forgive the way I'm dressed," she said, while her gaze told him she didn't care if he forgave it or not. "But I was just going down for a glass of water and didn't realize anyone would be about."

"Sam is still downstairs."

Bess's gaze filled with knowing amusement. "Is he? I thought he'd gone to bed long ago."

"It's only eight o'clock."

Bess laughed. "Is it? I don't know what I could have been thinking."

"Nor do I," Jared responded, knowing they both knew exactly what she'd been thinking. Now that her two bedmates were gone, Bess was looking for new prey and, judging by the way she was looking him over, just about anyone would suit her taste.

"I'll see you in the morning. I have to pack a few things."

"You could see me tonight, if you wished." Jared couldn't believe her gall. She'd followed him uninvited right into his room. "All of me if that were to your liking," she said as she allowed the material to slide again, exposing all any man might have wished to see of her breasts.

Jared watched her for a long moment. She was a beautiful woman with a body that matched her face in loveliness. There was a time when he might have sampled those huge breasts. Might have willingly, even eagerly pumped his body into hers, but not now. Not since Felicity and her shining hair and sparkling eyes. "I'm not interested, Margaret. You're wasting your time."

"Are you sure?" she asked, as she dropped all pretext of holding the bodice to her.

Jared thought he'd rarely seen anything quite so spectacular as this woman's breasts and still he felt not the slightest bit of interest. Knowing what she was, there was no way he would touch her. She'd taken on two only last night and as far as he knew that made her a whore of the first order. There was no telling how many she'd had before or since. Considering such a lifestyle, the woman might already be diseased. If not, Jared was sure she wouldn't remain free of the pox for long.

Bess grinned, believing the man wanted what he saw. But Bess was mistaken. She'd taken surprise added to the normal appreciation any man would know for a beautiful female form as acquiescence and advanced toward him.

"I'm going to marry your sister," Jared felt the need to remind.

"So? What difference does that make?"

Had he not been aware of the fact, her words would have proven her lacking of even a shred of decency. He knew only disgust. "I want you to leave."

"Can I be of some assistance, sir?" Marcy said suddenly standing in the room. Jared hadn't heard the door to their connecting rooms open.

Bess ignored the huge man's presence, her gaze on Jared. "We might not get another opportunity."

Jared turned from her near nakedness. "Marcy, would you pack me a few things? I might be away for a day or two."

Bess sighed her disappointment. Jared ignored the sound. There wasn't a doubt in his mind that this one was doomed to a bad end. All he could think was to keep Felicity from harm's way.

Twelve

With a hurriedly packed valise in each hand, Jared headed for the stairs and his promised drink with Sam when he heard voices below. He frowned, then grinned at the sound of Mary's voice. His grin was still in evidence as Bess ran past him, her dress in place, her expression one of disappointment mingled heavily with disgust.

"So, it seems I got here just in time."

"Thank you," Sam said weakly. He hadn't seen her in months and needed her desperately. And now that she was finally here, he dared not approach her, dared not take her in his arms.

Despite the fact that he loved his wife beyond his very life, his chances of surviving this night's temptation had not been all they could have been. He couldn't help but admit to being terribly tempted as the little whore twice backed him around the room, laughing upon being told he wasn't interested. It seemed nothing less than knocking the determined woman on her backside and hiding behind his locked bedroom door would have done the trick.

The idea was beginning to take on some real merit when Mary had knocked on the front door. Sam had almost run to answer the knock, only to blink in surprise at the sight of his wife, for her ship wasn't due for yet another four days.

Sam hadn't had a moment to think before Mary spotted the flimsily clad lady and moved quickly into the house.

"For what?" returned the small woman, who stood glaring at her husband, one hand on each of her hips.

"For saving him from a fate worse than death. Hello Mary," Jared said, grinning from the sitting-room doorway. "It's a good thing you arrived when you did. I couldn't stay and protect him tonight. My lady needs me."

"So, this is a sample of the horror of conflict. What with near-naked ladies running about, one can only imagine the conflict to mean which of you would have had her first."

"Not so, Mary. I am betrothed to another, while your husband has been pining away for the sight of you. All we ever hear around here is Mary, Mary, Mary. I for one am much relieved at your arrival. At least I will no longer be subjected to a review of your many attributes.

"As for the lady upstairs?" Jared lowered his voice as he spoke. "I'd appreciate your not mentioning this little episode to Felicity. She has no idea her half sister is so basely inclined."

Jared nodded toward his friend. "You don't mind if we postpone our drink, do you? I should get back."

Sam nodded, knowing his friend had allowed Mary just the right amount of truth without overly emphasizing his innocence. Hopefully it would smooth things over.

Jared closed the door behind him, with a grin threatening, while wishing he could tell Felicity of the evening's happenings. He might one day, but not now. She was too innocent, and he could hardly expect her to see the humor of the situation.

Inside the house, Mary watched her husband closely. He was obviously waiting for her move, unsure of what to say, how to act. Never being one to sidestep an issue, she came right to the point. "Were you tempted?"

"Yes."

Mary nodded, knowing any man might have been, for the woman who had tried to seduce her husband was indeed a beauty. "The question is, I think, would you have given in to the temptation?"

"I hope not. I was thinking about running for my room, just as you knocked."

"And your door has a lock on it?"

Sam nodded.

Mary's grin held a touch of wickedness, the anger and shock she'd known upon entering the house now completely gone. "So I saved you, did I?"

"Come over here."

"I came thousands of miles, Sam, I think you can make it the last few feet."

Sam grinned. "I hope you know I love you."

"Considering the woman you were trying to reject, how can I doubt it?" And Mary had no doubt that Sam had been trying to reject her. She knew well the look of passion on her husband's face and had not found a trace of it as he opened the door. He was dressed perfectly, his hair in place. He wouldn't have looked the same had he been in the midst of seduction. He wouldn't have answered the door within seconds of her knock had his mind been on enjoying the woman.

Besides, had he the intent of taking her, they might already be upstairs and in bed, for Sam was a gentleman with some strict moral code. He'd never seduce a lady where anyone might come across them. Only that one, Mary had known in an instant, could hardly be called a lady.

"Once I touch you, I'm not going to be able to stop."

"Good."

"Where are the children?"

"I left them on board. They were already asleep. Jenny is with them."

Sam nodded as he moved toward her, but Mary didn't get the kiss she expected. Instead he lifted her into his arms and started for the stairs. "You'll tell me all about her later?"

Sam didn't pretend to misunderstand. He knew well enough who she was talking about. He grinned, for the words were less a request than an order. "Yes, ma'am," he said as he opened

his door and kicked it shut behind him. "Only, if it's all right
with you, much later."

Felicity was obviously tired, having just come from the bed
at Jared's knock. Jared shook his head upon seeing her. "You'll
do her no good if you take ill next."

"What are you doing here?"

"What kind of a question is that? I'm a doctor, aren't I?"

Felicity smiled, almost, and then nodded.

"Besides, where else would I go? While I was packing a few
things for us, Mary came."

"Did she?" Her smile was a bit brighter this time. "Sam must
be thrilled. He was so anxious for her to join him."

"I imagine you're right about that."

"For *us?*" she asked, apparently having just realized his
words. "What do you mean?"

"I mean I'm staying with you." At that Jared walked into the
room and placed both valises on the bed. "Now that Mary is
here, I have no one to talk to."

Felicity chuckled softly as she closed the door and leaned
against it. "If you want to talk tonight, you'll have to do it to
yourself. I'm too tired." She yawned daintily. "I thought I
wouldn't see you again until tomorrow."

Jared shook his head. Watching her smile, he did not respond.

"You know, of course, that you cannot stay here."

"Can't I? Why not?" he asked as he took off his jacket and
hung it over the back of one chair.

"I mean, not in this room."

"You need someone to make sure you rest."

"And you're that someone?"

"I am." He smiled as he took off his cravat.

"I wonder if I'm going to like being married to a doctor."

"Why?" He was unbuttoning his shirt, and Felicity found her
gaze following the movement of his fingers. It was distracting
to say the least. "Felicity," Jared said when she did not respond.

"What?"

"Why are you wondering if you'll like being married to me."

"Oh, well, you are a bit domineering."

"You're a strong woman. I think you can take it." He pulled his shirt from his pants, but did not take it off.

Felicity knew only untold relief. She couldn't deny that the sight of his bare chest was doing some strange things to her stomach. Things she knew she shouldn't be feeling. "Meaning we'll argue from time to time?"

"On some matters perhaps."

"But we'll agree on others?"

Jared grinned. Then, allowing his gaze to move boldly over her, he said softly, "I think you might be safe in saying that."

He quite literally took her breath away. Especially now, standing in her room with his shirt open, his hair falling free of its tie, she thought him magnificent. "You really shouldn't be here." Felicity knew she was terribly breathless, and he couldn't help but notice, but she couldn't seem to catch her breath. She knew what he was about and found herself suddenly too tired to fight what he had in mind.

"I'm not here for that."

"For what?"

"For what you're thinking."

Their gazes held, and Felicity heard herself ask, "What am I thinking?"

"You're thinking I want to make love to you, and I do, but I won't. Not until this is over. Not until Carolyn is better."

Felicity didn't know what to think. He acted like a man who cared, only he wasn't supposed to care, at least not in this way. He'd said he wanted her, and because it was long past time for her to marry and start a family, they had made a pact. All should have been perfect, for both sides would find a measure of satisfaction in the agreement. Except for one thing. Felicity was trying, really trying, not to like him quite so much. It wouldn't do to like him too much, she thought. It wouldn't do at all.

"I only want to hold you, to see to it that you sleep."

She closed her eyes for a long second. "That sounds nice."

"I thought you might like it."

Felicity smiled and reached for his offered hand. With her hand in his, he walked toward the bed. He removed the bag and they both sat. His arm around her, he pulled her to lean against him. "I wasn't sure what you needed, so I brought one of everything."

"That was very kind."

"Shall I help you dress? I've brought your nightclothes along."

"No, I can do it," she said. "Just let me sit here for a minute." Felicity knew his careful attention toward her needs wasn't necessary, but was too tired to argue the point. Besides, it felt good to be pampered. Very good indeed.

A minute went by, and Jared felt her growing heavy against his side. He asked, "Felicity, are you asleep?"

No response.

He smiled as he gathered her against him and placed her upon the bed. At her side he watched her sleep until the candle burned low, flickered, and died, casting the room into darkness.

Snuggled close against her, Jared, maybe for the first time in a long time, felt truly content. Oddly enough, his contentment had nothing at all to do with sex.

He relieved David some time later. It wasn't until the sky began to hint of yet another morning that David returned and Jared crawled back into the bed. Felicity snuggled close against him. In her sleep (Jared could only wish to claim the same degree of ignorance), her leg came over his, her hand rested comfortably upon his stomach and every bit of Jared's former contentment disappeared. He dozed, ever aware of her at his side, ever aware of her movement, especially the movement of one hand as it sometimes lowered and sometimes rose, driving him half out of his mind.

Jared awoke two hours later at the sound of her gasp. She was sitting up, and about to leave the bed. He reached for her. "What is it?"

"I slept past my turn. I was supposed to . . . Why didn't he wake me up?"

"I took it for you. David is with her again."

"Is she . . . ?"

Jared shook his head. "No change."

Felicity seemed to breathe a sigh of relief. "Well, that's something, I suppose."

Jared could have told her that the longer Carolyn remained unconscious, the more obviously serious the trauma, but decided not to dash her hopes. It was too soon as yet to make judgments.

"I want to see her. Go back to sleep."

Jared only nodded and rolled to his side as she silently left the room.

Jared looked in before leaving for the hospital and checked in again that night, only to find Felicity even more exhausted than the night before. Exhausted, but with a brilliant smile.

"She moved her hand."

She might have moved her hand, but Carolyn was still unconscious. Jared knew this wasn't proof positive of imminent recuperation. Unconscious victims often had involuntary movement. Dr. Noble would be here in the morning. Together they'd make the decision whether or not to operate. Jared thought they probably would. "Isn't that good news?"

"I hope so. In the meantime, you're coming with me."

"Jared, I can't leave her alone."

Jared ordered a servant to stay with Carolyn and half dragged, half carried Felicity to her room. Once inside he said, none too gently, "What the hell do you think you're doing?"

"What do you mean?"

"I mean, you're almost dead on your feet. How long do you think you can keep this up?"

"I'm all right, and I have no idea how long I can . . ."

"Well, I'll tell you then. You'll be sick within a few days. You have to sleep."

"I slept last night. So soundly in fact, I don't think I moved a muscle."

"You moved. I can tell you that for a fact."

The tone of his voice brought her gaze to his. There was something in his eyes, something she didn't understand and most certainly did not trust. "Are you being hateful?"

Jared grinned. "No, just truthful. And I quite enjoyed it, thank you."

Felicity didn't have the courage to ask for particulars, and said instead, "Beast. Get out of this room."

"Get on that bed."

"Jared," she warned, her gaze narrowing.

"Felicity," he returned, following her example.

She watched him for a long moment before she realized the ridiculousness of this moment. A smile began to tease the corners of her mouth. "What do you want?"

"I want you to behave like a responsible adult."

"Meaning I haven't been?"

"Not in regard to your own health." Jared sighed at her look of annoyance. "What will happen is you'll come down with a cold and here we are getting married with you sneezing and coughing, and I'll be forced to make love to you with a dripping nose and watery eyes." He shook his head at her grin. "Quite distasteful."

"Why is it do you suppose that I don't believe you?"

"Which part don't you believe."

"The part about it being distasteful."

"Oh, well, I might have exaggerated there a bit."

"Just a bit?"

"Get out of those clothes and into your nightdress and robe."

Jared turned his back at her insistence, allowing her the privacy she demanded. He thought her modesty a bit much. "It wouldn't have mattered if I watched, you know." His back was to her as he sat on the bed, trying to see her in the reflection of the gleaming brass headboard. The distorted glimpses didn't offer much in the way of satisfaction.

"It would have mattered to me."

"We're going to be married next week."

"But we're not married yet."

"It's just a formality."

"It more than that, and you know it. All right, you can turn around now."

"Now I have a headache," he said collapsing dramatically upon the bed.

"Why? What's the matter?" she asked coming close enough to touch his forehead. Jared, never one to let an opportunity such as this slip from his grasp, caught her wrists. He pulled her suddenly upon him and grinned at her cry of alarm. A second later he rolled her to her back.

"I was trying to watch you in the headboard, and I think the strain ruined my eyes."

Felicity laughed. "Don't do anything. Not one single thing. I'm too tired, and it would be most ungentlemanly of you to take advantage."

"Just a kiss then."

Felicity frowned. "The trouble is, I know your kisses, and I don't think I have the strength."

"Just a small one?"

"A small one, then."

He touched his mouth to hers briefly and smiled. "Now that wasn't so bad, was it?"

Felicity chuckled softly. "It was lovely. Thank you."

"When did you eat last?"

"I had dinner in Carolyn's room." She yawned. "Did you get something?"

"I will. After you fall sleep."

Jared moved, allowing her to get under the sheet. He stripped away all but his trousers and a moment later he was beside her.

Felicity made a sound of appreciation as he brought her against him, her head pillowed upon his chest. Jared wasn't sure she realized the sound, nor her present position, for seconds later came the soft sound of snoring.

Jared dozed. Sometime during the night came a loud banging on the door. Jared, half-asleep, leaped from the bed and opened the door to David's grin. "She's awake. Thank God, she's awake."

Felicity, who had heard the knock, grabbed her robe and followed Jared to the door. At the sound of the good news she fairly flew down the hallway. Within seconds she was at Carolyn's side. "I hope you know you gave me the scare of my life. The next time this happens, have the decency to wake up right away, will you?"

Carolyn smiled at her friend's concern. "I'll try." And then she grimaced in pain. "How long have I been asleep? And what happened to my leg? It's killing me. And my head. Ow!" she said as she tried to move.

"Your leg was broken in the accident." This came from Jared, as he shoved his arms into his shirtsleeves and once again inspected the limb, grunting in satisfaction at finding no inflammation.

"What accident? Do something. You're a doctor aren't you?"

"Last I heard," Jared returned as he inspected the wound on her head. "Stay still and let me see." Jared nodded and made doctor sounds as he examined her. A moment later he said, "I can give you something for the discomfort, but it will make you sleep again."

"Leave it to a doctor to call this agony discomfort. I'm surprised you didn't say mild discomfort."

Jared grinned. "Well, nothing is wrong with her mouth."

"I don't care if I sleep again. Give me something."

"I think you should stay awake for a while. I want you to follow my finger."

"Why, is it going to do something interesting?"

Felicity fought back a laugh. David grinned. Jared ignored her sarcasm. "Are you dizzy?"

"A little."

"Can you see clearly?"

"I never could before. Why start now?"

"Do you have spectacles?"

"No. They're ugly things. Damn it! I'm in pain here."

"Move your toes?"

Carolyn murmured her annoyance as she did as she was told.

"Now your fingers. Raise your arm."

Jared nodded in satisfaction. As far as he could tell there were no lasting effects from the injury. He hoped it would stay that way. "All right, now tell me what you remember about the accident."

"I don't remember it at all. What happened?"

"You were hit by a cab."

"Where?"

"Just outside."

"Yes," Carolyn frowned. "I think I do remember that. I saw a cab coming. And then something hit me." She sighed. "I don't remember what happened after that."

Jared nodded. "It might come back, but it really doesn't matter. I'll give you some laudanum. Just enough to help with the pain. I want you to stay awake for a bit."

To David he said, "She should have some soup. She can have a little tea with it, but make it weak."

To Felicity, "Can you help her into her nightdress?"

Carolyn gasped at the last and looked down with a moan of pain. "Am I naked?"

The question went unanswered as Felicity brought her nightdress from the closet. Jared prepared the laudanum and water as the two women struggled with the gown. Once she was comfortable again he brought her a bedpan.

"I'm not using that. Take it away."

"You have no choice. You can't walk without splints. I'll get them tomorrow."

There was a long moment of silence before Jared said, "It's better, I think, than changing your bedding."

Carolyn moaned again. "Well, I'm not doing it in front of you, and I don't care if you are a doctor. Get out!"

* * *

Thomas Dryson sat on the edge of his bed, fighting off a wave of dizziness, and listened with a smile to the shrieks of children playing. Felicity was to be married today. He hoped by this time next year there would be a baby. Thomas could hardly wait for the joy of holding his own grandchild.

Thomas frowned as the floor swayed before him. Where was his usual strength? At first, after his body had begun to heal, he could feel it coming back, but lately, over the last few days, he felt himself growing weak again. Each day considerably weaker in fact. Felicity had waited to marry until he was stronger. And because he didn't want to ruin her day, Thomas kept his illness to himself.

There was a knock at his door. "Come in," Thomas called and smiled at the sight of his second daughter holding a small tray. "You didn't have to do this, Margaret. Becky would have brought me something later."

"It's no trouble, Father. I wanted to do it."

She placed the tray on his bedstand and helped him to a nearby chair. "I don't know what the matter is. Lately I've been feeling so weak. And my stomach. Lord, but it's cramping something awful. I should tell Jared."

"You might want to wait until he comes back from his wedding trip. Besides, you're looking ever so much better today."

Thomas smiled at her fussing. "I wish I had known you sooner. I wish things had been different."

"Don't worry, Father," Bess smiled into his blue eyes. "I'm here now. I'll take care of you."

Because she was hardly recovered from her accident, and as far as Jared was concerned should not have been out of bed at all, it was impossible for Carolyn to walk down the aisle of a church. Therefore, the church was canceled. Instead the minister had been asked to perform the ceremony in Felicity's home. Carolyn and Thomas would both be helped into place. Felicity would walk down the stairs unescorted and join her hand to Jared's.

The guests were arriving. Jared could hear them talking downstairs as he paced the hallway above. Finally out of desperate loneliness, he knocked on Felicity's door. Becky opened the door and gasped. "You can't come in here. It's bad luck to see her until . . ."

"I know that. Damn, I just wanted to talk to her for a minute."

"Don't let him in here." Jared recognized the voice as Carolyn's.

"Are you almost ready?" he called through the door.

"Almost," Felicity returned.

"Shall I tell Mrs. Hampill to start playing?"

"Go downstairs, Jared," Carolyn said, "I'll have Becky signal Mrs. Hampill when to begin."

The door closed. "God, I've never seen a man more anxious."

Felicity grinned, knowing she was just as eager. And how could she not be after the delicious night they had spent together and the promises he'd made to show her even more of the delight so far sampled. The night Carolyn had finally awakened played again in her mind. She couldn't forget it. Perhaps she never would.

After Carolyn had been dressed, fed, and finally settled for the night, Jared and Felicity had left her to David's watchful and loving ministrations and returned to the guest room. The moment he closed the door behind them, Felicity turned into his arms. Her arms moved around his neck, her mouth pressed against his throat, as she whispered, "I think you are wonderful. What would we have done without you?"

His arms came around her, even as he denied her praises. "Any doctor could have done as much."

"No, I don't think so. I don't think the others care like you do."

Jared smiled and rubbed his face into her hair. "She did most of the work herself, sweetheart."

"Jared," he felt the whisper against his chest, for in the darkness she'd grown considerably bolder and had taken advantage of his opened shirt. She kissed him there. "Make love to me."

Jared thought he'd never again hear such wondrous words. His body surged with longing, hardening at the knowledge that she was his for the taking. And after next week, despite her intent, his forever. Still a doubt plagued. He knew Felicity to be a moral lady, a woman of her time, caught up as most in the taboos of intimacy before marriage. She might know some need at the moment, but that need was confused with gratitude. In the end, she wouldn't be happy should he take her up on her offer. "Would you be saying that if Carolyn wasn't better?"

"I don't know," she answered honestly.

Jared knew she wouldn't have. He knew as well that to take her now would cause her some distress on the morrow, when she'd be thinking a bit more clearly. They were to be married in less than a week. He could wait. They both could. But in the meantime, just for tonight, because he needed to touch her so badly, he could show her a sample of the pleasure that lay in store. And with this sampling, she would have no choice but to want even more.

Blindly they moved toward the bed. Jared released her. After a moment's fumbling, he struck a match and lit the candle at their bedside.

Felicity was obviously puzzled and, judging by the look in her eyes, slightly alarmed. "Do we need light?"

He held her face in both hands tipping her mouth toward his. "I'm not going to make love to you, sweetheart. We'll save that for later, after we're married. But I am going to touch you. And I want to see what I touch."

She shivered at the dark hunger in his eyes.

"Are you afraid?"

"No." And then, "I don't know."

Jared smiled as he pushed his fingers into her hair. "You don't have to be. I won't do anything you don't want."

Felicity breathed a sigh at his words, and Jared knew he'd been right. She might not be afraid, exactly, but she was nervous. Now that she'd invited the moment she couldn't help but wonder if she were doing the right thing.

"Do you realize how lovely this is?"

"What, my hair?"

"Your hair, your skin, everything about you." He kissed her gently, feeling her sigh of disappointment as he released her mouth. He smiled, knowing he could have lengthened the moment and not have heard a murmur of complaint. But he didn't want her mindless with kisses. He wanted her senses heightened, but well aware of everything that was going on, eager to enjoy his touch, eager to touch him in return.

Her mouth was against his chest again. Her hands touching him lightly. "Is it all right if I touch you?"

"God," he said. "It's better than all right. Touch me anywhere you like."

Felicity realized a growing sense of power, something she'd never felt before. He wanted her to touch him, and yet had promised this intimacy would not end in consummation. The thought eased her mind somewhat, for although she might want to experience the mysteries between men and women, it was something she had never done before and she couldn't help knowing some trepidation at the thought. Now, because of his words, she felt herself relaxing, growing bolder, more confident of herself, more in control of the moment.

Her hands moved under his shirt and pushed the material over his shoulders and down his arms. The shirt fell unnoticed to the floor. "I've wanted to do this for a long time."

"I know. I saw the way you looked at me."

Felicity chuckled softly. She hadn't realized her wants were so obvious.

"And I've wanted you to."

His skin was smooth, the muscles beneath it hard and yet slightly giving against her mouth. She rubbed her face into his chest hair and laughed at the sheer joy of being allowed this intimacy.

Jared heard the soft chuckle. "What?" he asked bringing her face to his again.

"I like it. You feel better than I thought," she said as she returned to further investigate this phenomenon. "I didn't know a man could feel so good."

Jared moaned as her mouth lowered a bit, moaned again as her hands discovered the texture and feel of him. She kissed him, and when he moaned she kissed him again, allowing her tongue to sample his taste, to take in texture.

And then her hands were at his waist and then lower still, coming to his thighs and then, because he so obviously wanted more, moving boldly over the hardness of his arousal. She'd touched him there once before, but only because he had placed her hand there. She'd been a little afraid then, and a lot confused. Only neither of those emotions recurred now. Now she was hungry, obviously so, and Jared delighted in the fact, knowing the time wasn't far away when she might surpass him in the mindless ecstasy.

He took her by the shoulders, forcing her mouth from him, forcing her hands to fall to her sides, lest she innocently bring to a close a moment that might, if he had the strength, go on for half the night. "What?" she asked.

"My turn," he said as he sat on the edge of the bed and gathered her between his legs.

"But I wasn't finished."

"I know. I'll give you time later to finish."

His arms held her tightly against him as he rubbed his face into her softness. She felt delicious and smelled even better. Her robe parted, and, through the thin cotton of her gown, Jared took the tip of her breast into his mouth. He heard the sound of air being sucked between her teeth as her back arched slightly. "Do you like that?"

Felicity chuckled, a low and throaty sound. He might as well have asked if she liked sunshine, if she liked newborn babies, or the wind blowing through her hair as she rode her horse. The word "liked" hardly suited, for she longed for his touch and longed to touch him in return. And because he had allowed her the power, the ability to relax and enjoy this tender display, she was able to tease. "It's better than eating spinach, I suppose."

Jared pulled back in some surprise, then grinned at her dramatic, if feigned, display of martyrdom. "You know, some people believe women with red hair are witches."

Felicity laughed at the thought. "What do you believe?"

He didn't answer, but said instead, "And witches are said to have a mark, given them by the devil."

She frowned. "What kind of mark?"

"I don't know, but I'm sure I'd recognize it if I saw one."

Her frown turned into a smile that bordered on the amazed. "You don't know and yet you're sure you could recognize it?"

"It could be on your shoulder."

She shook her head. "It's not."

"I'd have to check it for myself to know for sure."

Felicity smiled as she reached for the ties of her gown, slowly pulling at the ribbons, slowly allowing him past this last barrier. She tugged the material to one side, baring a shoulder and then to the other. "See, I told you it's not there."

Jared moved the material so that it draped both shoulders at the same time. Next he leaned forward and brushed his mouth against her collarbone. Gently, he tasted the skin, delighting in its softness, in its clean flavor.

"Are you looking or tasting?" she asked, as his mouth, tongue and teeth dragged over the newly exposed skin from shoulder to shoulder.

"Both."

"You might hurt your eyes again. It's not good to be so close when . . ." She groaned a low sound, and found her neck unable to support the weight of her head. She closed her eyes and allowed her head to fall back. "Mm, that feels good."

"I don't see anything. Maybe I should lower it a bit."

"You wouldn't be trying to trick me, would you?"

Jared laughed. "I'm only looking for the mark."

"Is it a circle? I can tell you right now that I have one on my ankle."

"No, it's not a circle, and it definitely wouldn't be on your ankle."

"Why not?"

"Too easy to find."

Felicity didn't try to stop him when he lowered the neckline an inch. And she especially did not stop him when he did it again, since not a speck of skin went unadmired by the loving touch of his lips and tongue. "See anything yet?"

"God, I'm trying," he said a bit desperately.

She laughed, then looking into eyes gone black with hunger, she dared, "Are you sure you're looking?"

"I might need to lower it some more. Would that be all right?"

Her breathing was a bit labored as she imagined what would happen. Then she felt a surge of excitement, almost reaching for the garment herself, almost tearing at it in an effort to allow him to see what he would. She forced her hands to remain where they were, and said, "If you must."

"I think that's the right word. I must." Felicity might never know exactly how desperately he must. With her arms at her sides, it took only a flick of his fingers to see the gown fall to her waist. Jared leaned back and looked at her for a long minute, unable to believe the sight of this loveliness. He knew of course that her figure was lush. Those prim, but tight-fitting bodices couldn't deny that fact. And he'd caught a glimpse once upon entering her room, but he hadn't known how lush, how lovely she would be. He hadn't imagined what seeing her would do to his stomach, his heart, the jolt of lust that threatened to take his mind. Jared realized he wasn't breathing. He forced air into his lungs. This was definitely not the time to pass out. "I'm having a hard time breathing here."

"Perhaps it might be better if you didn't look so hard."

"I can't stop. If I had your body, I'd have eyestrain and headaches. I'd never leave the mirror."

Felicity laughed, knowing she pleased him more perhaps than he had expected. And surprised herself that she felt no shyness standing exposed to his view. Surprised herself again that she was able to speak, the way her heart was pounding. "I'm sure you'd grow used to it eventually."

Jared shook his head, his gaze moving to hers only to instantly return to the feast of loveliness before him. Her breasts were large and perfectly round. The tips were pink, very light pink, and Jared shuddered at the hunger they engendered, at the things he wanted to do to them. "I don't think so."

Through a haze of passion Felicity watched his gaze move over her. She knew some surprise that her natural modesty seemed to have disappeared. Never had she stood shamelessly before a man like this. Never had she felt so at ease, so sure of herself, so needy, so certain that he should look and touch where she'd never been looked upon or touched before.

Jared forced himself to breathe, forced his heart to resume its natural rhythm. All right, so he didn't do much of a job with either, but he tried. He could hardly get the words out, his voice trembled so. "I think I found it."

"What? Where?"

"Over here," he gasped. "There's a smudge of blue right here," he said, as his tongue traced a vein to the tip of her breast.

Felicity's eyes fluttered closed. Her voice was barely audible as she asked, "And that's it? The mark of a witch?"

Jared couldn't say more than "Mmm," as his tongue teased, and his teeth nibbled, then, his mouth hungry for still more, took her softness deep inside. He sucked hard and long, then, easing in urgency, he ran his tongue over her and sucked again, and each time he did, Felicity's legs grew a little weaker.

She held to his shoulders for support as his beard-roughened cheeks scratched at the sensitive skin and his tongue came again to soothe the tenderness. He needed a shave. "Jared, I'm having a bit of trouble standing."

He brought her to lie at his side, turning so he leaned over her a bit. "It's a wonder you can stand at all, what with the weight of these"—he placed a palm of each hand over each breast and rolled them gently against her chest—"pulling at your balance."

Felicity chuckled. "Yes, ladies do have their cross to bear."

"Crosses," he gently corrected, as his hand brought the soft flesh together and his mouth sipped at her, his tongue laving a path from tip to tip and back again. Jared wondered if he'd ever get enough of touching her, tasting her. He kissed her everywhere, leaving nothing of what was so beautifully exposed unloved. He placed her hands high over her head, so he might be allowed total access to all and took complete advantage of her gentle compliance.

His mouth was at her waist when he realized her gown was blocking any further discovery. Gently, without her notice, he pushed the fabric down until both drawers and gown were pulled from her legs. He wasn't going to make it. He'd promised her he wouldn't, but there was no way he could stop.

And then Jared realized he wouldn't be loving her after all. That it was too late. His sex had thickened as he'd loved her, thickened and lengthened to the point where there was no going back, no way he could stop what was to come.

Still in his trousers he rolled upon her, knowing only that he had to feel her softness beneath him or die. Their chests rubbed together, their mouths clung, and Jared dug his hips into hers, rocking just a bit before the shudders of ecstasy overtook him.

He lay heavily upon her, desperately trying to bring his breathing under some control. That she hadn't achieved near his delight was obvious in the confusion he saw in her eyes. Confusion and need.

"I didn't mean to do that."

"To do what?" she asked in all innocence.

Jared knew she was an innocent, that she hadn't known anything about the sex act. He should have expected that question. "To go that far."

She frowned, somehow expecting a bit more than what she'd gotten. "Did we . . . ?"

"No, but the thing is, you're just too irresistible, and I couldn't help myself."

Felicity didn't know for sure what it was he hadn't been unable to help, but took unkindly to her being at fault for this unstated weakness. "I think what I like most about men is their ability to take the blame for their own failings, rather than place that blame on women."

Jared grinned. "Can I help it if you're so adorable and tempting that you drive me crazy?"

"Do I?"

"Didn't I just prove it?"

"How should I know?"

Felicity seemed to have forgotten that she was lying quite naked beneath a man. And while lying naked she was sort of arguing over something she wasn't the least bit sure of. She frowned. "What are we talking about?"

Jared hugged her tightly against him and laughed. "I'm going to show you in just a minute."

And he did. He surely did.

"Felicity! What in the world is the matter with you?"

Felicity started at the sharpness of her voice. "What?" she asked as she turned from the mirror to find Carolyn limping on a crutch coming toward her.

"Didn't you hear me? I said Mrs. Hampill has started playing. Everyone is waiting."

David stood behind his lady, his arms draped loosely about her waist, ready to help her downstairs. "You'll be all right, won't you? I mean you're not going to forget to come down, are you?"

Felicity came to her feet and smiled. "I think I'll remember."

Thirteen

Felicity stood at the top of the stairs and allowed Carolyn the time, with David's assistance, to reach the minister in the sitting room below. It was then that she began her descent.

Amazingly enough, Felicity knew no fear as she walked toward the man she was to marry. She'd always thought that she'd be terrified, or at the very least shaken at this extraordinary moment in her life. Most brides trembled at the thought of the wedding night, but not she. If her cheeks were colored, it wasn't from a blush of maidenly shyness. It was sheer eagerness to see the magic that would be tonight.

Jared watched his bride move toward him. Her father was still too weak to accompany her, but he stood at Jared's side, ready to give his daughter away.

It took only a few minutes. Words were spoken, vows taken, and Jared knew his life had been inexorably changed forever. Only the change hadn't happened at this moment. It had happened the first moment he saw her. It was then that his fate had been sealed. He looked at his wife and smiled, as the minister said, "You may kiss your bride."

Jared willingly obeyed and grinned at the sparkle in Felicity's eyes as she purposely and wickedly, if only for an instant, slipped her tongue into his mouth. For a long moment he looked into her smiling eyes and both knew only joy and pleasure and maybe even more in what they saw. "Witch," he murmured at her enchantingly naughty smile.

Felicity laughed and turned to Carolyn and next her father. Bess came to kiss them both, although Jared would have bet an entire year's wages that she did not kiss Felicity in the exact same manner as she had him. He frowned as she tried to force his lips apart with her tongue. Damn, but the woman made his skin crawl.

Before he knew it, Jared saw his wife fully surrounded by an army of mostly men, each awaiting his chance to kiss the bride. It wasn't until he noticed the last man to kiss her only got back into line to do it again that he tore his wife from the long line of admirers.

The crowd followed them outside. A barrel of rum and another of ale stood in one corner of the terrace. Nearby were tables, covered with white cloth and piled high with food. The sun was bright, the day glorious, and Jared couldn't remember being happier.

Felicity had been nearly torn from his side and was at this minute talking to two of her friends. She laughed at something one of them said, then glanced at Jared. He had no doubt that whatever was said involved him and most likely the night that stretched before them. He moved to her side, only to hear, "I'm not telling you, so you might as well give it up."

Carolyn had joined in the conversation. "Why not?" she asked, then added in exaggerated slyness, "We weren't going to do anything."

Felicity shot the three grinning women a knowing look. "And my hair isn't really red, either."

Jared could have testified that her hair was really red. Just the thought of how he knew that for a fact caused him some intense longing, and he placed his arm around Felicity's waist, drawing her away from her company. "You ladies don't mind if I have a word with my bride, do you?"

He didn't wait for their response, and grinned at Felicity's wicked murmur, "He's just a little anxious," as he swept her away from her friends.

Felicity laughed all the way into the house.

"It's been exactly a half hour."

"Since what?"

"Since we were married."

Felicity grinned.

"Don't you think it's time we kissed?"

She smiled and moved a bit closer. "Are we always to kiss every half hour?"

"Always," Jared said as his mouth closed over hers. He was breathing heavily by the time his mouth moved from hers. Still, he managed, "On second thought let's make it every fifteen minutes."

Felicity chuckled a low, terribly wicked, sexy sound. A sound made sexier perhaps because she had no idea of its cataclysmic effect. It took just about every bit of Jared's strength not to cart her off to his bedroom upstairs. "I don't think that will give us much time to do anything else. It takes about five minutes for one of your kisses and according to my calculations, that leaves . . ."

Jared interrupted her teasing with yet another kiss.

She breathed a little shakily as he released her mouth and pressed his forehead against hers. "All right, fifteen minutes sounds about right to me."

Jared chuckled as he held her close against him, delighting in the fact that kissing her, holding her, was at last perfectly permissible, and it didn't matter who came upon them. "What did they want?"

"Who?"

"Your friends."

"Oh, they just wanted to know where we were going tonight."

He pulled back a bit, and asked, "You didn't tell them, did you?"

Felicity shot her husband a wicked grin. Where had she learned that? he wondered, totally enchanted by the sight of her smile. "There's more here, Jared, than just a pretty face."

Jared laughed. "And you know for certain that you have that?"

"What? A pretty face?" Felicity shrugged. "I look into a mirror now and then."

"It's more than pretty, you know."

She smiled again, and Jared swore his gentle compliment had just caused her to grow even more beautiful. It couldn't be, of course. Still, he couldn't deny the fact that she just about stole his breath with her every movement, glance, and devilish grin. "It isn't, but I'm happy you think so."

The party was still going strong some time later when Felicity kissed her father good-bye. With her hand in Jared's, the couple stole quietly away.

The light wasn't very good inside the carriage, but the lovers didn't need much light. It would be three hours, perhaps more, before they would reach Thomas Dryson's summer home. A small cottage near the town of Huntington, on Long Island. A cottage that stood high on a cliff over a white sandy beach. A cottage that servants had earlier stocked and made ready for their arrival.

"I spent just about every summer there as a child. I was as brown as a berry by the end of the season. Mother was always after me to put something on, but I liked to run around half-naked."

"I hope you still like it."

Felicity laughed at the hungry look in his eyes, but made no comment. "Once, when we were just girls, well perhaps more than girls, young ladies actually, Carolyn and I spent a week there, with Mrs. Carpenter and a few servants. One morning Carolyn and I decided to take a dip. We woke up at the crack of dawn and ran for the beach."

Jared smiled as he watched her animated expression. God, he could sit for hours and just watch her.

"It was hardly light out, so we didn't notice that the driver and his groom had had much the same idea. They were down the beach, so we didn't see them until all of us were out of the water and reaching for our robes." Felicity's eyes were filled with laughter.

"I wish I could describe Mrs. Carpenter's expression when she came across four nearly naked people on the beach. If she hadn't been so shocked, then so livid, I might have laughed myself silly."

"What were you wearing?"

"Me? I was in my shift. Modestly covered, I assure you."

Only Jared knew a wet shift was hardly any covering at all. He wasn't the least bit happy at the thought. "And Carolyn?"

"She wore only her drawers."

Jared grinned, knowing some relief at the thought. If Carolyn had been naked to her waist, it wasn't likely that either man paid Felicity much attention. "I can see why Mrs. Carpenter might have been a bit upset."

"It was all very innocent. The driver and groom turned away the second they noticed us."

"The second you noticed them noticing you, you mean."

Felicity shrugged. "In any case, we never went there again. It's been years."

"Tell me what it looks like."

Felicity described for him in detail the small house and its surroundings.

"And we'll be alone there? Really alone?" Jared asked enthusiastically.

Felicity almost grinned at his delight and shot him a narrowed, teasing glance. "We're sending the driver back, so I imagine we will be. Why? Are you planning to push me off the cliff?"

Jared laughed in amazement at her line of thinking, for his thoughts had the definite tendency to stray toward the intimacy that could be shared in a house while alone with his bride. "Well, I hadn't thought of it before, but now that you mention it, I might."

"Unless I push you off first."

Jared thought it just might be time to quiet that sassy mouth. "Get over here."

"What? And squash in beside you?"

"No, sit on my lap."

She managed to look quite shocked. "And wrinkle my gown?"

"Felicity," he sighed patiently, "I fully intend to remove that gown at the very first opportunity, and you won't be wearing it again, in any case, so what difference does it make if it wrinkles?"

"Here you are looking to remove it, and you haven't once said one word about it. You didn't say I was gorgeous, you didn't say I made a lovely bride. I might as well have worn a sack."

Jared hadn't said anything about her gown because he hadn't known how to voice his feelings. They ran so deep as to almost frighten him. Now that she had lightened the moment, he could grin at her teasing and respond with, "You're gorgeous. Now get over here."

Felicity nodded as if to herself and tapped her fingers on the seat beside her. "Mm, very romantic."

Jared laughed.

"Tell me something romantic."

"Like what?"

She shrugged. "Well, you could say, your hair is heavenly, your teeth pearls, your tiny feet adorable, your eyes dark pools of . . ." She shrugged. "I don't know, something."

"Actually they're not very dark. They're sort of honey brown, and they sparkle when you tease. I rather like that."

"Do you?" She seemed to enjoy that. "What else do you like?"

"You."

"I assumed that much. What about me?" She frowned and then grunted, "God, I've never worked so hard for a compliment."

Jared laughed. He found he'd been laughing quite a bit lately. Most every time he was in her company in fact. "I promise, if you sit on my lap, I will tell you everything."

Felicity did as he asked. "I'm not too heavy, am I?"

"Don't worry. I can take it."

Felicity shot him a warning look. "You were supposed to say you're as light as a feather, darling. Do I have to tell you everything?"

"I'm about to become romantic, Felicity, don't confuse me."

She sat primly, her hands folded in her lap, a smile teasing the corners of her mouth as she said, "You may begin."

"You are a beautiful lady."

"Thank you."

"Shut up before I forget what I was going to say."

Felicity giggled.

"I think your laughter is delicious, your mouth, the best I've ever tasted."

Her smile turned into a frown. "How many have you tasted?"

"Enough to know you're the best. I think I'm probably the luckiest man alive."

"What do you mean probably?"

"How am I supposed to talk romantic when you keep interrupting me?"

Felicity laughed and leaned a bit closer. "I think I should kiss you."

"Why?"

"Well, for one thing, I want to find out if you're the best I've ever tasted."

"I'm the only one you've ever tasted."

She sighed unhappily. "Yes, I forgot about that." She felt his hand move at the back of her neck. "What are you doing?"

"Opening these buttons. How many are there?"

"About a hundred. It could take you awhile."

Jared grinned, for it hadn't taken him long at all. The buttons were open to her waist. His fingers unpinned her veil and dropped it to the opposite seat. Next came the pins that held her hair in place. He slid them into his pocket, as long red curls cascaded down her back.

"I feel like I haven't seen you in days."

He had seen her for maybe a total of a half hour in four days, and it felt more like months as far as Jared was concerned. "I had to make sure Dr. Miller knew what his duties were."

"And you can stay away for two weeks?"

"Longer, if we like."

"We might like that," she said.

Jared slid the lace-covered bodice down her arms, slowly baring her to his view, not stopping until the material lay loosely at her waist. "Yes, you could be right. We might like that," he said, as his gaze took in her loveliness.

He touched her, cupping her softness, testing and retesting the weight of her in his hands. "You know, I was thinking."

Her eyes were closed, her head tipped back a bit, her back arched, obviously delighting in his gentle ministrations. "About what?"

"About all those clothes you brought with you. Do you think you'll need them? Three trunks? I mean, we are going to the country and . . ."

"Jared." She sounded as if she were admonishing him. "Father would have been shocked if I didn't bring something to wear. Becky would have told her lieutenant and our major might have found out, and Mary, God, I can just imagine how she would have blushed. I don't think she would have survived the shock."

He frowned. "What are you saying?"

"I'm saying, they're empty."

It took Jared a moment to understand. He repeated her words, still unsure of what she meant. "Empty?"

"Well, just about. Except one or two things plus something to wear home and a robe, of course." She shrugged. Jared was entranced, for the movement swayed her breasts. "I had to bring something in case of a fire."

Jared couldn't hold back his laughter. He hugged her tightly against him. "Do you mean to prance about the entire time naked?"

She shrugged, well, as much as his arms allowed, in any case. "I thought you wouldn't mind overmuch."

He kissed her long and hard. "God, you are so deliciously wicked. I think I'm going to love being married to you."

"I think I already love it," she said, her mouth against his neck, "but you got off the track, didn't you?"

He pulled back a bit and looked into her face. "What do you mean?"

"Well, you were very nicely occupied a moment ago and I thought I might remind you lest you forget that you have a half-naked lady sitting on your lap."

"I'm not likely to forget it. How much longer before we get there?"

"At least two hours."

"What do you think we might do to occupy our time while waiting?" he asked, as his hands returned to their original delicious chore.

"Well, we could sleep, I suppose."

"That's a good . . ."

"But I'll kill you if you try."

Jared grinned. "You wouldn't be a bit anxious, would you?"

"You mean to learn all the things you promised?"

Jared nodded.

"Maybe a little."

"Just a little?"

"All right. Maybe a lot."

"Well we should start then, don't you think?"

Felicity grinned. "It took you a while, but I think you're getting the idea."

Mr. Masters never noticed that the buttons running down Felicity's back had been hurriedly done up and a few were missing the hole they were meant to occupy. It never occurred to him that the bride's veil sat at an odd angle, not entirely centered on her head. It was dark by the time they arrived at the small house and even had he been of a mind to take a closer look, he would have noticed nothing in the near blackness of the night.

The house was quiet. Jared dismissed the driver before carrying Felicity inside. The three mostly empty trunks were left on the steps outside, alongside his small bag. Jared figured he'd bring them in next week . . . maybe. He bumped into a table and knocked it on its side, sending whatever had been upon it, by the sound of it something heavy, crashing to the floor.

"Careful," Felicity said about a minute too late.

"Why is there a table in the middle of the hallway?"

"Because this isn't a hallway. It's a sitting room."

"I need some light, before I kill the both of us."

"Put me down."

Jared did as she asked and waited until he heard the scratch of a match. A moment later a candle on the mantel was lit. He watched her move to a table in the corner of the room and light the lamp there. She closed the curtains.

Jared straightened the table and replaced the large thick candle in its pewter stand. "Start a fire while I find us something to eat."

The weather had been warm, but a cottage by the sea was usually damp, and this one proved to be no different.

Felicity took the lamp with her as she checked the larder. "I hope you know how to cook," she called from the only other room downstairs.

"Why?"

Felicity jumped, and Jared smiled at her dark look. "I didn't know you were behind me."

"Isn't there anything to eat?"

"Yes, but this won't last but a few days. Then we'll have to go into town and buy something."

"Don't you think you might startle the innocent citizens of the town, you being naked and all."

"I won't be naked then."

"You're not now either, and you did promise," he reminded her gently of their conversation in the carriage.

Felicity smiled. "Get the trunk."

"Which one?"

"The one with the leather straps. I want my robe."

"Are you telling me you're suddenly shy?" Jared couldn't believe her transformation. At first she had been a modest, shy maiden, shy enough in fact that a bold look brought a beautiful pink blush to her cheeks. Now her shyness seemed to have completely disappeared and she easily matched him in his eagerness to get on with the business at hand. He just might have to fight her off, once she knew of the pleasure. He couldn't wait.

"No. I have something in there for you."

Felicity prepared two plates of fried chicken, cheese, and bread. With it she took a bottle of wine and glasses into the sitting room and placed it all near the growing fire as Jared pulled her trunk inside the doorway.

Next she opened the trunk and took out a package. Inside the paper wrapping, Jared found a dark red silk lounging robe.

"Do you like it?"

"It's beautiful. Thank you. Did you make this for me?"

"No, actually, I made it for the stableboy, but I needed a wedding gift and thought he wouldn't mind if I . . ." He stopped her teasing words with his mouth.

Felicity breathed a sigh as his mouth released hers at last. "I think you'll look very handsome in it."

"Shall I put it on now?"

Felicity nodded.

"First, I have something for you."

Felicity never noticed that he'd taken a small box from his pocket and sighed happily. "I know."

Jared grinned. "I mean, I bought you something. A wedding gift."

Felicity's eyes widened as he handed her the box. Inside on a bed of black velvet lay a perfect cameo. A black velvet ribbon was curled to one side. "It's beautiful," she breathed.

"Shall I help you with it?"

Felicity smiled and nodded as she turned her back to him and lifted her hair aside.

The moment the cameo was secured around her neck, she grabbed something from the trunk and ran from the room. "I'll be right back."

"Jared, I've brought a fur blanket. It's in the trunk. You might like to spread it before the fire," she called this from the kitchen.

"What are you doing?"

"I'm changing into my robe."

Jared tore off his jacket and shirt and flung his boots to the other end of the room. He looked at his trousers and then shrugged as he pulled them off as well. She was bound to see him eventually. And he couldn't hide his arousal much longer. He only hoped she wouldn't be too afraid.

A moment later he sat upon the fur, naked beneath his silk robe. She'd thought of everything. Jared couldn't have been more pleased. He reached for his glass. The wine was light, clean, and crisp. Perfect.

"What's taking you so long?" he called behind him.

"I'm back," she said, and stood there waiting for him to turn.

Jared did exactly as she thought he might. He turned toward her, his mouth dropping open in surprise. He almost dropped the glass and cursed as some of the wine spilled on his new robe. He put the glass down. At least he thought he did. He couldn't take his gaze from her to be sure, but he hadn't heard glass break, not that he could have heard anything over the pounding of his heart. It took two tries before he finally managed, "Is that what you brought in case of a fire?"

Felicity smiled at his obvious appreciation. She didn't know herself anymore. She couldn't find even a shred of the shy maiden she'd once been, and reveled in the fact that with this man she couldn't remember the meaning of the word modesty. She'd never known such freedom, such absolute delight in being able to share these moments with him. "Do you like it?"

"I love it, but it doesn't cover much, does it?"

At his remark Felicity looked down at the garment. "Actually it covers all of me right to the floor," she corrected.

"Except that it's completely transparent."

"Oh that, well Carolyn gave it to me. She said I should wear it tonight. She was absolutely certain that you would like it."

He came to his feet. His voice told of his suffering as he tried to control the need to hurry this moment. "Remind me to thank Carolyn, when we go back."

The robe was of the palest pink. A dark pink ribbon secured the transparent fabric together just under her breasts. Jared figured he was probably going to need spectacles before this night was through. He couldn't stop staring at her. Her dark red hair lay over her shoulders, the ends curling enticingly at the tips of her breasts, and Jared knew he'd never seen anything half so lovely. He moved aside a lock of hair to better his view. "The first night I saw you, you were wearing pink. I thought then that pink made you look like a strawberry confection."

Felicity made a face. "How boring."

Jared smiled. "But I was wrong. Pink makes you look as if you just stepped out of an erotic dream."

Felicity's lips parted, and her heart hammered in her throat. She took a deep calming breath. Jared became enthralled by the gentle rise and fall of her breasts. "And here I thought you couldn't be romantic."

"Come closer to the fire." He held out his hand. "I want to see all of you."

"You've already seen that."

"I'm afraid once wasn't enough." Jared was afraid a thousand times wouldn't be enough.

"You're unbelievably lovely."

Felicity made another face. "What happened to erotic?"

Jared grinned at her question and watched with some amazement as she mussed her hair and allowed part of the heavy mass to fall over one side of her face. She bit her generous lips, bringing them more color, then wet them with her tongue. A moment later she struck up a provocative pose, leaning forward a bit. Just enough to allow the robe to part a fraction and display much of the barely veiled sweet globes of flesh to his view. "I've practiced this a dozen times. Is it working?"

Jared's voice was just a bit strangled. "Where did you practice it?"

"Well, I thought Mary and Sam might be a little shocked if I tried it in front of them, so mostly I did it in front of my mirror."

"I'm jealous of your mirror. I wish I had been watching."

"You're watching now."

"And you practiced this for me?"

"Of course, for you. Who else?"

"I can safely say it's working," Jared said, feeling a pulse throb in his throat. "I've never seen anything so sultry."

"Sultry is good." Felicity's eyes sparkled at the thought.

"Sultry is more than good," came his deep, ragged husk.

Felicity rewarded him with one of her smiles, and her gaze moved over the length of him. "I like you in that. You look like a man of leisure."

"I don't feel very leisurely right now."

Felicity smiled, noticing the trouble he was having with his breathing. "Do you think it would be too bold of me if I asked to look at you?"

"You are looking at me."

"I mean," she shrugged, "well you are my husband and all, and I was wondering . . ."

"What I looked like under this?"

Felicity only nodded. Jared's hands moved to the tie at his waist. "I don't want to scare you."

"I'm very brave," she said, her eyes dancing with merriment.

"Most ladies are not enamored of the male form."

"You're right, I think." She rested her hand flat upon his chest. "Why, I'd wager most would faint at the very thought of a naked man." Her hand moved aside, and her mouth grazed his skin, driving him mad with wanting more. "I used to be a lady. It's a good thing I'm not any longer."

"Are you sure you're not?" Jared wondered who had asked that. It hadn't sounded like his voice at all.

"I can't be, because I think your body is beautiful."

He sighed his relief. "Thank you, but men aren't supposed to be beautiful."

"And interesting."

"Interesting?" he asked, with a definite note of interest himself.

"Yes, I never imagined a man would look like this."

"What did you imagine?"

"I suppose I hadn't imagined it at all."

"What part exactly do you think is interesting?"

Felicity smiled into his hungry eyes. "Well, your thighs are very thick. I didn't think they might have hair on them." Her hands moved down his body as she spoke. "They feel very good."

"Thank you. And?" he prompted a bit anxiously.

"And this line of hair. I like the way it thins out like that from your chest." She shook her head. "I never thought . . . And your chest, your back." She touched him there, running her hands under the robe to spread her fingers over his back.

"They're interesting?"

"No, they're beautiful."

"What part is interesting?"

"Well, I'd have to say this part, most particularly." She took a half step back and allowed her gaze to move down his body and linger at his sex. Jared could feel himself growing thicker, longer before her eyes.

"Which part exactly? You could touch me there, so I'll know for sure."

Jared groaned as she cupped his sex at last. "God, I thought you'd never do this."

"You mean you want me to touch you there?"

Jared grinned at the thread of wickedness in what was supposed to be a totally innocent question. "You might have gotten that idea, although I can't imagine how."

She pretended to frown. "I wonder how I could have gotten such an idea?"

"It probably just came naturally."

"That might be true. Lately the most peculiar things have been coming naturally," she said on a delicious sigh, unable to resist kissing his chest again.

"What kind of things?"

"Well, for one, I'm standing here allowing you to see me, and I never would have done that before."

"That's all right. I'm allowing you to see me."

Felicity grinned. "Meaning, if you're allowed, I'm allowed?"

"Exactly."

"And then there are my thoughts."

"What kind of thoughts?"

"Well I've been thinking of you a lot."

There was a long moment of silence before he finally blurted out, "Tell me."

"I've been thinking what it would be like to touch you."

He closed his eyes with a groan. "What else?"

Felicity smiled at his apparent desperation. "And kissing you, just like you kissed me the other night."

"I think I'm dying. No, I must have done that already. This has got to be heaven."

Felicity's small hand stroked his erection, her fingers moving in the fashion he had silently taught. Occasionally she would move them away to discover all, then return again to what most fascinated. She couldn't hide her obvious delight in learning his body. "You're so different."

"If I don't sit down, I'm going to fall."

Only they didn't sit. They knelt. Felicity sat on her heels between his opened thighs and touched him everywhere and anywhere she chose. Mostly she chose the interesting parts. Mostly Jared thought he wouldn't live beyond this night.

Fourteen

He was dangerously close to taking this woman without a shred of tenderness. Wild erotic thoughts of shoving her to her back and entering her virginal flesh without a care refused to leave his mind. Jared had no choice but to bring to a close this most luscious moment. He hated to do it, but his hands covered hers, and he gently took them from his body. "You have to stop that for a little bit."

"Why?"

"Because it's driving me mad with wanting you and for your sake, for both our sakes, we have to go slower."

"Can I touch you later then?"

"You can touch me always, but not now."

"And not when we have company?"

Jared's gaze moved from the bow beneath her breasts to her laughing eyes. He grinned. "You're very wicked."

"Are you very disappointed? I confess I don't know what's come over me. Things just sort of slip out."

"I love it." He almost said, And I love you. Jared knew it was true. There was no sense in denying the obvious. How could any man not?

At first it might have been a case of simple attraction, but it was more than that now. Far more. He felt his heart squeeze at her glance, his stomach ache at her laughter, his breath disappear at the look in her eyes. He loved her, had loved her ever since the night she had come up with the ridiculous plan to marry, just for a time. She didn't know it yet, but he wasn't about to settle for anything less than her love in return.

Still, he managed to catch himself in time. Perhaps this should have been the time for proclaiming his love, but it wasn't. Not as long as Felicity thought this marriage only a temporary affair. He didn't want to argue with her. Not now. There were other things, better things than arguing, and Jared thought it was long past the time to show her exactly what he had in mind.

His fingers reached for the ribbon and he pulled at the end parting the fabric. Jared might have thought he'd seen all there was to see, but he was wrong. Her naked breasts, white and gleaming in the firelight, the soft pink of their tips, almost sent him over the edge. He swallowed, as he remembered their taste, aching for still another sampling. And Jared knew there was no need to deny himself the pleasure.

His mouth lowered to her shoulder, her neck, nibbling a path down her chest to the aching need awaiting him. Felicity moaned a soft sound of approval as he suckled. Releasing her, he ran his tongue over the tip and, as if he couldn't resist the temptation, groaned as he suckled again.

Watching him, her hands moved to his face, her fingers into the hollows of his cheeks. He teased the tip with light nibbles which brought another groan and then another as she arched her back and pressed her body into his mouth. "God," she groaned, as her hands left his face to lift her breasts toward this incredible pleasure.

And then she was on her back, her legs wide to his pleasure, and Felicity found not an inch of her was left lacking to the masterful seduction of his teeth, lips, and tongue.

He continued the torture. His teeth grazed the underside of her breasts and down her midriff, until she was trembling for more, for everything he could give.

"I love this. God, I . . . do . . . love this," she moaned brokenly as his mouth lowered to her navel and investigated the small indentation, to her hip, her stomach, her thighs. She squirmed, aching for him to come to her.

And then his mouth was where she wanted it most, and Felicity grew wild, her world greedy, terribly terribly greedy. He'd waited too long to touch her there, for too long had he teased, for too long had he kissed and loved and rubbed against her, driving her mad for more.

It took only the briefest touch of his tongue to send her spiraling into the madness. She'd known it was coming. She'd felt the tightening across her stomach, a repeat of the last time, but this had been harder, more hurting, the ecstasy more than anything she could have imagined as the ache turned into torment and her body had tightened into one hard agonizing need, surging forward, blindly, mindlessly searching for release.

"Oh God," she gasped, lost in the relentless, crushing waves of incredible pleasure. A pleasure her body had no choice but to accept again, again, and yet again.

Jared moved over her. There would never be a better moment. Her muscles were soft, relaxed, her body wet and ready. He entered her slowly, feeling the last jerking aftershocks of her pleasure squeeze around his sex. Gently he moved, sliding forward and down, just a bit farther. Just a bit, he promised himself. Soon he'd break through, and she would be his forever. His to love, his to hold and keep.

Felicity understood his gentle touch as he initiated her into the art of loving. She was on the brink of learning how to love a man. It was something she'd longed for, something she hadn't been able to put from her mind since that sensual night in her garden when he'd shown her for the first time what it was to want. Felicity thought to hurry him along, anxious for the expected pleasures, anxious to know for herself the secrets he held in those dark eyes.

Jared felt her stiffen as he broke through the tiny piece of tissue. In an instant he was deep inside. "It's all right, sweetheart," he comforted and gently soothed, holding himself back from her allure, refusing to allow himself the pleasure of further movement until her body could grow accustomed to his size. "That's all there is. It won't hurt again. I swear it."

"It only pinched a little, is all," she said, her gaze soft and adoring as it moved over his body to join his where their bodies merged. Jared wondered if she didn't love him a little. He wondered if she realized the soft look of love in her eyes. He wondered at her trust, her willingness to allow him the most intimate of pleasures.

She might not love him yet. But she felt something. It was there in her eyes, and it was a beginning.

"I can't believe how good this feels. I can't believe I've waited so long to find out."

Jared smiled as he looked into her eyes. "It's going to feel better every time we do it."

"Better?" she asked, her gaze filled with doubt, her body filled with his loving. "Better than this?"

"Much better," he said as he began to move his hips. Gently at first, fully conscious of his every movement. It wasn't long before he watched her eyes cloud over again, as she succumbed to the deliciousness, to the glory they'd only know when in each other's arms.

His mouth took hers, hard and insistent, demanding that she give all. His movements quickened, growing sharper, deeper, almost desperate. His tongue, matching the movements of his body drove deep, thick, hot, and wet into her mouth. Stealing her breath, bringing her to the edge of reason, as she moved into each mind-boggling thrust, and then it was there again, the tempting madness, daring her to come to him again, daring her to join him in the ecstasy.

And Felicity had no will to resist.

He felt the hard, aching squeezing of her muscles and fought back his need. He felt it again, stronger this time, harder, dangerously hard as it sought to pull him deeper into the delirium, into the magic that was her.

She groaned broken desperate sounds as her body strained forward, upward, daring him to leave the ecstasy. Taunting him to stay to love her as only he could. And then the last of the contractions eased, and Jared at last allowed himself the pleasure.

He swore there was nothing lacking. This was the way it had to be. He wouldn't lose her, couldn't lose her. She was his wife, the woman he loved, and nothing else mattered. Nothing but that she never suffer like Annie had. His arms tightened at the thought. Nothing but that he'd never lose her, never know that kind of pain again.

Felicity, having no knowledge of this act of love, thought nothing of the abrupt termination of their coupling as he tore his body from hers an instant before emptying his seed. In truth, because she had no way of knowing anything else, she imagined this was the way of things.

The slippery warmth of him covered her belly and felt delightfully wicked as it allowed her to move against him.

It took Jared a long moment to recuperate. It wasn't until he felt her moving that he realized he hadn't died of pleasure after all. He raised his head, and opened his eyes. It was then that he saw the most sensual smile in his life. Her arms were over her head, and she moved like a cat, sleek and feline, obviously enjoying the feel of him, the wetness, the heat against her.

Their eyes met, and a smile tugged at the corners of her mouth. She couldn't hold back her warm chuckle. "So this is what all the furor was about. Interesting."

Jared laughed, wrapped his arms around her and rolled to his back, bringing her with him. "Interesting? Does that mean it was better than spinach?"

"Mm," she sighed, and came up to rest her arms across his chest. "It certainly has possibilities, doesn't it?" She suddenly frowned. "Why in the world would a bride be so afraid of her wedding night? And what are the ladies talking about when they imply the last chore before finally being allowed to sleep? Are they insane?"

"Well, sweetheart, the thing is, most women do not much appreciate the marriage bed."

"Something is wrong with them," she said unequivocally as he tried to fight off a yawn, then added, "or me."

"There's nothing wrong with you. I can vouch for that." Jared reached for his long drawers and helped her to sit as he wiped her and himself clean. Felicity enjoyed even that and realized there was little this man could do that she wouldn't like. Perhaps that was the answer. Perhaps those other women only needed the right man, and they would have loved this as much as she. "You know what the problem is? They need a man like you."

Jared studied her for a long moment, basking in her compliment, knowing she didn't have the sophistication that would come out of experience. That she spoke from the heart and meant every word she'd just said. Of course women had complimented him before, but none had been quite so honest about her feelings. Had he been up and about, he would have no doubt swaggered like a peacock. "Do you think that's it?"

Felicity nodded, having no notion that the man was teasing her.

"You know"—he shrugged—"I was thinking. Just for the sake of those women, I could rent myself out."

Felicity shot him a look of warning and said very softly, but very distinctly, "I don't think so."

Jared's eyes rounded with supposed surprise. He should have known better than to tease her on this matter. Bent on seeing her smile return, he had yet to notice her stiffening, the way she pulled back. "No? Are you sure? Don't you feel anything for your fellow sisters, never knowing how good this can be?"

"And you wouldn't mind servicing them?"

"Well, except for being exhausted all the time, it wouldn't be much of a chore. As a matter of fact I might even . . . Ow! That hurt!" Jared rubbed the spot where she'd just pinched him and growled into her neck as he pulled her to him and rolled her to her back again. He sat on her hips, holding her hands over her head as he watched her struggle to throw him off.

When she realized her attempts were getting her nowhere, she glared. "Jared, if you ever, I swear I'll . . ."

His gaze moved down her body. She had to be the most beautiful creature ever, and he couldn't believe she was really his. He smiled at her warning. "You don't know me well enough yet, but once you do you'll realize I'm the faithful sort."

It was only then that Felicity realized what she was doing, what she was saying. One might have thought that she wanted him forever by the way she was acting. She'd almost forgotten their pact. What in the world could she be thinking? "I'm sorry. I didn't mean . . ." She shrugged, trying to make light of her odd behavior. "For a moment there I almost forgot our pact."

"What pact?"

She looked into his vague expression and frowned. "You know what pact. You wanted me. I want children. That pact."

"What about it?"

Felicity's frown deepened. "What do you mean, what about it? You're leaving after the war. You're to divorce me once you get home."

Jared thought he was already home. Anywhere she was was home. And as far as the war went, there were different types of war, he thought, and the best one just might never be over between them.

"Oh, that pact." Jared nodded. "You know, Felicity," he said as he leaned on one elbow and ran his free hand lightly up and down her body, as if without thought. "I was thinking."

"About what?" she asked, obviously accepting his touch with just a little more interest than he evinced in the giving.

"About the end of the war. What would you say if I decided to stay here?"

"Here? But you can't stay. How could we get divorced if you stay?"

"Well, I was thinking about that too. Maybe we shouldn't get divorced."

"Shouldn't get . . ." she repeated softly. "Why?"

"Lots of reasons. Suppose you don't get with child right away." Jared figured that was almost an absolute. Being a doctor he knew of other methods of birth control, but those involved Felicity's cooperation. And since her purpose for instigating this marriage was to have a child, he doubted she would willingly participate. Of course nothing but abstinence was foolproof, but this was the best he could do to keep her safe. "Suppose we have to work on it for a while."

"But I will eventually, and then what? Will you leave then?"

"I might have a practice by then. What would I do with it?"

"I don't know. What do doctors usually do?"

"They don't leave. That's for sure. A lot of people begin to depend on them."

And that was exactly what Felicity did not want. She did not want to come to depend on him. She didn't want to chance her heart. She didn't want to trust. Not after discovering the ways of men.

"Jared, I won't stay married to you."

"Why not?"

"Because I'll eventually love you, and if you did to me what my father did to my mother, I'll have to shoot you."

Jared grinned. "But suppose I never do what your father did. Suppose I remained faithful forever?"

Felicity shot him a look of disbelief. "And what am I to do in the meantime? Wait? Hoping this day won't be the one?" She shook her head. "My father adored my mother, and he did it. While you don't even love me."

"Why don't we just take things one day at a time?"

Felicity shook her head. "I won't love you."

"Why not? I'm a good sort."

"I won't. And you'll have to leave before I do."

"Suppose it just sort of sneaks up on you, and you find you already love me. What would you do?"

"Get over it."

Jared looked into her determined expression. "You're a tough lady."

"I have to be."

Jared might have told her that there was no need. That she could soften her heart. That he'd never hurt her. That he wouldn't be looking at another. That he wouldn't want another, ever. But he didn't. It was too soon.

"Are you hungry?"

Felicity nodded. "A little."

They lounged before the fire, eating, sipping their wine. He leaned against the trunks, cushioned by pillows. She sat between his legs, her back against his chest.

"This is very nice, isn't it," she asked, breathing deeply her contentment as she stared into the flames.

"What? Sitting here like this?"

She nodded.

"I, for one, am enjoying the view."

Felicity turned just a bit. Following the direction of his gaze she saw his view just happened to be her breasts, easy enough to see since all he had to do was look over her shoulder.

"Have you been looking there all this time?"

"I can't stop looking there."

"Even when I was telling you about Carolyn and the time we . . ."

"Carolyn who?" he asked vacantly.

Felicity laughed, knowing he had heard every word, knowing he'd asked her enough questions. He'd been listening all right. She turned to face him on her knees. "So I take it you don't want to talk?"

"Oh, well you can talk. I don't mind."

"I can talk, while you look. Is that it?"

Jared's grin was a masterful example of what a man could look like. A handsome man. A man who needed a woman. Felicity's confidence soared. Not just any woman. Her. He needed her. And that was terribly exciting, because she thought she just might be needing him as well.

"Why did you move?"

"Well." She shrugged. "I thought maybe you'd like to more than look."

"Do that again."

"What?"

"Shrug."

"You're being very bad."

"I can't be good around you. Don't ask."

"I wouldn't think of it," she said demurely. Jared wondered how she managed that, what with her being naked and all.

"Is there a tub around here somewhere?" The thought occurred to him that he could use some clean water and soap, but more than that, he might convince her to join him.

"There's a big one outside."

"Where?"

"Along the whole coast."

Jared grinned as he realized her meaning. "Do you think anyone would mind if we used it?"

"I don't know how to swim."

"I'll teach you."

Felicity laughed as she came to her feet and reached for his robe. Without asking, she slipped it on, leaving him to wear his trousers or go naked. Jared opted for naked, since he'd only have to take the trousers off again. She looked him over for a long minute, never thinking to ignore what the sight of her looking was doing to his body, and said very seriously, "Now I'll probably never learn."

Jared hugged her against him, laughing at her straightforward way of stating a fact as she saw it. He nuzzled his face into her hair for a moment before taking her hand and walking outside. The night was dark, illuminated only by a quarter moon, the air warm, the scent brisk and salty. The cabin, perched upon a high cliff, had a long backyard that disappeared into a sandy drop. The path, marked occasionally with tree trunks lying across it, allowed them a foothold. Soon they left the path and found themselves facing the gently swaying waters of Long Island Sound, bordered by a narrow beach. "I hope you don't get too tired."

Felicity glanced at him, silently waiting for him to go on.

"I don't think I could carry you back."

"I've climbed it once or twice before," she said, the truth being she'd climbed it since a child. "I think I can make it."

Felicity dropped the robe and ran into the water with Jared hot on her heels. They frolicked for a time, just like children, laughing, playing, slapping water at each other, diving to avoid the next splash.

Felicity stood suddenly alone. She knew he was nearby, ready to spring up from the water like a giant creature ready to drag his victim to a watery grave. The thought gave her the shivers. The water was very dark. She couldn't see a sign of him. No doubt his head was just above the surface as he stood crouched, waiting for the right moment to strike. "Jared, I don't like being scared."

Nothing.

"Jared," she called out, and a second later, just as she imagined he might, he lunged from the water with a mighty roar and great splash.

The trouble was, Jared had never scared her before. Well never really scared her. Anyone of her acquaintances could have warned him that Felicity Dryson Walker was not a woman who took to scaring lightly. That one took his chances doing as much. That one sometimes took great chances with his life, doing as much.

Jared didn't know, but Jared would learn and no doubt never forget.

Felicity fully expected him to come roaring at her. But expecting it did not in any way impede the sound of her scream, nor the way she swung out. The fact was Felicity was small, but most women were small. Jared was big. And when he jumped and Felicity swung out reflexively, her elbow contacted smartly with his most prideful possession. Jared saw a flash of light that might have been stars, but was more than likely the whole damn universe.

Having no knowledge that men not only prized this particular possession but sometimes found it sensitive in the extreme, Felicity thought he was still playing when he fell back into the water with a deep agonizing cry.

"That's it. I'm not playing anymore. I told you I don't like to be scared."

She said this, having no knowledge that she'd just laid the man low in waist-deep water. It took him a minute before he realized that he couldn't breathe. Jared jumped up again. Gasping, trembling from the shock of his pain, bent over, he stood there waiting for the agony to subside.

"There's no need to keep it up. I'm not even in the water anymore. You're wasting your time," she called from the rocky beach.

Jared only shot her a vacant look and groaned in response.

Felicity took a step toward him. "What's the matter?"

He only moaned for an answer.

"Are you still playing?"

"I wish to hell I were," he said softly, but since sound travels over the water quite easily, Felicity heard him well enough. She dashed back into the water. "What's the matter?"

"Nothing."

She made a tsking sound. "Nothing? Isn't that just like a man? You've hurt yourself and you won't admit it. I knew something like this would . . ."

"Felicity you just elbowed me in the balls. I did not hurt myself."

She frowned at his comment. She hadn't realized she'd hit him, having swung out reflexively in fear.

"Your elbow smashed into me."

"Did it? Oh, I'm sorry. When did I do that?"

"When I jumped up from the water?"

"Oh Jared, I didn't mean to hurt you. I sometimes, well, that's not entirely true, I suppose. Usually," she nodded at the correction, "I usually swing when I'm scared. I can't help it."

"I'll try to remember that," he said dryly, knowing he wasn't likely ever to forget.

"Put your arm around my shoulders, and I'll help you back."

Jared shot her a look that reminded her not only of her size, but his. How did she expect to help him back when he outweighed her by something like seventy-five pounds? "Wait a minute. It will be all right if I wait a minute," he said, thankful for the cool water. It seemed to be helping.

"Is it very bad?"

Jared took a deep breath. "It's a little better, I think."

When he was finally able to walk again, he hobbled back to the beach and out of the water. He sat with a groan, on the robe Felicity had dropped just before entering the water, shivering from the effects of the pain. Felicity watched him sit. He pulled his knees up, then lowered his legs again as if searching for a position that would ease the last of the throbbing. The night was warm, the breeze almost hot. He shouldn't have shivered. "Are you cold?"

"No, I'm fine. It's better now."

"Should I get you a blanket?"

"No. Just sit with me for a minute."

They sat side by side while Jared willed the last of the pain to leave. It finally did, and he leaned back, looking at the stars for a minute as he sighed his relief.

"All right now?"

"Yes."

Felicity finished the apology, adding that she'd make an earnest effort never to do anything like that again.

Jared nodded in satisfaction and told her that he certainly hoped not.

And then beneath the stars, alone in the world, with no one to gaze upon them but God, Jared proceeded to love her again.

Later, after he was able to breathe again, after he had recovered his strength, they took another dip in the sound. After

Jared's many many delightfully failed attempts to teach her to swim, they gave up and walked hand in hand to the beach. Felicity shook out his robe and again put it on.

"I'm glad you gave that robe to me."

"Me, too," Felicity said never noticing the note of playful sarcasm. "I'm starting to get cold."

"Why didn't you make yourself one?"

"I started it, but I didn't have the time to finish it."

Jared grinned as she proceeded him up the path. He thought he would have very much enjoyed the view had she not worn his robe. And wondered if tomorrow he couldn't convince her to leave it behind.

Inside the cabin, Jared added wood to the fire as the two of them rolled into the fur, warming themselves with each other's body heat. "Your feet are freezing," he said.

He wanted her again, but because she was new at this, and he didn't want her sore, they played at other equally pleasant ventures. During their play, Jared dribbled wine over her stomach and licked it off. He did much the same to her breasts, making sure she was thoroughly dry. He told her she could get a rash if she were left damp, and he had to make an especially good job of it. Felicity might not have believed him. Still, she found herself unable to argue the point.

She stretched and sighed her enjoyment. Her eyes were shining as she looked up to him. "How long do you think it will take?"

"What?"

"A baby."

Jared shrugged. "Sometimes it only takes once." He smiled, denying the guilt that surged through him. "But just to be sure, I think we should do this again tomorrow."

"Oh, yes, tomorrow and the day after and the day after that."

He lay down beside her, touching her as he pleased, and he pleased to touch her most all the time. "Are you in a hurry?"

"Well, I was thinking, if we could have a baby right away,

we might have the time to have yet another before you have to leave."

"And you like that do you? The way we make babies?"

Felicity only laughed. "One might say that."

Jared wondered if he could bear it should she like it more. Still, it wouldn't hurt any to hear the words.

Fifteen

Felicity groaned as Jared pushed aside her hair and nuzzled the back of her neck. "Go away. I can't do it again."

Jared chuckled. "I'm hungry."

"There's bread in the kitchen."

"What about some tea? Can you boil water?"

"Maybe. If I have a pot and a fire."

Jared rolled to his back and sighed. "I should have brought Marcy with us."

"And what? Locked him up until you were hungry?"

Jared remembered the preceding night and knew they never could have been as free or as daring with each other had there been the chance of another walking in on them. "All right. I'll get the water. Where's the well?"

"Outside and to your right."

He pulled his trousers on and went into the kitchen for a pot. Her wedding dress lay carelessly discarded upon the floor. Beside it her underthings and slippers. Jared smiled. It looked as if she had been in a hurry to get them off. As memories of her and last night came to mind, Jared had no doubt of her anxiousness at the time. "Add more wood to the fire," he called just before leaving the house.

"It looks like we're in a for a shower," Jared said entering the house and then fighting the door as a gust of wind tried to force it back.

Felicity bent before the fire, dressed in her chemise, poking at the blaze, trying to bring it to life again. They ate bread and cheese, and downed the food with hot tea.

Later it began to rain, a downpour actually, and Felicity convinced Jared that to venture outside would produce no ill effects, swearing she had done it a hundred times, when in fact she had done it but once and that time she'd been fully clothed.

"See, it's warm. I told you," she said, as they ran into the rain. Jared in his trousers, Felicity in her chemise, it took only a second or two before they were wet to the skin. She ran ahead of him toward the path, her intent obvious. Jared caught her halfway down. Holding her tightly against him, he forced her to stop. Water plastered their hair to their heads and streamed down their faces, making it difficult to see. But Jared figured anyone spotting his wife running half-naked about the place would make the effort. "It's daytime. And anyone could see you."

"No one lives around here. Town is miles away."

"I don't care," he said, as his gaze moved over the nearly transparent garment. "I don't want you running on the beach like this."

"I thought maybe we could make love on the beach, like last night."

Jared shook his head. "Tonight. When it's dark."

"Jared," she frowned, "I never realized you were so stuffy."

Jared didn't think protecting his wife was stuffy at all and was about to tell her as much when she boldly reached for him, finding him as usual in a semihard state. A response he was helpless but to allow, for it was impossible to look at her and not know longing.

"Oh, hello," she said with a wicked grin, then, continuing on in the way of last night, she teased, "At least you're not stuffy."

"Maybe, but I'm not going to," Jared returned. "And neither are you."

Felicity, having no option but to obey this time, thought they didn't need the beach in truth. The path to the beach had been cut deep into the cliff and offered a measure of privacy as the walls on each side rose some ten feet or more above them. The ground was soft under their feet. "No one could see us here," she pointed out, just before she ran her tongue over his nipple.

Jared's breath caught in his throat. He'd once imagined, upon her discovery of the delights in store, that she might become the aggressor, the initiator in their loving moments. Still he hadn't expected this degree of eagerness. He loved it, especially since her hand reached into his trousers and gently stroked him. He was lost, and he knew it. There was no way that he could refuse her, and Jared hadn't a doubt that by the end of this promise of passion, they'd probably be in the water.

They were. Felicity had argued there was no other way to get the sand off, and Jared, looking sharply about for a sign of any intruder, allowed her her way.

They stood waist-deep, locked in each other's arms. The hem of Felicity's chemise floated to the surface, leaving her bare beneath the water. She moved her silken legs against his, unable to touch him, or love him enough.

Jared couldn't resist the soft, wet silkiness of her. His body wasn't ready yet, but that didn't mean she had to go without. Holding her bottom with one hand, her legs wrapped around his hips, he brought her near-unbearable pleasure.

Once Felicity was able to stand again, they left the water and hurried now, for the rain and wind were picking up and cooling some, leaving her chilled. Her teeth were chattering as they reached the house. No sooner had they gained entrance than a carriage turned into the drive. Jared took the opportunity to rub himself dry before the driver knocked.

Felicity stood in the kitchen as she ran a towel over her sensitized body, hurrying lest she take a chill. She pulled on one stocking and was in the midst of pulling the other up her leg when Jared came into the room.

Felicity wasn't looking at him as she smoothed the second stocking into place. She asked, "What happened? You're not going back, are you? You said . . ." Her voice drifted to a close when she glanced in his direction. Jared was obviously upset. News from the hospital couldn't be that bad, could it?

"What happened?"

"Your father. He's taken a turn for the worse. We'd better go back."

There was no need to say the last of it. Felicity had already run into the sitting room and nearly tore the dress and underthings from her trunk. She cursed as they refused to move over her damp skin. Finally she managed the chore, but Felicity never remembered dressing, or closing up the house. The next thing she knew, the carriage lunged forward, and they were on their way back to the city.

"Who sent the message?"

"Sam."

"What exactly did he say?"

"Just that Thomas had been unwell, and this morning they hadn't been able to awaken him."

"You mean he's . . ." Felicity couldn't bear to say the word. She could hardly bear to hear the answer to her question.

"No. He's still alive. But he is unconscious."

She raised pleading eyes to her husband. "Jared, I can't . . ." One lone tear escaped to trickle unnoticed down her cheek. "I don't want him to die. Please, don't let him die."

Jared took her in his arms, settling her upon his lap. Leaning her against him, he sought to soothe her fears. "I can't see how he could be worse. Weak perhaps, but not ill." He groaned at her low sob, the sound tearing at his heart. "Sweetheart, don't cry. He might be much better by the time we arrive."

"Or dead," she shuddered. "He might already be dead."

Jared shook his head. "Sam must have called for another doctor. He wouldn't just leave your father alone. I'm sure things will be fine."

Jared might have said the words, but by his tone, Felicity knew even he didn't believe it. Sam wouldn't have sent word unless things had turned desperate. "I'll make him well again, sweetheart. I swear if I possibly can, I will."

This time his words brought some comfort. If they could make it in time, Jared would see to her father's care. She'd watched him care for others, others at least as desperately ill. He'd saved them. He'd even saved her father once. She knew, if anyone could do it, Jared could.

It was late in the afternoon when they arrived. Felicity nearly flew from the carriage, never waiting for Jared's help. Before he managed to get into the house she was already up the stairs and moving into her father's room.

A man stood beside the bed. Dr. Miller. She had met him briefly at her wedding. Jared hadn't been wrong. Sam had sent for a doctor. He was listening to her father's heart as she approached. Felicity waited for him to finish before asking, "How is he?"

"He's holding on." The doctor glanced in her direction, his gaze registering and sympathizing with her concern. "I'm sorry to have called you back, Mrs. Walker, but I thought you'd want to be here."

Felicity nodded, dismissing the fact that her honeymoon had been interrupted. The inconvenience wasn't important compared to her father's life. "What do you mean by holding on?"

"It means he's fighting to stay alive, Felicity," Jared explained from the doorway, not at all happy to find his patient still unconscious. "It means the outcome is mostly up to him."

Bess turned the key in the lock. Thanks to Frank, Lilly was gone. Bess knew it would happen. She'd warned him often enough, but Frank, being a man and men mostly believing a woman couldn't prefer one of her own kind, thought to dissuade Lilly of her erroneous ways.

The house had become a pigsty since. Bess didn't much care. She came here a few times a week for one thing only, and Frank was always ready and willing to accommodate.

She smiled at her thoughts, for by the sound of it, he was in the midst of accommodating right now. She moved from the hallway to the door of the sitting room and grinned at the sight before her.

Frank had wasted no time during her absence. He wouldn't admit to it, but it looked as if Alice had moved in. Bess shrugged, unconcerned. She didn't much care who he had taken up with, as long as there was enough left over to relieve her boredom. She couldn't imagine anything worse than spending the rest of her life with her *daddy* and *sister*. Even prison would be preferable to those two. She'd only spent a few weeks in the mansion. Still, she would have gone insane if it hadn't been for these afternoon visits with Frank.

Frank had heard her enter. He looked up and grinned, but didn't for a minute stop the movement of his hands, knowing how the sight of this was bound to excite. "I was hoping you'd be able to get away."

Bess laughed, not believing him for a minute. If he'd hoped she'd show up, it was only because he was low on cash again. "But just in case, I couldn't, you thought you shouldn't grow too bored?"

"I was just getting her ready for you," he said as he played almost absentmindedly with a naked breast, while watching Bess strip off her clothes. She never came here that she didn't immediately disrobe. It was almost as if she had to shed the garments in order to leave behind the stuffy world she now lived in. And could only breathe easily again when naked.

Bess moved toward the two reclining upon the settee and spent the next hour and more delightfully entertained. It was only after all three were completely sated that Alice left the two, complaining she'd been up all night and needed a nap. She went upstairs to bed.

Downstairs Bess puffed on her pipe and sipped from a glass of whiskey. Now that they could afford the good stuff, Bess kept a bottle for herself in her room, a pipe and tobacco as well. "What were you doing that she was up all night?"

Frank shrugged. "I had a few friends in."

The only thing that bothered Bess was that she had missed out on the fun. "Bring them back tomorrow afternoon."

Frank understood. He nodded as he joined her in a drink. "So how much did you get this time?"

"Twenty pounds," she returned while stretching languidly, hoping the movement might intrigue and take Frank's mind off his question. It didn't.

He took her nipple between his thumb and forefinger and squeezed not too gently. "How much?"

"Stop it, Frank." She made to shove his hand away.

"How much did you really get?" He increased the pressure slightly.

"Twenty-five, all right?" she returned with some disgust.

Frank smiled. "That's better."

"Five pounds. For God's sake, can't I keep a shilling for myself?" The truth of the matter being, Bess was slowly amassing a small fortune. She'd given over only half of everything she had begged or stolen from Thomas Dryson. Frank had no idea. Bess suffered under no delusions. She knew he would have killed her if he had.

Frank watched her face, wondering if she were telling him the truth. Wondering how much money she really had. The cold hardness in her eyes, the tightness around her mouth, gave him not a clue.

Bess figured it was almost time to see the last of this one. After her *father* died, she'd be rich. There wasn't any way she was sharing that kind of money. It was bad enough that she'd have to share it with Felicity. Frank might be well endowed, but so were others. She hadn't seen one yet, and she'd seen plenty, that was worth that much money.

Still, for the time being at least, she'd be taking advantage of what she had. She wasn't getting anything at the mansion, that was for sure. What with Mary in residence now and those three brats of hers always underfoot, she could hardly find a minute to herself, never mind time to indulge in her greatest pleasure.

"So how's the old bastard coming along?"

"He's unconscious," she said without a flicker of remorse or guilt. "I figure it won't be long now."

Frank's eyes widened with interest at her comment. They might as well have been discussing the weather for all the emotion involved. Frank, although just about the worst possible sort, was many things, but a murderer was not among them. It was one thing to plan this, but quite another actually to do it. He couldn't help a sense of disquiet that she could so calmly talk about another's demise.

The fact was Bess didn't care about anything or anyone but herself. At first that characteristic had excited him; in truth it had drawn him to her. Now, for come reason, it repulsed. Frank shrugged aside the thought. His feelings for her didn't matter. All that mattered was the easy scam they had stumbled upon. All that really mattered was the money.

A man and woman might love or fall out of love. But in the end they would age and eventually die. The only thing that remained, the only thing that was truly important, was money.

He smiled, imagining the trip they planned to Paris. In his time he'd known a few Frenchwomen and could well imagine the delights in store. Maybe, once he got his hands on the money, he could dump this one along the way. Not that he didn't enjoy her body. He did that, but there were always others to enjoy. Others who didn't try to steal from him.

Bess smiled as she blew out a thin stream of smoke, thinking much along the same lines as her soon-to-be-ex lover. Her thoughts were just as merciless and perhaps even more selfish with a touch of murderous intent. After all if she could kill one, why not rid herself of this one as well?

Bess was imagining the men she might enjoy, the many men who would visit her establishment, for Bess had every intention of opening her own house. A high-class house. The richest, best, and most expensive house in all of Europe.

"So when do you figure?"

"I don't know. If he wakes up, I'll give him another dose. That one will finish him off."

"You should have been done with it all at once. We might have had the money by now."

Bess shot Frank a quick look of disgust and disguised the emotion with an even quicker smile. "And face all kinds of questions?" She shook her head. "No, this is the best way. He took sick. No one knows for sure why. Even the doctors are baffled." She smiled again. "When he dies no one will suspect a thing."

"What did you tell them at the apothecary?"

"That we had rats."

Bess grinned. "Yeah, we had a rat all right." She leaned over a bit and played with his limp member. It was time to get more. Enough to last her until tomorrow.

Felicity sat at her father's side, knowing only guilt. Guilt because over the last few weeks she had hardly paid him any attention at all, plans for the wedding being uppermost in her mind. Guilt because she had put her own wants before her father's health.

She heard Bess come in, but the girl did not stop by to check upon her father's welfare. A few minutes later, dressed for dinner, Bess moved into the room. She stopped at the threshold, her eyes widening with surprise. "What are you doing here?"

"Sam sent word that Father is ill."

Bess had no doubt that it would have taken something closer to a catastrophe to bring her from the arms of a man like Jared. She wouldn't have cared if the old bastard died; she would have stayed right where she was.

"Why didn't you send for me right away?"

Bess frowned. Was that accusation she heard in her voice? Above all else, she didn't want Felicity to grow suspicious. Felicity had friends, important friends. Together they could cause her a lot of trouble. "You'd only been gone a day. He said he was feeling a bit weak. I made sure he rested."

Felicity wondered at the truth of that statement. How could

he have taken so grievously ill in only twenty-four hours? Granted her father's health had not completely returned as she'd hoped it might, but he was better. She'd been certain that he was on his way to full recovery. If Felicity hadn't believed that, she never would have left. She'd only been gone a short time. What could have happened?

"Have you spoken with the doctor?"

"Yes. And he won't give me a straight answer."

Bess almost smiled at that. The doctor wouldn't give her a straight answer, because he didn't know what the hell was happening.

Felicity sighed as she leaned her head back upon the chair and closed her eyes.

"If you like, I could sit with him while you go down to dinner." Mostly, since Mary's arrival, Bess took her dinner in her room. She didn't much like to sit there and watch the lovers make eyes at each other, knowing she would have no part in the real entertainment later in the evening. But tonight an officer had been invited to dine. The officer who would be living here once Sam and Mary moved into their new rooms. Bess thought she just might enjoy her meal for a change and maybe, if she were lucky, tonight as well.

Still, she knew it was important at least to appear to care about Thomas Dryson.

Felicity shook her head and smiled tiredly. "No, I'll stay."

"I'll look in on him again later," Bess said just before leaving the room.

In the hallway Bess grinned at the sight of Jared leaving his room. "Good evening, Captain. If you're going down for dinner, I could use a strong handsome man to escort me."

Jared had kept the vigil with Felicity for most of the afternoon and evening. He'd only left to shave, change his clothes, order Felicity a bath, and then dinner to be brought to Thomas's room. He was on his way back to his wife when courtesy insisted that he respond to the woman addressing him. "I'm sorry," he shook his head, "but I'll be eating dinner up here. Thank you, for the invitation, Margaret. Perhaps another time."

Bess shrugged, *or perhaps not,* she silently returned and moved past him, eagerly looking forward to meeting the new officer. She hoped he would be handsome, then laughed at her thoughts, knowing his looks didn't matter in the least. All she really wanted was for him to be open to her advances. She'd have to stay on a little longer. She couldn't just pack up and leave immediately after Thomas died. And if she had a young officer to share her evenings with, perhaps she wouldn't be quite so bored after all.

Bess was doomed to disappointment. The officer wasn't the least bit young, nor handsome, nor acquiescent. As a matter of fact, he seemed hardly to notice her at all. Bess thought that was just fine, for she wasn't interested in the likes of him.

Just about every word that came from the man's mouth was a line quoted from the Bible. If he said Alleluia once, he said it twenty, maybe thirty times during the meal's accompanying strained conversation. And with it he added Amen, brother, or sister, whichever the case might be, to the point where Bess thought she might surely go mad.

He was tall, thin to the point of being gaunt, refused to partake of spirits and, worst of all, told plainly his intent to see to it that this home became a God-fearing place where he might rest his head.

Bess almost laughed aloud at the words, since Sam and Mary seemed to take offense, for his manner appeared to suggest the present environment was a bit less than what he might have liked.

What was he doing here? Why wasn't he wearing black rather than the uniform of one of George's best? Why wasn't he thumping his Bible at some pulpit?

As it turned out, Captain Reeves did often use a pulpit, for he was the company chaplain. Bess sighed her misery, knowing yet another long night of boredom stretched ahead and figured if she had any luck at all, it was all bad.

* * *

Felicity gave in at last to Jared's insistence. She came to her feet with a nod and walked to her father's door. "You promise to call me, if anything happens?"

"I will. And take your time. Becky won't be able to get dinner up here for some time yet."

Felicity smiled as she entered her room, her eyes widening with surprise. Jared had thought of every comfort. So she wouldn't take a chill, a small fire had been started in the grate. The brass tub, filled with warm scented water, stood before it. Her robe and gown were lying upon the bed, while fluffy towels and a glass of wine stood upon a small table, within reach of the tub.

Felicity quickly disrobed and stepped into the water. A long sigh escaped her throat as she eased into the fragrant water, thinking as she did of her husband and his sweet concern. The water felt heavenly, and the wine eased her worries long enough to enable her to think a bit more clearly.

Something had happened here. Her father was obviously ill long before her wedding and the short trip taken afterward. Now that she had a chance to think on the matter, she wondered if he hadn't been growing weaker instead of stronger as each day passed. How could she not have noticed before? How could she have been so busy? She'd hardly a moment to spare what with the men coming and going in the chimney room, the plans for her wedding, and, of course, the constant need Jared had imposed upon her, a need that had caused all but his touch, his kiss to grow less than important. She'd never noticed her father's graying complexion, his inability to stand for any length of time, his growing confusion.

She never heard the door open. Jared standing at her side whispered her name.

Felicity jumped and swung out, but Jared expecting the reaction had already stepped back. Her heart was pounding when she glared into his amused expression. "Once was enough of that, sweetheart."

Felicity never noticed his smile, nor the fact that she had swung at him in her surprise. "What happened?"

"He's coming around."

"You mean he's waking up? Oh, God, thank you," she murmured as she just about leaped from the tub, spilling water over the floor as she rushed to get dressed. She tore her gown as she pulled it over her head.

"Easy. Dry off first."

"I haven't got the time," she said, and a moment later she was in her father's room, her robe only just coming around her. "Father. Can you hear me?"

"Of course I can hear you. Do you imagine something is wrong with my ears?"

Felicity heard Jared chuckle behind her.

"What are you doing here? How long have I been asleep?" He moaned as a cramp tore at his stomach.

"You're ill. Sam called us back."

"That was a damn fool thing to do. I wasn't ill at all. You woke me up."

"You were, sir," Jared said. "You were unconscious since last night. Becky found you on the floor."

Felicity's eyes widened. Apparently Jared had spoken with Sam. This was the first Felicity had heard. "On the floor," she repeated. "Oh, Father, what happened?"

"I don't know. I can't remember exactly. I know my stomach has been giving me some trouble."

"What else?" Jared asked as he took the weakened hand in his and felt for a pulse. His eyes were on his watch as he waited for a response.

"What do you mean, what else? Who are you?"

Felicity felt her heart grow cold with fear. What was the matter with him? Why was he asking questions, questions that he should have known the answer to?

"I'm a doctor. Your symptoms? What were they?"

"My throat and mouth hurt, but I've been vomiting a bit, so I imagine that's why."

"A bit?"

"Well perhaps more. I can't remember exactly. Felicity, are you going to tell me why you woke me up? Is something the matter?"

"No, Father. Nothing is the matter. Everything is fine," Felicity managed, although she couldn't have said how, what with her heart near to bursting with terror.

Jared didn't release his father-in-law's hand even after he put his watch away. Instead he ran his fingers over the unusual scaly texture of his skin. And as he touched him, he tried to understand what it was he felt. An idea dawned. The confusion, the pain, the vomiting. Jared turned the man's hand and checked the fingernails. Streaks. Damn, there was no doubt about it. Arsenic. The man had all the symptoms of chronic arsenic poisoning.

"Felicity, I want you to get your father some water."

"There's some in the pitcher," she said without thought.

"No, we won't be using that. And I'm going to need close to a tubful. Bring a bucket at a time."

Felicity didn't understand the order, but she figured Jared knew what he was about. After all, the man was a doctor. She nodded. "I'll ring for Becky."

"Get it yourself," he said sharply. "I want no one but you to touch it. And get it from the pump outside."

Felicity frowned. She was perfectly willing to do his bidding in most every case, but not when the man spoke gibberish. What difference did it make who brought the water? Jared could see she was about to argue with him. Gently he took her arm as he said, "Can I see you outside for a minute?" Felicity had no choice but to accede to his wishes as she was nearly dragged from the room.

"What are you doing? What's the matter with him? He's so confused," Felicity asked the moment they stood alone in the hallway. "He didn't remember you at all."

"I don't want you to drink or eat anything, and I do mean anything"—he gave her a little shake as if to emphasize his words—"unless you've gotten it yourself. Do you understand?"

"No. And I think you need a doctor as much as my father. What's the matter with you?"

Jared smiled and crushed her against him. There was no way anything was going to happen to this woman. Not if he could help it. Her words were muffled against his chest. "Would you mind telling me what is happening here?"

"Felicity, your father is suffering from chronic arsenic poisoning."

"Arsenic?" She pulled out of his arms. "What does that mean?"

"It could mean someone is trying to kill him, but it probably means something has been dropped by accident into the food or water."

Felicity shook her head. "But I'm not ill. You're not ill. How could . . . ?"

"He's been in bed almost constantly since returning home. He doesn't eat with us." His look was vacant, as if the words were coming, but he was thinking of something else.

"Jared, are you sure? Maybe it was some kind of medication."

Jared knew an arsenic compound was sometimes used in cases of dysentery, but Thomas couldn't have gotten hold of such. Nothing like that would have been prescribed in any case. "Miller said he gave him no medication at all, that by the time he was called, your father was already unconscious." Jared shook his head. "His fingernails are streaked. It's the one telltale sign. And another dose just might kill him."

"Is that why he's so confused?"

Jared nodded. "Confusion is one of the signs."

"What are we going to do?"

"We're going to watch everything he eats and drinks. And it won't be anything we don't prepare ourselves.

"Right how he needs water and lots of it. We've got to flush out what poison is left."

"But . . ."

"Hurry and do what I say. I don't want him to slip back."

The last words seemed to do the trick. Felicity fairly flew down the back stairs, heading toward the kitchen and out back for all the water she could carry.

As Thomas drank from the bucket Felicity had brought, Jared left the room to get more. He, like his wife, took it directly from the pump outside, knowing there was no way that this water could have been tampered with.

"God, I'm going to drown if I have to look at another glass of water."

"Stop complaining and do what the doctor says." Felicity could see his confusion was lessening. There were no words that could have come close to explaining her relief.

"You know," Thomas said between sips. "I always thought I'd like you to marry a doctor, but I think I've quite changed my mind."

"It's too late now," Felicity said as she boldly winked at her husband.

Jared, perhaps for the first time in his life blushed. Felicity's laughter was wicked. "You're a sassy lady, Felicity."

"She is," Thomas complained. "And I'm too weak to fight her off."

"Me too," Jared willingly admitted. His warm gaze told her the power she held over him. The intensity of that look quite stole her breath, and Felicity didn't know for sure what to think. His words, his look, spoke of the things they shared, their amazing night of loving. It didn't mean more than that, she managed to convince herself. He wasn't in love with her.

"Well we can't have that, can we? Someone has to be in charge around here."

"I think Felicity can handle being in charge. She did a mighty fine job of it while you were gone, after all."

Thomas was forced to admit to the truth of it. He shrugged. "Well, there is that, I suppose."

"The young girl you left behind has grown into a beautiful young lady.

"One more glass."

Thomas shot the glass a sick look. "You said that ten glasses ago."

Jared smiled and shot Felicity a look that caused her to understand his next words clearly. "Anything is easier if you can take it one step at a time."

Felicity almost laughed aloud at the words, for they might not have been directed at her, but she knew their meaning well enough. Jared had slowly seduced her into accepting him and his loving. And he'd done it so expertly that Felicity hadn't been aware of anything but her growing need for him. He had planned his battle well, she thought, for both had gained by his patience and skill. But she would win in the end. Just like her cause, there was no way she could allow herself to lose.

Sixteen

"Arsenic? What do you mean he's been poisoned?" Bess had returned to Thomas's bedroom after dinner. She imagined it might look suspicious if she did not. They stood in the hallway now as Jared and Felicity told her of his discovery. Bess had no option, of course, but to act the innocent, even while she raged inside at being cheated of the money that was almost hers for the taking. "Where would anyone get arsenic?"

Jared noticed she hadn't ask how but where? Wouldn't asking how arsenic had gotten into the man's food be a logical first question? Hadn't Felicity asked as much?

"Actually, it's quite easy to come by. Some use it in powders, especially ladies of fashion. You can buy it at the apothecary, I think, for controlling rodents."

"And it got into the food? Will we all get sick now?" Bess thought that last remark particularly good.

"Don't worry. You haven't gotten ill yet and probably won't. Tomorrow I'll look in the kitchen and see what I can find."

For instance, a can of arsenic might have fallen into a bag of flour. Bess almost grinned at how easy Felicity was making it for her. She'd almost put the idea into her head.

It was early in the morning. Jared and Felicity had been up all night making sure her father drank every bit of the water Jared had prescribed. His coloring had improved and the abdominal pains he'd been suffering had eased quite a bit. His confusion had greatly lessened as well. After hours of flushing his system, Jared had finally allowed Thomas to sleep, for he appeared already on the road to recovery.

Felicity left her father to sleep, while greatly looking forward to her own bed. She leaned against Jared tiredly and yawned. "You're exhausted, sweetheart. Go to bed."

"Aren't you coming?"

Jared nodded. "In a minute. I want to check the kitchen first."

"Jared, you've been up as long as I have. What will it matter if a few more hours . . ."

"Others could ingest."

"No one has so far."

"What about Mary's children? They could . . ."

"Lord, I didn't think." She straightened up. "I'll go with you."

"I want you in bed, right now."

"Jared, don't order me about. I don't much like it."

"Then do as I ask, and I won't need to order you."

"You can be insufferable."

"I never said I was perfect."

"It would have been a lie, had you bothered."

Jared chuckled as he pulled her against him again. "We're arguing over nothing. If you want to look the kitchen over with me, let's go."

Jared saw it almost the instant he stepped into the room. A long high shelf ran around the entire room. On the shelf stood cans of tea, oil, and such. Directly over the sacks of sugar and flour a can lay on its side. White powdery substance had fallen from the can and it was made to look as if it had also fallen into the flour and sugar. Perhaps some had, but Jared knew better than to think this was an accident.

He'd been in the kitchen a dozen times in the last eight hours. And not one of those times had the sugar or flour sacks been open. Above them no can had been on its side. Jared was sure of it. So sure in fact that he didn't hesitate to remark, "She's good, but not good enough."

"Who?"

"Your sister."

"What are you talking about now?"

"I'm talking about this." Jared reached for the can. Sure enough it was marked as containing arsenic. Bess had planted a beautiful scene. It was too bad he knew what it had looked like before.

"You found it! Well, that relieves my mind some."

"I'm afraid it only starts to worry mine."

"Why?"

"Because she put it there."

"Who? Margaret?"

Jared nodded.

"Why would she have done such a thing. Be reasonable."

"She is the only one beside the two of us who knows about the arsenic. She did it because she thought if we saw this, we wouldn't think your father was poisoned on purpose."

"Jared, that's an awful thing to say."

Jared shrugged. "Maybe, but I'm afraid it's true."

"You cannot possibly know that for sure."

"There was no can here before."

"You didn't look before."

"How the hell could I have missed it. It was so obviously in sight."

"I don't believe it. I won't believe it. Margaret might not be all she could be, but she's not a murderess. Besides, why would she try to kill . . . ?"

"Money," he said interrupting her question. "It's the best reason there is."

"But . . ."

"Has your father added her to his will?"

"I think . . ." Felicity remembered the lawyer's last visit. "Yes, he has. But she doesn't know it."

"What makes you think she doesn't? Your father might have mentioned it."

"This is all supposition. You can't prove anything."

"And she's smart enough to know it." He brought her close against him, his hands framing her face, his fingers threaded into her long hair. "I want you to be especially careful around her. You could be next."

"Why? She has nothing to gain if I died."

Jared thought his wife might be right on that score. If Felicity died her inheritance would come to him. Still, he wasn't about to trust her half sister. "Just do as I ask, please."

Felicity smiled at his concern. "I will. I promise."

Thomas made a spectacular recovery. Within three days he was well enough to leave his bed and spend long afternoons in his garden. Granted he had to rest periodically, but it was easy enough to see that the man was very nearly his old self again.

"You shouldn't work for more than a few minutes at a time."

Thomas sighed at his bossy daughter. Without looking behind him, he said, "Felicity, I've only been at this a few minutes. Give a man some peace."

"You have been on your knees exactly thirty-three minutes. And that's quite enough."

Thomas sighed and came to his feet, brushing off his knees in the process. "I enjoy working my garden."

"I know you do and I expect to see you doing as much for years to come. If you take care of yourself, there should be no problem."

"At least it will feel like years," the man grumbled.

"Your daughter is right," Jared said, coming up behind her and hugging her around the waist. "Rest a bit, then you can get back to it."

Thomas glared at his son-in-law. "You too? I'll be happy to see a grandchild of mine. Maybe then someone in this house will be on my side."

Felicity smiled as she smoothed a hand over her stomach,

hoping for exactly that herself. She pulled his chair farther into the shadows of a tree and handed him a glass of lemonade as he sat. "We're both on your side. Stop giving us a hard time."

Jared had been called to see an ailing officer and because he was so close thought he might stop by and see his bride for a few minutes. He had to get back to the hospital. He kissed Felicity and left only minutes after he'd arrived.

"Your man loves you something fierce," Thomas remarked as Jared waved from the edge of the drive.

Felicity knew the truth of the matter. Granted they did enjoy each other's company, whether in bed, or out, but that didn't mean he loved her any more than she loved him. No matter how much they enjoyed each other, love didn't enter into it at all.

"I hope you don't nag at the man as you do me?"

"Jared does not need nagging, presently." Felicity grinned. "But if the need should arise, I'm sure I could do just as good a job of it."

Thomas laughed, his daughter chuckled wickedly. "Have you heard anything?" he asked softly, lowering his voice even though they were quite alone.

Felicity knew he spoke of the war effort. Being confined to his bed and then the house hardly allowed him to keep up with abounding rumors. She nodded. "Cornwallis is entrenched at Yorktown. Word has it de Grasse has sent twenty-eight ships of the line toward the Chesapeake Bay."

Thomas Dryson closed his eyes and breathed a sigh, "Thank God for the French. If they hadn't kept these lobsterbacks from concentrating their efforts on us, we wouldn't have stood a chance."

"It shouldn't be much longer, I think." Oddly enough, Felicity found no delight in those words. With the conflict ending, Jared would soon be on his way home. She couldn't imagine why that thought should bring about this most unsettling feeling.

"It's been years too long as it is."

Felicity couldn't help but agree with that. The sight of an English redcoat had become common on the streets of New York. Six years common, and Felicity thought their occupation had lasted long enough.

"All right, that's enough rest. If we don't get at these weeds, the garden will soon be overgrown with them."

Thomas smiled at his daughter as she took a piece of canvas. Kneeling on it, she dug into the soft, sweet earth, her father soon at her side.

If Thomas had nearly recovered from his close bout with death, the same couldn't be said for Bess. Felicity bit her lip as she entered the woman's darkened room. Her sister had taken ill a week after the arsenic had been discovered. Terribly ill. Jared's suspicions had been unfounded after all, for Bess suffered much the same as had her father.

Only not quite.

Bess had taken a small, very small quantity of arsenic. Just enough to produce some symptoms, most of which were greatly exaggerated. Just enough for streaks to form over her nails. She thought the plan absolutely brilliant. No one would think to put the blame for the poisoning at her door when she herself suffered equally as much.

"Are you feeling better, dear?" Felicity asked as she approached the bed.

"I think so. I've been able to keep my food down all day."

"Jared will be happy to hear that," Felicity said with a smile.

Bess fought aside the need to glare. Jared this, Jared that. God, she was sick of hearing the man's accolades.

The truth was, Jared wasn't so much. Granted he was appealing to look at, but one might have thought her consumed with the pox for all the impression she made on him. "Could you ask him to stop by tonight? I'd like to get out of this bed. Maybe he could give me something."

"Have you been drinking the water?" Felicity was aware of Jared's prescription.

"Yes, it helped some, but I think I need something else." She was sure she needed something else, and Jared, if he had a mind, could accommodate a lady's needs.

Later that night Jared knocked and entered her room. Bess was ready for his visit. She was naked beneath her sheet, her body perfumed and powdered, just as it always was when anticipating a man. Lying in bed, awaiting his arrival she'd grown so excited for him, she could hardly control her need. And then, thankfully, he had come.

With businesslike efficiency Jared examined her, and to Bess's distress seemed to take no notice at all of her nakedness. He moved aside the sheet, checking first her heart and then the aching muscles of her abdomen.

She lay there naked to his view and he hadn't appeared to even notice. Not, that is, until she moaned at his touch. "Does that hurt?" he asked, his hand pressing a bit more firmly to her abdomen.

"A little," she said softly, her breathing growing ragged and labored.

Jared frowned in confusion, unable for a moment to understand what was happening. She shouldn't be having trouble with her breathing. The amount of arsenic ingested had not been so great as to affect her respiratory system.

And then he felt the slight movement of her hips and looked into her eyes. It was only then that he realized what she was about. Jared knew the look of passion when he saw it. Knowing nothing but disgust, he reached for the sheet and covered her again. "The pain will lessen a bit when you're up and about again." Jared had no doubt that he spoke the truth. Once she was up and about she could find herself a man. Obviously a man was the only medicine needed here. "Don't stay in bed tomorrow. You might find that trip to your friend will take your mind off your ills."

Bess's gaze locked with the man leaning slightly over her

bed. Did he know about Frank? *No,* she thought. *If he knew, he would have said something.* He suspected how she occupied herself during the afternoons. That was all. He only suspected.

Bess thought she might never get a better chance. She didn't hesitate to run her finger up the length of his thigh, growing bolder as he neither removed her hand nor stepped away.

Jared quite easily ignored her touch. She had to be made to know, once and for all, that he held no interest in her less than subtle advances. The truth was he could do wicked things, deliciously wicked things with his wife and never once had they left him with a feeling of disgust. Compared to this one and her heavy, cloying perfume . . . well, it just wasn't possible to compare the two.

Bess cupped his sex, finding it soft and unresponsive. "You're wasting your time, I promise you."

Bess laughed, knowing men never refused what was so freely offered. She pulled the sheet from her breasts and allowed him to look his full. And when that appeared to have little if any effect, she exposed all of herself. The trouble was Bess had never associated with decent men, or women for that matter and didn't realize that many, in fact, longed not for the easy and much-used body she offered but for the sweeter more gentle and slightly wicked delight found in the arms of their lady.

She touched herself and Jared was repulsed. He most definitely did not want this woman. How much more would it take before she understood that?

His gaze was filled with contempt as he took in her lush form. She was beautiful, he wouldn't deny that, but beautiful like some poisonous flower, like some black evil death. "If you're quite finished, Felicity is waiting for me." Jared moved away from her hand, hoping this last episode would clear up any misconception she might have had on a possible relationship between them. "I'll tell my wife you sent your regards," he said, as he closed the door behind his departing form.

Jared entered Felicity's room to find her coming from her

bath. Her body was pink and well scrubbed. He could hardly wait to touch her, to cleanse himself of the disgust he knew at Margaret's touch.

Felicity looked up at the sound of her door closing. She smiled as she reached for a towel. "Back so soon? Is she all right?"

"She's fine," Jared said while shrugging out of his clothes, his gaze on the bath.

"I'll have Becky bring more water," she said, realizing her husband's intent.

"No, I want to use your water."

Felicity's eyes widened at the purpose in his voice. "But it's filled with lavender soap."

"I don't care." Jared was naked by now standing before his wife, breathing in the deliciousness that was his wife. It was lavender he wanted. Lavender he needed to surround him, for nothing but her, the texture and scent of her, would suit. "Will you join me?"

Felicity laughed. "I've already bathed."

"Please?" he asked, taking her hand in his and guiding her back to the tub.

Felicity only smiled as she acceded to his wishes. "I have a special evening planned for you."

Jared settled her between his legs. "Do you? What kind of plans did you make?"

"Well first I was going to make myself beautiful for you."

"You already are beautiful." More beautiful than any foolish mirror could proclaim, for her beauty although obvious to any eye, came mostly from within. It glowed in soft honey eyes, in healthy smooth skin, in a tender smile, in a wicked look, in a burst of girlish laughter. And without his even knowing, it had stolen his heart.

Felicity smiled. "And then I was going to order you a bath and wash your back."

"You can wash it now."

Felicity giggled, since he handed her the soap and cloth but made no move to turn his back to her. "You'll have to turn around."

"I can't. I don't want to miss a minute of this," he said as he rubbed one wet finger over the tip of her breast. "If I lean forward a bit, you could reach around me."

Felicity willingly did as he asked. And as she did, Jared played with what was so generously offered to his view. Felicity made a sound of approval at his touch. "This is very nice, but I don't think my plans are going exactly as I thought they might."

"What else did you plan?"

"Well, I thought I'd wear my robe."

"The one you need in case of fire?"

Felicity smiled and nodded.

Jared took a deep breath, feeling his sex throb with the need to take her. "And then?"

"And then we would have dinner." She glanced at the small table.

Jared followed her gaze and saw for the first time the table, lone candle, and covered dishes ready for them. The wine that was cooling nearby.

"Is there a reason behind this special treatment?"

"There is. First of all, I think you deserve this and more for what you did."

Jared frowned. "What did I do?"

"You gave me back my father. Twice you saved his life."

Jared shook his head. "I did no more than any doctor might."

"But you aren't just any doctor, are you? You're . . ." There was a moment of hesitation here when Felicity realized she'd almost said, "You're the man I love." It was a good thing she hadn't said it, for Felicity was positive she did not love him. She might love his touch, even his teasing, and sense of humor, but she did not love him. Months ago she had steeled her heart against that failing. Felicity finally finished with, ". . . my husband."

Jared watched her look of confusion and wondered what she'd

been about to say. He smiled, knowing that whatever it was he'd know soon enough. "I wouldn't have thought that you'd realize the kind of rewards a doctor might expect."

Felicity chuckled at his teasing. "A certain man has taught me a lot of late. He's a doctor, you know."

Jared nodded in understanding. "I see. He's taught you well, I must say."

"He knew what he was doing, I expect."

Jared grinned as he cupped her breasts and brought the soapy tips against his mouth. "And you were a most eager student."

"He tricked me into that, I think."

Jared glanced into eyes that were beginning to glaze over and smiled.

"He knew how to tease, how to taunt and make me want more. What did he say once? Everything is easy if you take it a step at a time."

Jared smiled. "He was right. You're married to a very wise man."

"Wise perhaps, but a little shifty, I think."

Jared laughed in delight. "I think he just used whatever weapons he had at his command. After all, you are a luscious woman, and he couldn't help but want you. I wouldn't call that shifty."

"I'm sure you wouldn't," she returned, her voice wavering just a bit as his hands left her breasts to the enjoyment of his mouth, allowing them to slide beneath the water. "Jared," she said softly as he found the bud of her passion, hard and eager for his touch. "This isn't what I wanted."

"Shall I stop?"

"In a minute," she said, giving in at last to a temptation far too irresistible to refuse.

She flowered in his hand, her body's needs taking over for the moment as she strained forward, eager for the pleasure. The tightness was there spreading across her stomach, holding it firmly in its grip, forcing her to abandon the last of herself to his wants, to both their wants.

She leaned back, unable to remain upright, unable to do anything but lose herself in the moment. Her body opened fully to his ministration and Jared delighted in the ease in which he could bring her this passion.

His hands moved over her, touching her, loving her, his fingers an extension of his heart. And then sliding into the heat of her, he felt the response he'd waited for, felt the muscles contract, and then ease only to contract again in almost painful waves of pleasure.

It took a long moment for Felicity to regain her senses. When she did she eyed him with one brow raised as if annoyed. "I hope you're satisfied."

"Not yet," Jared said honestly and with a definite leer. "But I expect to be."

Felicity laughed. "I hadn't thought we'd indulge until later."

Jared leaned back against the tub. "From this minute on, I'm in your hands. I won't do a thing until you tell me I should."

"All right, now that we've got that settled, just give me a minute."

Jared grinned and to his delight watched as she soon came from the tub, dried off, and, remaining naked, bent to see to his bath. She soaped the cloth and spread it over his chest, neck and ears. While working over him, her breasts often rubbed against his shoulder. Jared loved it.

He especially loved it as the cloth rubbed the soap down his chest. Then, discarding the cloth entirely, she dipped her hands beneath the water to bathe him as every man longed to be bathed.

Jared leaned back, helpless but to enjoy her every touch. A low moan escaped his throat, and Felicity realized she was perhaps dallying a bit overmuch. She had more in mind, much more in fact, and was loath to see the intimacy end so quickly.

"All right, you're finished. Stand up."

Jared obeyed her command and stepped from the tub, only

to find his wife with a towel in her hand. He made as if to take it from her, only to hear, "No, let me."

Jared didn't need further entreaty, for he was most willing to succumb to her sweet seduction. He trembled to be sure, but managed to keep his footing as she dried him most thoroughly and as she dried each portion of his body, her mouth was there to taste and test the scent and texture of his skin.

On her knees she dried his legs and then her mouth was suddenly against him, kissing him where he wanted kisses most. Her tongue touched upon him and ran the length of his shaft. Jared groaned again, then swore he'd do his best in the future to control these sounds, for it brought the moment to a close, a moment he might have enjoyed for some long minutes.

She dressed him in his red-silk robe, leaving the robe open and hanging at his sides. A moment later she secured the ribbons of her transparent robe under her breasts.

They weren't dressed, but they weren't naked either. Well, not exactly. And somehow their attire only intensified the already barely controlled passion. Jared swore he needed no heightening of his senses. He'd been dangerously close to losing it all the moment he stepped into this room.

Felicity smiled.

Jared swallowed. He was afraid to say anything, lest it ruin what ever might come next.

"Now you have to sit on the bed."

Jared did as he was told as Felicity brought the covered dishes to the bed. The wine was poured, the glasses placed upon the bed stand. Felicity then proceeded to feed him, occasionally washing down his food with a sip of wine.

Jared leaned back and took a sip of wine. The position was a bit awkward, and a drop or two dripped down his chest as Felicity tipped the glass to his mouth. Felicity without a moment's hesitation licked it away.

Felicity heard his gasp and then a moment later he took the glass from her fingers and dribbled a bit of the cooling liquid where he needed cooling the most. He watched the growing knowledge in her eyes for a long moment before, with a low chuckle, her head dipped and she loved him as a man could only dream of being loved.

"God," he said luxuriating in the feel of her hair across his stomach, her lips and tongue moving over his sex. "I hope your father gets sick again, real soon."

Felicity laughed, even as she raised her gaze to his and said, "Don't be mean."

"I only meant so I could cure him again."

"I know what you meant," she said between luscious delicate tastings. "And you already saved him twice."

"Twice?" Jared tried to keep his moan at bay. It was beyond his ability, only this time the sound didn't seem to do anything but stir her on to further darings. Thank God. "Oh yes, I forgot." A pulse drummed in his throat as he asked, "What kind of reward does that entitle me to?"

Felicity nuzzled her face against him. "All kinds. This is just one of them."

"You mean you might do this again?"

"I imagine I might," she said, then grinned wickedly just before she took him deep into her mouth.

Jared closed his eyes concentrating on the pleasure. "God, I can't tell you how good this feels." A few minutes went by before Jared realized he was allowing too much, that before long it would be too late, and he hadn't yet begun to do the things he had in mind. "I can't believe I'm saying this, but you had better stop."

Felicity knew what he was about, knew her ministrations had brought him close to release and like her he wanted to prolong this night of intimacy. She chuckled as she crawled up the length of him to kiss his mouth with all the fervor and care she'd used on other parts of his body. Her mouth was hot, burning hot, and Jared wanted nothing more than to lie among the flames.

He rolled her to her back, knowing this time wouldn't be good for her, and he'd wanted it to be the best ever. "I'm sorry. I can't wait," he said just before entering her pliant, ready body.

Felicity groaned, her eyes rolling back, the lids fluttering closed at the force of his thrust. Jared might have thought he'd hurt her had it not been for the movement of her hips and the nails that dug into his shoulders, urging him on, silently pleading for more.

Jared was wrong. It was good for her. She, too, tottered on the edge of madness, and it took only the right movement to send her over the edge. He felt her body convulse after only three or four thrusts, her soft wordless cry muffled beneath his lips. Jared trembled with the knowledge that he need not hold back, that she was already lost in her own release.

Jared gasped for his every breath as he lay heavily upon her, his face against her neck. "Oh God, you just about killed me, this time."

Felicity smiled and moved her hips in an upward motion toward his. Teasing his body, his mind, to dare to take her again. "I think I created a monster."

Felicity laughed. "Are you complaining?"

"I wondered if this might happen. I thought you would turn into a wanton seductress and I'd have to fight you off, lest you tamper with my virginal body."

"I haven't a doubt that you're telling me the truth, but it wasn't what you thought, it was what you hoped. Am I right?"

"Both." Jared grinned to her delighted laughter. "Do you mind if I thank you for thanking me?"

"You're welcome."

And then he remembered something. "Felicity, you said first of all. Why else are you thanking me?"

Her eyes lost the last of their passion and grew bright, almost sparkling with happiness. "I think I'm going to have a baby."

Jared felt every muscle in his body stiffen with dread. He'd been so careful. It couldn't be. Only he knew it could. His form of birth control was far from foolproof. He pulled her against him, tightening his hold until he came close to hurting her, burying his face into her throat as he begged God, not to do this to him again. He couldn't bear it this time. This time he'd die along with her.

Jared had loved his first wife, but he'd never known it was possible to love like this. It couldn't be that God would give her to him, only to tear her away. No, he wouldn't allow it. No!

And then he realized he was no doubt worrying for nothing. It was too soon. She couldn't know her condition for a fact. Jared counted back. It had been just over three weeks since their first night. Three weeks was far too soon to know anything for sure.

"So soon?"

"Well, I think so. My monthly time hasn't come and my breasts are aching a little."

Jared said nothing. There were a dozen things that could have delayed her course. Worry over her father for one. And as far as her breasts aching, Jared thought his enthusiasm might have been the culprit there. Jared prayed his silent conclusions would prove true. They had to be true.

"Aren't you happy for me? God, I'm so excited."

"Very happy, sweetheart," he said as he deposited a dozen kisses over her cheek, nose, chin and lips. "I just don't want you to be too disappointed if it doesn't happen right away. I want you to remember we have time. Plenty of time." They were going to have forever if he had anything to say about it.

"You don't seem happy, Jared. What's the matter?"

"Nothing."

"Do you think now that I no longer need your services I'll ask you to leave my bed? I won't, you know. You can stay with me until you sail for England."

Jared breathed a sigh. "No, it's not that," he said while rolling from her.

"What is it then?" she asked coming to him, snuggling up against his length.

"I should have told you this before. I was married a few years back."

Felicity's eyes widened in shock, in horror. Her body stiffened and she forgot to breathe. He was married! He was married and yet he'd married her. He was married and between them they had conceived a bastard? No, she'd kill anyone who dared to call her child that.

Felicity was about to jump from the bed, to shower this beast with her rage, her insults, when her growing rage was suddenly stilled by the thought that he had spoken in the past tense. She frowned as she asked, "You're not married now?"

He frowned at the question, having no idea the thoughts that had been careening through her mind. "I'm married to you now."

"What happened?"

"She died in childbirth."

"Oh, Jared. God, how awful."

Jared nodded as he watched the flickering light of a candle upon the ceiling, almost smiling at the understatement, almost moaning at the remembered agony. "Yes, it was that."

"Did you love her terribly?"

"No, but I did love her."

Felicity frowned at his answer. She hadn't thought there were degrees of loving. She'd always believed love was love plain and simple. That all who fell under its spell felt the same. Now, at his calm, but certain response, she could only wonder at those beliefs.

He was very silent, and Felicity thought perhaps she understood. "Are you worried for me? Are you afraid it might happen again?"

"It won't," he said, crushing her suddenly against him. "I swear to God, it won't." He rolled her to her back and glared into her surprised expression, his fingers biting into her shoulders. "I won't allow you to die. You understand me? I won't ever allow it."

"Jared, a lot of women have babies, and most don't die."

Jared nodded as he listened to her words. His soul seemed to absorb them to be forever imprinted on his heart, for he felt desperate for even the slightest reassurance. "And you won't either."

Seventeen

It had been more than two weeks since Bess's brush with death, and until this morning, Felicity believed the matter behind them at last. She had believed it until she found Fluffy's lifeless body just outside her doorway. Somehow, some way, her pet had come across yet another source of the poison.

Jared was sweetly comforting, promising her that her dog had not suffered, but had ingested a goodly amount which had brought about a quick and painless end. He didn't much believe the words himself, but thought Felicity would only suffer all the more if she knew the pain involved in arsenic poisoning.

Carolyn had come for tea that same afternoon. She sipped at the brew as they discussed Felicity's sad finding. "Have you searched everywhere? There isn't any more of it in the house, is there?"

Felicity nodded. "Jared took care of what we found in the kitchen a few weeks back, but apparently another source had been overlooked. He and Marcy are searching the rooms upstairs right now."

Felicity sighed. "There's no explanation for what happened. Father and Margaret, just the two of them. And now Fluffy. The poor little thing. He never harmed anyone in his life."

Carolyn nodded. "I know, dear," she said sympathetically, knowing there was little else she could say, for there was no way to soothe her loss. "And no one will admit to bringing it into the house?"

Felicity shook her head. "Becky and Milly swear they know nothing of the matter. Perhaps it was left behind by one of the officers. Only I can't imagine why one of them might have had it in his possession." She breathed a sigh. "When I think of the children. Lord, we could have had a catastrophe on our hands. I can tell you Mary is breathing a sigh of relief. She worries for Sam since his offices are still here, but at least the children are in no danger, now that they've found a house to rent."

"What does Jared think?"

"He doesn't know what to think. At first he thought Margaret was behind it all. Since this mess began sometime after her arrival, it would seem logical, I suppose," Felicity shook her head, never noticing Carolyn's frown, "but I knew it wasn't true. He doesn't like her very much, I think." Felicity shrugged, as if she couldn't control the likes and dislikes of those around her and had given up trying. "But of course with her taking ill, Jared had no choice but to admit she couldn't be at fault." Felicity sighed unhappily. "And now Fluffy. It has to be an accident. No one would purposely kill my dog."

Carolyn nodded, then frowned again as a picture flashed through her mind. A picture of a dark carriage moving away from her. The same picture had come often over these last few weeks, gone in an instant, slightly out of focus, it always left Carolyn with a feeling of apprehension and confusion, but more than that it left her with the most unsettling feeling that she needed to remember something. Only Carolyn couldn't imagine what that something might be.

Felicity noticed her friend's pained expression and, because she was ever on guard since the poisonings had begun, glanced at the tea and then her friend. "What's the matter? You're not taking ill now, are you? There's nothing wrong with the tea, is there?"

Carolyn smiled. "The tea is perfect."

Felicity breathed a sigh of relief. "It's getting to the point where every time I drink or eat something, I wait to see if it might have killed me." She nodded toward her friend. "For just a second, you looked like you were in pain."

Carolyn smiled. "I'm fine. Once my leg is better, I'll be perfect."

Felicity grinned. "Is that David I hear?"

"Well, he tells me that all the time. Can I help it if I'm starting to believe him?"

"When are you getting married?"

"As soon as Jared takes this ugly thing off my leg."

Felicity squealed her delight and, quickly putting aside her tea, hugged her friend tightly. "When were you going to tell me?"

"Today. He only asked me last night."

"What is this," Felicity's father asked as he stepped into the sitting room.

"Carolyn is getting married," Felicity said proudly.

"And I've come to ask if you would give me away, Mr. Dryson."

Thomas smiled at his daughter's longtime friend, a young woman who was almost part of his family. As a girl, she had been in his home more often than her own. He couldn't remember a time when Carolyn wasn't somewhere underfoot, causing mayhem and always including his daughter in her mischief. "Of course. I'd be honored."

As the three spoke downstairs about the coming nuptials, Jared and Marcy searched through the rooms above. There had to be an explanation. Arsenic had been brought into the house. Fluffy was dead from the poison, while Mr. Dryson and Bess had taken ill. There had to be a logical reason for that most illogical happening, and Jared figured that the best way to find out was to look into the matter himself.

Together they searched the rooms on the second level. Nothing. On the third level they searched as they had the second. Marcy started at one end of the long hall, Jared the other.

Jared closed the door behind him, his nose wrinkling at the

cloying scent of heavy perfume. He rubbed his nose and resisted the urge to sneeze.

His gaze moved over the room, the bed, the small tables at each side, the chest of drawers, the armoire. The answer had to be here somewhere. It couldn't be anywhere else.

Jared didn't care that Bess had fallen ill to the same poison as had her father. He figured there was no better way to ward off suspicion than to take a bit herself? She had to be the one behind the poison. Somehow he knew it in his gut. No doubt Fluffy had entered this room and come across the stuff by accident.

He had just closed the last drawer when he heard something behind him. Jared spun around and found Bess grinning. "Are you waiting for me?"

It had been uncomfortable enough to face this one every day. He hadn't wanted to get caught in the act of searching her room. Jared gave a mental shrug, knowing he now had little choice in the matter.

"Perhaps you've had second thoughts about my offer."

The memory of her touch a few weeks back still sent shivers of disgust through him. "Actually, no, I have not." Jared's words and tone couldn't have been more positive. "Where were you?" he asked, more because he couldn't think of anything else to say rather than because he cared.

"How is my coming and going any of your concern?" she asked as she removed her jacket and then started on the buttons of her blouse.

"Margaret, perhaps we should talk."

"About what?" she had her blouse off and Jared was feeling distinctly uneasy. The woman seemed to have no care that her brother-in-law was standing there talking to her. She was undressing as if she were very much alone. Hadn't she even a shred of decency?

Jared couldn't help but remember their last encounter when she had lain naked before him trying to tempt him into joining her in bed and knew of course that she had none. Still, she was

Felicity's sister and, perhaps, just perhaps he'd expected too much from the woman considering her background. Suppose he was wrong in his suppositions. Suppose Bess was innocent. Jared almost laughed aloud at that thought. Well, at least innocent of the poisonings. He should try, for Felicity's sake, to create a bit of harmony between them. It couldn't be so hard to simply be civil to one another, could it?

She was working on the skirt now, having undone the tabs she allowed the material to fall to the floor. Jared frowned, wondering what her game was? Did she think to walk around her room in her underwear while he was present? Did she think he would stay and watch this show, even knowing he couldn't stand her?

And then Jared suddenly realized her game. She was purposely trying to get him to leave. Trying to get him to run, in fact. And there could only be one reason why. Obviously there was something here she didn't want him to see.

"Where is it?" he asked, all forms of supposed civility now abandoned.

"Where is what?" she asked, unable to hide the flash of fear in her eyes.

Jared grinned, watching as she controlled her fear. Had he any doubts, that look, that momentary slip had just cured him of them. "I know you poisoned Thomas, and probably took the arsenic yourself, no doubt to throw suspicion off."

"You're insane." It was all that stupid's dog's fault. If he hadn't been in her room putting his nose in places it did not belong, all would have soon relaxed their guard and she would have been able to finish Dryson off with one massive dose. Now she'd have to wait again. Wait for this scare to be over, but first, before he found the incriminating evidence, she had to get him out of her room.

"Am I? Then why are you undressing? Could it be you have some left and don't want me to find it? Could it be you thought I'd run, leaving you the opportunity to dispose of it?" Jared laughed, for they both knew her act hadn't worked. "You should have gotten rid of it right away, Margaret. You shouldn't have waited." He smiled. "But perhaps you were hoping for yet another opportunity."

Jared had hit the truth on the mark, only she couldn't tell him that. Bess had no choice but to play the innocent.

"There's nothing here. You're wasting your time."

"I don't think so. Is it in the closet, Margaret, behind some little trinket perhaps?" Jared opened the closet and blinked at the large candlesticks. The silver candlesticks that had formerly graced the dining room table. Jared laughed. "Well, well. A thief as well as a whore and murderess. Who would have thought?"

"I didn't put them there." Bess felt cornered, and would have done anything or said anything to get out of this. The arsenic was under her mattress. He couldn't find it. There was no way that she could let him find it.

"Of course not. Becky probably did that. No doubt she brought them up here to be polished." His voice dripped sarcasm. "Or have you thought to earn your keep by taking on polishing the silver?" Jared shot her a look of disgust, knowing she lived the life of leisure and wouldn't have thought to lift a finger to help out around the house. "I have no doubt she brings all the silver up here." And then as if to himself he asked, "I wonder what else is missing from the house."

"No, I . . . I . . . needed light. I couldn't see when I went downstairs the other night. It was very dark, so I took . . ."

"Two candelabras?" Jared chuckled at the thought. "It must have been dark indeed."

"It was all I could find. Jared, please, you've got to believe me."

"You said you didn't put them there."

"What I meant was, I knew what you would think, and I didn't steal them."

Jared laughed. He knew her for the liar she was, but he'd rarely heard lies told in so poor a fashion. Clearly she was desperate. He continued his search.

Jared saw the small bag in the back of the closet. He took it out and emptied it. He laughed at the articles that fell to the bed. Among them were Felicity's watch, most often worn pinned to the bodice of one of her gowns, a small bottle of perfume, a necklace of exquisite perfectly matched pearls, and the cameo he'd given his wife on their wedding night. A diamond hatpin, emerald earrings, and silk scarves finished the collection of obviously stolen articles.

Jared glanced at Bess, knowing some little surprise to find her wearing only her drawers and stockings, her breasts naked to his view. He shouldn't have been surprised of course, for she had exposed herself to him on more than one occasion. She wasn't the least bit self-conscious about her half-naked state, and he didn't doubt that she often exposed herself to men. He shrugged aside the thought, completely unconcerned. "I imagine you needed these for light as well?"

Bess knew the game was up. There was no way that she could deny having Felicity's personal items in her possession. She might say she had no idea how they had gotten there, but the chance she'd be believed were little to none. There was only one way to extradite herself from this sticky mess. One tried and true way.

She moved toward him. "All right, I took it," she said. "I needed money."

"I'd say you needed quite a lot of money, by the looks of it."

"It's Frank. He made me do it." Bess had practiced this often enough. Tears glistened, then streamed down her lovely face. "I swear, I never would have done it except that he said he'd kill me if I didn't get him money."

Jared watched her carefully, not trusting anything she said or might do. "Put your clothes on."

"Look," she said turning her back to him. "Look at what he did to my back."

Jared looked over the many scars running the length of her back, but noticed right off that they were old scars. She'd been beaten, he hadn't a doubt, but not for a long time.

"Where did you get them really? Did one of your customers like it rough?"

Jared was closer than he knew to the truth. Terrified that she'd gone through these weeks of stifling boredom all for nothing, almost able to see all that lovely money slipping from her hands, Bess tried another tack. "Jared, we can work this out. I promise I won't take anything else. All right?"

"I'm afraid it's not all right."

"And I'll make restitution. I swear it."

"How? By using your trade?"

She shrugged, knowing it was useless to deny his accusation. "Men pay well for the pleasure I bring them. I could show you if you like, Jared. I could show you how much men want me. How they liked to be touched. I know all the tricks."

"I'm sure you do. Get dressed."

"They love to touch these." She lifted her breasts for his inspection and Jared, a man who particularly enjoyed the sight of a woman's breasts, experienced only a slight sense of nausea. "Touch them. You'll see, you'll love it to."

"I want you out of here today. Felicity thinks you're a decent, normal person."

"Felicity is a fool. With those ladylike ways of hers, she wouldn't know the first thing about making a man happy. I could . . ."

"Shut up!" Bess was wrong on that score. She couldn't have been more wrong, in fact, for Jared had never known such happiness even existed. His voice lowered to a whisper as his eyes glared his distaste. "Here's my offer. Get out today and never let me see your face again."

"And . . . ?" Bess prompted wondering what he might suggest she'd gain by her efforts.

"And I won't tell anyone about your being behind the things missing around here."

Bess felt panicked, her voice raised far louder than it should have. "And I'm to get nothing?"

"I think you've already gotten more than you deserve.

Thomas will no doubt continue your allowance. It might be enough to set you up in rooms of your own."

Except for Dryson, she'd never hated anyone in her life. For what had become of her mother, she'd hate him forever, for she held him personally responsible, believing her mother would never have turned to others if Dryson would have kept her for himself. But even the hatred she knew for that selfish old bastard didn't compare to the emotion she now felt. If it were possible, Bess would have killed this one on the spot.

Jared never noticed the door open, but Bess did. She caught a glimpse of Felicity's blue skirt just before she buried her face in her hands, her quick mind taking in the coming scene and using it to her best advantage. She was going to take care of this one and eventually, she'd get the old man as well. This son of a bitch hadn't an inkling of who he thought he was threatening.

Jared only frowned for the sudden gloating in her eyes seemed totally out of place. But what was even more out of place were her next words. "Jared, please. We have to stop this. I love you, but you have to stop coming up here." She produced one perfect theatrical sob, and then, "Felicity is my sister. I don't want to hurt her."

Jared was still frowning as Bess lifted one side of her mouth into a smirk, the side that couldn't be seen from the doorway. It took him only a moment to realize they were no longer alone. His gaze moved from Bess to the doorway to see Felicity, Thomas, and Carolyn, all standing there, silent and obviously dumbfounded.

He understood then what the woman was about. She'd noticed seconds before he that the door was opening. It was her chance to get even, he supposed and she was giving it her best shot.

Jared forgot the others. His gaze moved to his wife, his dark eyes pleading with her to believe not what she saw, not what she heard, but his silent denial. Of course it was a useless endeavor. Especially when Bess gasped and reached for her discarded chemise, as if she'd only just now noticed the intrusion.

Especially since her face became a picture of suffering and guilt. Especially when she said those final damning words, "Oh, Felicity, I'm so sorry. Jared said you'd never find out and I . . . I didn't want to do it. I swear I didn't."

Felicity looked from her sister to her husband. She watched him for a long moment, remembering how he had pressured her. How she had so thoroughly enjoyed that pressuring. How she too hadn't been able to resist. And that she supposed was the one damnable fact. The man was irresistible. "Yes, when he puts his mind to it, none of us have much of a chance, do we?"

Jared never said a word in his defense as Felicity suddenly turned and left the room. A moment later Carolyn, with the aid of her cane, and Mr. Dryson followed suit.

The door closed behind them, leaving Jared alone with a woman and a rage that was very nearly out of control. Carefully, very carefully, lest he do her in on the spot, Jared waited for the worst of the emotion to pass. Silence filled the room. Terrible deadly silence. And Bess was beginning to think she just might have pushed this one a bit too far. He walked toward her, absolutely expressionless. It was that lack of expression that instilled terror in her heart.

Jared backed her against the wall, only he didn't stop there. His hand reached for her throat and he lifted her from the floor as if she weighed nothing, putting most of his weight behind his hand, it totally closed off her ability to breathe.

She dangled there, her face growing blotchy, her lips holding just a trace of blue, her eyes huge as she fought an impossible task. She clawed at his hand, but she might not have bothered. There was no way that she could breathe. And until he was ready, no way he would let her go. Her face was even with his as he leaned just a bit closer and whispered menacingly, "You bitch." He applied a bit more pressure and smiled as he watched the terror grow in her eyes. He'd crack her neck for sure and there wasn't a thing she could do to stop him. "I could kill you right now and no one would give a good damn." He took a deep breath as he struggled to resist the temptation. "If you're still here in one hour, I swear before God, I'll do it."

With that he dropped her to the floor. Jared never glanced at her crumpled form. He never heard her choking and gagging as he swooped Felicity's things from the bed and gently closed the door behind him.

He ran down the stairs. There wasn't an instant to lose. He had to talk to Felicity. He had to explain before she came to believe the things she'd seen. Jared entered her room, with such force that her door smashed to the wall behind it.

Felicity sat at her dressing table, staring into the mirror, seeing nothing, but the lies, knowing nothing but the pain that tore through her heart. She tried to breathe regularly, but there was some sort of constriction in her chest. And for some insane reason, agonizing pain. Felicity frowned wondering why that should be? Surely she wasn't suffering because of the scene she'd walked in on. Felicity almost laughed at the thought. She wasn't hurting because her husband and sister were having an affair. She couldn't be. Suffering would mean she loved him and she didn't. Luckily for her, there hadn't been time to grow to love him.

She'd been surprised, was all. She hadn't expected him to be faithful. She knew men and wouldn't expect faithfulness of any one of them. It was just that she'd thought he'd wait awhile before turning to another. It was just that he touched her so gently, loved her so sweetly, she'd thought . . . Well, she couldn't help but think . . . Felicity jumped as the door to her room crashed open.

Jared stood very still, not knowing for sure how to begin, not knowing what to say. How was he to convince her that it had all been lies. Not them, not the things they had done together, but the woman upstairs. God, please, he silently prayed, begging for the wisdom, for the right words. "My dear . . ."

Felicity turned in her seat, her lips growing into a wide smile, a smile that never touched her eyes. He'd never seen eyes so empty of all but sadness and felt his heart twist in pain, in fear that he might lose her. "Actually, Jared, it's getting late and I thought I would change for dinner. We could talk later if you wish." Her voice couldn't have been more steady, her smile more serene.

"Now, Felicity."

She was as cold as ice. How was he supposed to convince her of anything when he was positive he hadn't a chance of even being heard. "Will you listen?"

"Of course." She smiled that smile again, came from her chair, and proceeded to search through her closet as if her life depended upon finding something suitable for dinner.

Jared took a deep breath, holding to almost no hope as he began. "Have you noticed things missing? Your watch, your pearls, and emerald earrings? The cameo I gave you?"

"Yes, well now that you mention it, a few things are missing," she said almost absentmindedly.

"I was searching Margaret's room for the arsenic."

Felicity nodded, but said nothing.

"I found this in her closet." Jared dropped the items on her bed. "She's been stealing things from the house probably since the first day she got here."

Felicity glanced at the articles, and shook her head, while a long sigh preceded, "Isn't that sad?"

"It's hardly sad, Felicity. What it is, is criminal."

"It's sad because she thought she had to steal things in order to have them, when Father would have given her anything she needed."

"Are you saying you feel sorry for her?"

"Of course. Don't you?" Felicity thought that question over for a second before she realized she shouldn't have asked. "I'm sorry. You wouldn't, of course. I imagine it's other things you feel for her."

"You're right about that, and hatred tops the list."

"Now, Jared, if you're talking about what happened upstairs, there's no need for you to be upset. I apologize for barging in like that. It was entirely my fault." Her heart was breaking. No it wasn't!

"What the hell are you talking about, barging in?"

"Well, we heard voices. It sounded like an argument, and I didn't think to knock." Had she ever known such pain?

"Felicity, my God," he groaned with building fear. How could she be so calm. Could it be she truly didn't care?

"We both knew this marriage wasn't a permanent affair. Believe me, I don't blame you. I know men and their desires. I understand." It took all of her strength to say those words. Had anyone ever hurt like this before?

"You don't understand a damn thing. I do not desire anyone but you."

Felicity smiled that fake smile again. "Thank you, that was very sweet. Now, if you'll excuse me, I'd like to dress."

Jared repeated sarcastically, "That was very sweet. All right, let's see if you think this is sweet. Your sister took off her clothes believing it would distract me from searching her room."

"Why are you telling me this? I promise you, it doesn't matter."

"It bloody well does matter. She tried to seduce me, thinking if I enjoyed her charms, I wouldn't give her away. You can ask Marcy, if you don't believe me. He saw me practically kick her out of my room on one occasion. I've never had a thing to do with her. The damn woman makes my skin crawl."

"Jared, this is very unkind of you."

"Right, a gentleman never tells, is that it?"

Felicity shrugged.

"All right, don't believe me then, but you might as well add this to your list of things not to believe. I love you. I have no intentions of going back home. I'll be staying on here indefinitely."

Felicity shook her head. "That wasn't the plan."

"To hell with the asinine plan. I love you. Do you hear that? Do you understand that?"

"Yes."

"So what are you going to do about it?"

"Nothing."

"Nothing? I don't . . ."

"The plan was to marry, to get me with child, and for you to leave. I'm sorry if you've fallen in love."

"Tell me you haven't done the same."

"You know I haven't." Felicity wondered if she was telling the truth. If she didn't love him, then why was her chest threatening to explode, why did she feel this agony? It was shock, is all. It was just shock. She didn't love him. She wouldn't love him.

"Damn you, Felicity. You're ripping my heart out with your pride. Admit that you love me!"

"I'm sorry. Truly, I am."

Jared took a deep breath. "No, you're not. You're not sorry at all. What you are is a little coward. You're hiding behind that wall you've built around yourself, so as not to get hurt. You're afraid, afraid to really live, afraid to take the chance."

"Jared, I'd really like to dress." She glanced at the clock on her dresser. "I'll be late."

Jared sighed and ran his fingers through his hair in frustration. "All right," he forced a calmness he was far from feeling, "let's assume I did have an affair. As far as you're concerned, it wouldn't have mattered, am I right?"

"You are."

"Because, as you say, this marriage was only temporary anyway. Correct?"

"Yes."

"So why would I lie? What gain is there for me if I tell you I didn't when I did?"

"Perhaps you thought to keep our arrangement amicable during your stay."

"Meaning I might insist on my husbandly rights?"

"You might, but I can tell you now, you'd be wasting your time."

"You know, I went along with this plan because I thought eventually things would work out between us . . ."

"And they have."

Jared ignored the interruption. "I thought I could convince you to love me. Only I think now that you haven't the capacity. Some people are like that, I expect. Some just haven't got what it takes and it looks like you're one of them."

"When was the last time you caught me in a gentleman's chambers, while that gentleman was half-naked?" She laughed again, this time the laughter was hard, bone-chilling hard. "You might be right, Jared. Perhaps I don't know how to love, but I do know one thing. I'm better off for it."

"Better off living out your life alone? I doubt it."

"Better off living it with no pain."

Jared said nothing more, but walked out of the room, slamming her door behind him. It was the second time in less than fifteen minutes that he'd left behind a woman crumpled to the floor, gasping for her next breath as pain tore through her chest.

Felicity, so engrossed in that pain, never heard the hobbling footsteps, aided by a cane. The only sound in the room was the ticking of her clock and Felicity's stifled sobs of misery. Suddenly Carolyn entered Felicity's room, again smashing the door against the wall. "I remember. I finally remember," she announced, in her excitement she'd never thought to knock. An instant later she gasped as she saw her friend on the floor. "What happened? What's the matter?"

Felicity wiped her eyes and crawled to her knees. She managed to stand, but only for as long as it took to reach her bed. She sank upon it. "What do you want?"

"Why were you on the floor?"

"I fell."

Carolyn moved closer and inspected her friend's face as she sat at her side. "You're crying. Why? Surely you didn't believe that little scene upstairs."

Felicity sniffed and wiped at her eyes with the dress that she'd taken from the closet and held crumpled in her hands. "It doesn't make any difference."

"What doesn't? That the little hussy was trying to seduce your husband? Do you mean that you don't care?"

"That's exactly what I mean," Felicity said, lifting her chin and straightening her shoulders.

"I think you'd better tell me what's going on."

It took some prodding, but Felicity finally blurted out the truth. The reason for the marriage, her and Jared's relationship, their most recent confrontation, her belief that he would have cheated eventually anyway and that it was better this way. At least it was all over.

There was a moment of silence before Carolyn said, "You little fool."

Felicity shot her friend a dark look of warning. "If you want to remain my friend, I think you won't call me that again."

"If I weren't your friend, I'd probably have slapped you." Carolyn sighed. "I can't believe this. The man told you he loves you and what do you say? 'I'm sorry?' Are you mad?" Carolyn took a deep breath. "Women have killed for a lesser man than that one. Felicity, wake up and listen to me. Don't let him get away. You'll never forgive yourself.

"He's not involved with Margaret."

"How can you know that?"

"Think a minute. When you stand half-naked in the same room with him, does he remain at least ten feet away?"

"Well, no, I suppose . . ."

"Do his eyes remain clear, or do they fill with passion, perhaps grow a little glazed, while you work your wiles?"

Felicity frowned. "Who said I work . . . ?"

Carolyn, having had a bit of experience herself over the years, knew the look of passion in a man's eyes and had found nothing resembling the emotion in Jared. "Do they?" she insisted.

"Well, I suppose."

"Remember his eyes, Felicity. Remember the disgust in them?"

Felicity shook her head. She hadn't actually noticed his eyes. All she could remember was the sight of her sister, her half-naked state and the tears. "I don't know."

"Well, I do. He wasn't excited. A man cannot deny his excitement. It only takes a glance, and one can see that for a fact."

"It doesn't matter."

"What does that mean?"

"It means he would have cheated eventually. It's just as well that it's happened now. It would have been terrible if I had loved him."

"And, of course, you don't love him." Carolyn sighed dramatically. "I'm sure you're right about that. Why as far as I can remember, I've never seen two people less in love."

"There's no need for sarcasm."

"There's every need as far as I can tell."

Felicity did not want to talk about love. She did not love her husband. It didn't matter what Carolyn believed. "Why did you come in here?"

It took Carolyn a second before she realized the subject had been changed, "Oh yes, that. I remembered."

"What?"

"Ever since awakening from that accident, I've been getting flashes of memory. One particular picture would come to me at the most unsuspecting times. It was something about the cab, something I couldn't remember. And then after we walked in on Jared and that little bitch, it all came back.

"Not right away of course. At first I was probably as shocked as you."

Felicity truly doubted the possibility.

"But after you left, for just a second I saw the look of victory in her eyes and then it all came back. It was the look that did it, I think."

Felicity frowned. "What came back?"

"The picture of the cab, the window in the rear and the woman's face. I saw a woman in the cab that hit me. She turned in her seat as I lay upon the ground. She looked back at me. It was that same exact look, and then she tipped her head back as she laughed. The woman was Margaret."

Felicity gasped, her fingers coming to her lips, her shock clear in her rounded eyes. "No!"

"Yes."

"Maybe you only imagined . . ."

"I imagined nothing. I saw her face as clearly as I'm seeing yours."

"My God."

Carolyn laughed as she jumped from the bed. She limped around the room a bit as she spoke. "I've already told Major Wood. He's sending for the authorities. She'll be in prison by dark."

"I don't think so," Jared said from the doorway. "She left just after you ran up the stairs."

"Left?" Carolyn asked as Felicity's gaze locked with his. How much had he heard? Had he been there when she told her story and listened as Carolyn called her a fool? Had he heard her less-than-emphatic denial when accused of loving him?

Jared nodded sadly, his gaze never leaving his wife's face. She'd been crying. That had to be a good sign. At least he hoped to God it was. Her tears had to mean she cared. He wouldn't rush her, he swore. If she cared just a little, it would be enough for now. "I'm afraid I'm at fault here. I sort of persuaded her that her evil face wouldn't be a welcome sight if I saw it after an hour. I was a mite upset at the time."

Carolyn laughed. "I imagine you were." She shrugged. "No matter. The authorities will find her. Mr. Struthers has her last address. I hope she enjoys the little freedom she has left."

Eighteen

Bess ran into the small house and sighed her disgust at the sight of mostly naked men and women lounging about, enjoying the entertainment. Not now. She hadn't the time now. Damn Frank and his parties.

Where the hell *was* Frank? She had to get him and their money and make herself scarce for a while. She moved quickly up the stairs. The two rooms upstairs were occupied in much the same fashion as those below; Frank was in one of them.

"What are you doing back?" he asked, coming from the bed as another man quickly took his place. He grinned as he noticed her clothes. "And why are you dressed?"

"I need the money right away."

"What happened?"

"I've been found out." Bess touched the marks on her throat. "I was asked to leave. And none too gently I might add. The bastard." She spat the word out in disgust, while silently swearing she'd get even.

"What? With nothing?"

Bess nodded, her eyes wide with fear. "The bitch found out. The one we ran down. She remembers."

Bess had not been privy to Carolyn and Felicity's conversation, but she had heard the report given to Major Wood as she moved silently down the stairs. Thankfully she'd been able to sneak out the door before they saw her.

Frank cursed long and hard as he searched the room for his

clothes. He was shoving his legs into his trousers when he asked, "Now what?"

"What are we going to do?" Bess asked.

"First, we get out of here. I have to think."

An hour later Frank and Bess sat on a squeaking bed in a rented room, counting all the money they had between them. All the money he was aware of, at least. It came to less than a hundred pounds. Frank threw the pound notes down and sighed his disgust. "We should have had more than this."

"We might have if you didn't have a party nearly every day."

"I had the parties for you. You're the one who said you were bored."

"All right, yelling at each other won't help matters. We've got to come up with something. We'll have to get out of the city soon. The Drysons have too many powerful contacts."

"You got any you didn't tell me about?" Frank asked, his gaze narrowing with suspicion as he looked at her and her carpetbag and back again.

"I told you . . ."

"I know what you told me, but let's take a look in that bag, just to be sure."

"All right, so maybe I did put a little away. It's a good thing I did, isn't it?"

"How much?"

"Two hundred."

Frank grinned as he made himself comfortable on the bed. His hands were locked under his head as he stared at the water-stained ceiling above. "All right, that gives us three hundred pounds. Enough to book passage to the islands. And then later we'll make our way to France."

Bess sighed at the thought of getting out of this city. She hadn't realized until this very minute just how frightened she'd been. "That sounds like a good idea."

"Or," he said, leaving whatever he was about to say unfinished as an idea began to form.

"Or, what?" Bess prompted when he didn't appear of a mind to go on.

"Or we could wait here, in this room for things to cool down."

"And?"

"And in the meantime maybe we could come up with a plan. A plan that might leave us richer than either of us have ever imagined."

"What are you talking about?"

"How much is Dryson's daughter's life worth?"

Bess laughed. "You're asking the wrong person. I wouldn't give you a shilling for her."

"But Dryson would. He'd probably give us more than a million shillings. Maybe even a million pounds."

"What? You want to kidnap her?"

"What do you think? It's worth a try."

"He doesn't have a million pounds."

Frank frowned. "Everyone knows he's a millionaire."

"Yes, but his money is in property and ships as well as that big house. He doesn't have a million pounds sitting in his desk drawer." Bess knew that for a fact, for she had personally investigated those drawers. The man had no more than fifty pounds on hand at any given time.

"Maybe not in his drawers, but he has it. How much do you think we can get?"

"Maybe a thousand, I don't know."

"You're not thinking big enough. How much would you give if your only daughter's life were in jeopardy?"

Bess shrugged as she began to disrobe. "Ask me after I have a daughter."

"All right, we'll think that part over later. Right now, I've got to find someone I can trust. We can't do this by ourselves."

"If we don't, then we'll have to share the money. I don't want to do that."

"Greedy little bitch you are, Bess." He said the words almost lovingly, well with at least as much love as his stunted emotions allowed.

Bess laughed, knowing the truth of that statement. They didn't come any greedier.

Back in the house on Lexington, Mr. Dryson, Mr. Struthers, Felicity, and Jared, as well as a group of officers met and spoke for most of one hour. Just before the meeting, the records at City Hall had been opened, at this late hour, thanks to Major Wood's order.

It was determined, during the conversation, that Margaret Rhodes was in fact Bess Rhodes, Margaret's half sister. That Margaret was dead, that she had died, according to the city's records, within a few days of her mother. That Bess Rhodes had been living with a certain Frank Stoltz, before arriving here, and that Mr. Stoltz was a small-time crook. Deferring to the lady present, they did not mention the word "pimp," but said that he oversaw a few women and collected from these women a portion of their nightly wages. Apparently Bess had at one time been his most popular attraction. Felicity understood.

They did not mention that the rest of the women on the whole were a sorry-looking lot and, to date, Mr. Stoltz had not done well with his endeavor. They did mention his last venture into business, that being an insurance scam. For he'd threatened more than one shopkeeper for a monthly payment lest they find their businesses suddenly destroyed by vandals or fire.

"Meaning he would destroy the business if he wasn't paid?" Felicity had never heard anything so cold-blooded.

"I'm afraid so, ma'am," an officer returned, his blue gaze warm and appreciative as it moved over Felicity's face.

The meeting was breaking up. A warrant would be issued for both Bess Rhodes and Frank Stoltz. The men were leaving. The officer who had looked so kindly upon Felicity appeared to linger for a moment, obviously wishing a word with the lady.

Jared at her side, instinctively placed his hand on hers. Felicity allowed the possessive action without thought. She never noticed their fingers intertwined, for her mind was on matters other than the man at her side.

The officer noticed. His gaze moved from the two hands to Jared and his look clearly told Jared he was a lucky son of a bitch. Jared only smiled, wishing, or hoping he truly was.

As it turned out, Jared had a way to go before he could consider himself lucky.

It was late. Jared had remained downstairs talking with Sam. He had locked up after Sam left for the night.

Felicity was in her room, undressing for bed, when the door opened. She had only gotten so far as to remove her shoes and stockings when she blinked in surprise as Jared stepped inside. "Yes?"

"Yes, what?"

"What are you doing here?"

"I'm getting ready for bed. What else would I be doing here?"

She shook her head. "Jared, I thought you understood."

"You're married to me."

"Perhaps, but not for long."

"Forever. We might as well get that straight right now."

"We might as well get this straight, you mean," she returned taking two steps toward him, then realizing the danger standing too close might entail, took another back. She glare at him. "I don't want you here. And I won't be staying married to you."

"The fact of the matter being, you are my wife and your wishes hardly enter into the matter."

"Fine," she said, watching him throw his clothes around her room. "If you won't leave, then I will."

She walked toward the door, only to find herself suddenly lifted and thrown through the air. She landed upon the bed with a bounce. Jared looked at her for a long moment, knowing it was going to take time, perhaps a lot of time. He only prayed he had what it took to wait, to convince her to see to his way of thinking. Finally he breathed a long sigh as he said, "You win." And without another word, walked out of her room.

Felicity never realized how very long a night could be. She watched the candle burn down. She watched the darkness, she watched the sun rise in the morning. And never closed her eyes longer than it took to blink.

She looked awful the next morning, only it didn't matter. She wanted to look awful. Perhaps if she looked bad enough, the man would leave. Perhaps then she could resume her life. Perhaps then she might find some peace.

Felicity left her father to his meal and ran up the stairs, hoping she'd make it in time. The door had just closed behind her when the first heave assaulted. With her hand pressed hard to her mouth she finally reached the chamber pot, and her stomach emptied the few bites she had taken of her morning meal.

Felicity groaned at the weakness that enveloped as she sat upon the floor of her room. The nausea had eased, but had not completely abated. Every morning. How much longer would this go on?

Felicity thought she'd visit a midwife today. She knew she was going to have a baby. Her earlier suspicions had proved true. What she needed was to know what she might expect during this time. What she needed was to feel a measure of safety.

Carolyn knew Mrs. Adam's address. She'd visit with her friend this morning and get it.

Felicity smiled as a servant answered her knock. "Hello, Alice, is she in?"

The servant nodded and glanced up the stairs.

Felicity, very much at home in Carolyn's house needed no one to guide her, nor a formal announcement of her arrival. The two women came and went in each other's homes as if they

belonged there. Felicity knocked and without waiting for a response, entered Carolyn's chamber.

Carolyn was lying upon her bed, with Jared leaning over her,
examining her leg. Apparently he'd just removed the splint, and
judging by the look in Carolyn's eyes, she couldn't have been
happier. "I was going to surprise you today. How do you like
it?" Carolyn asked as she raised her leg a bit and displayed the
smooth line of bone as well as the small scar where the bone
had broken through the skin. "He did a wonderful job of it
didn't he?"

"A wonderful job," Felicity said a bit glumly, obviously unhappy to have encountered Jared. It had been three weeks since
their last confrontation. They had hardly seen one another since,
with the possible exception of passing on the stairway or in
coming and going at Felicity's front door.

Jared worked late, and most always missed the evening meal,
while Felicity purposely stayed in bed until after he left the
house in the mornings.

Her evenings were spent visiting friends or in her room, reading. She made it a point, an obvious point, Jared couldn't help
but notice, to avoid him at every opportunity.

Jared had thought to give her some time, but as far as he
could see he was accomplishing nothing by being patient. All
his efforts had managed to date was to further their estrange-
ment. It was time, he thought, to see to the end of this separa-
tion. Well past time.

Jared studied her face as she spoke with her friend, doing her
best to ignore his presence. She hadn't been sleeping well, he
thought. There were smudges under her eyes, and she appeared
wan and tired. And then his gaze moved from her face to her
small frame. She'd lost some weight, he thought, although the
loss had not lessened any of her curves. In fact, because her
waist appeared smaller than ever, her breasts seemed empha-
sized as they were even more full, more tempting. He couldn't
imagine how he had managed to stay away from her, especially
at night, knowing she slept one door from his. This rift between

them was driving him mad and, according to his coworkers, had not improved his sense of humor in any marked degree.

Jared promised himself it would soon be over. There was no way that he was going to wait much longer, perhaps not even beyond this very night.

Carolyn came to a sitting position and with Jared and Felicity on each side of her managed to limp around the room, trying out her newly healed leg. "Use the cane for a bit," Jared suggested. "You'll know when you don't need it anymore."

Felicity fetched the cane, and Carolyn smiled as she walked on her own and without splints for the first time in weeks.

"Let me know if it gives you any problems," he said as he gathered his supplies and replaced them in his bag.

He looked at Felicity for a long moment, his gaze studying her every feature as if he couldn't get enough, as if he'd never get enough. "I'll see you at home tonight," Jared said just before he walked out of the room.

"Wow," Carolyn said, "that was something, wasn't it? What do you imagine he meant by that?"

Felicity didn't want to think what he meant and decided he meant nothing at all. "I don't know what you mean."

"I mean, the way he looked at you and what he said. It was almost a promise."

Felicity tried to laugh, but the sound came out more a garbled groan. "You're imagining things."

"I take it you two have not reconciled."

"I told you there was nothing between us." She shrugged. "Nothing real, in any case."

"It looked real to me."

Felicity smiled, and perhaps for the first time since entering this room with some feeling. "That's because you are a hopeless romantic."

Carolyn grinned. "I can't believe it. Two more days, and he'll be mine forever. Did you get the alterations done on your gown?"

Felicity nodded. "I finished them last night."

"You should eat more. I don't think it's good for you to lose weight now."

The thought of food almost sent Felicity searching for Carolyn's chamber pot. "Please," she swallowed. "Don't talk about it."

"Does Jared know?"

Felicity shrugged, not at all happy to talk about Jared. "I mentioned the possibility some time back."

"But he doesn't know for sure."

"I don't even know for sure."

Carolyn laughed at that comment. "Have you seen anyone yet?"

"No, that's why I came here today. I thought you might give me Mrs. Adam's address."

"Felicity, your husband is a doctor and you're going to a midwife?"

"I want a midwife," Felicity said, leaving Carolyn no room for argument.

The two visited for an hour or so, talking about the wedding that was to take place the day after tomorrow, and the wedding trip that would follow. Carolyn could barely control her anxiousness, her joy, while Felicity centered her thoughts not on the flimsy devotion of a man, but on the baby she would soon hold in her arms. The real and only constant love of any woman's life.

Felicity returned home at teatime, her spirits greatly lifted. All was well. She was about three months into her term. In another six, or a bit less she'd have her baby. Mrs. Adam had promised her the morning sickness would soon stop, that her appetite would increase and she'd grow wonderfully fat and lovely as her baby grew within.

It was Felicity's habit to stop in the chimney room at or just before teatime every day. There was always someone there, some poor lost soul who had escaped from the hell houses the British called prisons.

Brian still brought them regularly, but since her marriage, he no longer came to her room at night. They were just suddenly there. Felicity saw to their care, sometimes for a few days before they were suddenly spirited away, just as silently and, as they had come, without warning.

Two men sat in the small, dark room. She brought them water and hot tea as well as a meal that might have to last them some time and a bag of bread. She was just leaving her charges when Brian entered the room.

Felicity knew he wouldn't have come unless something terrible had happened, for to come and go in broad daylight was chancing much. "They found us out," Brian said, his face white to his lips as he leaned heavily against one wall. "Joshua is dead."

"Oh my God! What happened?"

"The bloody guard. He set us up. They were waitin' for us."

"But it's daytime. You never before . . ."

"I know. We were told a whole shipment of men were being taken to the *Jersey.*" Felicity as well as every man woman and child in the New York area had heard if not seen the hellish ship anchored in New York's harbor. Many died there, most in fact, and it was assumed once a man set foot on the *Jersey* all hope was lost. Not one, to her knowledge, had ever escaped.

"As it turned out the wagon was filled with soldiers. They got the jump on us easy enough. Shot Joshua down like a dog. The bastards. Killed five of us."

Felicity moaned at the terrible loss.

"Don't worry, I lost them a ways back. They don't know I'm here. And I'll be leaving once it's dark."

Felicity nodded.

"I'll need your help tonight. You up to it?"

"What do you need?"

"Caleb Brewster will be working these waters looking for these two and five of them redcoats we got ready for him. I don't have anyone else now that Joshua is gone."

Felicity nodded. The two escapees were too weak to do much

more than see to their own care. Brian couldn't manage five soldiers without help. "I'll go."

"I wouldn't ask you, lassie, but that I'm in a bit of a fix."

"Don't worry about it. What time will you need me?"

"Eight o'clock. We're to meet at nine."

Felicity nodded again. "I'll be ready."

Felicity had her dinner alone and early. Professing to be tired, she told Becky, her father, and Alvina that she was going up to bed. What she needed, she said, was a good night's sleep. She had no doubt that Jared would hear as much as soon as he returned to the house. Whatever the man had in mind for the night, and Felicity had no doubt that he did indeed have something in mind, would have to wait.

Alone in her room, Felicity dressed in her father's clothes, just as she had the night she and Brian had kidnapped Jared and forced him to minister to Joshua. Felicity sighed as she readied herself. Jared had saved Joshua's life only to have him die months later at the hands of Jared's countrymen.

She checked the time. It was ten minutes to the hour. Felicity moved into the closet and shut the door behind her. A moment later her hand reached for the hook holding her coat. A turn and the wall slid open creating a doorway. Felicity moved into the hidden walkway and down the stairs to the basement. Another latch, and the wall to the chimney room stood open. Brian was there waiting for her. The men gathered together the bread and two bottles of water and all four left the house.

So as to bring no notice upon them they moved one at a time from the shrubbery against the mansion's brick wall, into the street of the city, heading for the narrow strip of water that separated Manhattan from Long Island.

Two miles away, in the low-lying waters that lapped gently against the city's shores, hidden by tall grass, Caleb Brewster waited in his longboat for his next group of passengers and their subsequent journey to Connecticut.

In a shack, hidden in woods, not a half mile from the water, five red-coated young men lay with their arms bound behind their backs, shackled to one another, as well as to the iron bars that secured the windows and doors of the shed.

Brian had the key, but as each man was loosened from the iron, his arms remained secured behind him, allowing none the liberty to remove the gags over their mouths.

The moon was bright tonight, and Caleb would be in a hurry to make himself scarce, she was sure. One of the soldiers looked at Felicity, then seemed to gasp his surprise. She didn't remember the man, but no doubt they had met at one social function or another throughout the city. Apparently he recognized her. It didn't matter, for he wouldn't long remain in the city.

The men wore leg irons. It was slow going. Just as well, Felicity thought, since the two Americans were not as strong as they might have been and were even now having a time of it keeping up.

Felicity and Brian faded into the darkness, lost in grass tall enough to hide any man, and breathed a sigh of relief as the longboat pulled away from shore.

Somewhere a bell chimed the hour of eleven, and because the usual sounds of the city had been put to bed for this night, Felicity could hear faint words of a town crier calling out that all was well. Felicity smiled in agreement, for all was very well indeed.

She and Brian walked back, retracing their way. They were not stopped until three blocks from Felicity's home. Brian had left his carpenter tools in a small wooden carrying case at Felicity's, hidden in the bushes at the side of her house, for there was no way to carry them and keep his weapons aimed at the soldiers. Had he had the tools with him, these two soldiers would have realized the man and his helper were on their way home for the night and let them pass with no further delay.

As it turned out Brian was questioned and Felicity, praying

for help, could only stand there and listen to the lies. "Let's bring them in."

"No, wait, I can't, my wife will worry," Brian said.

The soldier laughed, telling clearly his disregard. "Will she now? Then we shouldn't keep you too long."

Brian knew there was only one way out of this. They couldn't be taken in for questioning. Both he and Felicity had weapons upon their person. If those weapons were discovered, all would be lost.

The largest of the two reached for Felicity. Brian pulled his gun from his pocket and shot the man without a second's hesitation. Next he turned the gun toward the remaining officer, and shouted to Felicity, "Run!"

Apparently the words worked better on the soldier than they did on the woman they were intended for, for the young officer screamed and ran for all he was worth, disappearing seconds later as he rounded one of the city's corners, leaving Felicity to stare with no little shock at the wounded man moaning at her feet.

Brian dragged her away and into one garden, over a brick wall, and into another. They moved silently down an alley, so silently in fact that they never disturbed a sleeping dog at the far end, hid for a moment in the shadows of a carriage house and then over another wall and one more. Felicity found herself in her own garden.

It was only then that she had the sense to ask, "Did you kill him?"

"No, lass, but they would have done us in, if given the chance." He pushed her toward the wall of her home and said, "Go in now. Get some sleep. I'll be in touch."

It took Felicity some time to mount the steps to her room. She knew the way, of course, so it wasn't the darkness that hampered, rather the shock of seeing a man shot before her eyes and the terrorizing fear this night had brought her.

Soundlessly, Felicity entered her closet. A moment later she opened the closet door. In the safety of her room she leaned against the door for a moment. It was only after she raised her gaze from the carpet that she realized she stood facing her astonished husband.

Nineteen

It took no master of detection to realize what Felicity had been about. The hour was fast approaching midnight, and here she was just coming in, although for just a second he hadn't a notion as to how she had accomplished that feat, through her closet. There was a hidden doorway, obviously, but he couldn't go into that now.

Jared couldn't think beyond the horrifying sight of blood. Her face was splattered with it, and Jared felt his stomach tighten with terror. Was it her blood? His learned gaze moved over her for a long minute before he realized her clothing displayed no stains. The blood wasn't hers.

Jared knew relief so intense it threatened his ability to stand. And then the relief was replaced by an anger of such magnitude he wondered how he was able to keep his hands at his sides? His wife had actually killed a man tonight. The sweet, shy, demure miss he had married was a murderess.

"Is he dead?"

"Who?"

"The man you shot?"

"I didn't shoot him. Br. . . ." She caught herself in time. "Someone else did, and no, he isn't dead," she said too weary, too relieved finally to have reached her room, to deny what was obviously so true. She'd been in a gunfight, just like the hero of some exciting novel. Right in the middle of one, if the truth were known. Only it hadn't been exciting at all, it had been terrifying. Had it not been for Brian pulling her away from the fallen soldier, she would have no doubt still stood there, staring in shock at what had happened.

"You have his blood on your face."

"Yes." She wiped at the reddish brown blotches with the sleeve of her coat, smearing what had not already dried down her cheek. "I was standing close."

Jared took a deep breath, releasing it slowly. "How often have you done this?"

"What? Gone out like this?"

"Serving your cause, no doubt," he said with no little disgust.

Felicity ignored not only his last comment, but the sarcasm behind it, and said, "This is the first time."

"This is not the first time," Jared reminded, for they both knew she'd done as much before.

"Oh, except for that," she agreed at the knowing look in his eyes. "Except for kidnapping you, it's the first time."

"But more importantly, I think, Felicity, it's the last time. You will swear it, Felicity. You will swear on your mother's grave that you will never do something like this again." Jared felt slightly amazed that he was able to speak at all, never mind keep his voice low and his words fairly rational.

He'd been sitting in her room for most of the night, waiting for her return, after being told she was in bed asleep. He'd thought at first to awaken her with his kisses to take from her what she would not give him while fully awake, but to his surprise he'd found her bed empty. Apparently she had gone out perhaps to Carolyn's, to go over the final preparations for the wedding. He'd never expected her to return by way of her closet, nor to find her dressed as she was, with blood splattered over her face. It took just about every inch of his self-control not to beat her, for he'd never known one more deserving of a husband's wrath.

He turned away, lest he suddenly give in to that need, and moved across the room, to the bottle of wine he'd brought into the room while awaiting her return. He poured two glasses and returned to her side as she removed her jacket. In the waistband of her trousers were two pistols. Jared shook his head in amazement at the sight of them, wondering how he'd ever gotten involved with such a woman? How he'd ever allowed himself to fall in love with her?

He handed her a glass and watched as she swallowed the whole of it in three thirsty gulps. Felicity sighed as she wiped her mouth with the back of her hand and returned the glass to Jared. "Thank you."

"Here, take this one as well," he said, offering her his glass.

She was in the midst of drinking it when he relieved her of her weapons. Felicity ignored his action and finished the glass.

Jared put the guns in her drawer. "I suppose asking you to show me how you got in here would be a waste of time."

Felicity did not respond, but said instead, "Did you hear that Cornwallis surrendered today at Yorktown?"

Jared figured he'd find the opening later, find it and seal it permanently. "I did," he said, the whole city did in fact.

"The war is over."

"It will be awhile yet, I think."

"But the fighting will stop now."

"Probably. But until peace is signed in Paris, we'll be staying on, I expect."

"What does that mean? That you'll be staying on?"

"I'm staying on, no matter the outcome. You've known that for some time."

She poured water into a bowl and washed her face and hands free of the blood. She was wiping them dry when she said, "You're not welcome here."

"I don't believe you."

"You should. It's the truth."

"Felicity, you wouldn't know the truth if it hit you in the face."

Felicity laughed at that as she kicked off her boots. "Meaning I'm hiding again?"

"Aren't you?"

"No! I told you from the first that . . ."

"I know what you told me," he interrupted as he watched her walk behind her screen. "But that doesn't matter anymore. Things have changed."

"What things?"

"The fact that we love each other."

"We don't. The fact is, you think it's love, but it's only wanting."

"Is it?"

Felicity gasped as Jared was suddenly behind the screen with her. She stood there clothed only in her drawers. Her shirt was on the floor. She reached for her robe, but the movement was brought to a stop as Jared took both her hands in his. "I won't deny that I want you. I won't deny that you are the most beautiful woman I've ever known, but it's not only wanting. I love you. Sometimes, like tonight while watching you come in through your closet, I wished to hell I didn't, but I do."

Her hands were held in his. There was no way that she could protect herself from his hungry gaze.

"Jared don't." She tried to pull away, but Jared only pulled her firmly against him.

"I love you. You are my wife." There was no doubt in either mind of this man's intent. Felicity tried to back away. She didn't want this. She'd gone out of her way to make sure nothing like this would ever happen. And yet she couldn't deny the almost-depraved surge of excitement that suddenly filled her.

There was a possibility that he would take her without her consent. Felicity shivered at the look in his eyes, for the possibility was even greater that he'd convince her that she wanted this as much as he. Felicity feared the latter, for to want him made her weak, and the weak could only suffer, caught up as they were in the inexplicable bonds of love.

Jared pushed one hand into her hair and pulled down forcing her face upward, her lips within inches of his. "I'm not, no . . ." she managed, before her words were lost in the seductive promise of ecstasy that was his mouth. Felicity felt a jolt of amazement that it took only his touch, his look, and, curse the man, his kiss, to make her want him, want this. The thickness grew in an instant to bind her abdomen, to crave more, for all he could give. The force of the emotion left her helpless, her knees barely able to hold her weight, and yet somehow stronger than she'd ever been before. It filled her mind to overflowing, drowning out the softly whispered echoes of caution. And then she was in his arms, hers wrapping tightly around his neck, pulling him closer, closer, and all reason and thought vanished as would a single raindrop in a desert.

She gasped for air, but her lungs, her mind, her senses were filled with him. And as she absorbed taste, scent, and texture, her strength increased. She pulled him tighter to her, her lips parting at a single touch, until mouths grew wide, needy, hungry for the rapture that could be given, for the ecstasy that would be taken in return.

This man could make her strong, she thought wildly, crazily, for there came upon her a sudden strength so powerful that she knew she could conquer anything. She'd been mistaken. Touching him, wanting him did not weaken the spirit. It was only when love was involved that . . . that . . .

She was in his arms being carried to the bed, but Jared didn't find her a receptive or acquiescent partner in this passion. He found her greedy, perhaps more so than he. He put her on the bed, but it was she who shoved aside her remaining clothes. It was she who tore his shirt in her anxiousness to touch. It was she who reached for his sex and directed him unerringly to her warmth.

There was no teasing of the senses here, no time for arousal, no loving sweet, or gentle moment. This was hunger. Pure animal lust that could not find appeasement, but in one final, explosive act.

She drew him into the madness, the heat, the tightness, the joy of loving her once again. Jared gave willingly of his mind, his soul, unable to hold back even if it meant his life.

His sex was thicker, stronger than ever before. It pulsed with blood, with life as his body plunged deep into the mindless joy of loving her. Never had there been a moment like this, never a woman like this.

He had no strength against her. He had no will but to keep her with him always, to love her to the end of his life. He might have thought to lengthen the torment, to drag out the moment, to heighten the ecstasy, but in the end it was she who took control.

She who had been without for so long grew wild in her touching, she who swore she didn't want, wanted more than her very life. She bit his shoulder, wild in her need, sucking until he was marked as she. She pulled at his hair and bit her nails deep into his back, urging him to do her will, then, when he had no will but to obey her silent, anxious demands, she locked her legs around his waist, locking him forever into the madness as she strove higher and higher toward the offer of magic.

Jared was aware she had reached no climax, that her body strained forward still, but he was lost in her need, lost like an animal who hungered for the scent of his mate. He couldn't stop what was to come, but he could bring her with him.

He reached between their locked bodies, his finger rotating the tiny nub, and Felicity became only a mindless hungry beast desperate to reach the light.

He couldn't pull away this time. This time her body held him in place, sucking him deeper into the mindless joy, the pain that was only glory.

And then she laughed, a wildly wicked sound, echoing the frenzy of both mind and body. Her head flung back, her teeth bared as if she could stand no more, as joy washed over her and he felt the sucking crushing waves of rapture come to draw him deeper, deeper into the maddening euphoria. And then he knew nothing but to love her, to love her until the madness, the rapture, the blinding light became one with her.

Jared couldn't move. He'd never known a release so powerful, a climax that shook his very soul. A pleasure so deep it had stolen his heart forever.

It took him a few minutes before he had the strength even to raise his head. And when he did, he saw in her eyes the knowledge of what he'd done. That he'd been so caught up in the fire that he'd forgotten his vow to protect her and for the first time Felicity understood the truth, understood as well the pleasure he'd denied her.

"Wait a minute. Don't get upset."

"You bastard."

Jared shook his head. He couldn't get his thoughts together. He needed to explain, to tell her why, but found he was unable to put together two barely intelligible words.

"Felicity, please."

"Get off me."

"Will you give me a minute, damn it!"

"Why? So you can make up a lie?"

"No, so I can tell you the truth, so I can say the words and make you understand."

"Oh, I understand all right. I understand that you are selfish to the depths of your soul, that you used my body for your own pleasure never caring if I found pleasure in return. Get off!"

"Listen to me."

She slapped him, and Jared sucked in a breath at the stinging blow. A moment later he had her hands bound within one of his and above her head. "I hate you. Let me go."

"No, you don't. Listen to me." He shook her then, until her teeth rattled, until she grew suddenly calm. He waited a moment before going on. "I know you think I was selfish, but the truth is, there is no greater pleasure than loving you. If I denied you, I denied myself as well."

He saw the confusion in her eyes. She didn't understand. If there was no greater pleasure, why then had he held back? Why had he denied them both the pleasure?

"But there's more than the act. There's loving you, you, not only the body, but the entire person. Your laughter, your teasing, your anger, everything about you that makes you wonderful. I couldn't chance losing you. My first wife died in childbirth. I couldn't ever allow that to happen again."

"You couldn't this, you couldn't that. What about me? What about my choices? What about our bargain? You entered it with a lie. You never intended to give me a child."

"It was selfish, I know, unfair at the very least, but I never expected to be found out."

"Oh, and I suppose that makes it all right? You can lie, steal, or murder, just don't get found out?"

"No, Jared, it wasn't just the lie, it was the deceit behind the lie. How can I ever trust you?"

"Yes, if I would have thought on it a bit, I might not have done it. But it never occurred to me that I might lose all control and forget to protect you."

"Is that what happened? You lost control?"

"God," he groaned as he rubbed his face into her neck. "I've never been so out of control in my life."

"Let my hands go," she said with perfect calmness.

"Why?"

"Because I want to hit you again."

Jared smiled, certain now that he could convince her. He heard the softening in her voice. She might not understand exactly, but she knew his intent was to bring no harm. "Felicity, listen. I know I was wrong, but I couldn't chance your life. I couldn't live through losing you. That happened once before, and I couldn't let it happen again."

"Oh? Am I supposed to feel sorry for you now? Am I supposed to say, that's all right Jared, you tried to rob me of one of life's most perfect joys, but I forgive you?"

"Well it appears, no matter my attempts, you won't be robbed of it in any case."

"That's right. No thanks to you."

Jared chuckled. "Actually, it's every thanks to me."

"Beast. I'll never forgive you."

"We have our whole lives before us, sweetheart. I imagine you can find it in that steely little heart of yours to eventually forgive me."

"Little heart? Is that what you think?"

He nodded. "It couldn't get smaller and still keep a woman alive."

"Oh how easy it is to find fault. You do something despicable, and I'm wrong because I won't forgive you."

"Well, it is the Christian thing to do."

Her eyes narrowed as she sought further insults. And then she asked, "How many times have we made love, do you think?"

"Oh, maybe a hundred or so."

Felicity nodded. "That means I owe you ninety-nine slaps. Perhaps after the last one, I'll think about forgiving you."

"And in the meantime?"

"In the meantime what?"

"While I'm waiting for your forgiveness? What shall we do?"

"Nothing."

"Nothing? Not even this?" he asked as he leaned to one side and with his free hand ran one finger from her neck to her chest. Jared was not unaware of the catch in her breathing as his finger brushed over the tip of one breast and then continued on its journey to her thigh. He smiled.

He shouldn't be able to do this to her. His touch shouldn't mean so much. It shouldn't be this easy. "I'm going to get even. I swear it."

"How?" Jared couldn't deny a distinct sense of unease.

"I don't know yet, but I'll find a way."

Jared rolled to his back, taking her with him. Her hands were released and he lay there totally open, exposed and waiting for whatever punishment she deemed fitting. "Hit me, beat me, I don't care. Just get it over with."

Felicity couldn't hold back her smile. She came to a sitting position, her legs straddling his hips. "What do you mean?"

"I mean I can't stand the thought of you lying in wait, ready to spring something on me."

Felicity grinned as she leaned forward, her hands on his shoulders supporting herself above him. Her breasts swayed a bit as she leaned forward. "Are you afraid of me, Jared?"

"No, I wouldn't say I was afraid exactly. I think what I feel is more like terror."

Felicity laughed. "You're only saying that so I'll forget my anger and you can have your way with me again."

"I'm saying that because it's true, and, actually, I was hoping you'd have your way with me this time."

Felicity shook her head. "Lord, what have I gotten myself into here? Not only have you lied to me, tricked me, and gotten me with child only by accident, but now you expect me to make love to you?"

"Well, I don't expect it, exactly. But I was sort of hoping."

Felicity ignored the hopeful look in his eyes. "Tell me about her."

"What? About Annie?" Jared smiled at the fond memory. "Annie was a good wife, sweet and giving. A man couldn't want more."

Felicity's eyes narrowed a bit at the woman's many attributes. Oddly enough, now that she'd asked, she didn't want to hear about them. "When we discovered she was going to have a baby, we were happy." The happy memory faded from Jared's eyes as their depths filled with distant pain. "The pregnancy was hard. She was uncomfortable, and I was terrified. I knew the baby was too big. I knew she would die unless I did something."

"What did you do?"

"I went to Europe and consulted with doctors there. One suggested a procedure. Said he'd had some luck in it. I was to take the baby, by operating. I was sure it was her only chance." Jared sighed at the memory. "I was too late. She was in labor when I came home. In hard labor, and the baby was too far along. It was too late."

Jared sighed again, remembering his despair. "She was too small, her hips too narrow. It couldn't be done, and I stood there and watched both the child and her die." He looked at Felicity for a long moment, his voice barely audible when he said, "You can't know what that's like.

"She was pregnant because of me, and she died because I, as a doctor, could offer her no help."

Felicity nodded in understanding. Because of what had happened to Annie, Jared hadn't wanted her to have a baby. Perhaps he hadn't gone about things the right way, but his motives had been worthy. Well, sort of. At least his deception had come from good intent. "You don't need to worry about me. I'll be fine."

Jared rolled her suddenly to her back, his body crushing her into the mattress, holding her tightly against him. "You will be. I swear it."

A moment later Jared rolled them both from the bed and, with his arm around her waist, brought her with him to the washstand. He turned her toward the mirror that leaned against the wall, standing behind her he watched her body for a long moment before he reached for a cloth and began to wash them both of the stickiness his loving had caused.

And then the cloth dropped away, but Jared seemed not to have noticed, for his hands continued moving over her. Felicity watched his hands, his long fingers, the back of each sprinkled with dark hair. She'd never noticed before how beautiful a man's hands could be.

They moved now over her midriff, her belly, her hips, and her neck, her shoulders, coming breathlessly close to where she wanted touching most, only to move away again. She watched until she could no longer hold her head up, or keep her eyes open. Her head fell back against his chest, the tips of her breasts tightened, the pale pink grew dark and tight with building desire as she arched her back in silent offering and groaned his name in growing urgency.

"Open your eyes, sweetheart. Watch my hands."

"You're making me weak. I can't."

"Open them," he said again, and Felicity had no will but to obey. His dark eyes bored deeply into hers. The intensity she saw in their depths nearly stole her breath. Had any man ever looked at a woman like this?

"Jared," she said softly, suddenly afraid of the tempting depth of emotion. Afraid she might lose herself forever. It was going too far, too serious, too meaningful. "Jared, I didn't want this."

"I know," he returned. "I think I didn't want it either, at least not at first, but I couldn't stop it. Not after knowing you. Not after the laughter, the teasing, the loving we've shared. It's a scary thing to love this hard."

She shook her head. "I don't."

"Were you happy without me, Felicity? Did you laugh? Did you smile?"

"Smiling isn't so much," she answered, her words telling exactly what he wanted to know.

Jared nodded. "You could laugh now. If you would let yourself go, you could laugh for joy right now."

She shook her head. "I can't. You're asking too much."

She was afraid, more afraid than he might have imagined, and the deceit she'd discovered tonight might have been all she needed never to trust him again. She could go on dangerous, life-threatening missions, but she couldn't promise to give herself, her heart, to a man. She couldn't promise to love. Jared figured he'd never known a woman more complicated. "You don't think that Margaret and I were involved, do you?"

"No, I know you weren't."

Jared breathed a sigh of relief. At least he had that much to offer her. At least she could believe him to be faithful. And then he thought of a new tactic, a way perhaps that might bring them together forever. "All right, let's forget about love for now. You don't have to love me, do you? We could have a life together, couldn't we? Maybe you would never love me, but we could be happy. I know we could."

Felicity seemed to think that over for a minute. Upon reflection, the idea seemed to hold some promise. After all they'd been together, well mostly, for some months now and she hadn't lost her heart. She hadn't grown to love him as she had once feared she might. Perhaps they could be happy together. And maybe, with nothing more than what they already had, together they could create something that would last. Love didn't have to enter into the matter, did it?

Felicity raised her gaze. And in his eyes she saw the promise that it would be all right. That anything, any way she chose, would be all right. She nodded and for the first time in weeks smiled at him. "I think you're right. I think we could be happy. When do you want to start?"

Jared whispered a silent prayer of thanks. It was all he could do to keep from crushing her against him. Instead, he smiled. "Well I was thinking that right now might be just about perfect." He sighed with pleasure as she turned into his arms. "Ah, sweetheart, standing like this, I can't help but think of other things as well."

Felicity laughed softly, the sound bringing an ache of longing to Jared's gut. He'd almost begun to lose hope that he'd ever hear it again. "Me, too."

"What kind of things?"

"I wouldn't want to shock you."

"I love being shocked."

Felicity laughed again. "Well if you really love it, I could show you."

Jared pretended to be shocked as she kissed his neck, his chest. His gasps and moans and occasional astonished, "Oh dears," seemed only to spur her on as her mouth moved slowly down his body.

She laughed at every sound and because she laughed and because Jared loved hearing the sound he kept up the playful teasing.

"If you don't stop making all that noise, I'll never get to the most shocking part."

"If there's one thing I know how to do, it's to shut the hell up."

Twenty

Bess waited nervously as a knock sounded on the door. Frank led the man inside the rented room. He looked no different than most street toughs, except that he might have been a little cleaner and better-looking. No different but for the cold, almost-dead look in his eyes. Bess felt a shiver of fear as he looked her over without a flicker of emotion, and she knew instinctively that he had none, no emotion at all.

This man was the sort to kill on command, if the money were right. Kill quickly, cleanly, and without regret. And he wouldn't hesitate to kill a woman, any woman.

Bess wasn't happy with Frank's choice. Like anything in life there were degrees and Frank had found the lowest sort to do their work.

There couldn't be a mistake here. Felicity couldn't die. To kill her outright would have been no problem, but to kill her for gain . . . Bess shook her head at the thought.

Dryson as well as Jared would know from day one who was behind the kidnapping. Bess knew the man cared deeply for his wife. The world wasn't big enough to hide them should something happen to her.

Frank introduced the man as Mike. Last names weren't mentioned. They sat at a small scarred table in the corner of the room.

"So who you lookin' to grab?"

"You don't need to know her name. I'll point her out when the time is right."

Mike shrugged, not at all concerned. Frank was right not to trust him. In his line of work it was best never to trust.

"I need a place to put her. A place where she'll be safe. Nothing can happen to this one."

Mike nodded. "I know a place. How much?"

"A third of the take."

"A third? I do the grabbing and hiding. I take all the risks and I only get a third?"

Frank shrugged. "I can't do it myself. There can't be any mistake here."

Mike was silent.

"Fine, you don't want in, I'll find someone else."

"I never said that." Mike figured by the looks of these two, it would be simple enough to take it all when the time came. Who the hell would stop him? The man was soft, a little jowly, and showed nothing in the way of muscle. By the looks of him, he spent too much time between the sheets.

The woman might give him a bit of trouble, but he figured he could take care of that. He almost grinned at the thought of how easy that would be. "When do you want it done?"

"We're working that out right now. I'll have to let you know."

Mike frowned. "You been thinkin' about this long?"

"Why?" Bess asked.

Mike looked at her for the first time since entering the room. He didn't usually mix business with pleasure. In his business the mix could be dangerous. Besides, his business usually brought its own kind of pleasure. Having the power and the will to snuff out a life brought him the greatest satisfaction. Sex could only come in as a weak second when comparing the high, although it was usually needed immediately after the happening.

Still, there was always a chance he could change his ways. At least for as long as it would take to stick it to this one. " 'Cause you ain't got nothin' figured."

"We will. Where can we meet?"

"You know Duncan's place on Twenty-second?"

"Yeah."

"If you want me, you can usually find me there."

Mike came to his feet and walked out without another word spoken.

"I don't like it," Bess said. "He ain't normal."

"What does that mean?"

"Did you look in his eyes? God, it gave me the shivers."

"What the hell are you talking about?"

"He'd kill as easily as swatting a fly."

"So would you, 'cept you hide it better."

"And who did I kill lately?"

"You mean, who did you try to kill lately?"

Bess shook her head. "That was different. I hated both of them."

Frank shrugged. "He'll do what he's told. Motives don't matter. The only thing that does is money. And when this is over, we'll have more than we've ever dreamed of."

Carolyn made a beautiful bride, but to Jared's way of thinking, Felicity made an even more beautiful matron of honor. Matron meaning woman, and in this case a married woman. Jared thought the word might be almost as beautiful as the lady herself.

She was his, his to keep, to love and cherish for all time.

He was crazy for her, absolutely mad, and he loved every minute of it. He couldn't touch her enough, love her enough, tease and play enough. He hated every minute spent from her side, and knew some terrible jolts of jealousy if she simply looked at another man, never mind spoke to one. And she was speaking to one at the moment.

He'd watched her move freely about the Carpenter home, stopping to say something to a few of her friends and then laughing as a man he hadn't met before joined the small group. Jared had been talking to Sam, only for the last minute or so he hadn't remembered much of their conversation. His gaze had followed Felicity around the room, followed her to where she stood right now, followed her to the man who smiled, bowed, and kissed her hand, his mouth lingering as far as Jared was concerned, far longer than necessary.

Sam looked slightly surprised and then grinned as Jared moved directly to his wife, offering no excuses as he left his side. Mary came upon her husband and smiled, having noticed the abrupt leave-taking. "I'd say, it looks as if your friend has found something a bit more interesting than your company."

Sam grinned at his wife. "He could have said excuse me at least."

"He probably thought he did."

Sam grinned at the tiny woman standing before him. "Did you ever notice how strange a man can act when he's in love?"

Mary leaned into her husband, her laughter soft warm and delicious.

"When did you tell Jenny to expect us?"

"Not until late."

"I have a carriage outside. I thought we might take a ride around the city. You haven't seen much of it yet."

"Carolyn will be upset if we just leave."

"She'll never notice, and we'll be back in a few hours."

A few hours alone with her husband. The thought was far too tempting to resist. Even with help, they often found little time for privacy, time away from three demanding youngsters. "I wonder if these people would think anything amiss if I raced you to the carriage."

Outside the mansion carriages lined the drive. Across the street, in a lot filled only with trees and undergrowth, two darkly clad figures scanned the guests as yet another group arrived. Frank had no idea what Felicity looked like, and he needed to be able to point her out, if their plan was ever to be put into effect. "Haven't you seen her yet?"

Bess glared her annoyance. "I told you she probably arrived

early. The paper said she was matron of honor. She's probably inside, and we're wasting our time."

Frank grumbled a curse. He'd been standing here for two hours. His back was beginning to ache, and he needed a drink.

"I told you we should have waited. By the time she comes out it will be too dark to see anything. It's almost too dark now. We could have rented a cab and waited outside her house."

Frank nodded. He hadn't wanted to create any suspicion and thought a cab sitting outside her home on Lexington might have done just that. He'd thought to watch the wedding instead, and after Bess pointed her out, he could set his plan into motion. "All right, we'll start tomorrow. She visits her dressmaker on Mondays, doesn't she?"

Bess nodded. "In the morning." A second later she made some sort of sound, bringing Frank's attention to the couple across the way. Two people appeared to be hurrying from the party. The light was fading and they were far enough away so she couldn't be sure, but the woman did have red hair and the man was a tall English officer. "That looks like it might be them."

"What do you mean, might be?"

"We're too far away to know for sure, but she's small and has the right color hair."

Frank grinned. "You never told me her hair was red. Is it real?"

Bess shrugged unconcerned. "Maybe you'll get the chance to find out for yourself."

Frank licked his lips in anticipation. The Dryson bitch and her husband were leaving the party alone. Maybe, just maybe, if luck were with them, they wouldn't have to involve Mike in this matter at all. Maybe they could take care of this little business themselves, and keep all the money.

Bess and Frank mounted their horses and watching the carriage pull out into light traffic began to follow.

Inside the carriage Sam grinned at his lady. "Why are you sitting over there?"

"Where would you like me to sit?"

"Well, I was sort of thinking you might be more comfortable if you sat over here."

"I'm perfectly comfortable here, thank you."

Sam laughed as he reached for her hand and guided her to sit upon his lap. "Isn't this better?"

Her arms went around his neck. "Well, now that you mention it."

Sam kissed her, a long wet, slow kiss that left both of them shaken. Mary snuggled closer and sighed in her happiness. "I love you. Tell me again what you're going to do after we go home."

"I'm retiring from the service and buying a farm, a very big farm about twenty miles from London. It has a large manor house on it with plenty of room for the children. I have it picked out already, but I want you to see it before I sign the papers."

"I'm going to love it."

The next thing Mary knew, the coach came to a sudden stop and Mary found herself on the floor. "Ow," she said, as she quickly smoothed her dress into place. "What happened?"

Sam called out to the driver as he helped Mary gain her seat again. "What's the trouble?"

"People are fighting up ahead. I can't get through."

Sam pushed aside the curtain and leaned out the window. "Stay here," he said, as he jumped from the carriage.

Frank grinned as he watched the officer leave the coach. He'd never get a better chance. He moved forward and adjusted his neckerchief to cover his face, while motioning for Bess to do the same. Dismounting he reached for the coach door and snapped it open.

Mary was on the opposite side of the coach. Standing, bent in half, the upper part of her body was sticking out the door's window as she strained to see what the commotion was. She never heard the opposite door open, and she jumped as someone reached for her skirt, trying to pull her back inside. Mary knew it wasn't her husband. She could see Sam's tall form over the crowd about a dozen yards down the street.

Someone was grabbing at her, trying to pull her from the coach.

Mary's arms wrapped themselves over the doorframe. She held on for dear life. Her head and shoulders outside of the coach, she screamed for help as her dress was torn at the waist. She kicked behind her and knew only a moment's satisfaction at the low grunt she heard in return and then the door suddenly opened and she was hanging outside the coach, hanging halfway through the coach window.

"Help me! Somebody help me," she said just as her skirt was pulled again, swinging the door closed. Her hold gave out and she was dragged through the coach and out the other side.

Mary was forced toward a horse, a hand held over her mouth, muffling her screams as she fought her abductor every step of the way. Mary was a small woman, but a bundle of fury and the man holding her was not having an easy time of it.

Bess knew they had already taken far too long. At any second, the crowd would realize what was happening. They'd stop Frank then, and one way or another prevent any means of escape. They had to get out of here and they had to get out now!

A man muttered, "Hey, what are you doing there?"

Another, "Leave the lady be."

Frank heard someone shout "Mary!" and then a man worked feverishly to part the crowd of ten or fifteen restless people, his arms stretched out, his hands coming dangerously close to grasping Frank's throat, before the thickness of the crowd finally impeded. Frank was jostled forward, the force bringing him up against the horse, who had grown skittish, taking his cue from the anxious, angry people surrounding him. The horse whinnied a sound of fear and took off.

Frank, desperate for escape pulled his gun and shot into the crowd. People screamed and tried to get out of the way. A second later he shoved the woman toward the wild-eyed man still fighting to reach her. In an instant, he was running. He didn't have time to search out Bess. She'd have to make it out on her own. All he could do was run for his life.

Frank didn't stop running until he mounted the steps to the small rented room, a mile or more from the attempted kidnapping. He opened the door and closed it hard, leaning weakly against it, as he tried to control the burning pain his breathing caused his lungs. That had been close. Much too close.

Frank listened to the sounds of the house for a long moment. A baby cried down the hall. On the floor above him a man yelled at his wife. A woman somewhere at the back of the building laughed. Frank breathed a sigh of relief. He figured he'd probably made good his escape. As far as he could tell he hadn't been followed. He'd raced up and down a dozen alleyways and along three avenues before slowly coming to a stop and circling back. He found no crowd chasing after him. Only the usual pedestrian traffic lined the city's wide sidewalks.

Bess came in a half hour later after returning the horse to the livery. "Did you see anyone out there?" Frank asked as he peeked from a corner of the covered window.

"No. The streets are quiet."

Frank breathed a sigh. "Damn, the little bitch gave me such a hard time. I never would have believed she could fight like that."

"That's because it wasn't Felicity."

"What?"

"You heard me. You almost took the wrong one."

Frank sat heavily upon the bed.

"I think you were right about bringing in Mike. Kidnapping isn't so easy a chore. You should let him take care of it."

"I have every intention of letting him take care of it." Frank rubbed a small lump on his jaw. He'd only just now realized the ache. The woman had hit him, and during the ruckus he'd never noticed.

* * *

A servant brought Jared a note explaining that Sam had been shot. The note explained it was naught but a flesh wound. Still, Mary would appreciate it if Jared could look at her husband at his first opportunity.

Felicity left the party with him.

Mary was cleaning Sam's arm when Jared and Felicity arrived. The two were arguing. "I'm telling you it won't hurt."

"Wait until Jared gets here."

"What won't hurt?" Jared asked as he walked unannounced into the small rented house and the sitting room just inside the front door.

"He wants a drink."

"Give him one," Jared said as he knelt before his friend and examined the injury. It was minor. The bullet had clipped the skin on the outside of his upper arm. It might hurt a bit, and even grow a little stiff upon the morrow, but no real damage had been done.

"What happened?"

"Damned if I know." Sam shook his head. "Someone tried to kidnap Mary and the bloody . . ." He shot both his wife and Felicity a sheepish grin, "Sorry. And the bloke shot me."

"What are you talking about? Why would someone want to kidnap Mary?" Felicity's eyes were wide at the horror.

"Been trying to figure that out myself," Sam said and then grinned, his eyes warm with emotion as they settled upon his wife. "If she were a comely wench, then maybe . . ."

"Behave yourself," Mary snapped, "or I'll clean your wound again."

"You won't let her near me, will you, Jared?"

"Why don't you tell me exactly what happened?"

"We went for a drive."

Jared nodded, choosing not to comment since he figured he knew why they had left the party. "And?"

"And the coach came to a stop. There was some trouble in the street."

"What kind?"

"A mob had gotten hold of a few Tories. They were going at them with sticks." Sam sighed. "It took me a minute to straighten it out, luckily a few of my men were nearby, and we soon got the fight settled."

"And?" Jared prompted again.

"And then I heard Mary screaming. I didn't realize it was her at first, but by the time I got back to the coach, a man had dragged her out . . ."

". . . and was trying to get me on his horse," Mary added.

Both Jared and Felicity looked at Mary with shock. "Are you all right?"

"He tore my dress," was all she said, turning a bit so the tear at her waist could be seen and Jared assumed if that were the worst of it, Mary had been lucky tonight, very lucky indeed.

"Why?"

"We can't figure that out," Sam said. "As far as I know I haven't made any enemies, at least no more than any officer might make. We haven't anything, if ransom were on their minds. What could they have wanted?"

"They?" Jared asked.

Mary shuddered. "There were two of them. One stayed on his horse."

"I almost had the bastard," Sam said as Jared bandaged his arm, this time he forgot to apologize to the ladies for the less than polite word. "I was this close"—he held up two fingers about three inches apart—"and then he shot me. The next thing I knew he shoved Mary at me, almost knocking her down, he pushed her so damn hard." Sam's look told of his intent should he ever get his hands on the man. "It gave him the chance he needed to get away."

"And you didn't see . . . ?"

Sam shook his head. "He was masked."

"They both were," Mary added.

Jared came to his feet. Sam would be fine. He couldn't say the same for Mary as she paced nervously, a wild look in her eyes. To say that she'd been terrified was to put it mildly, and Jared thought only time and perhaps a mild sedative would help.

He prescribed a drink for both Mary and Sam as well as a good night's rest, and left a sedative in case she couldn't sleep. Moment's later they left the young couple to comfort one another.

Felicity was not unaware of the fact that Sam's small house was surrounded by well-armed sentries. She thought Mary should find some security in that fact.

Felicity sat at Jared's side during the short ride home. "What do you think? Why would someone want to take her?"

"I've got two thoughts at the moment."

Felicity turned in her seat waiting for him to go on.

"One, it could have been a spur of the moment happening. Mary is a pretty woman and all sorts of degenerates can be found in a city the size of this one."

Felicity shuddered at the thought.

"And second, have you ever noticed how closely you and Mary resemble each other?"

"We don't look alike at all, and what has that got to do with . . ."

"I said resemble, not look alike. Both of you are small, both have red hair. Both are married to English officers, tall English officers."

Felicity frowned. "What has that got to do with anything?"

Jared shrugged. "It was just a thought, but I think it's possible they tried to take the wrong woman."

Felicity stared at him for a long moment before she laughed, the sound low and throaty, stirring within him an instant and powerful need. Jared mentally hurried the coach back home. "Jared, one day you're going to have to get over this preposterous notion of yours that every man who sees me wants me. If that were the case, I wouldn't have waited until I was very nearly an old maid before marrying."

"One has nothing to do with the other. You were the one who did the refusing. That doesn't mean men didn't want you."

Felicity sighed. "It's a complimentary thought to be so desirable as to drive men to desperate measures, but unless the man is in dire need of spectacles, I think you're wrong."

"It was dark. By the time the coach was stopped, it was probably impossible to see inside."

Felicity shook her head at the preposterous notion that she could have been the target. "Jared."

"All right, I could be wrong, but tell me why they tried to take Mary? Everyone knows they have hardly enough to support their family as it is. Surely they could have expected no great reward for their efforts."

"Perhaps it was as you said, a spur of the moment happening. Perhaps they thought to take her for reasons other than money." Felicity shivered at the horror of that thought, for there could be no other reason then to misuse her terribly.

Jared nodded and brought Felicity closer to his side. Her head nestled against his chest. Jared might have appeared to agree with her, but the truth was, he thought his suggestion held some merit. Had Felicity been the target, the possible gain might have been great. Her father was a rich man, a very rich man.

Jared's arms tightened at the thought of what might have happened. It would be a long time before he would be able to give up the thought, before his fear would ease. In the meantime, Jared figured it wouldn't hurt to make sure nothing like this ever happened to his wife.

Felicity was bound to give him some grief here, but he thought if he hired on a few men, men who knew how to keep their distance, even as they protected, she shouldn't be too upset.

Only she was.

"I don't mind telling you he scared me half to death," Felicity ranted as she paced angrily before her husband. Jared sat one hip on a small table in a little room off the largest ward and watched his wife's flushed face and delicious form. She was six months along, and her belly was rounding nicely, even as her breasts slowly approached gigantic proportions. Jared was delighted. And except for the fear he knew concerning her delivery, a fear that threatened to consume him at times, he couldn't have been happier.

She was dressed in a green walking suit that was trimmed in fur at her throat, cuffs, and hem, and held in one hand a matching fur muff. Jared thought she wasn't likely to ever look more beautiful, especially when her color rose as now, and her eyes flashed with fire.

Upon noticing the man following her, and being closer to the hospital than home, Felicity had made a run for it. Even now, after realizing she had nothing to fear, she was still slightly out of breath.

"He was only doing his job."

She watched him for a long moment before saying, "I'm so angry, I can hardly speak. How dare you hire a bodyguard and never tell me?"

Angry or not she seemed to be doing a pretty good job of speaking, of raving, in fact. "I knew you'd give me trouble on that score. He wasn't supposed to be obvious."

The fact that Jared seem unconcerned at her distress did not lessen her anger in any marked degree. The truth was, Jared was not unconcerned, but thought that her fear would pass soon enough while his wasn't likely to ease until the culprits behind Mary's attempted kidnapping were discovered. Until that day, Jared thought his fear the greater of the two, and Felicity would just have to put up with a little inconvenience.

"No, I imagine having a man follow me into every store and sit three tables from mine in the teashop couldn't be considered obvious.

"Poor Alvina. I'm sure she didn't know what to make of it as she watched me run from the place."

Jared grinned imagining the old woman's alarm. "I'll talk to him."

"Don't talk to him, fire him."

Jared smiled.

"Jared, he chased me all the way here." She rubbed her protruding stomach and then glared at his grin. "And I can tell you a lady in my condition cannot run very fast."

Jared thought to lighten the moment. He teased, "You couldn't run very fast before either, or you might not have found yourself in this condition."

Felicity was hardly in the mood for teasing. "I tell you I was quite desperate by the time I entered this building."

"I'm sorry you were frightened, sweetheart. You weren't to know. But once he realized you were aware of his presence, he should have told you what he was about."

"No doubt," she said snidely at what she considered a gross understatement. "How long has this been going on?"

"Since Mary's attempted kidnapping."

Felicity's mouth dropped open. "Three months? And you never said a word during all that time?"

"I knew you'd be upset."

"Call him off, Jared." It wasn't a request. It was a direct order.

Jared only shook his head. "Not a chance."

"You'll be sorry, if you don't."

Jared was well aware of the meaning behind her threat. He knew women had but one weapon, and Felicity wouldn't hesitate to use it. He shrugged, knowing he would have done much to avoid her anger, but in this case he preferred anger to the possible alternative. No, her anger didn't matter. It only mattered that she'd remain safe. "You might as well get that out of your mind right now."

"Get what out?"

"Holding back your favors. I love you, and I won't see you come to harm no matter how you fight me."

"Jared, please," she said so prettily that he almost gave in on the spot, especially since she had moved to stand between his legs and deliberately ran her hand over his sex.

"Witch," he said, as he pulled her into his arms and buried his face in her sweetly scented neck. Jared was giving some real consideration to the fact that there was after all a table in

this room, a table that might be put to the best use it had ever
known.

She turned her head and ran deliciously sweet kisses along
the side of his throat and her tongue was playing against his
ear. "Please, I could make you very happy," she whispered
softly, the heat of her breath sending shivers down his spine as
she purred in her most seductive tone.

It took some doing but Jared managed to keep his senses
about him. His hand was under her dress, his palm cupping the
sweetness of her through her drawers. "You've already done
that and more," he returned, "and there's no way anyone is going
to take you from me."

Felicity shoved herself from his arms and stood there a long
moment glaring her resentment. She had forgotten how easily
the need could come upon her. It took only a glance to realize
her husband was equally as affected. Equally affected, perhaps,
but just as stubborn as ever. Seduction would serve no purpose
in this instance. He'd take what was offered, to be sure, and in
the end still refuse her plea.

Jared grinned as she tried to compose herself. She muttered,
"Beast," to his sexy grin. And then a light of impending victory
entered her eyes. "I'll pay him more than you can."

Jared laughed and folded his arms across his chest. "I told
him there was a possibility of that happening. If he knows what's
good for him, he won't take it."

"Nothing is going to happen to me!" she said, her voice rising
just a bit in frustration.

Jared's arms were still folded across his chest and he nodded
in all confidence. "I know."

Twenty-one

"It's been three months. When the hell are we going to get on with it?" Bess asked as she shoved a piece of wood she'd stolen from the O'Connor's pile down the hall into the small fireplace, her hands reaching toward the flickering, always-evasive warmth. The room was freezing, and no matter how much wood she stole, she could never get it warm.

"Mike said we had to give them time to relax their guard. He knows what he's doing."

"You'd better get me a few more customers. We're down to our last shilling, and there's nothing left to eat."

Frank's little side business had come to an abrupt stop, some weeks back. He'd gone to collect as usual, but all he'd gotten for his efforts was a beating, and hadn't tried again, for the shopkeepers had joined together and hired their own toughs. Since then Frank had been forced to resort to Bess and her talent. She brought in a pound or so a week. After paying their rent, there was little enough left over. The truth was, they were near to starving to death, and Frank hoped Mike would be about their plan soon. He nodded at her comment. "I told Ed you wouldn't mind servicing him this afternoon."

Bess groaned at the thought. Of all her customers, she disliked servicing Ed Fountain. He more than most was disagreeable in the extreme, for he lacked in some much-needed everyday hygiene. He had but one redeeming factor, that being he was over and done with his business within seconds. Bess shrugged at the thought, knowing his money was as good as any. And money could make any encounter palatable. "That's not likely to send us over the top."

"I told him it would be an extra shilling this time."

Bess nodded at the thought. They were late with the rent again, and most of what she made today would go to Mr. Cox, the landlord, but for the first time in weeks there might be extra. With it they'd be able to buy tea and the makings for a stew tonight. And maybe even a loaf of warm crusty bread from the bakery. Her stomach growled at the thought. "What about tobacco? I ran out last night."

"Stop smoking."

"Oh, there's a good answer. Should I stop drinking as well?"

"All right, I'll run downstairs and see if I can find someone. Fix your hair and wash up a bit, will you? You ain't likely to make much looking like you have lately."

Bess sighed, knowing Frank was right about that. Still, what did it matter what she looked like? A man was only interested in one particular part of her body. And if that part were eager to do his bidding, what did he care how she looked?

The plan had been to make herself scarce. It had to be believed that she was no longer in the city, lest blame fall to her when Felicity turned up missing. Besides, as far as she knew, they were still looking for her, because of that bitch Carolyn.

The enforced seclusion found her growing increasingly lazy. She never went out and, therefore, never found the need to fix herself, but lounged around the rented room in her robe for most of every day. Except for the trip to the midwife to abort either Frank's or one of her customer's kid, she'd never know which, she hadn't walked out of this room in almost three months.

Bess glanced at her slovenly reflection in the cracked mirror. The mirror hung over a table that held a pitcher and bowl, both of which were empty at the moment. The thought of bringing another bucket of freezing water and the remnants of a bar of harsh soap to their third-floor room hardly induced delightful thoughts of cleanliness. She sighed, "All right, just hurry up. I need a drink."

Mike sat in the tavern not a block from the rented room, his big hand wrapped around a tankard of ale as he smiled at the man opposite him. Tonight. They'd make their move tonight. If there were guards, they would have grown negligent by now. And if not, well, one precisely placed bullet should easily do the trick.

Mike nodded at the man opposite him as he repeated his instructions. He needed Jack to drive and deliver the ransom note. He didn't need Frank or Bess for anything, except to take the blame. Mike grinned at the thought, for he had every intention of leaving the city with all of the money in hand. "The boy will bring the note. I'll be waiting with the cab. How do we know she'll take it?"

Mike frowned at the question. They'd been over this again and again. "I told you a dozen times already. The note will say her man has been hurt. She won't think but to run for the nearest cab."

Jack Spencer nodded as he remembered. "Yeah, I forgot."

"And then?" Mike prompted, wondering if he shouldn't have chosen another. The more they spoke, the more Mike realized this one hardly had the intelligence of a field mouse. Mike shrugged, knowing he couldn't have it both ways. If Jack had had any sense at all, he would have demanded more than the few pounds he was getting for his part in this job. And Mike, a greedy sort, wanted all he could get. "Do you remember what you're supposed to do then?"

"Sure. I'm supposed to drive the cab to the shack."

"Where is it?"

"By the river. Why are we going over this again? You'll be inside the cab, won't you? If I forget, you can tell me."

Mike nodded. "We're going over it again because I want no mistakes," he said, as he leaned back in his chair and took a long swallow of the bitter brew. He touched his pocket, feeling the crackle of paper inside, the note the boy would deliver tonight. "We have two hours. Nurse that," he said referring to Jack's ale.

"It's cold outside. Besides, I can hold my liquor."

Mike nodded. "Nurse it anyway."

Early that evening the cab sat in front of the mansion on Lexington. It was only six o'clock but already dark. A light snow was beginning to fall.

Inside the cab two men and a woman sat huddled against the cold. All three were masked. From the uncurtained window they watched in some anxiety as a boy approached the mansion's door. He knocked, and handed the note to an elderly woman. The boy walked away, jingling in his pocket the two shillings he'd gotten to deliver the note.

Alvina frowned at the note addressed to Felicity as she returned to the sitting room. Felicity was sewing a thin strip of lace to a baby's dress and smiled at her friend and cousin. "Who was it Alvina?"

"A boy with a note. It's addressed to you."

"Who could have . . . ?" Felicity began as she tore open the envelope and stared for a moment at the scrawling words, apparently hastily penned. Her heart came to a sudden stop at the horror and then pounded double time as she came to her feet and ran wildly for the hallway and front door.

"Where are you going?"

"Jared is hurt."

"What happened?"

"I don't know."

"Wait! Call Jed. Don't go alone," Alvina said as Felicity ran down the few steps leading to the sidewalk. "Felicity," she called after her young cousin. "Wait!"

Felicity never heard her cousin's cautioning words. All she

could think was that Jared had somehow been hurt, that he needed her. A cab stood parked before her house.

The cloak she swung around her was barely in place as she ran down the few steps that brought her to the sidewalk. She addressed the cab's driver. "Are you waiting for me?"

"Yes, ma'am," Jack said in response, and all three inside the cab smiled beneath their masks as Felicity opened the door and was dragged into the dark vehicle.

Within seconds the cab was moving, and Felicity had only the chance to make the smallest of sounds before being instantly subdued.

For just a second Alvina thought perhaps she hadn't seen what she'd seen. And then for another second wondered what to do about it.

In the mansion's kitchen a man stood near the fireplace sipping at a bracing cup of tea. He'd have to relieve Christian in a minute. Damn, but he hated these long nights, especially when duty meant he'd spend most of it outside in the cold.

Alvina ran into the room, her dark eyes wide with fear, her mouth working silently as she tried to convey her anxiety. That the old woman had been running in the first place was enough to bring her to Jed Masion's attention. But it was her wild look of fear that shot a surge of adrenaline throughout his body. Something was wrong. Something was very wrong. "What's the matter?"

"She went off?"

"What?"

"Mrs. Walker. She left."

"When?" the man bellowed as he threw his cup to the floor without notice, causing the old lady to jump and then tremble as his obvious anxiety only multiplied her own.

"Just now. She got a note and left. I told her to wait for you, but she didn't hear me."

"Is she on foot?"

"I saw someone pull her inside a cab."

"Sonofabitch!" the man said, forgetting a woman was present. Jed wasted no time as he shrugged into his greatcoat and then reassured himself by touching the pistol as always secured in his belt. "Get word to Dr. Walker. Tell him what happened. Tell him I'm right behind her."

The cab hadn't turned a corner before Jed was out the front door. A man lay in the shadows of the building, a bruise forming along one side of his face where he'd obviously taken a serious blow. Jed suffered under no delusion. The lady of this house had just been kidnapped! Without taking the time to give his partner more than the briefest of looks, Jed ran for the stable out back and took a horse. A saddle was a luxury he couldn't afford at the moment. He swung himself on the animal's back. In the next instant he was riding down the drive and out into the street.

Jed came to a sudden stop.

There were three cabs within sight, one to his left, two to his right. Unless it had already turned off the avenue, Jed figured the farthest was probably the one that had carried her off. He prayed it was.

He followed, careful to keep his distance and yet remain within sight of the vehicle. He wouldn't approach the cab now. It could be dangerous not only to himself but to the woman inside, if he did so. His orders had been to protect the woman, yes, but there had been a suggestion that if there were a possibility of catching the culprits, he might find it profitable to do so. Of course, something like this had not been expected. A confrontation would have been a hell of a lot simpler. Still, there might be a way.

A half hour later Jed was positive of one of two things. He had either followed a pair of lovers who had paid the cabby to wander the streets of New York aimlessly, until their liaison was brought to its inevitable close, or he had chosen the right cab and the driver was purposely driving at a moderate pace, but randomly up one street and down another in order to throw off any would-be followers.

None too happily, Jed was beginning to think that the former was a distinct possibility when the cab left the city behind and finally came to a stop at a shack some distance down a rutted dirt road. Two men and two women exited the cab before it immediately drove off again.

Jed frowned. What the hell? Two men and *two* women? Were three involved in this? Four including the driver of the cab? Or had he chosen the wrong cab and inadvertently spied upon four who had no ulterior motives but to enjoy an illicit evening? Jed couldn't imagine why else they would have chosen so secluded a place, unless their intent was slightly out of the norm.

Jed remained where he was, easily hidden by the darkness and grass tall enough to disguise a standing man. They were within yards of the river, and he wasn't sure what to do. Should he go for help, even knowing they might be gone before his return? Did he dare leave Mrs. Walker to a gang of three? For that matter, was Mrs. Walker among them?

He had to get closer. He had to look inside, to know for sure.

Jed left his horse and crept closer to the dilapidated building. Someone lit a lamp inside and Jed instinctively ducked lower and then smiled knowing no one could see him especially now that a lamp had been lit.

It was snowing harder, but Jed felt none of the cold that bit into his exposed hands and face. All he could feel was sweat forming under his arms and down his back. All he could hear was the pounding of his heart and each silently taken breath.

He reached the building at last. Close to the wall, but careful not to lean against its flimsy construction, lest he give himself away, he bent forward and looked through the broken window. A piece of wood covered most of the opening, but there was a crack where the wood didn't exactly reach one corner. Jed could see nothing but the far wall. Still, between the crack and the thinness of the walls, he could hear clearly enough.

Inside the small shack, Felicity sat huddled in the corner farthest from the window. Her hands were bound behind her. With a gag tied around her mouth, she wasn't able to do more than moan. She was freezing, freezing and terrified. Jared had been right. She'd been such a fool to ignore his worries for her. If she ever got out of this, she swore she'd never again ignore his fears for her safety.

She glanced longingly at the shack's only door, if she could somehow . . .

"Don't even think about it," a steely voice said. "You're not going anywhere."

Felicity shivered at the coldness in that voice, at the flatness in the eyes behind that mask. The man stood looking down at her without a glimmer of emotion. The lifeless quality of those eyes told her she had every right to fear this man, for he had it in him to kill. This one wouldn't be bothered by the killing any more than if he squashed a bug.

Three of them. It would be next to impossible to escape. And even if by some miracle she managed the impossible, how would she get back home when she had no idea in which direction home was? All she could do was pray that by some miracle she'd be found. Found before it was too late.

The three spoke among themselves, ignoring her for the moment. She heard the mention of money and realized then it was ransom they had in mind. Felicity couldn't help but relax at the thought. Granted, she didn't have to remain alive in order for them to gain their ill-gotten riches, but there was a good chance she might, especially since their faces were covered and she could not identify anyone. Perhaps, if God were to smile down a blessing upon her, money would be all that was lost on this night. Lord please, she silently begged.

She looked around the room. A dirty mattress lay on the floor in one corner. In the room's center stood a table and one chair. A small coal stove and chimney sat to the right of a broken window.

"Frank, do something about the stove. God, it's freezing in here."

"What did I say about names?" the man, Felicity had silently named Cold Eyes nearly thundered, causing her to jump and then shiver at the hardness and instant fury in his voice. "If she knows our names, I'll have to . . ." Cold Eyes let the sentence hang. He didn't need to finish. Felicity was well aware of his meaning. She could hardly breathe for the terror that rushed through her entire body. Terror that tingled to both fingertips and toes alike.

Mike didn't care much if she came to realize who the other two were. She'd know that later, in any case. Everyone would eventually know who had been behind her kidnapping. But if either of them mentioned his name, he'd have to kill them all. There was no way that he was going to rot in prison because of their stupidity.

"Sorry," Bess said. "Do something about that stove," she repeated.

Frank nodded and crushed up paper, added kindling, and within minutes Felicity could feel the stove's warmth begin to force the cold from the shack. If the floor hadn't been of dirt, perhaps her rear might have warmed as well.

"How long are we going to keep her here?"

"Until the money arrives."

"Here? Are you having someone bring it here?" Bess grew visibly excited at the thought of seeing and touching all that money. She could hardly wait.

Felicity frowned. Apparently all three were not privy to the same information. Felicity thought they should have been. After all, if she were involved in a kidnapping, she'd want to know everything.

"Don't worry. You'll have what's owed to you soon enough," she heard a man say.

Felicity realized the true meaning behind his words. This man, the apparent leader of the gang, wasn't about to share. She knew it, and could only wonder how the other two had missed the sinister meaning behind those words.

"Go outside and walk around a bit. Make sure no one followed us."

"What? Now? It's snowing outside," Frank returned, obviously amazed that his cohort had issued so unthinkable an order.

"Aye, now," Mike said. "I've been fixin' to have a go at her." He nodded toward Bess. It wasn't unusual for Mike to need a woman. Most every time he succeeded in a criminal act, he felt much the same need. The exhilaration he knew at accomplishing his intent needed an immediate outlet, and he wasn't particular who he got it from.

Frank laughed. "I don't need to go outside for that. I don't mind watching." Frank often did as much, for the watching only added to his own excitement. "Maybe I'll take a turn after you're done."

Mike didn't much care if he watched or not but he did care about checking outside. They weren't going to get caught. At least *he* wasn't. "Go," Mike said. "And make sure you give it a good look."

"What about her?"

"Drop the bag over her head. We can take the masks off then."

Jed moved silently from the building. It was snowing more heavily than ever. He knew any sign of his presence would be covered within minutes.

As Bess accommodated both men, then soon enough accommodated them again, Felicity listened to the sounds of sex, torn between shock, embarrassment, and fear that they would use her next.

At first she'd been so terrorized, she hadn't realized the woman's voice was familiar. It took some time, but Felicity knew Margaret—no, her name was Bess, wasn't it?—was one of her kidnappers. Why hadn't she listened! Why hadn't she taken Jared's warnings seriously?

While Bess serviced the men and Felicity sat perfectly still, dreading what was to her mind the inevitable, Jed rushed back to the center of the city. As he forced the horse toward the house on Lexington, Jared walked from the hospital, and turned the corner of his home. At that moment a man rushed by him, mounted a parked cab and snapped the reins over the horse's head.

Jared frowned, for the man had nearly run him down and never once glanced in his direction, nor offered a word of apology at the near accident he'd caused. Jared sighed tiredly. It had been a hard day, and he longed for Felicity and her gentle touch. He needed a bath, a drink, and his wife, well perhaps not in that exact order and hoped she wouldn't mind washing his back.

Jared had just reached the door and was about to turn the knob when the door was wrenched open and Thomas Dryson stood there with a wild look in his eyes.

Jared was just about to remark on the coincidence when he noticed the man's look. "What's the matter?"

"They've taken her."

"Taken who?" Jared asked, but he might not have bothered, for he knew in his gut something had happened to his wife. Something terrible. It was for this reason that he'd insisted on the guards.

"Where? Who? When?" he asked in rapid succession, knowing even as he asked the man could give no answer. "Where the hell is Jed?"

"He went after them, I think."

"What do you mean, you think?"

"Calm down and have a drink."

"Thomas, tell me right now. I want to know the whole of it."

They were in the sitting room. Alvina sat in a chair, moaning and crying into a small lace handkerchief. Jared ignored her.

Thomas paced as Jared stood-stock still, praying his entire world was not about to end.

"Alvina saw her. She left without telling Jed. She took a cab. Jed followed. I hope to God he found her. He hasn't come back. We found Christian outside. He was unconscious. Still is, I think."

Jared poured himself three fingers of rum, despite the obvious look of displeasure shot his way by the reverend who had weeks ago taken a room upstairs. He gulped it down. "Exactly what did you see?"

For the third time that night, Alvina again told what she'd seen.

Jared frowned, knowing this woman, who was most always drunk, was hardly to be trusted. How much of what she said was the truth? How much imagined? "How long?" he asked, as he wiped his mouth with the back of his hand. "How long has she been gone?"

Thomas returned with, "I don't know. An hour maybe. This just came."

It took Jared longer than it should have to read the note. He might have suspected what his wife's disappearance was about, but actually reading the sinister words was just about more than he could bear. The pain, the fear he knew was not to be borne. And this note made it all real. Far too real.

The money was to be delivered at twelve tomorrow night. Dropped at the park and left in a black bag. Felicity's life depended on their cooperation, only Jared doubted he'd live till tomorrow. The way his heart was pounding, he wasn't going to make it beyond the next hour.

Suddenly the front door crashed open and Jed rushed into the room. "Where is she?" Jared swore he'd kill the man with his bare hands if he dared to say he didn't know.

"They have her in a shack by the river about three miles outside the city."

Jared almost collapsed with relief and clung to the desk before him, as he waited for his strength to return. Thomas fell into a chair with a soft moan. Alvina cried all the harder.

"Who took her?"

Jed shook his head. "They were masked. How is Christian?"

"He'll be no help. I think he's still out." This came from Thomas. "What are we going to do?"

Jed was obviously thinking. "I'll have to go back to the office. I've got to get help."

"I'll go."

Jed shook his head. "I need someone with experience. She could be hurt. If they start shooting, so could you."

"I said, I'll go," Jared returned, as he started for the front door.

"All right," Jed said, knowing the man would follow in any case, and it was best they did this with some order. Not that he knew what the hell he was going to do exactly. "Do you have a weapon?"

Jared remembered the two pistols he'd put in Felicity's room. Those would suit him fine. He nodded and ran for the guns.

By the time he returned, Thomas had gained his strength again and insisted on joining them. Horses were saddled, and the three were soon on their way out of the city.

Felicity cried silent tears. Something was indeed lacking in her, for she'd only just now realized that she loved her husband to madness. Now, as she silently willed him to come to her rescue. Now that she might never see him again. Why hadn't she realized it before? Why had she insisted on being so stubborn? Why hadn't she told him?

Lord, she silently prayed, *Give me the chance to tell him. Please.*

"I told you, I ain't touching her."

Mike grinned as he watched the tiny woman in the corner tense and then relax only to tense again as he said, "Well I ain't afraid of her husband."

"You should be," Bess said. "I ain't never seen a man more taken."

"Hand me that rope," Mike said. "I ain't never had myself a little mama before."

Felicity whimpered behind her gag, as Bess threw the rope in his direction and Mike chuckled as he bent and took it from the floor.

He stood before Felicity a long moment before throwing the rope down. There was no reason to tie her. She couldn't fight him, at least not in a way anyone would notice. She was such a little thing, and with her hands tied at her back, she wouldn't be no trouble at all. Her face was covered, she'd never even know which of them had done the deed. If she lived through this night, she'd never be able to tell. Mike chuckled at the thought.

Felicity screamed as someone touched her foot. The sound muffled behind her gag. A man laughed as she kicked wildly, blindly before her. A moment later he had both her ankles and she was being pulled to the floor to lie flat upon its cold surface. She screamed again and would have begged for mercy had she been able.

All she could think about was the baby. God, please, they couldn't hurt her baby! *Jared please, help me. They can't hurt our baby!*

Felicity grunted as the man leaned his weight fully upon her. Her hands were crushed to the floor behind her, sending excruciating pain up her arms. She moaned as the agony momentarily blocked out his fumbling.

And then her skirts were raised and her bodice torn and Felicity knew he'd penetrate her body at any second.

He tore at her underthings, leaving her body exposed to all in the room.

"She's a piece ain't she, mate?" the man leaning over her grunted.

Frank kept his distance. There was no way that he was going to touch that one. Her husband would find him, he knew. He'd search forever to find him, and Frank wasn't about to live with that kind of fear.

Felicity remembered the night of her wedding when she had inadvertently laid her husband low. Could she do it again? Would that give her the time she needed? She raised her knee, hard, coming dangerously close to the man's crotch, hitting him in fact high on his thigh.

Mike, realizing her intent, swung a thick fist and punched her just once. It was all that was needed.

Felicity never saw the blow coming, of course. Suddenly something from out of the blackness jammed into her jaw, something incredibly hard. She saw the flicker of tiny lights and groaned the softest of sounds, then knew only the blackness that lingered at the edges of her consciousness. She was limp, barely conscious. Still she knew what was happening but found herself unable to do a thing to stop it.

All eyes were on the beautiful woman and the man who was about to rape her. No one realized the door was opening. No one heard the footsteps on the dirt floor.

Jared froze at the sight. A bag was over his wife's head, but he knew it was she. It took less than a half second for him to realize Felicity was bound, her clothing torn. She was lying half-naked beneath a man whose trousers bunched around his ankles. He held a gun in his hand and almost pulled the trigger, but at the last instant realized Felicity could be shot in the doing. He roared the sound of the insane, sending shivers down every man's back.

Mike paused, turning to see where that maniacal sound had come from and found himself faced with the boot of a man flying through the air. He grunted at the unexpected impact. His nose broke, and at least two of his front teeth came loose. His mouth filled with blood, and even as he rolled to his back from the force of the blow, he gagged on the thick metallic taste. Half-naked he lay there for just a second before gaining his wits, before reaching for his gun. It wasn't two feet from where he fell, but it might have been a mile.

Jed kept his gun aimed at the two on the mattress, while Thomas ran for his daughter, talking to her in soothing tones as he covered her nakedness. Bringing her to lean against him, he pulled the bag from her head and began to untie her.

Jared wanted to kill the man more than he'd ever wanted anything in his life, but he was a doctor and had sworn to heal, to treasure every life. Maybe even this bastard's. The room took on a red glow as he struggled against the need to kill. Jared might have sworn an oath, but nowhere did it say he couldn't make sure animals such as this never practiced their evil again. "I hope you enjoyed my wife, mister, 'cause she's the last woman you'll ever abuse." And with those words, Jared forced his heel down on the man's groin, all of his 175 pounds of weight behind the blow.

Mike screamed and writhed with pain as Jared ground his heel to the floor and then turned to Felicity. Thomas handed over his daughter to her husband, and Jared rocked her gently against him, unashamed that tears of relief ran down his face. His arms trembled as he brought her close, knowing he'd come closer than he cared to think to losing her.

Mike groveled upon the dirt floor, the pain excruciating, all-consuming, very nearly unbearable. All was lost, and he knew it, but he wasn't going down alone. He might die on this night, but he was taking at least one of these bastards with him.

Just before the last stages of the throbbing agony began to ease, his fingers reached around the handle of his gun. An instant later the room exploded with the sounds of gunfire and screams. In the deadly silent aftermath, a small neat, but gushing hole came suddenly into being in the center of Mike's forehead.

Felicity groaned at the sight and turned her face into Jared's chest as all eyes turned to Jed and the gun he held in his hand. He threw the gun to the floor and took the second into his right hand. The two on the mattress, believing they were next, called for pity, swearing they had nothing to do with the lady or her abuse. They were merely innocent bystanders.

Jed cursed, knowing it would be a stretch to call either of these two innocent. He knew they were just as guilty as their partner. He'd take them to the authorities. Justice would be done on this night.

Mike was dead, his lifeless body thrown over Jed's horse. The others, if Jared had his way, would be spending the rest of their years in prison.

Jed tied Frank and Bess together. They'd be walking back to the city tonight. After again checking to see that Felicity suffered no ill effects from this near-disastrous night, Thomas and Jed started back.

The cabin was empty but for Jared and Felicity. She sat on his lap. Jared thought they should stay a bit, before moving her. He wanted to make sure she was all right. Really all right. There was no telling what damage might have been done. It was best to wait a bit, necessary in fact, lest the abuse and trauma she'd suffered cause the baby a premature birth.

He smoothed her hair back into place before settling her comfortably against his chest. "You'll be all right, sweetheart. I promise you will be," he soothed. "Once I get you back home, I'll examine you and make sure, but I know everything will be fine."

Felicity trembled against him, her relief knowing no bounds as she cuddled into his warmth. She'd lived for what felt like hours in a world of blackness, only hearing, only feeling. She could hardly believe it was over. She could hardly believe she was safe at last.

"I'm just so glad you're here. I was praying so hard, willing you to know where I was." She'd stopped crying some time ago, but the memory of this night sent a shiver through her again and she clung desperately to her husband. "How did you ever find me in time?"

Jared sighed his misery, sighed for the pain she'd known, for the abuse she'd taken. "I'm afraid I wasn't in time, darling. But it doesn't matter. I swear to you, it doesn't." He groaned knowing all would have ended well if he'd only been there a few minutes sooner. If he'd only been a bit faster. Just a second or two faster, he might have prevented the worst of it.

Felicity pulled away from his chest, her eyes misted with still more unshed tears. She wiped them away and frowned. "What are you talking about?"

"I'm talking about . . . about . . ."

Felicity made a tsking sound as she realized the way of his

thoughts. "Jared, he did not abuse me. At least not in the way you think." She touched a hand to her discolored jaw. "He did punch me, though. At least I think it was a punch."

"I saw him, sweetheart." Jared figured she was hysterical, even though she appeared unusually calm. Had she somehow forgotten what had happened? Had this night's events done something to her wits? His arms tightened around her. "It's all right. We never have to talk about this again."

"I think we should, Jared. I think you should know the man didn't follow through. Not that he wouldn't have, I'm sure, but you stopped him in time. Perhaps, I think, with only a second or two to spare."

He grabbed her suddenly by her shoulders, his fingers biting deep into her soft flesh, his eyes widening with delight, with absolute amazement that the woman he loved had somehow escaped the horror. "God Almighty, are you sure?"

"As sure as I am that if you squeeze me any tighter, I'll pop."

Jared laughed and crushed her against him. "I thought . . . I thought." He shuddered, "Well you know what I thought."

"Stop thinking, I can hardly breathe."

Jared laughed again as he came to his feet and lifted her into his arms. There was no reason to stay here any longer. Except for her fear, the lingering moments of terror that sometimes caused her to tremble, and taking a blow to her jaw, Felicity hadn't been damaged. "Are you sure you're all right? You can ride?"

"I'm fine. I told you, didn't I? And you know, I've been thinking."

"Have you?" Jared asked as he moved the horse slowly back to the city. The night was cold as snow gently covered their huddled forms. Cold and clean. It smelled wonderful. "About what?"

"About the fact that I love you and almost didn't get a chance to tell you."

Only silence followed her declaration.

The silence dragged on long enough for her to ask, "Did you hear me, Jared?"

"I'm not sure."

Felicity turned and smiled at her husband's shocked expression.

"The thing is, I've been waiting a long time to hear you say the words. And now that you have, I thought maybe I was imagining them."

She nodded. "Well, it took me a long time because I didn't want to love you. I think you tricked me into it."

"How did I do that?"

"By being wonderful, by being you. That was very underhanded of you."

Jared laughed as he cuddled her closer against him wrapping her tightly against the night's cold. "When did you know?"

"I only realized it tonight. But I've loved you for a long time. Since before we were married, I think. It sort of crept up on me, like you said it might."

"That's the way it happened to me."

"Did it? We're very lucky, aren't we?"

"Luckier than I could ever have imagined," he said, as he tightened his hold, wishing he'd never have to let this woman go.

Epilogue

"All right, now breathe!" Jared commanded, ignoring Felicity's sneering look.

"Will somebody get him out of here?" Felicity said a bit louder than she might have had she not been in the midst of a pain that just about drove all thoughts, but for agony, from her mind. The pressure came again and drove her to bear down, she prayed for the last time. This was killing her, and all the stupid man could do was tell her to breathe. All he was doing was bothering her. Put your legs up, put them down, move over here, over there. Turn to your right, your left. Didn't he know? Hadn't he ever seen a baby being born before? This had been going on for hours and he hadn't given her a minute's peace.

"I think you're making her nervous, Doctor," Mrs. Adam, the midwife said.

"He's making me more than nervous. Get out!"

Jared couldn't leave. She'd never know the terror he felt at watching her writhe in pain. She couldn't know his dread. She couldn't know that something terrible would happen if he left her side for even a second.

There was no way on earth that he could make his feet move beyond this room. "I'll be quiet, I promise," he said, coming to her side and taking her hand in his. In doing so, to Felicity's relief, he allowed Alvina and the midwife to see to the actual birthing. "Let me stay, please?"

Felicity didn't hear him. Her face turned beet red, for she was unable to resist the next need to push.

"Here he comes," Mrs. Adam said, standing at the bottom of the bed. "One more push should do it."

Felicity almost broke Jared's hand as she tightened her hold and pushed and pushed and grunted and growled and pushed some more.

And when the pushing was over at last, when a small, warm, wet screaming baby slipped from her to lie helplessly between her thighs, Alvina laughed. "It's a boy, Felicity."

"Oh God," she said, breathing heavily, one gasping breath after another, and then on an exhausted sigh, "Thank you, thank you." Felicity wasn't so much thanking God that He had given her a boy, but that this boy, obviously as stubborn as his father, had finally made his entrance into the world. She'd never known exhaustion to equal this. If it meant her life, she couldn't have lifted her head from the pillow.

"We have a baby, sweetheart." Jared couldn't believe the feelings surging through him. Had he ever known such happiness, such relief, such blessed peace and love? Was there ever a woman so strong, so perfect, so . . . He blinked as if trying to concentrate and then sounding rather confused, he said, "I feel so odd. I wonder . . ."

Felicity watched with some surprise as Jared slipped suddenly back from the bed and collapsed upon the floor.

Felicity looked at her husband's unconscious form, rolled her eyes toward the ceiling, and sighed. "At least he's finally quiet."

Both women smiled at the unconscious man, then ignored him as they went about the chore of seeing to mother and child. "You won't be saying the same for this little one," Alvina said as she handed the mother her newborn son.

Jared's faint only lasted a few seconds. Upon awakening, he rolled instantly to his knees and leaned over the bed, obviously a bit dizzy, but asking in a sharp tone, as if she had been the one to faint, "Are you all right?"

The baby was at her breast, fussing a bit and taking the time

to suck, only to lose his hold and fuss again. "Don't worry,
sweetheart," Felicity told him. "I've heard it gets easier after
the first time."

Jared watched his little son suckle hungrily for a minute before her words dawned. It was then that he pressed his face into
the pillow, knowing he had no will to resist her, especially in
this.

TANTALIZING ROMANCE
FROM STELLA CAMERON

ROMANCE FROM FERN MICHAELS

DEAR EMILY   (0-8217-4952-8, $5.99)

WISH LIST   (0-8217-5228-6, $6.99)

AND IN HARDCOVER:

VEGAS RICH   (1-57566-057-1, $25.00)